Mad Mischief

<<< A NOVEL >>>

Mad Mischief

►◄ A NOVEL ►◄

SUSAN ST. JOHN

MCP Books
2301 Lucien Way #415
Maitland, FL 32751
407.339.4217
www.MCPBooks.com

ISBN-13: 978-1-63505-264-0 - H
LCCN: 2016914775

FIRST EDITION

Distributed by Itasca Books

Printed in the United States of America

To my dearest friend, Genya Soovajian, and my brother David P. O'Malley. This dedication is best understood by knowing that each made a trip many years ago that in all likelihood saved my life.

David rarely saves me from myself anymore, unless, of course, I let him; and Genya died in April of 2006. On her deathbed, she looked at me plaintively, threw her arms up in her typical 'what-can-we-do-about-this' gesture, and said, "You have to go back to Africa so I can rescue you."

PROLOGUE

The door flew open and a tall, soaking-wet figure catapulted into the room wearing a confident grin on his ruddy face. Protecting a slide carousel under his well-worn leather bomber jacket, he landed next to a Kodak projector, his drenched boots touching down on the conference room's plush carpeting. He clicked his slide tray into place.

Sarah and Peter, who lived in California, were guests of a prominent Atlanta couple who had invited them out for a weekend of fishing and golf. When rain washed out those plans, their hosts suggested they watch a presentation by a well-known private safari guide, a guide they themselves were going to go to Africa with as soon as their schedule permitted. This was what accounted for Sarah and Peter now being in the well-appointed conference room of their host's business.

With the faint residue of a Scottish burr spicing his speech, the guide introduced himself. "Hi, I'm Max Einfield. Sorry to be so late, but I rode my motorcycle across town as fast as I could. It's a bit wet out there!"

Sarah became spellbound, even seduced, for although there were traces of an Atlanta rainstorm all about this famous guide, to Sarah, he was dripping with charm, accented by the scent of musk and leather.

She looked over at her husband, Peter, rigid in his determination that he not be moved against their plans to only travel to East Africa with Abercrombie and Kent, as planned. When Max began to speak, Sarah sensed that those very plans, which she had so meticulously organized, might shortly be undone. It was a premonition arising out of her once infallible sixth sense.

After casually flicking beads of water from his face and hair, Max removed his jacket, revealing a faded blue cotton short-sleeve shirt. His Levi jeans showed the early signs of being worn through.

The unusually high regard in which Max was held resulted from the fact that he had earned a PhD in Zoology and a master's in teaching, giving him an advantage over other guides when it came to understanding and predicting animal behaviors, thus bestowing to his clients a studied appreciation of their sightings. He had also received private flying instructions as a gesture of appreciation from a wealthy repeat client, thereby allowing him to become a licensed pilot; soon thereafter, he purchased a six-passenger plane. He was a self-taught, world-class photographer, and, not insignificantly, was reputed to be one of the most effective game spotters in East Africa.

Straight, bluntly cut red hair fell over his forehead like a burnished Celtic helmet. Max could be forty-five or fifty-five; there was youth in his step but statesmanship in his stance. His expression suggested mid-forties. His creased face said over fifty. No single factor betrayed his age, a fact that further enhanced his intrigue.

He made his way around the conference table exuding an air of assurance, his badly scarred right arm moving as his advance man. "Hi there. I'm Max. And you are—?" he asked in one form or another, managing to elicit a smile from every handshake.

When he reached Sarah, his roughened hand took hers and, glancing at her pale skin, he smiled into her eyes.

Max completed his circuit, then picked up the projector's remote switch and commanded the lights to be turned off. Like a gunslinger shooting cans along the top of a fence, he began to punch the forward button, triggering a succession of *National Geographic*-quality images. For Sarah, sitting still in her seat, the lifelike pictures became a magic carpet, transporting her more than nine thousand miles away to the East African veldt. The subjects were unfamiliar, yet for reasons she could not understand, they struck a haunting, personal chord.

One moment the peripatetic Max was at the side of the projector. The next, he was at the front of the room, standing beside a crisp close-up shot of a lion's head, pointing to the magnificent animal's whisker pattern.

"Every one of these configurations," he informed the group as he traced the facial hair and the ears of the beast depicted on the screen, "is different, unchanging, a unique fingerprint. It's their personal identification."

Image after image pulled Sarah deeper into their thrall. Nature, without Max to interpret it, would never hold the same allure. Even a series of pictures depicting a monstrous crocodile lunging at the belly of a zebra and exploding its stomach in midair only heightened Sarah's growing desire to be on the river's far shore. She whispered her enthusiasm into her husband's ear. "I can get us out of the Abercrombie arrangements. We must do the safari this way, with Max! He could help you get just the type of quality pictures you want."

After almost twenty years of accommodating Peter's overbearing personality, she realized the risk in altering their journey.

Peter sighed in that way Sarah knew to mean he did not want to have this conversation. "A trip with Max would be a unique adventure and yes, I could get great photographs with him, but this is nothing like the safaris we've read about. This is hard work. I can't get pictures like we've just seen without hours of waiting around, and I don't want to have to deal with you."

Sarah could well understand how someone, some other person in the room perhaps, might look at her and judge her as an improbable candidate: the makeup, the perfume, the perfectly coordinated outfit, the hair pulled back into a tight chignon secured with a black velvet bow. "Peter, you of all people should know I can handle anything, and that I have."

Of course Peter knew that Sarah could handle all that was thrown at her, she thought with subdued frustration. That is why he had married her instead of all the other women he might have chosen. And perhaps when he witnessed her handling everything that a safari would entail, he would be reminded of why he had wanted her to be his wife. Maybe this safari would bring them close together again. A personal safari with Max would be intimate. And, Sarah dared to hope, perhaps she and Peter might be intimate again on what would be their biggest adventure. The issue of going to Africa with Max or with a more conventional operator came down to a match of wills. "Peter, this is not a coincidence, our being here. It's fate. There are no coincidences. We're meant to go on safari with Max."

Sarah could see that Peter was beginning to bend, perhaps not because of her but by the unflagging strength of Max's conviction in himself. This was a trait that Peter identified with. He shrugged, and Sarah breathed a sigh of hope.

She looked out through a small parting in the curtains of the boardroom. The rain had stopped, and a sliver of sun spread across the screen, lighting up the savanna.

CHAPTER 1

THE FIRST RELEVANT QUESTION

Sarah has stayed on in Nairobi after the safari so she can write in her journal, conduct interviews, and check facts that seem to elude her. And, she has been planning her own going-away party for the following week. But her days have been eaten up by Max and his endless requests for favors, which, for some reason she cannot grasp, she feels obligated to grant.

But at last, the day would be hers. Sarah's hand rests on the proof of it: a large brass handle protruding from the thick mahogany door. She releases the gold safety lock, feeling like a thief, for she is taking the first moment of time that will belong entirely to her.

To announce the irony of her plan, the phone peals out insistently just as the latch chain releases. The concierge had phoned earlier to inform her that her driver waited downstairs. Sarah is thirty minutes behind schedule and thinks the ringing is a courtesy reminder.

"Sarah, this is Eric, the pilot who flew you to the Aberdares. Has Max's lawyer been in touch with you?"

"No, I haven't heard a thing. Why? What in God's name is wrong now?"

Eric's lips sound as if they are pushed against the mouthpiece to shelter his voice from others. "Max has been arrested. The authorities grabbed him the minute he landed here at Wilson Airport with his group."

Sarah has already squandered her allotted time extension in Nairobi. She cannot afford another day that ignores her purpose for having stayed on in this frantic city. "Okay, Eric. I've got a driver waiting downstairs. I can be there in twenty minutes."

"Sarah, whatever do you imagine you can do?" he asks, sounding so damn British.

She has no idea what she is going to do. All Sarah knows is that she has managed to escape her husband, responsibility, and sanity, the effect of which is she esteems herself capable of anything.

Downstairs, Moses introduces Sarah to her driver, who, like most others in her service thus far, has been given the first name of a biblical figure or American president. He is Joseph.

Joseph opens the back door of the cream-colored Mercedes-Benz, motioning Sarah inside. She declines his offer in favor of riding in front with him, a position of proximity the social norms frown upon, and which she relishes all the more for this very reason.

The driver is almost six feet tall. His frame is sturdy, as if his muscles have been hard-worked and well-tested before settling down into a strong physique. A somewhat passive face bears the suggestion of extraordinary serenity. He comports himself with self-assuredness, a quality that stands out in marked contrast to Sarah's anxiousness, as she delivers instructions contradicting the trip sheet he holds up as if it is a winning lottery ticket.

"Joseph, we're not going to the museum or the library. I need to go to Wilson Airport, and I want you to get me there in fifteen minutes instead of twenty-five. Can you do that?"

"Yes, Madam. And shall I wait for your flight to return?"

"I'm not flying anywhere. I'm going to Wilson because a man's been arrested, and is, I'm afraid, in a great deal of trouble."

"And Madam, you are able to fix this problem?"

"I don't know. It's an immigration issue involving his visa and Kenyan work permit."

"Oh, then I will help you. I have a relative at the Immigration Department. I will take good care of you. Yes, Madam, this is why I am here: to help you. And after I am done and have solved the problem, I would like you to be my wife."

Ordinarily Sarah would have judged his remark to be impudent, but he has delivered it in far too earnest a manner to receive any reprimand. Joseph—almost angelic in his appearance of wanting to do good—defies any harsh word. "I think you are asking quite a lot for helping me. Let's just get Max out of jail before we start making any long-term plans." Sarah laughs, certain he understands her effort to diffuse his intentions.

But the imperative has shifted, for he is now pushing the car beyond the pace of Nairobi's traffic jungle, adding to the volume of sound by his unrelenting use of the horn. He steers the vehicle deftly around an overcrowded matatu minibus, dodging rusty, skeletal bicycles, skimming past throngs of moistened bodies crossing the busy streets, and creating scenes of chaos.

The colors of countless lavender Jacaranda trees swirl together with the effusive purple bougainvillea flowers hanging over gray cement walls. Yellow-green bananas and orange-yellow mangoes are piled high on fruit stands set back only slightly from the street. Blankets of variegated green leaves cover the sidewalk. Blacks, Asians, and whites whirl against the tightly rigged canvas of an intense blue sky.

Joseph is racing madly to create a tornado of blurred color. He has understood Sarah's directions perfectly.

"This person we will help, he is your husband?"

No, Sarah thinks. Her husband is gone, and within the shocking context of this realization, she has to ask herself, "What am I doing here? Why am I forcing this gentle man to break the law, to speed along the dangerous, madly congested streets of Nairobi, to help Max, a man who has expressed such obvious contempt for me?"

The answer is the same excuse she has used to rationalize every other action she has taken throughout her life: because it's the right thing to do. "No. He's not my husband. He was my safari guide."

"Ah, I see, Madam. He is your very good friend?"

"No, actually, I don't think I even like him anymore. But he was the reason I was able to so completely experience the areas we visited, the animal behaviors we observed, and even some of the history of your country."

"I am very sorry, Madam, but I do not understand. If you don't like him anymore, why, then, will you help him?"

"Because, Joseph, he's an American citizen."

"Yes, I see. Then it is a very good thing to be an American citizen. No one would help me so much."

There it is again, Sarah acknowledges, the persistent conviction seemingly bred into every Kenyan man, woman, and child she has encountered thus far, that everything about America is unequivocally good.

Joseph speeds past the guard gate, the car's trunk barely escaping a hard slap by the armature's red metal limb. Sarah directs him to the last hangar in the long row of gleaming, corrugated tin. Here, he screeches to a stop, scattering dust about as if trying to disguise their arrival. This is a place Sarah has come to know over the last several weeks. Once again, she is at the home base for private charters, Kenya's Wilson Airport.

"Where should I be?" Joseph asks before unlocking and opening the door.

"Stand right behind me. Be close enough for me to turn around and grab you, okay?"

"Yes, Madam."

Sarah spots Eric immediately. He scratches his head, as if agitating his memory to recollection. The last time he saw her, he was looking over his shoulder from the cockpit of his plane to the backseat where Sarah was putting ink to paper thousands of feet above the sprawling Kenyan countryside.

"They just left for Nyayo House with Max. They're going to detain him until his trial."

As she heads back to the car with Joseph, Sarah's heart spasms in irregular palpitations and perspiration forms rivulets down her face. Somehow she must bluff through the next crucial stage: rescuing Max. He has inspired Sarah's picture of Nyayo House—the government building housing the offices of immigration and customs— during the safari, describing it in terrifying terms.

With Joseph again at the wheel, the car careens around corners and obstacles, as if attempting to shake sense into her, the horn screaming for all to hear. Sarah vaguely understands that there is no rationale for her rescue of Max, but she is operating on the very edge of reason, a place where her actions make perfect sense.

Joseph's worn shoes press hard on the accelerator, his broad shoulders swinging from right to left and then back again in a ride of professional daring. He bends the car to his own will and passes every impediment in the way of his single purpose.

At last, they approach a building reaching over twenty-seven redwood stories high, emboldened by a length of granite bearing large, white, badly soiled lettering: NYAYO HOUSE, Nairobi Provincial Hall. So this is it, Sarah realizes. Nyayo House. As Max had explained to her one night on the safari, at some point in history, in the lower hold of the building, prisoners were stripped naked, beaten, and made to suffer indignities. Cigarettes had been used to burn skin. Razors made to slash. Food and water withheld. It was Amnesty International's classic description of human rights abuse. The worst of these horrors may have been reserved for political prisoners, but it is, nevertheless, the building where Max is now being held.

Before stopping, Joseph elevates his body above the driver's seat, reaches into his back pocket, and withdraws a fat, dilapidated wallet. He fishes out a tattered business card. "I'm taking you to see my cousin, Cecil. Put this card in your purse. When I introduce you, take it out and give it to him. Tell him you are a good friend of this man. Then he will be sure to help you. Get it back from him but don't do anything to let him see it belongs to me."

Sarah inspects the card inscribed with the words UNITED NATIONS and a name, under which bears the title "Representative to Kenya."

"Joseph, who is this person?"

"He is a man who is my friend. I was his driver and his bodyguard for many years, a long time ago."

No parking space is available, causing Joseph to position his vehicle illegally along a wedge-shaped piece of ground adjacent to the government building's lot. He motions for the nearest policeman. When the guard appears in front of Joseph, he is given the car keys along with a fifty-shilling note.

Then they are there, within the chamber of Nyayo House, running upstairs, turning through dank stairwells, moving past throngs of disconcerted foreigners, ex-patriots, black and white Kenyans. All are clamoring to be heard, their hands reaching out forcibly with fistfuls of paperwork, frayed files shoved under their arms.

They smoke, swear in their disparate languages, huddle, sweat, wear expressions of despair or frustration or, more often, fierce distrust, as if Sarah's and Joseph's legs will take them to their desired results faster than the others might reach theirs.

At the top of the seventh floor, Sarah finds a corridor that appears to be more abyss than hallway. The office belonging to Cecil is directly ahead. Joseph hovers a moment at the open door, saying nothing, his eyes lowered in a tactical effort to prevent Cecil from glancing up and becoming alarmed at the large, bulky intruder standing in his doorway.

Cecil finally takes notice, and when he does, there is an expression of abject surprise. Joseph begins to speak their common language. In a jocular voice, Cecil invites, "Oh yes. Come in, cousin. Come in."

Joseph and Cecil speak again, still rapidly, in the lingua franca of Kenya, Kiswahili, so that they alone understand what transpires between them.

While they banter unintelligible words, Sarah studies Cecil and, occasionally, he studies her. His pale gray pin-striped suit is contemporary and impeccable. He looks like a dandy, and yet his appearance reflects a radiance of childlike mirth, as if firecrackers in his soul were once lit and continue to sparkle. Bright teeth flash against his charcoal face, a contrast as compelling as the sun unexpectedly bursting through dark clouds.

He turns to Sarah and clasps her hand with both of his. Holding on in this personalized clench, he pumps her arm up and down in a careful, calculated manner. "I am so very, very glad to meet you, really. Joseph, my cousin, whom I have not seen in many years, has just told me about you. I know who you are, and why you are here. I think you have nothing to fear, really. I would be only too happy to be of service to you. But, first, let me tell you what I must do. I must obtain the file on this Max person. Then, it will be necessary for me to speak to 'the big man upstairs.' Quite coincidentally, I am about to see him soon, for a meeting in town."

With an exaggerated flourish, he picks up the receiver from the old-fashioned dial phone and brings it to his ear. In the demeanor of a man comically displaying power, he speaks words that result in a woman wearing a florid dress to enter his office, Max's file in hand.

Cecil asks Joseph and Sarah to step into the hallway. He sequesters himself inside his small, functional space only to open his door a few minutes later. "I will be out for a while, so please, go to lunch. Come back in about an hour, and we shall work everything out."

Sarah realizes she has not yet given Cecil the business card. She quickly withdraws it from her pocket, allowing him to study the implicit message. When he has reviewed it sufficiently, she takes it back. "Could I speak to Max for a moment, just so he'll know everything's going to be okay?"

"Oh no. Max isn't even here yet. Don't worry." He skips down the steps with the file neatly packed into his black leather briefcase.

"My God, Joseph, what did you tell him?"

"Madam, I told him you are the mistress of my friend, the UN Representative. He was very impressed."

"You did what?" Sarah interrupts. "How could you have said such a thing without my permission?"

"Please forgive me, but you are an attractive white woman. He would have made this conclusion once he saw the name of my friend, even if I had said nothing."

Sarah is appalled, but his logic acts like a sharp slap across the face, awakening her to the street smarts Joseph possesses and she so obviously lacks. "Did you also tell him you want to marry me?"

"I only told him, Madam, that we had spoken of it. Shall I drive you somewhere for lunch?"

"No, I don't intend to move. Christ, if we leave and Cecil returns, he'll think we've eloped! Joseph, you stay here in case Cecil comes back. I'm going to walk around."

"All right, Madam, but please, if people talk to you, never appear afraid. They like very much to intimidate foreigners."

"Joseph, you have nothing to worry about. In fact, your fears should be the other way around."

"I am sorry. I don't understand."

"I cannot be intimidated! If anything, you should be concerned with just how boldly I might act."

Her reply brings his first smile of the day.

As Sarah walks up a flight of stairs, a pungent ammonia-like odor fills her nostrils. When she reaches the eighth floor, she looks directly at a white plastic nameplate affixed to a door. Its black letters read: J. Z. ONDUKO, ASSISTANT PRINCIPAL IMMIGRATION OFFICER. Underneath is a second, black plate: PERSONAL ASSISTANT TO THE PRINCIPAL IMMIGRATION OFFICER.

Onduko is the very name Max used whenever he spoke of the person whom his lawyer was endeavoring to reach. Onduko is where the bribes stop. Onduko is "the man."

Sarah opens the door to find the same professional-looking woman who had earlier brought Max's file to Cecil. "Pardon me, I'm waiting for Cecil. I believe he's gone to a meeting with your boss. Do you know when they're expected back?"

"No, you are wrong. Cecil is not with Mr. Onduko. Mr. Onduko has gone to lunch alone."

"Are you absolutely sure? Cecil told me he was just going to a short meeting with your boss."

"Yes. But they are not together. I am certain."

"Then could you tell me where you detain individuals who are awaiting their hearing?"

"No, I cannot." She returns robotically to her typewriter.

Sarah's anger heightens, as evidenced in the clutched sound of her voice. "If I'm not mistaken, you're the secretary to the second most important man in this building, and you can't tell me where they hold people?"

She nods that this is so, and without looking up, her nails continue pecking at the keyboard, sounding like a blackbird working its beak feverishly on cheap metal.

Sarah rushes down the stairs to find Joseph propped up, as if he is a leaning sentry, his face blank, exactly as she had left him. "Goddamn it, what the hell's going on around here? Cecil didn't go to a meeting with 'the big man upstairs'!"

Joseph looks at Sarah with the same vapid look she just witnessed on the secretary. She feels every symptom of her low blood sugar, each one ushering in a concern that she is part of a shadowy something she cannot fully comprehend. Her shaking is not fear, but anger submerged in an underfed, exhausted body. "Never mind, Joseph. I'll handle this myself."

Joseph hears her, but his bland face makes it clear he does not intend to reply. He stands there, an enigmatic, ebony puzzle wrapped in pressed khaki slacks and a sporty short-sleeve striped shirt.

Sarah tries to open Cecil's door without success, then attempts the door to the right. Locked, it shelters several men whose voices can be heard within. With a force of desperation driving her, Sarah bangs on the door with her open hand, increasing the intensity of each thump. At last the door opens, revealing a tall wiry black man with sick, fluid eyes, yellow in the area that is usually white.

His open mouth gives way to badly discolored teeth. His anger holds him erect until he falters and sways toward her. His breath reeks of alcohol. Behind him, in his small, stuffy office, sit two other men who have taken off their suit jackets and draped them across the back of their chairs. Bent over, shirtsleeves rolled up, they are picking from a pile of rancid-smelling French fries spread on sheets of grease-stained wax paper.

"Why do you knock on this door? Stop. It is my lunchtime. I don't have to talk to you now."

"Just tell me where they keep someone when they bring them here, before their trial."

"No!" He thrust the door in Sarah's face with a force she did not anticipate from one so inebriated.

She pounds again with both hands. Moments feel like forever until the man abruptly reopens the door. "Tell me where Max is and I won't bother you again!"

"I don't know about any Max. You are not to knock again or I will call someone to take you away." He pushes the door into Sarah's face with a final slam.

She turns to Joseph and notices a delicate woman in her early twenties leaving an office at the far end of the hall, locking it behind her. Sarah walks up to the young woman, gathering her shredded composure. "Hello. I am from the American Embassy and I want to visit a citizen who's being held until his trial tomorrow. Mr. Onduko said I could see him, but I forget what floor he said he was on. Can you tell me where the American might be?"

The girl covers her small mouth, hiding her poor dentistry. She giggles, embarrassed at her fascination with Sarah's makeup and gold earrings, which must strike her as amusing in contrast to Sarah's stained and crumpled safari outfit. "I do not know which room he is in, but he would surely be somewhere on this floor."

"Really? Thank you so much." Sarah returns to Joseph who, at a distance, looks as if he already knows Max might be on this floor. But perhaps, she thinks, it is just her imagination.

"Joseph, I don't know what the hell's going on, but I can assure you that I am very much up for the game. You better think about whether you want to stick around, because I can't predict what might happen."

Joseph shakes his head affirmatively. He leans back against the wall, the slightest smile lurking behind his face.

Sarah begins at one end of the hall, shouting, "Max, are you in there?" She plunges from one door to the next, knocking hard and bloodying her knuckles.

At the very last room, at the opposite end of the hall from where Sarah started, she is rewarded by the words, "In here."

She scans the door for a way to see him. A panel of glass at the top appears to be the only way this might be accomplished. Sarah motions for Joseph. "Put your hands together so I can stand on them. I want to see if I can reach up there."

Sarah is unable to gain the necessary height. Without words, Joseph points to the linoleum beneath their feet. She sits down and bends her head to the floor. From this lowly vantage point, sprawled out on cold prefabricated squares blotched with the permanent scars of accumulated filth, Sarah sees a hunched figure rocking on the edge of a mattress streaked with dirt, the squalid centerpiece of an otherwise bare room. Sarah's eyes are drawn to the nervous, twitching fingers belonging to Max, the once supremely confident guide who conducted her private safari just three weeks before. These are the hands she remembers ably pointing out all variety of game, after which would come an explanation of the order, family, subfamily, genus, species, and subspecies. Here are the fingers on the hands that had come together repeatedly to amplify bird calls or animal vocalizations, the hands that had wrapped around complex camera equipment in a kind of private catechism.

Those hands Sarah had known so personally now knot and unknot in pained distress. He is incarcerated in Nyayo House, the very government hellhole he has so ardently tried to avoid.

"Max, get down on the floor so you can hear me. I've found someone here to help you. Everything's going to be okay."

"Sarah, I don't want you here pulling one of your goddamn 'wobblies.' Get the hell outta here. You're just going to make everything worse. We're talking about my life, and you could fuck up everything I've worked for."

Sarah is not surprised. There has been little evidence of humanity toward her during the last several weeks. Unwittingly, she continuously managed to rub him like a brass lantern, always releasing the worst of his many genies.

"Thanks for the warm welcome. How could things possibly be worse, Max? Why don't you direct your anger at your goddamn lawyer, the one who ought to be here instead of me?"

* * *

First, there is just one man, and Sarah can see him clearly as he stands alone, profiled against the long hallway. But then there are more, so many that she cannot make out where one man starts and the next begins. She is looking at approximately ten figures, each dressed smartly in suits or jackets and pants. All of them stare with hardened faces.

Together, they represent one office or another of the bureaucracy that constitutes the seventh floor of Nyayo House. They chant their recrimination.

"Go away from that door."

"You have no right to be there."

"It is not allowed."

"Get away from there at once."

They move forward, stop, and then move back again. Sarah must subdue an urge to laugh, for each of the men is somehow ridiculously oversized, like putty characters of evil either grotesquely stretched up for tallness or sideways for great girth, depending on the whim of whomever pulled the clay.

After a time, their individual words fuse together: "Go away."

Despite Sarah's initial rounds of controlled entreaties, then stronger, louder, wilder protestations, she is not being allowed to see Max. Her incantations continue, rising periodically over Max's repeated instructions to leave him alone, go away, and be damned to hell.

Time passes; men come and go. Even Cecil, the glib gray suit on whom Sarah had attached earlier expectations, eventually returns, looks angrily at Joseph, then bolts into his office.

Sarah screws her bottom to the plastic floor. And there is Joseph, watching her in a steadfast gaze that expresses pride, for as he has directed, his charge is not being cowed by the men looking down at her.

Sarah studies her untidy safari clothes, removes a camera from the top pocket of her shirt, and pretends to take pictures of the antagonists before her. This is an act calculated to incite the mob, but still no one opens the door to Max.

After goading these officials without results, Sarah takes out a cigarette and methodically lights it. She begins to tear empty pages of her journal from their spiral spine, crumbles them, and assigns them to a carefully constructed pile. She flips ashes atop the paper heap, thus, she imagines, threatening to ignite a fire for her audience of men, one of whom finally crosses the invisible line and approaches. In a voice of heavy concern, he both states and questions, "You are causing quite a disturbance, you know. I can tell you there is going to be a lot of trouble for you. What can I do to make you leave this place?"

Sarah looks at his young, willing face, and replies evenly. "You can do this: You can go to 'the big man upstairs,' Mr. Onduko, and you can tell him I am attached to the American Embassy, that I am a personal friend of President Clinton, and that I want this goddamn door opened in the next twenty minutes or I will call the President of the United States. Do you understand me?" As she delivers the words "goddamn door," Sarah hits it soundly with her fist, giving substance to her empty threat.

The man looks at her intently and turns around; he is heading to the eighth floor.

Sarah is fighting Max behind the door that separates them, the faceless men in front of her. Her throat is dry; swallowing has become increasingly difficult. There is nothing to drink. She continues to drag on cigarettes, consigning their ashes to the paper pyre at her side.

Forty minutes after the delivery of her ultimatum, the biggest man of the assembly appears, and for a moment Sarah thinks she might laugh hysterically. The man is so tall she indulges in a long, slow gaze to comprehend the magnitude of his height. This could only be "the big man upstairs."

But it is not a time to laugh. Onduko is in a raging fit of temper, his arms flailing out in every direction, his eyes shooting off several rounds of steel-cold indignation. When he opens his mouth to talk, he disgorges questions like the rapport of bullets from a short-range pistol. "Who are you and what are you doing here?" he demands belligerently. "Why do you risk yourself for this person? Is he your husband? Is he your lover?"

Sarah tries to answer what Max is to her.

"Is he your lover?" Onduko demands again. "Answer me! Who is he and why are you here?"

Indeed, Sarah asks herself, how is it that she arrived in Nairobi with her husband, her health, her sanity, and her journal, and now finds herself alone, sick, and quite mad, throwing out insults and infuriating officials.

Why, she wonders, is she risking her life for Max, who has so adversely affected hers? Although she is barely able to think clearly, the shadow of an answer forming around the edges of what is left of her mind suggests

17

that all her life she has been a caregiver, ministering to the real or imagined needs of others. And that is why she is here now.

CHAPTER 2

THE TEMPLATE

Sarah's mind time-traveled to the stretch of the Serengeti where the scents of nature allied to perfect intoxicating perfumes. Confined as she now was, she could only inhale the stench of human waste.

She reflected on the animals that had looked upon her in varying degrees of assessment. There was no hatred in them such as that which now bore into her from the suited men held at bay by an invisible force.

Where there had been endless openness, now there was only the narrow passageway of the building with its bureaucrats. Flickering florescent lights replaced the bygone blue sky.

"The Big Man" interrupted her flow of memory. He bent over her as if he might strike her. Even then, she could not bring herself to care. Had he dared to do so, she only knew she would slap him back. Such was her false sense of fearlessness.

* * *

September 1993, several months after meeting Max Einfield and hiring him for their private safari, Sarah and Peter deplane at Kenyatta International Airport in Nairobi, Kenya.

Claiming their possessions at the luggage platform, they take their first steps into East Africa, each of them carrying the maximum-weight twenty-five-pound duffel bag on one arm, Peter with his camera in his free hand, and Sarah with a small blank notebook in hers.

It is 9:00 AM and already the effect of the intense equatorial sun has rendered the building's fan system useless. Outside the steamy, frenetic Immigration area, Max stands restlessly, trying to pick out of the crowd two faces he saw only once, months earlier.

Peter calls out Max's name, bringing him and his exaggerated smile immediately to their side. Max slaps Peter fraternally on the back, welcoming him to Kenya. He removes the weight from Sarah's shoulder, greeting her with a stiff one-armed hug and a sandpaper kiss.

"God, am I glad I found you. Your travel agent didn't give me any information except the airline. No problem, though, I figured it out."

They have only just arrived and already Max has secured their gratitude with the same diffidence as a porter matching suitcases to claim checks.

* * *

Clean and rested, Max, Sarah, Peter, and a second imposing couple stand beneath the porte cochere of the historic Norfolk Hotel, a relic of colonial times, with public and private rooms stiff from history, tradition, business deals, romance, and gossip. Right now, there is no opportunity for Sarah to contemplate the past, for the antiquated London taxi whistled out of traffic by the transportation captain putters its anxiousness to be off.

"Are you ready?" questions the man dressed in green livery.

"I was born ready!" Max responds. He will ride shotgun alongside the taxi on his motorcycle.

With the taxi door opened, the four enter, sitting on the edge of sun-parched leather seats. The taxi's first gambit is a quick U-turn and then a brief jolt to the end of the street. The taciturn driver turns again, making his way into the heart of the jumbled-up downtown area of Nairobi, a place of incongruities, where each sight stands alongside its definitive counterpart.

Sarah peers out at a freshly washed black Mercedes reaching the stoplight just inches ahead of a splintered wooden cart pulled by a dust-coated black man whose frame curves downward, his eyes fixed on the buckled pavement beneath his callused feet.

The hands of the other drivers on the street apply pressure to their horns, blasting loudly in protest of the unmoving traffic. These sounds compete with the urgent voices of mothers laden down by one or two babies strapped to their back, maneuvering between children and elders who are begging, and momentarily grateful, for anything their solicitations produce. Venders scramble to sell one of their innumerable trinkets.

An armed policeman can be seen apprehending a small child whose companion has jumped on the back of a white woman, tearing a chain from her neck and making off with it. The child, judged to be an accomplice, lies crouched under the raised stick of two uniformed men who have witnessed the attempted robbery.

The driver explains, "We don't want crime. It is very bad for tourism. I should not have come this way."

"But why must they beat a child like that?" Sarah demands to know.

"Oh, the child? He would only sell the stolen necklace and buy glue to sniff behind some building. He will die anyway, and probably very soon."

Others in this kinetic picture take a few shillings in exchange for something tangible. The sale of Chiclets in colored boxes appears to be monopolized by children with pronounced deformities. Able-bodied teenagers rush cars at traffic signals, eagerly hoping to sell yesterday's newspapers and week-old magazines at a steep discount. Headlines scream of brutal killings, kidnappings, bold robberies, surprise attacks, and political strife, while visitors leaving for or returning from their safari look out in bewilderment from behind the closed windows of their air-conditioned tour buses.

Corporate advertisers hawk their products from billboards, cinder-block structures, and the side of buildings. Philips, General Electric, Coca-Cola, Pepsi, Gillette, they are all here, waiting to pass off merchandise that Sarah will learn has little or no remaining shelf life, flowing through distribution systems comprised almost exclusively of white men.

Old-fashioned storefronts stand in formation alongside modern edifices, like defeated militia unable to pass inspection, with their faces of deteriorating paint, bones of broken bricks, and eyes of shattered glass.

The neo-cosmopolitan skyline starts to light up as numerous small bands of homeless people begin the nightly ritual of igniting fires in the city's parks, creating a source of heat against the coming cool of Kenya's night.

In the midst of all this activity, boys and young men are seen leaning on crumbling walls, sitting upon cracked curbs, or standing on the sidewalk against a building, causing a pattern of irregular dark stripes. Here are once hopeful men, gone from villages in a quest for jobs and a desire to work in a city that is without sufficient means to employ them.

And on every block, Askaris, drab-green-uniformed figures, wearing dark olive berets pulled low and clenching long wooden batons or rifles, can be seen. They are poised to deter the crime awaiting any opportunity within the jagged pieces of this scrambled scene.

Altogether, Nairobi is an energized dichotomy of past and present, a strange cavalcade of mixed messages daring the foreigner to understand. It discharges energy capable of igniting a flame. Sarah is aglow. She is falling passionately in love with this city. Falling in love in the way one does when infatuation is sudden, inexplicable, because of a look, a sound, a fragrance, a gesture— striking and combusting without reason or logic, just love for love's sake.

The seduction is interrupted when the cab stops in front of a whitewashed building with windows spilling rusty orange stains.

* * *

The group arrives at the Haandi restaurant, named after a cooking utensil with a concave bottom for the even distribution of heat. Peter has selected this place for dinner after carefully reading from an assortment of guidebooks.

The room is filled with sophisticated locals, businessmen, politicians, and Asians and their families, all glancing about, occasionally casting eyes upon the open kitchen and Indian clay ovens. There is a swirl of turbans, beards, long black hair, bald heads, fair- and dark-skinned patrons, sarongs, safari outfits, suits, khaki slacks, and words spoken in foreign tongues. Smells of curry, herbs, and ground spices hang pungently in the air. Tea is passed at tables, oils sizzle, and waiters move about with specialties in covered dishes.

Max follows the maître d' to a table in the very center of this rich Punjabi cuisine. It is only now, after the challenge of ordering, that there is time to settle in, to learn more about Max, the plans for the next two and a half weeks, and to become acquainted with Thad and Julia, who have become Sarah and Peter's last-minute safari companions.

To Sarah, the couple appears especially dramatic, with their tall muscular bodies and fresh-faced good looks, as if nature had a special interest in how they were portrayed.

Sarah judges that Thad is above six feet tall and probably weighs in at well over two hundred pounds. His head juts forward so as to hear every word. His ears look like a pair of catchers' mitts, making the sentences of others into baseballs each glove reaches out to catch. He has the appearance of a yuppie poster child for the forty-something success story that he is. The group soon learns that he has the financial means to indulge in off-road biking in the summer and downhill skiing in the winter. He drives a sport-utility vehicle when he could well afford a Porsche, even if his large physique could not.

He grins gamely and makes one thing clear: extracting the full measure of the days ahead is his single objective. His Nordic blue eyes hold a steady, animal-like alertness, conveying an acute concentration that Sarah judges will be expertly deployed during the safari.

Inspired by Thad's powerful physique, light blond hair, stubble of a beard, and newly purchased safari clothing, Peter has already begun to address him as Indiana, short for Indiana Jones.

Julia, Thad's girlfriend, is in her late twenties. She is tall enough to look him directly in the eye, and blessed with classic good looks that are emphasized when she removes her oval tortoiseshell spectacles and releases shoulder-length blond hair from her thick ponytail.

She exudes a charming naiveté and appears eager to please Thad, but not, Sarah guesses, at the expense of erasing herself. Bereft of all pretensions, Julia unabashedly refers to the safari as her first "serious trip."

Thad states for an invisible record that he was once divorced, noting that he is inclined to maintain the status quo. Julia shakes her head as if it is a neck exercise she has become accustomed to doing. They appear perfectly suited, but for their differences on the matter of matrimony, which will often be in the margins of what they say.

Peter sits uncomfortably, and Sarah knows that it is because he is always the one in charge. But for the next eighteen days, Max will run the show.

Peter's unease did not begin tonight. At his insistence, Sarah had sent Max innumerable questions prior to leaving for Kenya. Just days before leaving, Peter insisted on having Sarah ask Max to allow him to review the maintenance records on Max's plane, a request that Sarah finally refused, leaving his worries to form a feeding frenzy around the issues inherent in regular safety checks.

Looking at her husband, Sarah's imagination unfurls. With his silver hair and gray mustache, Peter, fifty-five, is about to push his Jewish heritage into the bush, looking somewhat like a slimmed-down version of Ernest Hemingway. Now, in an era of conservation awareness, when it is more acceptable to hunt with a camera instead of a gun, Peter will shoot with his Canon EOS II. Sarah knows that, claiming his photographs as his prize, he will be every bit as content as was Hemingway triggering his custom-made Springfield.

"Try this sauce," Max suggests to Sarah.

"What is it?"

"It's called garam masala."

"It's fabulous. There are so many different flavors. Cloves, cumin. I can't figure it out."

Max takes a pen clipped to his shirt and reaches in his back pants pocket for a small tablet. He writes down the recipe and pushes it towards Sarah. While spooning out generous portions of Navratan Biryani and Murgh Tikka Tandoori, Max blazes with boyish enthusiasm, fielding questions and asking several of his own.

"Hey," he asks, "where were you when I asked your travel agent to reach you about Thad and Julia joining us?"

"We were in the middle of the Baltic Sea, headed for St. Petersburg," Sarah answers.

"Why there?" asks Julia.

"Peter and I have traveled quite a bit to different parts of Europe, but I've always hoped to go to Russia. Peter took me on a cruise there for my forty-fifth birthday. My heritage is Russian, and I have been fascinated by Peter the Great for years."

"Why him in particular?" Julia wants to know, her face expressing genuine interest.

"He was just the most amazing man, interested in astronomy, agriculture, architecture, the construction of vessels. He traveled to the major shipbuilding cities of Europe dressed like a commoner and swore his attendants to secrecy regarding his true identity in order to avoid the ceremonies of court, but it was actually impossible for him not to stand out. He was a giant, so much taller than most everyone! He was six eight and—"

"No, Sarah, he was not six eight. He was six five," Peter, who has not read about Russia's czar, corrects her.

Conversation stops. Sarah's momentum and conviction are arrested.

"Peter, I've read every—"

"He was six five, but it's not important. Go on. It doesn't matter whether he was six five or six eight."

"If it's not important, why did you interrupt me?" Sarah sighs, experiencing the usual false hope that no one has noticed her small humiliation.

Max rushes in. "What do you guys know about Africa? Have you read anything?"

Thad, using his arm to wipe a thin line of beer foam from above his lip, is first to respond.

"I've been on the road for six months straight. Haven't read a thing but my company's P&L reports. I don't know what to expect, but I'm ready."

"I've read several novels to get a feel for Kenya," Sarah volunteers. "Of course I've read Hemingway's stories, and I've read about Beryl Markham, Elspeth Huxley, Dian Fossey, and the stories of the Leakey family."

"She's rather compulsive. You'll see what I mean. She can't help herself," Peter informs them, as if sharing a burden he has carried for too long. "She once spent a summer memorizing the entire Webster's dictionary."

Sarah would not have revealed this about herself; if questioned, she would have to admit that it was because she was put back a grade upon entering a new boarding school and that her only idea for dealing with the embarrassment was to become smart. Memorizing every word in the dictionary was, to her understanding, the way to accomplish this. She was on the Honor Roll the first semester after returning to school and every semester thereafter. The more subtle effect of her exercise was to instill in her a certainty that her intuition could be counted on to finesse any situation she would confront in the future.

"Julia, what about you? Have you read anything?"

"I haven't read too much, but I subscribe to *National Geographic* and I watch Animal Kingdom and The Discovery Channel all the time. I know a little something about animals; I train horses for a living and I hang out with vets. The only book I could find about Africa to read on this trip was *I Dreamed of Africa*."

"Uh-huh," Max expels disdainfully. "You know, I really didn't like that book."

There is a moment's lull as Max's voice shifts into an innocent, yet mischievous tone. He leans his head toward the center of the table over the aromatic dishes. "Do you know the three things that trigger man's survival mechanism?"

"Fear?"

"Jealousy?"

"Confrontation?"

"Lost luggage?" jokes Julia, whose bag, along with Thad's, is missing, explaining their crisp, new safari outfits.

"Nope. The three things are the sensation of falling, loud noises, and snakes."

Peter announces, "Well, the black mamba's the worst. It's absolutely deadly." Then, with subdued curiosity, he asks, "What's the likelihood of our running into one?"

Max deadpans, "Not significant. But the black mamba isn't what you should be worried about. If one bites you, it's likely I can save you, depending on the amount of venom injected. The puff adder's the most lethal snake, Peter, and they're definitely out there. Run into one of those babies, and man, it's curtains. If you're bitten, you bleed internally, and then die of exhaustion. You could accidentally provoke it, and then naturally, it's going to react in self-defense. Yeah, we'll have to be on the lookout for those guys."

"I must tell you, I am going to be very nervous."

"Do you have any other particular fears, Peter?"

"Well, I'm allergic to bee stings, so I brought along a special kit—"

Max looks at Peter with deep flexing eyebrows. "Oh, you get that nasty anaphylactic shock reaction? Well, if anything happens, I'll just 'trach' you with a straw!" Max laughs raucously at his own humor.

"God, this is going to be so great!" Thad proclaims.

Sarah is feeling invulnerable, thinking of herself as old enough to have experienced everything that life could throw at her. No, Sarah thinks, we will not encounter any difficulty. Not on this adventure.

"What are you afraid of, Max?" asks Peter, searching to even the score.

"What I fear isn't out there. It's right here in Nairobi."

Everyone strains to hear.

"It's a place called Nyayo House. Let's just say it's your worst nightmare."

Sarah notices that Peter's eyes are cast down. He no longer participates in the conversation, and she watches him withdraw into his private den of silence and thought.

Peter reaches for a small jar of peppers, but the slight tremble of his hand upsets the crockery. It drops and splinters in front of him, scattering the red-hot contents on the white tablecloth.

With this single unintentional act, the template has been etched.

CHAPTER 3

EPIPHANY

"Get up. The door will be opened." It was "The Big Man." "Unlock it. Find the key. Let her see this Max person."

An immediate scattering followed the orders, the bureaucrats breaking rank like soldiers flying from an onslaught of pelting bullets. But the key was nowhere to be found.

* * *

According to Eric, the pilot, the Piper Comanche and its "cargo of five souls" (as he radioed in to the control tower) are flying north, from Nairobi to its destination high in the Aberdare mountain range. Max had asked Eric to fly his group this morning because he had sudden urgent business, but used the excuse of tracking down Thad and Julia's luggage. He had left it up to Eric to inform the group when he picked them up at their hotel that morning.

From the air, crop formations appear in rectangular, triangular, strip, circular, and semicircular patterns.

Gradually, this auburn land transitions to brown fertile soil swelling with mother-lode crops of coffee and tea.

The safari group's route courses above the area both history and lore refer to as "The White Highlands," a part of Kenya representing thousands of acres appropriated from the inhabitants by the British and Europeans who then proceeded to cultivate not only the earth but also a lifestyle that earned them the sobriquet "The Happy Valley Set."

Once a railway was built, the commissioner of the protectorate of Kenya intended that the line pay its own way and produce a return on the five million pounds it cost. One ambitious plan to help achieve this objective was the parceling out of a million acres of land to settlers who would cultivate farms in the highlands. In 1903, a commission granted 999-year leases, attractive to those of London's British officer class and sons of Europeans who could not benefit from primogeniture, the practice of leaving one's estate to the first-born male.

Canadians, Australians, and South Africans followed. Next came increasing scores of adventurers possessing indomitable spirits, people driven by passion. They came to be emancipated from the constraints of the restrictive society codes too civilized for their temperament. They came to escape or to avoid scandal. They came for the opportunity to make their fortune. Whatever their reason or motivation, the settlers came.

Fun and a certain bohemian abandonment flourished, while society norms, as these newcomers had known them in the countries of their birth, expediently disappeared. The White Highlands became a vast playground where repressed urges slipped out from behind stiff upper lips.

Extreme behaviors took root and grew, yielding bountiful harvests of cocktail parties serving hors d'oeuvres, drinks, and cocaine. Thus, the players in this colorful, wild sandbox were known as "The Happy Valley" set.

As the crops rotated, so did the couples. Affairs flourished. Divorces and remarriages were recorded like the entries in a farmer's ledger. It was a country for agriculture and a land of unabated intrigue. The Happy Valley was a den of iniquity covering several thousand square miles of Kenyan landscape.

And here is Sarah, flying above its history.

* * *

Approximately forty-five minutes after leaving Wilson Airport, the single-engine plane banks steeply. Like a vulture assessing the opportunity of a banquet, the plane twice circles the cluster of buildings below, signaling an approach.

After having buzzed the Aberdare Country Club, a celebrated golf resort lying lazily on the richly vegetated slopes of Mweiga Hill, Eric targets a spot within the arms of the Aberdare Mountains, a range of cavernous depressions and protrusions rising fourteen thousand feet.

The few people on the ground gaze upward in unspoken acknowledgment, and with this exchange, Eric stabilizes the aircraft, negotiates his descent, and glides forward to an open pasture, planting the craft deftly upon a scratch of dirt.

He sets down with one gentle thump. The wheels meet the ground and the plane taxies, slows, and stops parallel to a dilapidated building sheltering two dark figures within from the midday sun.

Thad thrusts his bulky frame out of the copilot seat, planting his hiking boots solidly onto the crusted dirt. Eric deftly assists Peter and Julia from the plane, then reaches over the two middle seats to extricate a somewhat green-faced Sarah.

Their possessions are disgorged from the belly of the plane, after which Eric arches his back and strikes an erect stance, suggesting a former military background. He informs his charges, "You will be met shortly by a driver from the lodge. A van will be here in a few minutes to take you to the country club."

His cadence is abrupt. His voice hints at his being inconvenienced, which, when combined with his stiff demeanor, discourages any questions. Peter's jaw sets in self-imposed control, attempting to conceal the fact that he does not want Eric to leave until they have been met and transferred. His attempt at restraint fails. "This isn't really appropriate, is it? Shouldn't you wait till someone picks us up?"

Eric repeats his terse assurance.

The group was an unexpected addition to his full day's flying schedule, for Eric had only been contacted sometime after Max's decision to remain in Nairobi. Eric manages a curt good-bye as he hoists himself into the plane. He snaps together the tarnished metal seat-belt buckle, adjusts his headset, turns over the engine, and guns down the runway far ahead of the group's faint farewells.

In the shadow of majestic Mount Kenya, the Aberdare mountain range, and the thirteen-hundred-acre wildlife sanctuary, the four travelers stand under an intense equatorial sun in a dusty pasture cluttered with animal droppings and dotted with five small weather-beaten planes tied down to makeshift moorings.

There is no breeze. In this stillness, the tattered wind sock of the landing strip is motionless. The only discernible movement is a slow-walking old woman dressed in a conflict of colorful clothing. Her gnarled hand grips a crooked tree branch used as a staff to support her as she feebly makes her way just one step ahead of a ragtag goat herd that stops intermittently to graze on tufts of faded grass.

Minutes pass and still no one comes. Peter and Thad retreat, scratching their heads, kicking the dust, and spitting out colorful epigrams to vent their frustration. Nothing else is audible except the crackling of an incomprehensible conversation, a spray of words generated by two guards leaning against corrugated metal walls propped up in imitation of a shed.

The black men who do belong here occasionally survey the confused white group who do not. They throw out unfriendly glances, causing the concerns of the new arrivals to intensify as they stand helplessly in the abandoned field.

"How could this happen? What are we doing here?" ask Peter and Thad, although the only two people who might provide answers speak no English.

At last, Peter and Thad approach the men in the shed and point to the phone. One man abruptly thrusts the dusty instrument into Thad's unprepared hand.

"It's dead, Peter. They can't reach anyone."

"What are we supposed to do now?" Peter asks the two men, who still speak no English.

Thad looks away, fixing his glance on the road. "There's an old man over there," Thad points. "Maybe he can help." He waves to an elderly man who pauses for a moment to be certain it is really he who is being summoned.

The gaunt figure turns. He is dressed in a mismatched outfit comprised of the torn brown striped jacket of one suit and the ripped gray pants of another. His only source of shade is a wide-brimmed dusty panama hat, a residual token from the period of colonial rule in Kenya. Strays of tightly crinkled gray hair escape from underneath the unraveling relic.

Thad addresses him, asking carefully, "We need a ride to the lodge. Can you walk there and tell them we are waiting?"

A smile breaks over the old man's face. His eyes brighten with anticipation. His voice is low and his English meager, but the exchange is sufficient. "Yes, I will go for you. I can get someone to take you there."

He makes a small gesture as if he is about to disappear, but instead, bends down and patiently rolls up each pant leg to the middle of his withered calf. "I will bring you the help. It will be one hour."

He walks determinedly toward the road. They watch in astonishment as he breaks into an even-paced trot.

Three quarters of an hour pass and the aged messenger reappears, riding in the front seat of a rundown pickup truck. Sitting between the driver and another man, he sustains an almost toothless grin.

Thad leans through the window and slaps the frail hero on his shoulder, grabbing his knobby hand in a rush of relief and appreciation. The smile, revealing still more of his gums, expands another half inch. Never has he been so completely acknowledged for anything.

The truck, rusty and battered with dents, is quite obviously not from the lodge. A makeshift windowless camper sits behind the cab, bolted to the sides of the vehicle, rattling insecurely. The four rescued travelers climb inside and crouch to avoid hitting their heads during the ride.

A strong odor of sweat arises from the three men in the front of the truck. The human smell wafts to the back of the cab and, combining with noxious fumes from the vehicle, assaults the four Americans. The truck jerks forward as the driver pulls at the wheel, turning the vehicle back in the direction from which it came.

After ten minutes, Thad's enthusiasm at being picked up shifts into another gear. "We don't even know what these guys are saying. We don't know where we're going."

He would continue his concern but for the unexpected sight of a pristine golf course. Stark white pin flags mark holes on lush greens, standing in magnificent relief to fairways filled with indigenous tropical growth. Graceful giraffes and compactly built zebras stroll lazily across the rolling course as if looking for their caddie, inspiring Peter to joke, "Hey Thad, I bet you have to play fast on this course. The animals out there may not let you play through!"

As their laughter dispels the tension, the pickup stops in front of an imposing country-style building of dark wood and stone, supported by stylized colonial columns.

Numerous porters wearing crisp white uniforms pace the spacious lobby. Soldiers in military garb clutching automatic rifles are intentionally visible.

The driver opens his door and removes the bags, tossing them on one side of the veranda where they become a part of the heap of luggage generated by other guests. A large man whose black skin shines with microscopic beads of perspiration approaches Sarah, smiling in so grand a fashion as to reveal the entire width of his toothsome greeting. "Jambo, Mama."

Sarah nods, pretending to understand.

Thad steps forward to give the old man who acted as their emissary a monetary token of appreciation. When the same offer is made to the driver, he declines indignantly, demanding to be paid a higher fee for the ride he has provided. Thad presses him, "Here, take these shillings."

Still the driver will not accept, turning the gesture into a loud scene. As voices rise on both sides, attracting the attention of guests in the lobby, one of the porters steps forward from his station to clarify the specific amount of money demanded by the driver.

Thad inquires, "What would the normal fee be if the lodge driver had picked us up, as we had arranged?"

"It would be two hundred and fifty Kenya shillings for each person in your party, sir."

By this calculation, the driver expects half again what the lodge would have charged. The porter does not offer further assistance. The attendants behind the desk do not move from their registration forms, and when Thad asks about the manager, he learns he is not available.

Fearing that unless the problem is quickly resolved, Peter will plunge into hostility toward this country to which the next two and a half weeks have been committed, Sarah pushes her husband forward to help Thad negotiate. But Peter will not be drawn into the drama, and handing her a fistful of bills, instructs, "Here, just give them the extra money and let's get the hell out of here. I refuse to negotiate with them."

Sarah presents the additional filthy shilling notes to Thad. "It's only ten extra dollars. Here."

Thad remains resolute, refusing to compromise. Julia leans into Sarah's ear. "With Thad, it's not about the money; it's the principle. We could be here all day."

Finally, contentious passions spiking between the two warriors, Sarah's nerves ready to snap, she takes the crumpled notes from Thad's outstretched hand and delivers them defiantly into that of the driver's. "Take it or leave it."

The driver's hand closes around the bills.

* * *

Beyond the frustrations experienced in the lobby lies a beautifully landscaped carpet patterned with a variety of mature, verdant bushes, many of which sprout bright flowers in oranges, yellows, and reds. The manicured lawn is flanked by the forest on one side and, on the other, steps leading to the veranda of the club's restaurant.

Although seated on a porch shaded by the overhang of the dining room, the promise of drinks and lunch in evidence, Peter is not appeased. "I feel as if we've been left to flounder out here on our own. This should never have happened."

Thad takes off his safari hat, revealing flat hair matted down by the day's heavy heat, and allows Peter to vent his anger.

"Obviously they don't think it's their problem, and I have a feeling the manager disappeared intentionally. Wait till I get a hold of Max."

"Well, it's over now," Thad says to Julia, who nods in recognition of the worst being behind them.

"Welcome to the Aberdare Country Club," voices an immaculately dressed waiter. He records their order for four Tom Collins cocktails, then informs them, "After lunch, you will board a bus and be transported to the lodge."

Checking her watch, Sarah excuses herself to return to the lobby, where she locates the well-stocked souvenir shop, assessing the neatly arranged shelves supporting a small selection of photography books, guide books, and a variety of T-shirts embroidered with small, colorful animals, which she buys, suspecting that when she gets home, they will have no particular significance to the people for whom they are intended. Her purchases also include two packages of cigarettes and a pocket-sized book about the animals of Kenya, featuring the definitions of a limited number of words in the country's native tongue, Swahili.

Upon Sarah's return, Peter loudly unleashes his displeasure over her disappearance. "Where've you been, for Christ's sake? The waiter came back with the drinks and was ready to take our lunch order. Now he's gone and

God knows when he'll be back. Stay right here, damn it. Don't move again."

"I'm sorry," Sarah apologizes nervously. "Here he comes now. There's no problem, Peter. Please calm down."

Sarah fumbles in her purse for the cigarettes, wondering how something in her purse can be on top one moment and shuffle to the bottom the next, giving the impression that she never knows where things are, even in her own small space.

Although Peter continues to work his cigar, he stares Sarah down in unmistakable disapproval as she lights her cigarette.

"Just a little something to soothe my nerves," Sarah explains.

Steak sandwiches are consumed voraciously despite the tough, tasteless beef burrowed between fresh-baked bread. The waiter returns for the last time bearing the check. "You must finish lunch now and go to the lobby where you will board a bus. Departure is in ten minutes."

Peter pulls out his billfold ahead of Thad's draw. No one will pick up a check with Peter in their midst.

Sarah looks at Peter's billfold with a sense of sadness. She is all too familiar with its contents and the small horoscopes of helplessness within, for his wallet only contains one credit card, a driver's license, a Social Security card, a health insurance card, and his AAA card. There are three old business cards on which he has compressed phone numbers above and below his name and former title on the front, and on the entirety of the reverse sides of each.

These are phone numbers of women, but they are each disguised as men. "Nick" is Nicole. "Judd" is Judith. Sarah has not yet figured out this latest ploy. Despite Peter's transgressions, she wants to believe they are the names of golfers he calls when he needs a partner, Peter's effort to reach out to others and to organize his days in patterns meant to keep him busy. She is smart, strong, and not naïve, but she has endured a great deal to keep the marriage together and her mind will not—cannot—embrace the possibility of its falling apart.

For Sarah, the troublesome aspect of his wallet is the picture of her from when she was much younger, made permanent in the yellowing plastic, as if Peter would have her be that age forever. Very decent pictures have been taken over the past decade, but they are not included.

Two photos lie back to back. They are of his son. One depicts him in uniform during the Gulf War; the other taken just months after his release, wearing an expensive tweed sports jacket, part of a new wardrobe lavished upon him after his return to the States. The pictures freeze his son's manhood into two moments in time, lost for years to an addiction to alcohol and descent into cycles of rehabilitation and relapse until, many years later, he managed to pull himself up by his singular will, the unconditional love of his mother, and his insatiable need for his father's approval.

There is no picture of his overweight daughter.

Sarah often wonders what exactly is necessary to claim a spot within the plastic Hall of Fame Peter carries with him everywhere.

* * *

In the lobby, scores of individuals and groups are eager to board one of several refurbished school buses. Just before entering the fray, Julia assesses the situation with a sarcasm Sarah will increasingly come to cherish. "It's great to be on a private safari with a personal guide, isn't it?"

"Julia, you're very young, but you have great promise," Sarah tells her.

The bus ascends over a road, climbing from cedar, hagenia, and bamboo to peat, bog, and patched vegetation: the many ecosystems of the Aberdare National Park. Sarah's nose presses against the window, her eyes sorting out occasional appearances by animals she cannot yet identify. Rickety-fenced, thatched-roof shambas sit on farmland, and cattle encroach upon the park, speaking visually of the struggle to balance Kenya's need for grazing land with the requirements of preserving habitats for the diminishing wildlife, the country's trump card for attracting tourists.

When the bus stops at a summit, the driver stands and drones instructions through a sputtering microphone. The passengers slowly tread across a long, narrow gangplank supporting foot traffic high above a dense green glen. At the end of this bridge is the entrance to a wood-and-glass triangular structure resembling an ark. At the opening to the ark, names are surrendered to lodge personnel in return for assigned rooms and directions down narrow halls. They will spend the next eighteen hours in this dry-docked vessel.

Peter and Sarah open the door to their designated room, adjacent to the accommodations reserved for Thad and Julia. They discover two simple cots and one small dresser. A wood box rests between the beds with a conspicuous alarm switch explained by an instructional plaque. It informs them that if the switch is in the upward position, guests will be awakened during the night by a buzzer in order to witness one of the "Big Five"—elephant, rhino, buffalo, lion, or leopard—if such animals should come into the vicinity.

Peter responds to the invitation with an unhesitant gesture, flipping the switch down. "If I can manage to get to sleep in this goddamn place, I sure as hell don't want to be awakened."

Sleep. Sleep is one of those "regulars," like eating breakfast, lunch, and dinner at prescribed times, having each meal followed by scalding hot tea, going to bed at ten in the evening and awakening each morning at seven. Habits and rituals make up the substance of Sarah and Peter's days and nights, and she worries that much of their life is slipping away like liquid through a slotted spoon. Sarah knows the rules, the procedures, the necessary things. Peter has made her believe that keeping track of them is part of her responsibility as his wife, and she imagines that she has been doing a good job. Of the two of them, she alone thinks this to be so.

* * *

Emptying the contents of her duffel bag and spreading her things atop the bed, Sarah extracts clean clothes to change into before dinner.

"Why don't you read the instructions for your Pentax?" Peter asks Sarah. This is a camera he purchased for her when she indicated that she too wanted to take pictures on their trip.

Her patience is thin and her attention span waning. "No. I want to look around. I'm too excited now."

She had wanted to practice with her camera well before the safari, but Peter had gone to Alaska, taking all his camera gear and hers as well, learning to use her new Pentax during his trip. When he returned, there was no time to read the instructions nor to practice, for he continued to provide never-ending lists of things for her to do.

* * *

This is the first night for the four travelers outside the city of Nairobi. It is to be their initial introduction to animal behavior, and being trapped within these walls is the last place they want to be. Why, Sarah wonders, didn't Max hire someone to wait for the baggage rather than volunteer to become a high-priced porter?

Sarah has resolved not to be the first to comment on the obvious. She will not complain, because of the time years ago when she and Peter were at Christmas Island, a spot on the Pacific Ocean fifteen hundred miles from the equator. They were there in order to catch the elusive fighting bonefish.

But this was also where the hydrogen bomb had been tested. Everything remaining on the island appeared to have survived the fallout by mutating into a horrifying Jules Verne adaptation. Jungle vegetation entangled the island, frigate birds morphed to the size of small planes, and below, on the runway, hundreds of white crabs marched forward like a well-fed Aryan army.

As Sarah walked amongst the invading crabs and took in the overgrown landscape, Peter's friend had remarked in a burst of humble appreciation, "Peter, it doesn't get any better than this!"

Sarah had stopped, amazed. Was that the voice of their traveling companion, or someone stranded there from an Old Milwaukee Beer commercial? Her worst nightmare was another's dream come true. She had been ready to complain, but decided right then never to express dissatisfaction on a vacation.

However, at The Aberdare Ark, while sitting down for dinner at a community table, it becomes evident that her travel partners share the same negative point of view concerning Max's decision to remain in Nairobi.

Thad is the first to suggest, "You know, I wouldn't be surprised if Max just didn't want to be caged in here and used our missing luggage as an excuse. I bet he's got some heavy action in Nairobi!"

Julia seconds, "Yeah. Can you really see Max cooped up in this place? He knew he could just stick us here for one night. We're safe, and he gets another evening in the big city."

Peter strikes a different note. "I'm definitely going to speak to him. I don't want him to get the impression he can get away with this shit."

After dinner, Peter excuses himself to smoke a cigar outside on the deck, taking his camera, set on photographing something before retiring for the night. Sarah recognizes the clench of his jaw, set in determination, remembering the many times she has watched him from the shore as he turned blue in cold lakes, his arm repeatedly moving a fly rod from air to water and back again in competition with the very fish he has sworn to catch and then release. Remembering how she waited for endless hours on many a boat's deck until he reeled in the particular fish he envisioned at the time he applied the lure. Remembering him play three consecutive rounds of golf in climates so hot the others eventually dropped out from heat exhaustion. She recognizes Peter's pattern of persistence.

Sarah joins Peter outside, clutching her journal, looking forward to lighting up while he is diverted. As Sarah's match meets the cigarette, Julia sits down by her side. "Can I bum one off you?"

"Yes, of course," Sarah apologizes. "I didn't realize you smoke."

"I don't."

"Oh. Well, it's okay. I don't smoke either," Sarah informs her while trying to light Julia's cigarette despite the strong breeze.

"Nerves?" Sarah suggests.

"Yeah," Julia confesses with smoky resignation.

"Well, let's just get through tonight. Tomorrow we'll be with Max, you and Thad will have your luggage, and we'll be staying in tents. It's bound to be more like a real safari experience than this."

"I hope so, because Thad isn't going to be able to deal with coming all this way just to stay at some African version of the YMCA."

Then, a sound breaks into the clearing: the soft rustle of foliage. The evening show is about to begin. Peter's camera is in position, and as Sarah turns, she sees the massive head of a female elephant stepping slowly, cautiously, through the thicket of bushes and trees into the spotlight.

Click. Click. Click.

Behind her follow several more elephants: three other females and two small calves. Each of the mammals is deliberate and contemplative as they move toward the water, pausing only to look up. Then, turning from their targeted trajectory to stand facing the balcony, they gaze at their audience with stares that do not see into the distance. The pointing trunks pick up a scent, confirming the spectators' presence.

One of the small calves nudges the grandmother with its infantile trunk, raising it to blow a word in the elder's great, fig-like ear. After listening, the massive head moves down, causing her agile trunk to fall between her legs where it brushes the ground, hitting each of her two front feet.

The elephants rotate back onto the path leading to the water hole. They stop at the very edge of the pool where their trunks draw in the murky liquid. They raise their heads, pouring the libation down their pink throats like orators throwing back stiff drinks to calm their nerves after a filibuster.

Peter has placed his cigar on the railing and is carefully snapping successive shots, desperate to minimize any motion.

Sarah slumps down in the chair, any recollections of the day's trials entirely displaced by the magnificent elephants. She is filled with the awe of being here, whatever the cost, regardless of the many inconveniences.

She reaches for her journal, hoping in some way to record the scene she is witnessing.

Julia, watching pages of Sarah's journal rapidly fill, asks, "Are you writing a book?"

"No, I think I'm just keeping a journal. We shall see. Maybe it will become a book."

Thad's arms are on Julia's shoulders. He is standing tall behind her, his chest full, as if inflated with pride for having decided to take such a trip.

"If it were to be a book, what would be its title?"

Sarah thinks of the elephants, mammoth symbols of survival, silhouetted against a moon-bright sky. She senses the enormity of the animals' story.

"I suppose it would be entitled 'My Epiphany.'"

CHAPTER 4

SAMBURU DAY

Max's loud sighs could be heard under the still-locked door. Sarah slumped further against the wall. Each notch downward was calibrated to measure her mounting impatience with the ineptitude of the bureaucracy responsible for the misplaced key.

More time passed, and "The Big Man's" anger was temporarily averted from Sarah and cast out instead over his minions, not one of which appeared able to execute his order to release Max. Her brief reprieve ended when he returned his attention to her.

"Why did you come to Kenya?"

"I was on safari," Sarah answered, the words propelling from her mouth. And indeed, that was why she had come. But it had become so complicated. It had become personal. Very personal.

* * *

Yesterday is behind them, replaced by a fresh day and the sheer delight of being in Max's six-passenger Cessna 207 as it hums along the edge of a magnificent September morning. Sarah celebrates the moment while looking out the window at a small slice of Kenya, enjoying the pulsating notes of Ravel's "Bolero" being piped through the plane's earphones.

Here, East Africa is a dry land, perforated intermittently by pale green scrub, open savanna, and hills that are small yet pronounced in character for the relief they provide. Max and his passengers are in-flight to the Samburu National Reserve, north of the central mountains and the equator.

The music ends with Max's alert. "Okay, guys, we're heading down. Zip-a-dee-doo-dah, zip-a-dee . . . Watch this."

He steadies the aircraft, taking it lower, directly toward a herd of gazelle-like animals. The plane's shadow and the sound of the engine jar the ten fragile creatures to full alert. They cluster together, several standing on hind legs, their front limbs braced gingerly against trees with branches like the spokes of standing umbrellas. The animals' elongated necks are fully extended, providing their velvety lips access to lush green leaves. In this stance they resemble delicate underfed waifs, with small hands resting upon the windowsill of the town's finest restaurant, their gazes riveted on the tantalizing dishes within.

Through binoculars, Sarah fixes on buff-colored ears twitching straight up, marble eyes widening. The herd turns their angular faces to the open savanna, then gracefully they shoot off, like arrows fleeing from a bow.

"Yeeeeehaw! Look at them go. Aren't they great? Meet *litocranius walleri*, commonly called the gerenuk," Max explains playfully. "And that was a grove of acacias where they were eating."

Having dispersed the herd, he directs the aircraft away from the now deserted acacia grove, levels off, and heads toward a stand of stalwart trees reaching skyward, pulling up over the timbers and slanting the right wing of his Cessna above the small tent camp staked out along a narrow, muddy riverbank dotted with shiny black Samburu bodies.

Max takes the Cessna past the encampment to a rudimentary runway bisecting an open meadow. The plane gently kisses the ground before he sets it down in the face of a wind gust sufficient to gently rock the craft before allowing it to rest.

Numerous flight considerations have been checked and attended to: mixing fuel; switching tanks, throttle, prop pitch, and vertical air speed; gauging temperature and pressure, trip time, and navigational instrumentation. But no activity, Sarah observes, has absorbed Max at a conscious level. Every aspect of his flying and landing are inconspicuous, easy.

"Good flight, Max," asserts Thad.

"Any flight you walk away from is a good flight," Peter jokes.

A large customized Leyland Motors Land Rover waits on the dirt road marking one edge of the meadow. The driver is dressed in blue with accents of red and white, including his navy Nike baseball cap with matching Keds tennis shoes. He is a member of the Samburu tribe, but he has replaced his native shuka with sportswear and chic Ray-Ban sunglasses. His all-American image extends to his salutation.

"Hi! I am Francis."

The Land Rover's passenger side discharges a trim white man standing over six feet tall. He has a delicately aristocratic air despite his almost ungainly stature. In the heat of the midday equatorial sun, he is cool and crisp, attired in a short-sleeve khaki safari shirt and freshly laundered pants with a crease running down the front of each leg to meet classic-style safari boots. His words resonate with an engaging British accent. "Hello. I'm William. Hello there, Max. We're all ready for you."

Max hastens from the plane to introduce each member of his group to William, then returning to it, jettisons duffel bags from the cargo bay, employs all the men to push the machine forward, wedges the front wheel against a wooden chock, locks the doors, covers the plane in tarpaulin, and finally, strokes the aircraft tenderly, as if to reassure it of his eventual return.

Everyone but Sarah is already in the Land Rover ready to depart. She stands alone on the airstrip, fighting the contents of her purse for a pen in order to make furtive journal entries on a myriad of first impressions. Max jumps down and pushes his arm through Sarah's, escorting her to the Land Rover as he confides loud enough for everyone to hear, "Sarah, we're outta here."

The wheels rotate forward, tracking along the rutted dirt road to the camp a short distance away.

"It's okay to stand up on the seat," says Max. "If you're looking out through the open hatch, you'll see more, and while you're at it, smell this air."

It seems clear to Sarah that Max is a man who is returning to nature and eager to make love to his mistress. At any moment she expects him to slump down on a riverbank, giving himself up to this seduction. And so this first of many metaphors is emblazoned in her journal.

Everyone secures a footing and gazes upon vegetation ranging from sloping scrub to trees with trunks gnarled into complex, foreboding patterns. Animal life springs from the earth like floating leaves catching a ride on the wind.

Max, observing the enthralled expressions, promises, "Boy, I'll tell you what, we're going to see more game than you can possibly imagine, and what's out there now, those reticulated giraffes, that herd of Grévy's zebras, and that blue-shanked Somali ostrich, they're just a few appetizers."

In the space of less than a mile he points out four different birds, including a beautiful lilac-breasted roller, red-billed hornbill, brown-throated barbet, and a white-headed mousebird, all flirting with the blossoms of flowering acacia bushes.

The air is heavy with the musky scent of animals having marked their territory, blended with fresh spores, grasses, trees, and the thin condensation of evaporating morning dew.

Francis steers past a gatehouse where two uniformed men wave him through, and the group enters a private tent camp situated about one hundred feet from the bank of the Uaso Nyiro River. Duffel bags are again unloaded and then brought to the appointed tents. Francis works for William, the Englishman who, along with his family, owns the vehicles, pots, pans, tents, furnishings, and other camping accoutrements. William's team will set up each of the three separate camps over the next two and a half weeks.

"Okay, let me give you a brief tour, if I may. Then, I expect you'd like to wash up. We'll be serving lunch in an hour. Afterwards, you can rest a bit, and at two thirty this afternoon, we shall head into the park."

William's initial stop is at the largest of the green tents. It covers a rectangular table dressed in a white embroidered linen tablecloth. There is an antique hand-cranked phonograph with its wide signature brass mouthpiece. A table is piled high with vintage books about game hunters and old Kenya. Persian rugs pick up color as the sun's rays spotlight striking patterns woven scores of years ago. Several couches are draped with tribal blankets and spotted with colorful silk pillows. It is a pasha's den, muses Sarah.

"So, here you have it. This is the mess tent. All our meals are to be served in here. There's a small refrigerator over there, and you're welcome to help yourself to whatever you want. The table next to it is the bar," he explains, pointing to bottles of Jack Daniel's, Absolut Vodka, Harvey's Bristol Cream, and Dewar's Scotch.

A few feet further on, William resumes his orientation, flamboyantly opening the flap of the first small tent. "This one's for you, Thad and Julia. We've placed two lanterns on the table outside. They'll be lit at dusk. Carry one of them about, and leave the other here so you can find your way back. We placed your water bowls right inside the canvas," he says, pointing to sticks of wood crossed, bound, and balanced to hold a white ceramic bowl, a threadbare washcloth, and a small bar of Ivory soap.

"They will be filled in the morning and evening with hot water for washing. Let's go inside, shall we?"

As he talks, he makes his way to one of the beds. Here he fastidiously fluffs the pillow before continuing.

"This is the sleeping area, and beyond it, over there, is where you dress. All the flaps should be zipped to keep out mosquitoes, monkeys, and such. Beyond the dressing space, there is a toilet of sorts. Basically, it's just a hole we've dug in the ground with a seat over it. After you're finished with your business, take the shovel at the base of the seat, toss some dirt over it, and, well, that's your flush. Behind the bathroom is the shower tent. There's a bar of soap in the canvas pockets on the interior."

William moves past the canvas bathroom area into the last partition, stepping into the shower and up onto the flimsy, overturned wooden crate intended to prevent one from standing in the mud while the water is running.

"The way it works is quite simple, actually. Pull this end of the wire for water, after camp attendants have filled the container on top of the tent, of course. You have almost four minutes of water."

Peter, accustomed to first-class accommodations, stares at Sarah.

"Have you any questions?" William asks.

Peter does. "I want to ask about the safety of my things. I also want to know how to have my laundry done, and what I have to do to get hot coffee in the morning."

Sarah holds her breath in anticipation, hoping that William's answers will sufficiently satisfy her difficult husband.

"Ah yes, safety. Well, that's a bit tricky, actually. I would say quite honestly, in general, your things will be safe in the tent, but it would be prudent to keep your money on you. No need to tempt the chaps, eh?"

William shuffles for a moment, then continues. "You can place your dirty laundry in a bag on the bed. It will be picked up, washed, ironed, and sent back to you the next day. The women are asked to do their own laundry—personal things, that is. The attendants are quite modest, and they'd kick up a fuss if they were asked to handle your undergarments.

"Hot coffee or tea will be brought to you around dawn. So if that's all, I shall see you at lunch. Be sure to zip up your tent when you leave, because there will definitely be monkey business otherwise!"

"Start unpacking my things now," Peter instructs Sarah, once in their own tent. "I want this side of the tent and these drawers."

"I'll get right on it, Peter," Sarah responds, actually intending to do it in her own good time. The first plastic bag she pulls from her duffel bag contains her medication: Valium for her nerves, Paxil for depression, and the antimalaria drug Lariam, which both she and Peter are to take once a week. The second bag contains five lightweight water-repellent shirts: two khaki-colored shirts, one green, one yellow, and one red. The shirts are long-sleeved, with mesh air vents under the arms and across the back.

Observing that Max is still wearing the same faded blue short-sleeve shirt Sarah had seen him wear when she first met him in Atlanta, she decides to give him one of her new khaki-colored shirts.

Max is sitting outside his tent playing solitaire with a pack of tattered cards.

"May I enter your territory?" Sarah inquires.

"Yeah, sure. What's up?"

Holding out the shirt like a premature peace offering, she says, "Your skin looks pretty fair. I wondered if you'd like this. It's designed by a dermatologist for protection against the sun."

Max takes the shirt from her, grabbing it with the swift, retractile motion of a chameleon's suction-cup tongue. His head is cocked to one side and his eyes look at her curiously. "I can use it, but why are you giving it to me?"

"I brought four others along: another khaki, a green, a red, and a yellow one."

"Too bad, because you can't wear red or yellow out here. My brochure specifically states not to bring any bright colors. The animals will spot you. You're an easy mark in any bright color."

Although Sarah scrutinized the instructions before packing, determined not to make any mistakes that might affect her safari experience or precipitate Peter's anger, she is aware of no such warning. In the succeeding silence, Sarah wants to tell him she has been in the business world for twenty years, that she knows how to read a brochure, that she has meticulously—at Peter's insistence—checked off every item packed against the list in his brochure. Instead, she confesses, "Well, I don't know what to say. I read the information thoroughly, but if that's the case, I need the shirt back."

"Nope."

"No?" Sarah asks, dumbfounded.

"No way."

She feebly manages the last words on the subject. "I see."

Back at her tent, Sarah seethes over Max's behavior. She feels desperate in the knowledge that if Max had not somehow already come to matter to her in some way, she would have had at least three shirts to wear, as she now had to fold the yellow and red shirts to put away.

She reaches for a cigarette and attempts to light it, but the shaking of her hands extinguishes the small blaze. With no improved results the second time, Peter comes close, flicking his cigar lighter. His gesture surprises her; his words do not. "Sarah, you're going to burn the goddamn tent down. If you're going to smoke, at least go outside. Why are you smoking anyway?"

"I'm smoking to keep away the mosquitoes."

Peter sighs deeply. "I'm going over to the meal tent. I need a drink." Then, alarmed, he asks, "Now that you've mentioned mosquitoes, when is our next dose of Lariam?"

"Tuesday, Peter. We take the pill every Tuesday."

"How do I know you'll remember? I've got enough problems without getting malaria."

Sarah has prepared an itinerary with a page for every day. Each sheet reflects the date, location, and description of their locale; Tuesday's pages include a boldface notation to take the Lariam.

"Peter, I look at our schedule daily. The three Tuesday pages include a reminder about the medication."

"Are you sure you know where the pills are?"

"Yes." She holds up the appropriate plastic bag sitting on the bed next to her bag of antidepressants.

"We take the Lariam again tomorrow," Sarah says, thinking of the accompanying nausea, one of the medication's more immediate side effects.

Sarah takes two drags of her Marlboro, replacing the tightly packed tobacco with quivering gray ash. She reapplies blood-red lipstick rather than unpacking Peter's clothing.

At lunch, Max rocks back and forth. He has asked Sarah to sit at his left across from Peter. Thad and Julia sit next to one another, with William taking the seat at the other end of the table. Max's dominant seat allows him to act as host at each meal, jumpstarting stories, maintaining the tempo, setting the mood, and directing the details for their communal time.

Sarah observes that Max appears shorter than he actually is, as though someone mischievously cut an inch from the legs of his chair, and she suppresses an urge to laugh. Oblivious to this, he begins, speaking in the voice of one formally opening a summit session, "Did everyone zip up their tents? If you didn't, you're going to have a problem with vervet monkeys. They get inside and throw things all over the place, and it's just holy damn hell when they're finished."

Sarah was the last to leave their tent, and is not confident she has closed the flap. She quickly diverts the subject to her new journal, showing Max the small binder of thick, multicolored sheets recently purchased in

London where she and Peter spent two days recuperating from the transatlantic flight. She plans to carry the journal with her each day to record her impressions and make notations that will help her identify the location of the pictures Peter will shoot.

On close examination, Max notices that the manufacturer intends the pages to be used to transform signatures into ghastly figures of its signers. The vacant notebook is labeled "The Ghosts of My Friends," and directs the user to "Fold the paper in half, open it, and sign your name along the crease with a full pen of ink, then double the page over without using blotting paper." The outcome is either a skeletal figure with its face and hair indeed resembling a ghost, or the abstract imprint of a Rorschach test.

Max appraises the spiraled pages as if they are sinister phantoms designed to entrap him. He tosses the journal back to Sarah, almost hitting her.

Sarah now decides that it is she who is shrinking, sliding down in her chair, disappearing, becoming invisible. Contemplating Max's behavior, she recognizes that he is much more complicated than she has assumed, and that beyond his charm is another, perhaps more sinister side worth exploring. She will add her observations to her journal, and he will be captured within it after all, she decides.

William, feeling uncomfortable at Max's slight, addresses him. "There's a buzz we've got ourselves a lactating cheetah in the area. It would be quite something if we could catch a glimpse."

"The drier it is, the better the viewing. The animals are forced out in the open," Max explains. "They take more risks. Cheetahs are relatively uncommon in these conservation areas because of the number of other predators, such as lions, leopards, spotted hyenas, and jackals."

As Max reaches across the table, he winces with pain. William observes the flinch, inquiring with concern, "Max, what's wrong with your arm?"

"I was sideswiped by some idiot in Nairobi last night while I was on my motorcycle. Now my arm hurts like hell and my neck is out of whack. What I need is a great massage. Not going to get one out here though."

Peter provides a solution, pointing to Sarah. "She gives great massages. Her hands are strong as a son of a bitch. She can also cut your hair if you need a haircut."

"Would you give me a massage?" asks Max.

His tone and sheepish manner are boyish, expunging all traces of the earlier shirt and journal incidents. She succumbs to her ingrained nature of attempting to please, despite his previous slight.

"Well, all right. I could do that."

"Wow, this looks good enough to eat!" Max jokes as the food is presented.

Great portions of sliced beef, ham, and cheeses are handed around while a third server offers fresh hot bread and another provides a choice of salads. Thirsts are quenched with frosty cold Tusker beer.

Following lunch, Max and the others move outside the dining tent, bringing their chairs and arranging them in a tightly configured semicircle. Attendants process orders for tea or coffee, with or without honey, with or without sweetener and, in the classic English style, with or without hot steamed milk.

The fortifying meal seems to have provided Max with greater height, for he now sits straighter, regaining his stature.

"Would you take off your shirt so I can give you that massage?" Sarah requests.

Max jumps abruptly in his seat as if Sarah holds a jagged shard of fractured glass at his jugular. "Not now! I don't want it now. You can do it later."

His reaction leaves Sarah feeling deflated and awkward. She stands there, purposeless. His words flood her with all-too-familiar memories of efforts rejected. She has never learned to obliterate the effect of these feelings.

She manages to reclaim her seat while others sip their hot beverages. Peter, Thad, and Julia use their binoculars to observe naked Samburu men and children playing in the river.

Julia glances wickedly over her shoulder and then telescopes her hands like a fisherman overstating the size of his unsubstantiated catch. Thad, somewhat annoyed at the focus of her attention, requests only somewhat tolerantly, "Julia, will you give it a rest?"

A full hour passes. The sun, which has been boiling directly above, is now at its 2:30 PM position in the East African sky.

"Okay, guys," orders Max. "Let's hit it. You've got five minutes."

Sarah hurries to the tent. The flap is open! She inches the canvas back by degrees. Her heart is pounding hard and her throat constricts as she considers the scope of Peter's anger if he should come upon this scene. Suddenly primal fear reaches out to grip her as a black-faced white-bodied Abyssinian colobus monkey springs forward. It lurches from the cot, leaping past her shoulder, its soft fur grazing Sarah's hot cheek. Sarah cups her mouth with her hand, smothering a scream.

She has reached the tent just moments after the monkey entered, for it has only had time to dislodge her makeup bag from its place on top of the bed. The damage is limited to a lipstick rolling on the floor and a mascara wand protruding from under the pillow.

Stumbling inside, her body vibrating with fright, Sarah slumps in a heap upon the cot. As she tries to reclaim her composure, Peter enters. "What in hell's the matter? You look as if you've seen a ghost. What's your lipstick doing on the floor? God, you're not going to put more of that crap on out here, are you?"

"I'm fine. No, I'm not going to put on more crap."

Passing Thad and Julia's tent, Sarah and Peter pick the couple up along the way as Max, coming from another direction, starts for the Land Rover, his waving arm held up like a flag. His walk is brisk and filled with positive purpose: his signature gait.

Sarah claims the front seat, next to William. He has agreed to act as driver for this first outing, in place of Francis, who is busy refining the camp setup. Peter and Max assume the middle seat. Thad and Julia climb into the back, unconsciously mimicking the innate behavior of animals establishing their particular territory.

The Land Rover's immaculate interior camouflages its age. Within are many useful items, including soft drinks, bottles of water, suntan lotion, lip protection, Kleenex, flashlights, a first-aid kit, a knife, and a two-way radio. There are several nature books covered with old leather describing flora and fauna. To these staples, Sarah adds five PowerBars sealed in a small plastic baggie to use if her blood sugar gets low. Max appraises the PowerBars, his eyes seeming to stake a claim on them, though Sarah cannot be sure.

The suntan lotion is passed around, but Max refuses to use it, his freckles and lined skin speaking of his disdain for the practice in general.

They roll out of camp at fifteen miles an hour, past the gate, and into the Samburu Game Reserve, entering a working ecosystem. By day, they will be amongst the living and the dying of wildlife in this semidesert. By night, they will all sleep under the common blanket of the Samburu sky, bound by the stars and serenaded by animals that sound their presence in the dark.

Just outside the gated area, a thin young girl milks a scrawny nanny goat directly into a calabash, while agile teenage boys with tall spears herd approximately twenty painfully lean humpbacked cattle. Each cow's skeletal ribs are visible underneath its mangy hide. With no fattening fodder or steroids to bulk out their frames, these are the cattle of Kenya and, probably, Sarah realizes, the tasteless beef of yesterday's lunch.

"Those kids are Samburu, one of the tribes related to the Maasai," Max explains. "They're required to tend their clan's herds, a custom designed to teach them discipline and responsibility. Everyone has a job to perform; it allows them to experience value, worth, and social standing. After they're circumcised, they'll become warriors. Then, eventually, they graduate to elders. The problem here is that you can't raise stock on the same land apportioned to wild game, and it's usually the wildlife that's sacrificed."

Max surveys the immediate area, contemplating which direction to take, when William volunteers, "Max, do you think we should head over beyond the riverbank to the stand of acacia trees? We may have a shot at seeing the cheetah if we go in that direction. She can get a bit of water and shade there. It's hot enough that she probably needs both."

"Sounds good. Let's go get 'er."

A short distance later, Max points to a ribbon of indigenous acacias dripping with hundreds of oblong nests made of dry grass, hanging like Chinese lanterns, grasping tightly to branches at successive levels of the trees.

"These nests are constructed by male weaver birds. They nest in flocks. Their nests help 'em to compete for females, so those suckers put a lot of effort into their little habitats!"

William shifts the vehicle into park. With the motor idling, Max stretches his head high above the hatch, his binoculars pressed close to his eyes so that nothing, not even tint on glass, will come between him and his purpose. He lowers his field glasses, refocuses, returns the binoculars to his eyes, refocuses again, and announces, "Cheetah at two o'clock, fifty yards. God, this is unbelievable. She's got three cubs with her!"

Max assumes total control, and William downshifts to driver-only activity. "William, go up the road a ways and turn in." Seconds later, "Okay, stop right here. Turn off the engine. See them? Oh, Christ! Not these guys again."

Three Abercrombie and Kent tour vehicles and their stylish passengers, many of whom clasp expensive cameras, appear from windows and hatches. They head past Max when their drivers, recognizing him, back up, and come to a stop next to the Land Rover.

Max sighs loudly in disgust. "They never would've pulled over if they hadn't seen me. They would've missed her."

The cat and her cubs blend into the terrain, making it difficult to differentiate them from the thicket of tall, parched, golden grass in which they lie. The cheetah is sleek, blazing with alertness, while displaying a wild, hungry demeanor. She wears a luxurious coat, dappled with irregular, half-dollar-sized circles of black, an outfit in conspiratorial harmony with her surroundings. Her brood is still swaddled in soft fuzziness, through which their legs and tails protrude like small, independently moving parts.

Max instructs William, "Back up several yards and take the side road. That should put us in front of the cheetah's probable escape route."

William maneuvers to a new position, but predictably, the other vehicle follows. Max stiffens. William whispers to Sarah, "Those poor chaps have to show them something for their money. They probably haven't spotted anything decent all day."

Indifferently, the cheetah rises, turns toward the main road, and crosses the vehicle's bow, her three cubs scampering behind. She lies down languidly under a sparse tree, proudly displaying the design of her deep chest, svelte body, and long legs. She accommodates the photographers' need for variety and unflinching stillness with each new pose. Her head twists over her left shoulder, her face perpendicular to her body, eyes looking at her tail, simulating an advanced yoga position.

Max interprets her suddenly keen glance. "She's lactating. Mothers have to hunt, and they have a much higher success rate than their non-lactating peers. Guess what, boys and girls, I do believe we might see a kill. Hot damn!"

This is the first of Max's predictions to be realized over the course of the safari.

The mother's young charges stop their frolicking long enough to feed, aggressively nudging one another for the best seat at the milk bar. Although there are the beginnings of defined markings on the cubs' legs, when they snuggle in to grab a nipple, their identity is lost in the cheetah's stomach.

She must rest. Snatching a short break from the cubs tugging at her, the cheetah rolls onto her other side and faces the direction she could expect to run if a savory something catches her eye. Undaunted, the cubs scramble on top of her and frantically resume their sucking. Their meal concluded, they lumber away, allowing Mom to roll back over. Released momentarily from her maternal obligations, she sits up on her back legs, inspiring Max to explain a basic law of nature. "All predators are opportunists. If she saw prey now, she'd go for it."

As the cubs begin to wander off a few feet to play amongst a cluster of rocks, the cheetah gracefully moves away. While they scamper between the hardened sediment, their mother eases slowly into open terrain and calculates the best vantage point, then settles herself atop a termite mound for better viewing of the sprawling ground below.

Max fires one shot from his camera and checks the meter reading. "William, maneuver the Land Rover and give us some space to shoot, away from the other vehicles."

William manages the Land Rover into an off-road site tight enough to ensure relative isolation from the other safari groups.

"There, that solves the shade problem. Good. You're ready. Watch her feet. See how she depresses her feet and leaves an impression of them along with her claws, which—unlike those of most other cats—are only semi-retractable? These are the marks of a cheetah track."

There are Grant's gazelles in the immediate area. Seeing that the cheetah is intentionally ignoring them, Max observes indignantly, "She doesn't even seem to notice that her lunch is right over there!"

The predator is up, but not looking at the Grant's. Instead, her sights appear to be set on another prey.

"Christ Almighty!" Max states disdainfully, following the cheetah's gaze. "It's a lowly African hare. She's going to go for it instead of the Grant's! No wonder she lowered her head!"

His gaze returns to Peter and Thad, who move their cameras into position. "Get ready to start shooting. Pay attention to depth of field. Shoot that. Don't open it up. Stop it down for better depth. Thad, give your camera to me. Don't stop down."

He handles Thad's camera brusquely, making a few rapid adjustments, then passes it back.

"Peter, give me a meter reading. What speed is your film? 100 ASA, okay. Go to manual focus. Go to manual function, I said. Tell me what you've got when it's centered. Overexpose by one stop."

Click. Click. Click.

Max fires commands to Thad and, impatient at his response time, demands, "Give me the camera again."

The camera swiftly passes over to Max, who takes a split second to reassess the cheetah. "Okay, with 100 ASA, use a stop of F8 at 500th of a second when you're using a long lens. Don't go slower than the focal length of the lens. You're well within range now."

Click. Click. Click.

The cheetah remains crouched, her head hunched to her shoulders. Then, undetected by the hare, she stalks forward as Max continues with his lesson. "She has a seventy-meter striking capacity."

As if to validate his calculations, the cheetah's muscles release and she breaks into a trot. The hare looks up. The cheetah freezes, lies low, then rises and accelerates her gait to a full gallop.

Within attacking range of the hare, she thrusts herself forward, her back legs powering the sprint, as Max playfully imitates a track announcer, calling out, "And there she goes!"

She leaps forward in one premeditated, fluid motion, allowing a hundred and twenty pounds of muscle to pounce atop the ten-pound hare, detonating an explosion of dirt. When the dust settles, the head of the cheetah is moving violently from right to left, shaking her victim.

Click. Click. Click.

"She's employing the characteristic cheetah throat hold for a quick kill. She's achieved her objective," Max explains.

Julia is enraptured, her mouth open in awe. Thad is unabashedly impressed, his head moving about as if to unload some of the weight of what he has witnessed. Peter is trapped in concern. Did he have all the settings right? Did he get the shots? Sarah's reaction is to contemplate the natural wisdom of this creature, so clear about her mission that she abdicates the uncertain glory of a Grant's gazelle for the absolute satisfaction of the hare. "Be wise," the cheetah might have said, "not proud." Sarah senses that the message is personally meant for her, and thus, records the lesson in her journal.

The cheetah drags the booty nearer to the cubs and, uttering a high-pitched growl, commands her preoccupied brood to join her. They jump off the playground of rocks, cross in back of the vehicle, and chase each other to catch up. They are allowed to investigate the prize, while Max points to the limp hare and the cubs toying with it.

"Look, they can't open the package!"

As if in direct response to Max's remark, the cheetah steps in and snaps off the hare's head, providing her youngsters the first mouthfuls of raw flesh. The cubs leap into the body to feast, while Mom sits back on her hindquarters, her stomach expanding and contracting after her effort like billows fanning dying embers.

Click. Click. Click.

"She may be the fastest land creature around, but her burst is pretty brief, and it takes just about everything out of her."

The cubs' snouts are crimson. One has a piece of the hare stuck on its chin. The hare has transmuted into an elongated, lifeless form, with a portion of one ear still intact.

Now the hunter partakes. Other than the clicking of cameras, only tearing sounds can be heard. It is an unusual noise, amplified by the contrasting silence of the plain. This awful, audible crunching is maintained for several minutes, until the cheetah has decimated most of her meal.

As she records the word "noise" in her journal, Sarah's past memories are unconsciously triggered and she remembers the noises of her childhood. They had been frightening, loud, and seemingly endless. They were the sounds of her parents' nightly fights. Occasionally, when the battles raged on, either her mother or father would punish the other by driving off with Sarah and her brother and sister, Daniel and Rebecca, hiding for days at a time. When one parent left, the other did not know the children's whereabouts until the child-thief, tired of the game, would return home.

From the vehicle, zooming lenses continue to reach out, focusing on small, bloodied muzzles, while Sarah writes in her journal about the remainder of the hare's ear being drawn into the cheetah's mouth.

Max, in the voice of a general testing the newest recalcitrant member of his regiment, orders, "Sarah, stop writing and watch what's happening."

Like a commander deploying troop reinforcements, Peter sends in backup. "Sarah, for Christ's sake, you can write when we get back to camp. Put that damn journal away."

Under his breath, William whispers consolation. "Don't be put off. Max pushes a bit hard. If this were my safari, you could write all you want. It will be far too dark to write when we get back. Sorry about that."

The cubs lick the hollow carcass. They tussle with the skin, playing a child's game of tug of war. The hare has been devoured with an efficiency that precludes the hyenas and vultures from participating in the feast.

"She went for the hare instead of the Grant's because of the risk versus reward. There's no danger in going for a hare. She won't be attacked or hurt by another predator, a lion or a hyena, for example. The hare's a freebie. She's gotta eat something. Practicality drove her decision. She's going to have to hunt and eat again today, but for now, the show's over."

Then, as if Max were going to place a call to Central Casting, he assures the group, "I'll get you a lion and a leopard next." The cockiness of his statement challenges any doubt. Sarah is enamored of Max's confidence and, inexplicably, also by his disparagement of her.

Attentive to Max's cue, William starts the engine.

A safari vehicle emerges from nowhere, trying to close the distance, traveling as fast as the park's speed signs permit. The driver, doggedly chasing William, finally pulls alongside the Land Rover. The guide at the wheel leans far out his window. "Did you see the kill?"

Max, appearing through the hatch, grins widely at the unnerved man, and delights in responding before William can speak. "Yeah."

The other guide is agitated, and, looking directly at Max, asks, "Did you see the hunt too?"

Max is loud enough for the man's entire group of passengers to hear. "Uh-huh."

Without his sunglasses, the questioner cannot bluff away the envy in his eyes. "You got lucky, huh?"

Max, having visibly enjoyed the round, ends the game with the score in his favor. "No, not really. I don't depend on luck. Ever."

CHAPTER 5

THE MASSAGE

After twenty-five minutes, the key was found. The frustrated figure of "The Big Man" fought the lock until the door opened. He kicked it soundly and it fell in, revealing the naked room and the fatigued figure of Max.

"There. Come out."

Max and Sarah's eyes met for the first time in days. His were the eyes of a shark, filled with fury and frenzy; Sarah's were torches of triumph.

* * *

All is being made ready for the day. Fire fills spaces between large logs outside the cooking tent. Eggs are scrambled and quickly piled onto awaiting pewter trays. Hot slices of newly baked bread crisp in tin pans placed on last night's embers. Potatoes have been peeled, sliced, and are fried in scalding oil, embellished by small pieces of bacon and green peppers, seasoned with salt and pepper.

The smells signal morning to the congregation of five stretching in slow motion to meet the dawn. Here, cold hands snuggle up to cups of strong coffee, as they engage in the first ceremony of the day: waking up.

With the clatter of serving breakfast, it is as if last night has been lost in the immediate urgency of now, for there is only talk of the day ahead, talk of an adequate supply of film, pictures to be taken, animals to be spotted, a schedule to be kept.

Shortly after dawn, thick with sleep, Sarah wanders outside to the fresh, warm water of the porcelain bowl, cleaning off the residue of night with waterlogged Ivory soap.

Max emerges from his tent as Sarah's head surfaces, making a point of passing by her indifferently on his way to the newly enlivened fire.

Alas, she thinks, where is the acknowledgment of last night? Not a word of it is mentioned nor referenced by any look passing between them. But, she knows, his dismissal of last night, and of her, does not erase the fact of it, and of its having been recorded on pages lit with the meager wattage of a small flashlight. Colored sheets containing a message of the massage, of muscles with an encrypted compression of tightly wound emotions, of a secret hidden by Max's shirt, and something of the ways of these Samburu.

Yesterday, after the day's dust, all took showers and sat around the campfire. At first, Max drank little, crossing his legs and arms in reaffirmation of his carefully crafted persona.

Thad, in contrast, sprawled over his chair, unable to be confined within its frame. Julia also sat in unstructured relaxation, her body daring anyone to organize it, her chair pulled so close to Thad's that the side arms nicked away at one another, splinter by splinter.

Peter struck a contrived casualness, balancing a cigar in one hand, alternating it between his lips and fingers, blowing smoke that merged with the campfire's. In his other hand, vodka sloshed amongst rocks of ice, drained in measured sips into a body begging for a buzz.

Sarah sat on the very edge of her chair, pivoting to whichever set of ears would indulge one of her stories or beget a response.

Then, the group was initiated to dining in camp, an adventure compiled with carefully assembled ingredients from the markets of Nairobi. Cooks produced gourmet dishes, including a Caesar salad, spicy Moroccan lamb, mashed potatoes, string beans, and apple pie, all impressively and immaculately served by the camp's attendants, dressed in crisp white waiters' jackets.

The combination of a fine meal and the raw wilderness formed a unique dining experience. Candles dripping wax tears listened as stories were delivered between sips of vintage South African wine, the lubrication of tired, wagging tongues.

One intrigue of the palate followed another, with Kenyan coffee chasing down the meal, after which Courvoisier in glass brandy snifters was savored slowly. At last the goodness of the day, the food, the liquor, was all too much. And when Thad announced, "It's time for me to check Julia for ticks," everyone laughed and said their good nights, walking with heavy bodies toward their tents, dragging large lit lanterns behind them.

Sarah followed this procession for a few steps when a rough palm rested on her arm. She turned to face Max. The skin around his eyes was engraved with fatigue. In a subdued tone, he asked, "Sarah, can I have that massage now, in my tent, before I fall asleep?"

In spite of her exhaustion, she felt compelled to end the day on a positive note with Max. "Let me ask Peter. If it's okay, I'll grab some oil and be over there in a few minutes."

Peter's intoxicated state dulled his ability to comprehend her question, and Sarah gleaned that permission was granted, or, at least, not withheld.

She concocted a brew of oil, mint toothpaste, and tea bags. With lantern, flashlight, and her special snake oil elixir, she departed for Max's tent.

"Turn that damned lantern off," he said as she stepped within. Sarah wound down the flint, extinguishing the light, replacing it with the limited visibility of a flashlight. "Turn that off too," Max demanded.

He was already on the cot, undressed, beneath covers pulled up just below his well-defined waist. She uncorked the plastic bottle, sat down at his side, and began to administer the balm to the back of his neck, shoulder blades, and sides of his body. Under his skin, stubborn knots of tension challenged her fingers, defying her to undo them, smooth them, cure them.

Angled in a contorted, uncomfortable position, Sarah settled on the cot with one knee on either side of his narrow hips. She straddled him from above, dropping down each time she reached out for his body. Her thumbs rode the entire length of his spine, pushing and kneading, vertebrae by vertebrae, then up again to the base of his skull, down to his tailbone.

He made sounds of discomfort, sounds of relief, sounds he stifled, and, just when she felt she could go no further, sounds that implored her not to stop.

As she began to feel a sense of confidence, she inched her fingertips to what she imagined might be acupuncture points, pressing firmly, as if she could push a button and change the course of Max's pain.

Sarah eventually became acutely aware of the scene's sensuality: the dark, the sounds of nature, the private confines of the tent, the sensation of Max's body beneath her. She tingled awake and realized how long it had been since she and Peter had felt desire. There had been the other women, and for the longest time, Sarah imagined there were just too many people in the bed, too many to compete with. Peter had begun referring to sex as "fucking," and his description left her cold. With Max below her and the opportunity about her, she moved just a small step out of her sexual repose. What if? she questioned herself.

Sarah rubbed her hands together to regain circulation while Max slowly turned over and asked her to continue. She began at his collarbone, forcing blood into surrounding cavities, and was working her way down when her left hand fell into an unexpected depression on the lower right side of his rib cage. "What is this?" Sarah gasped.

"It's nothing. Just keep going."

"I realize it's nothing. That's the problem. It's supposed to be something. What happened to you? Did an animal gore you?"

"I had cancer. They cut it out. Shut up, okay?"

"No, I won't," Sarah insisted. "Is it all out?"

"I don't know. They removed what they could, and I never went back."

"You haven't been back for further testing? I thought you were so damn smart. Why would you take chances with your life?"

"It wouldn't change anything. It wouldn't alter a single aspect of my life or the way I live it. So it doesn't matter if I know or not."

He guided Sarah's hand to his navel, below which, the sheet began to rise. But the effect of the indentation in his body had sobered her. He must be desperate, she realized, to take a chance with a married woman. She wondered if he believed he would be doing her a favor. Could I go through with it? Sarah questioned, equivocal about the answer.

"Your massage is now over."

"Okay, but stay awhile and talk to me," he pleaded in a voice succumbing to oncoming sleep.

"Why are you so tense? What's really going on?"

"I can't talk now, I'm too tired. Maybe I'll tell you tomorrow night. Okay?"

"Are you asking me on a date?" she asked, with a tint of humor.

"Yeah, sort of."

"Why?"

"I like your taste in shirts."

Would Max continue to be his funny, somewhat endearing self when alone with her, only to become the darker Max when he was around Peter? Sarah was confused about the answer, but clear about the fact that she wanted to find out.

Sarah knew that Max would not bother to contemplate what might have happened had she stayed. He would go right to sleep. It was a woman's work, she thought, to consider all the possible interpretations of thoughts expressed and those that were not.

Although she was tired, she wanted to take pleasure in massaging the slants on every word spoken. This was the time for her to return to her tent, rescue her journal from the dresser, return to the fire, and figure everything out.

The fire extinguished the cold, but not the curiosity she experienced over the sudden change in Max and the elongated shadow whose footsteps she heard in soft approach.

It was William, checking the camp before retiring for the night. He stopped before her, squatting down. "Are you all right? I thought everyone was in their tents."

Sarah, in a state of hyperstimulation, replied, "I can't sleep. There are too many sounds."

William looked into the navy night, as if he needed to listen before rendering his judgment. "The sounds are lions. They usually hunt after dark. There are elephants out there too, close to camp. The figures you see are the Samburu men who guard us throughout the night. They police the area, keeping out everyone and anything trying to enter."

Although Max's behavior had captivated her attention earlier, she realized that if William would only allow her to talk to the Samburu, she might be able to add pages of personal notes to her journal. "I would love to talk to them for just a few minutes. I'll never have this opportunity again. Please."

He contemplated her request, then nodded in slow affirmation. "All right, but ask me the questions and I shall translate for you; this must not take too long. If Max finds out, he'll be livid."

William lured the guards into the lair of the fire's heat and, warmed by its embers, the Samburu told their story. They are cousins to the Maasai and are pastoralists whose flocks of cattle are their form of currency, representing their wealth and giving them position amongst their clansmen. A boy passes into the age-set of manhood at circumcision if he can withstand the knife without so much as a single flinch.

If he shows any sign of discomfort, he and his family will be humiliated. It is possible they will be shunned and may even be forced to leave their clan. If a boy does not pass this test, his face forever reflects his disappointment and failure through the final stages of his life.

Sarah asked how they prepared for the pain and learned they ready themselves their entire life, not with medicine, but with fear and anticipation. Their desire is to move forward, to the next phase of being Samburu. It is the understanding of their intended destiny that prepares them.

"You have heard a great deal from us this evening. We are now warm and rested so we shall go back to the trees and protect you while you sleep. Will you rest now?"

Sarah rose slowly, stiffly. "Yes. I shall dream of what you have said."

"One last thing we share with you, about religion. We are spiritual, not religious." They nodded and retreated into the night.

"Spiritual, not religious," thought Sarah. Well, we have that in common.

"William, thank you so much. Now, can you tell me about Max? I really can't figure him out."

"You will not get to know him. I have worked with him for over fifteen years, through every situation one could imagine. I will tell you this about him," he said, looking at the ground, "he is the master of calculation and the manager of chance."

In the morning, as Sarah yawns over breakfast, she realizes that between the massage and the Samburu, she was left with only four hours until the break of dawn.

Thus ended the day her itinerary so casually referred to as "Day Three: Samburu."

CHAPTER 6

BUFFALO SPRINGS

Sarah's reward for Max's release was her ability to review him, assess him, judge him, as he had done to her. She saw shadows lying firmly under Max's swollen eyes. The straight shoulders had fallen ten degrees; the purposeful walk had slackened and, naturally, the bowie knife that had hung at his belt like a gleaming punctuation mark had been confiscated.

"Come with me, I said," demanded "The Big Man," haughty and certain of his ability to reduce Sarah and Max to his will.

Sarah climbed up from the floor slowly. The long hours of sitting had stiffened her limbs and pinched her nerves. She reached up for a helping hand from Max, but he pushed past her. She was on her own.

* * *

On day four, the Land Rover forges the Ewaso Ng'iro River at its southern bank. This ten-mile waterway courses a strict divide between Samburu National Park and the conservation area now being entered, the Buffalo Springs Reserve, a Paleolithic box of sights as exotic as its name: The Northern Frontier Province.

It is early morning. The sun beats down, oblivious to its many effects: the reddening of white skin, the persistent sucking of moisture from bodies, the crinkling of eyes into uneven slits. The sun is the intense light of an intense land. It is the brightness of Kenya's people, the fuel of its flora and fauna. It is a rare constant among variables.

Max bursts into Sarah's daydream, bringing everyone to attention. "Hey, listen up! Birds. Birds are warm-blooded, even inside their eggs. Out here, in this hot climate, there's a danger of the unborn overheating. Like, well, see that fellow over there? That's a blacksmith plover. They actually stand over their eggs so their wings can provide shade for the little guys before they even break out of their shells!"

The sky is freckled with formless clouds, a soft white contradiction to the loud parade of quarrelsome carrion dressed in black feathers awaiting the dance of death.

Here Sarah stands, half her body outside the hatch, eyes riveted on a mutilating feeding frenzy.

It is ten o'clock in the morning. It has been well over an hour since Max first uttered the words, "Wow, look over there," indicating his sighting of what Sarah imagines is a golden something moving inside a form of black-and-white stripes deep within the gilded grass.

Binoculars and cameras fix on a massive predator and its victim: a shabby male lion dragging the remains of a dead Grévy's zebra. The manner in which Sarah perceives the lion bearing the zebra is so unexpected that Sarah constantly has to reevaluate what she is seeing because she fears that she might be hallucinating.

The lion, she writes, *is positioned inside the carcass of the slain, striped African horse. He wears the partial remains of skin still clinging to the zebra's fully intact skeleton as a bloodied royal cloak. The lion's noble head presses against the inside of an empty cavity that hours earlier had been the zebra's jaw.*

The smug cat with its tattered mane looks up angrily. He pulls forward in a slow, debauched stride. Occasionally, the lion stops to eat, then picks up the carcass and pushes it a few paces. Once, he comes so close as to be within striking distance of the vehicle. The lion pants, expelling his fetid breath. The onlookers hold theirs.

Peter is fully extended out of the window when the predator passes the vehicle. Everyone remains motionless while pressing the appropriate button on their cameras.

Click. Click. Click.

Together, they continue to move forward, the lion and the fallen prey protruding by only a nostril, not even a nose. This relationship between the conqueror and the vanquished stirs Sarah. How like the zebra I feel, not running with the herd; neither had the zebra, and the cost was its life.

Sarah's mind becomes crowded with frenetic imagery. She imagines the lion to be a symbol of the British Empire of the nineteenth century. White men Christianizing and colonizing the black man, with Britain and Germany apportioning East Africa, planning away at her riches of coffee, tea, pyrethrum, sisal, and pineapple. Then, like the lion with the zebra, Britain began to eat at Kenya, first structuring it as an investment, the Imperial British East Africa Company, later making it a protectorate and, finally, a colony.

White administration gave black men jurisprudence, parliamentary rule, discipline, medicine, religion, some learning as well as commerce and, in return, took much of their resources, the territorial boundaries of their individual clans, dignity, and self-confidence. After World War II depleted English coffers, the British could no longer continue to carry the colony, just as the lion will soon be incapable of carrying the zebra.

Sarah strains to rid her head of metaphors as the satiated lion now faces his competitors, including the advancing females of the pride, each of them demanding their pounds of flesh.

Thad announces, "I've gotta get in on this." He arches out of the hatch.

Click. Click. Click.

"It's unlikely the lion made the kill," Max clarifies.

"The kill," Sarah thinks, remembering the day when Sarah's mother swept up her children from their school playground to sequester them in a hotel on the outskirts of Los Angeles. Her mother had shouted hysterically, "Your father has threatened me with a gun!" as if this were explanation enough.

Each morning Sarah's mother departed at dawn for work, leaving Sarah and her brother and sister with an aged black nanny. One evening, two weeks into hiding, Sarah's mother returned from work and marched her children into the room with two twin beds. She sat on one bed, her offspring crowded together on the other, like tiny soldiers facing their commander. "Your father has committed suicide," she stated matter-of-factly, doing little to soften the message of how he died. (One bullet through his head.)

Max interrupts Sarah's memory. "The females of the pride, or even hyenas, probably made the kill. Lions are usually guided to carcasses by the sight of vultures looking over the carnage from overhead and the cries of hyenas below."

Hearing this remark, Francis, who has resumed his responsibility as driver, informs Max in perfect English, "I once followed some lions at night. The hyenas made the kill of a zebra, just like this. Then the lions came in and took it and the hyenas stood away while the lion ate. It looked to the people as if the hyenas were the scavengers. That is what everyone thought but me. Because I had seen it all, it was me who told them what happened."

With Francis's story complete, Max continues his. "The Grévy's zebra is about eight hundred pounds. The stripes around its sides and neck all meet at the mane. Those alternating stripes are designed for camouflage; the white is sort of like the light of day, and the black is like the dark of night. At dusk, when day and night come together, the zebra is pretty much protected from the lion, which normally awakes about that time to hunt. People eat zebra meat, but it's not particularly good, except to the lion."

Sarah feels certain that the aging lion appreciates the zebra's usefulness, for it now feeds the senior member of the pride, strengthening him for the continued defense of his realm. Later, it will fortify the females and their cubs, gifting them another day, another chance for survival. Finally, scraps will fill the bellies of these rapacious jackals and vultures, which will fastidiously remove every morsel from the table of the environment.

All traces of Sarah's earlier revulsion is now abated, replaced by fascination and understanding. Feeding on a kill is an example of nature's hand at work, cleaning house and restoring balance.

"The Grévy's zebra is diminishing 'cause they're competing for water with domestic stock," Max continues. "Nomads have settled near their water sources, and water flow has been reduced by irrigation. The Samburu people control this reserve, so it's not under the jurisdiction of the Kenya Wildlife Service. Management practices around here aren't coordinated with the other conservation areas, and guidelines reflect the Samburu's own self-interests over that of the game."

"That's a sunbird," Max states, his voice changing. "It's got a long tongue divided into two parts, from the middle down, so it can lick up nectar with a quick thrust into the flower."

Then he laughs, as if he could go further with this imagery. He looks at the guys. "No comment from the peanut gallery, please."

Insights are being recorded in rapid, sloppy strokes across the pages of Sarah's notebook when Max chastises her once again. This time, his voice rings with advancing disrespect. "Sarah, listen up. I don't want to have to keep saying this, but put down that journal and watch what's going on. You can't observe if you're always writing, and every time I look at you, that's all you're doing."

"Max, I am watching. Let me read what I've written and judge for yourself."

"I don't want to discuss this. It's not possible. I know from experience that you can't do both: write and watch. Just do as I say."

"For Christ's sake, will you follow his instructions, Sarah?" Peter allies himself with Max.

"Okay, Max," she surrenders, sensing that she is unable to fight one, let alone two, alpha males. She feels as if the inability to write is leaving her as empty as the journal's unfilled pages, voiding the impressions of these animals and their behaviors in their natural habitat.

"Good. I'm glad you're finally with the program."

Sarah's brain is storming with confusion. She tries to comprehend why she is unable to put the journal down, why she feels an uncontrollable need to push her thoughts onto pages once intended for simple, shorthand descriptions. To whom can she explain that her mind is being flooded with metaphors and recollections? How can she explain raging compulsion? A last remaining shred of logic forces her to wonder why she is being prevented from experiencing the safari with words. Why are photos and the endless waiting to capture them more acceptable than glancing down to write what must be written?

Satisfied with Sarah's compliance, Max turns to the approaching Toyota Land Cruiser with exaggerated disappointment. "Well, too bad. There goes the neighborhood."

The vehicle is filled with white human cargo and, in particular, two passengers who instantly captivate Sarah.

A well-groomed man pushes through a window frame, inexplicably ignoring the fully raised hatch. He wears an immaculate white shirt, partially covered by a multicolored, finely striped knit draped across his back, its sleeves knotted across his chest, collegiate style. It is a Missoni sweater, Sarah notes.

A loose-fitting gold-link chain encircles his neck, sparkling above a chest full of dark, curly hair visible through his half-unbuttoned shirt. His right wrist is cuffed with a Rolex President watch. On the small finger of his left hand, a thick band supports a blinding diamond, causing his hand to flash in the sunlight as he maneuvers his compact video camera to capture not the lion, not the zebra carcass, but the oncoming lappet-faced vultures.

The bare, pinkish heads and scrawny necks of the vultures transfix the man. Their brackish-colored bills tear stray pieces of what little remains of the zebra. "Those are the biggest vultures I've ever seen. Look at those faces and bald heads. It's a beautiful thing. A beautiful thing."

Max is disgusted. "Vultures, vultures, vultures! That's all he talks about. I wonder if he knows how many guys have been killed when one of them flies into the propeller of a plane."

The man's camera records the birds approaching by land and those descending from the air. He considers no subject other than the impatient birds dressed like so many Draculas, awaiting the moment their appetite for blood will be satisfied. The man is mesmerized as a vulture rides a thermal down from the sky. Its large talons are pulled up close to its chest, like the white rims of an airplane's wheels about to unfold for landing.

Max begins a heated conversation with this man, neither one hearing the other. Their voices are obliterated by the sounds of the lion gnawing, jackals cackling and hissing, and the yelping and grunting of an increasing number of feathered carnivores despoiling the zebra remains. Life gone, life continuing, thinks Sarah, and her mind loosens, falling backward again into her memories.

Upon hearing of her father's death, Rebecca, Sarah's younger sister, sobbed as if she might drown in her own flash flood of tears. Daniel, the youngest, sat on the bed, frozen. He could not comprehend the permanent implication of being a boy who would grow up without a male figure. Sarah had been the closest of the three children to her father, yet her reaction was the least demonstrative. Her eyes fluttered closed as she experienced a numbness that would brace her for what lay ahead. That closing of her eyes and the anesthetized sensation had been replayed in subsequent years, whenever emotional pain had threatened her carefully constructed fortress.

Sarah observes the woman nestled next to the man. Her chestnut hair falls from under a canvas cowboy hat tied beneath her chin in a small bow. Her ears display magnificent earrings. The slender fingers of her fragile, cream-colored hand gently curl around the window frame, revealing a bright red manicure. On her wrist resides the sleek and unmistakable Cartier rectangular timepiece known simply as "The Tank Watch."

An explanation of the zebra's dissection is in progress, and though Sarah understands that she should be attentive, her binoculars remain fixed on the woman's handsome watch, with its diamond-studded frame and simple black alligator-skin wristband. It is the precise model that had bewitched Sarah seven days earlier in London when she had discovered it sitting upon its white satin throne within its trademark red box in the window of Cartier Jewelers.

Moments ago she was enraptured by the hand of nature; now it is this woman's hand that mesmerizes her. Which world, she wonders, is she in?

Max shakes his head. "Christ Almighty, they want to know when the vultures will get their chance to eat! Sweet Jesus, why don't they stay in Beverly Hills?"

Their guide does not react. He neither speaks, nor points, nor attempts to interpret the activity before them. Instead, his head sinks back and his eyelids slide downward as he strains to stave off sleep.

The passengers disregard their guide's nodding indifference. They ignore his slouch and his lack of explanation of the changing sights before them: the deterioration of the carcass, the jackal's loud hysterics, the lion's fierce protection of the looted meat, the conspicuous absence of one large cone-shaped incisor from his upper jaw. They are not alerted to the oncoming approach of the lionesses inching toward the prize. They are only conscious of additional vultures being carried down by a warm thermal, like an ethereal conveyer belt transporting morticians.

While their guide dozes, Max tells stories. His group will depart enriched with knowledge; the other group will leave impoverished.

Within these few seconds, the pelvic girdle has been separated from its spinal column.

Click. Click. Click.

"Look at those dancing ribs!" Max insists. "But remember, you guys, the predator is the underdog. Why? Because there are more zebras than lions."

Peter, continuing to snap pictures, pauses. "Nature is incredibly efficient."

"Boy oh boy, yes, it is. You're absolutely right, Peter. Hey, where's that zebra? In three hours, when the red blood on those bones turns to brown, people like these idiots will come by and say, 'Oh, this is nice—it must have been eaten by jackals, insects, and mice!"

Sarah's mind slips again. After her father's death, she and her siblings adjusted to a mother whose normally volatile character was further aggravated by being the sole provider. Sarah was put in charge of her sister and brother after school, and made responsible for cleaning the house, doing the laundry, and preparing dinner. She found herself trying to please a woman who appeared to bite off satisfaction from her children in tiny morsels, then, finding them unpalatable, spat them out.

Sarah pushes herself to reenter the present. Max, she realizes, managed to rhyme the last sentence. Then, pretending to enlighten those passengers he mocks, he feigns helpfulness, pointing out, "You guys, look. Vultures catching a thermal!"

Max picks up the remnant of his last thought, laughing at his jokes the way he plays solitaire: holding all the cards. "Look at Mr. Zebra now, his jaws just flapping away. And here goes his nose. There! It's gone."

The lionesses stop feeding, moving deliberately and wearing the sediment of the zebra's wine all about their mouths and tongues.

"Don't worry, you guys, we're staying right here for the next few minutes. The vultures are going to keep the pressure on till the jackals give it up and go home to regurgitate everything they've just eaten so they can feed it to their little rug rats."

Now, it is the vultures' turn. Forty carnivorous birds finish the few leftovers in mere minutes. Max looks at the other safari group, commenting, "I wouldn't be at all surprised if those guys begin applauding them. Vultures! Christ, let's get the hell outta here."

Bumping along back to camp on the same dusty, unpaved road used this morning, Sarah fixates on irregular stone markers identifying alternative courses of travel. Stockpiles of bleached bones in varying lengths, widths, and shapes lie in disarray along with the litter of fresh elephant droppings studded with acacia thorns and beetles. They resemble great irregular clusters of clay, dotted with shiny pebbles. There are trees split and damaged by elephants. Some of the trees are growing through termite mounds surrounded by spoor.

As the group begins to cross back over the river between Buffalo Springs and Samburu National Park, a herd of elephants, ranging from massive to infant-size, drink, bathe, and play games. The matriarch sloshes around till the remaining cows follow. They pause, entering the water tentatively, but once in, decisively cross over.

Click. Click. Click.

"By six months old, those little 'tottos' can swim with their front legs on top of Mom," Max informs them.

A pair of bull elephants spars on shore, playfully interlocking hundreds of pounds of precious ivory. They tangle tusks and then disengage their heavy treasure, repeating the sport until all are convinced that this is just a game, not the more customary fight for dominance of the herd. One steps into the river to quench its thirst, soon followed by others.

Max explains, "It may be thirty or more miles before water's available for them again."

The wet creatures turn the murky color of the water, but upon ascending to the bank, the cast of their skin shines as green as the water's moss. One small elephant stops after swimming over and looks back to the other side, calculating how far it has come. The matriarch, having forged the river, laboriously mounts the muddy steps, followed by sister cows, each one crossing to the opposite bank with an individual style.

On the other side they stand with prominent, irregular watermarks across the stomachs of the herd's youngsters and across the thighs of the larger ones, like two-tusked mastodons in a muddy swamp sloshing through eons of time. Yet they are here now, Sarah realizes, points of relative constancy in a universe of dynamic change.

A medium-sized elephant takes a branch bearing hundreds of thorns and consumes the limb in its entirety.

"Such an animal will consume about three to four hundred pounds a day—grasses, herbs, and woody plants—spending anywhere from eighteen to twenty hours eating. Over fifty percent of what they eat goes straight through them. Elephants get six sets of molars in a lifetime. When the sixth wears out, they can no longer eat, then become nutritionally deprived and die."

Max continues to feed his audience. "Tusks are an elephant's front teeth; they do most of the work. So if the right tusk's shorter than the left, then it's right-handed. Did you see how he grabbed that branch? It's easy for them, a piece of cake. They have a hundred thousand separate muscles and three thousand separate muscle bundles in their trunk! With that tool, they can reach higher than a giraffe. That's what they greet each other with.

"See the 'totto' sticking its trunk in the mother's mouth? It's testing what Mom's eating. Those little guys are three hundred pounds at birth. They demand a lot of attention. They need to be touched all the time; they can't live without it," he asserts, as if this need applies only to these creatures.

Max continues before Sarah can extrapolate meaning from the word "touch."

"There's a twenty-two-month gestation period. An elephant's childhood lasts as long as ours. A calf can be raised by a related elephant."

A huge bull elephant helps himself to the abundance of available dust, throwing it about as if it were so much brown talcum powder applied after a shower. His color transforms into the tint of fine silt.

Click. Click. Click.

"He's protecting himself from parasites and the rays of the sun. It's unusual because bull elephants seldom move with the herd. It's a matriarchal society, led by the grandmother."

The beast walks through a thicket of foliage and dissolves in a grove Max identifies as Boscia Garasses trees.

With the bull's sudden disappearance, Sarah exclaims, "He looks exactly like the baseball player Shoeless Joe Jackson being erased by the ears of corn in *Field of Dreams*."

Max watches Sarah's fascination with this scene, realizing that she has become as lost within it as the elephant in the thorn trees. He points at the herd, his arm extending directly under her nostrils, the hairs upon it tickling her nose. He explains as she sneezes, "Their hide is so thick, they don't feel a damn thing. That would absolutely filet human skin."

Having completed the careful movement of the vehicle across the river, Max and his charges now find themselves adjacent to the pachyderms. The imposing matriarch elephant stands staunchly, not six feet away, appraising the relatively small Land Rover. The vehicle rests precariously on an elevation of wet embankment that slips away by small degrees as its passengers try to find the best vantage point for a photograph.

The matriarch's ears, each shaped like the continent of Africa itself, are fully spread, fanning forward and back. The head rears, the trunk is up. It is the presentation of a contemplated full-on charge under the outstretched branches of one more acacia tree. Eye to eye with Sarah, she backs up a few steps, spreads her ears, and trumpets several menacing notes. Max wants to take a picture. Intending to accommodate him, Sarah climbs atop the vehicle to allow him an unobstructed shot.

Click. Click. Click.

"It's a fine line of trust, Sarah. You shouldn't have exposed yourself so far out of the hatch. Inside, you're okay. Step out, and you've crossed the line. You're fair game."

The elephant's ears fold back. She grumbles a reverberating warning of distress. Max cups his hands together, bringing them close to his mouth, then sends her a lulling, rolling, purring sound. She responds with docility, viewing her audience with the inquisitive stare of a gentle giant.

Max relishes his triumph. "See, Sarah, you crossed the line and I saved you."

Although the elephant is formidable, her baggy skin, expression of submission to Max, and her uncomplicated gaze beneath unblinking eyelashes cause her to emanate a human-like quality.

"Don't you guys start getting sentimental," Max says, looking first at Sarah, then at Julia. "Don't think that they're like us, because they're not. They're animals, just animals."

"But there are so many stories that might lead to a different conclusion, Max. Roman audiences in the Coliseum rose in the stands and demanded that the elephants pitted against armored assailants be spared. Many of the wounded elephants voiced their pain but refused to attack, and the audience, the very Romans who thrived on blood sports, showed sympathy for them," Sarah exclaims.

"Yeah," Julia adds. "There are stories of elephants grieving, throwing sand, dust, and branches over the carcasses of their dead, vigils lasting hours. And what about the rumors of them carrying off bones and tusks to burial grounds?"

"Joyce Poole, a biologist here in Kenya, says elephants' behavior toward their dead leaves her with little doubt that they experience deep emotions and have some understanding about death," says Max, adding, "On the other hand, the neuroscientist Ledoux maintains you can't prove that animals feel anything."

"Maybe women are just freer to express their feelings about these things than men," says Sarah.

"You're dead wrong. There's no difference in the way males and females respond to nature. I can feel the same things you do."

"Max," Sarah says, surprised by the strength of her conviction, "you can't possibly tell me you have the emotions I have now."

"Yes, that's exactly what I'm saying. You have no scientific proof I am wrong."

Sarah considers the matter, struggling to come up with more weight to tip the teeter-totter so that she will be grounded and Max will fly out of his scientific seat. But attempting to conjure up her limited knowledge, Sarah realizes, is no better than a fool striking a match to provide light for the universe. She knows nothing, and nothing was truly knowable before now.

Except, she believes, that the universe most likely put Sarah into Peter's orbit, such were the probabilities against her ever meeting him. Her first job was with a new division of an international talent agency. Peter, a top agent, hired her as one of his assistants. Soon she would dare to speak to him, a word here, a word there. Sarah's goal was to relieve Peter from the necessity of behaving seriously. All the while, she willed that her intellect and personality would eventually encourage consideration for being promoted to an agent in her own right so that she would no longer be expected to deal with the mundane activities expected of her: getting coffee, taking out laundry, setting up appointments, and shielding Peter from unwanted phone calls.

In the meantime, she felt she could draw his attention to her in a positive way, maybe a personal way. There was nothing realistic about her conviction, for he was moving up the company ladder like an ascending star, blasting past obstacles as if they were mere sprinkles of stardust.

She is momentarily brought back to the present by a small speck of a plane flying overhead. Its engine emits a background buzz above the herd that now shares the riverbank with the most recent arrivals: supine crocodiles lying about as if they have risen from the murk. They wear sinister smiles and possess an incorrigible air of infinite endurance, for they have enjoyed survival in excess of one million years.

As Sarah dug further into the role of being an agent, she somehow found the strength to stand up to Peter's frequent tirades, going toe to toe with him in a dance in which she was able to hold her own and, on occasion, even lead. She was young and thin, with waist-long black hair pulled back in a businesslike chignon. Dressing conservatively, she managed to sustain the appearance of being self-assured and unattainable. It was the unattainable aspect that interested Peter.

Twelve years after hiring Sarah, Peter asked her to marry him. For Peter, no period of getting acquainted on a personal level was necessary. He had observed her capacity for work, for putting up with untenable situations, for dealing effectively with him.

Sarah and Peter were considered well suited for one another. Sarah could handle Peter's volcanic temperament; he was one of the few men not intimidated by her spirited personality and force of character. But sometime within the first year of their marriage, Peter decided there was no more play left in the game. He strolled off the field, returning to his briefcase and reports. There was uncertainty for Sarah as to how to be her own person in Peter's shadow, for no partnership existed in the spotlight aimed on Peter.

Sarah tried desperately to resurrect her own career track in the agency business, which had been derailed as a result of her marriage to Peter. Additionally, she cooked, entertained, played the role of stepmother on weekends to Peter's two children, and took care of their separate finances. She hoped these visible exertions would somehow ingratiate her back into her husband's affections. Instead, her efforts became expected, and both she and her career suffered.

Arguments became increasingly acrimonious, and Peter used them as a justification for finding a private place within him to hide, a place where he did not have to speak or reach out for days at a time.

Thirty years after her father's suicide and eight years into her marriage to Peter, every pressure in Sarah's life imploded. She contrived an overly complicated plan to take her own life. Her scheme involved the straightedge razor she used for cutting Peter's hair and an overdose of Valium and sleeping pills. She drew the blade through her right tendon and then, somehow, managed to cut her left wrist.

Seven hours later, Peter discovered her caked in blood, with no discernible pulse. She was removed by paramedics in a zipped body bag. Despite the zero odds, medical teams were assembled, and five days later, Sarah was miraculously pulled from her coma by the sheer determination of the intensive care crew, her brother, Daniel, and most particularly, Peter.

Sarah, stripped of clothing, hairpins, and makeup, experienced a confused, dependent, entirely heartfelt love for Peter, who sat in her hospital room hour after hour, day after day. But before time turned the flame-colored scars white, the fighting had resumed.

Max notices Sarah's attention on the crocodiles. "They're able to survive because of their adaptability." His words snatch her back to the present. "They can last as long as a year without eating by going into a state of estivation, a period of short-term self-induced hibernation. When the eggs are laid, they're not males or females; their sex is determined by the temperature. If it's cooler, more males, and if it's warmer, females."

Despite Sarah's fascination at the influence temperature exerts over the gender of these creatures, it is the newly arrived five giraffes she now becomes fixated on. They are coquettish, perpetually flirting with their sensuous black lashes. Small protruding horns sit atop their heads like natural skull-bone crowns. They demonstrate unmistakable grace in contrast to their size. Their charming diffidence is altered only when they reach down for water, front legs splaying awkwardly. Black tongues unfold to ladle water, some of which mixes with saliva and slips back out of their soft mouths in long, silver strands. Having had their fill, they gather themselves up and glide off, spotted masts unfurled as they sail the savanna.

"Giraffes have no sweat glands, so their urine and saliva are very concentrated."

Max looks up and then back at the elephants, noticing that they are unaffected by the drone of a plane. "Nature's yielding to today's technology. It's economically smart to do so. The planes disturb the elephants—it's another impact on the environment—but, hey, the tourist trade keeps these big guys in business.

"Speaking of technology, did you know they once spotted elephants by plane for hunting parties? Denys Finch Hatton had the idea of providing this service for hunters, but he was killed before he could really try it out on paying customers.

"Beryl Markham actually picked up the idea. She'd spot 'em, scribble a note, and drop it in a weighted message bag aimed at the hunters. One of her more challenging assignments was spotting elephants for Baron von Blixen's safari with Winston Churchill."

Beryl Markham's book was one Sarah had read. Beryl described how the elephants had learned to outsmart her aerial sighting efforts. Sarah volunteers, "Didn't the elephants form a circle, hiding the tusks of the bull so—"

Max cuts in, taking over the story. "Yeah, at first. She'd fly her blue and silver plane scouting for herds until she'd locate the guys with big tusks. That tactic didn't last very long because the elephants outsmarted her. A huge elephant would stand in the open with its tusks buried in the brush, but when spotted at close range, it turned out to be a decoy. A large female cow instead of the bull the hunters were after!"

Max's interruption of Sarah complete, he changes subjects. "I told you we'd get lucky with this dry weather. There are hundreds of bird species here. Look at all those sandgrouse. And over there, by the riverbank, scores of helmeted and vulturine guinea fowl. They're great eating. We'll try to have a taste before you leave."

As Sarah looks about her, she feels a subtle conviction that this is heaven. It is a place of thick, hot dung, its pungent odor blending into the unique, heavy fragrance conceived by blending savanna scents. Yes, she decides, this is definitely heaven. My heaven.

But she stops herself. No thoughts of heaven, she reasons, for she is here, in the land where humans are said to have evolved from apes, not far from the Great Rift Valley, the Cradle of Mankind.

What would Max say? Sarah wonders. As a scientist, does he permit himself the indulgence of contemplating a spiritual view of creation?

Never mind, Sarah resolves. She will ask him later. Perhaps in his tent.

CHAPTER 7

MOM

Sarah and Max were directed by "The Big Man" into an office two doors down from Cecil's. They stepped into a room equal to at least a tenth of the entire seventh floor. A large couch crowded up against the far wall, but went unoccupied. The bureaucratic contingent that had taunted Sarah earlier found their way into the rear of the room like spectators filling the gallery. They stood near the furniture, not daring to sit. Cecil appeared and stood by the door, his curiosity uncontainable within his drab office.

* * *

Samburu. The group has shared blistering days together, and each knows the humbleness of constantly dirty fingernails, filthy sweat-streaked faces, the experience and mixed results of four-minute showers, the ineffectiveness of deodorant at the equator, the paucity of one-ply toilet paper, and the indignity of bathrooms that are but holes dug in the dirt. Nothing is off-limits, and the camaraderie they experience at the end of the day sets the mood for telling life stories.

Julia asks questions of Max, exploring what she believes to be the paternal relationship Dian Fossey had with Dr. Louis Leakey.

"No, Julia," Max gently chastises, "Louis Leakey wasn't like a father to Dian Fossey at all. He gave her an opportunity, yeah. You might even say he capitulated to her demand for it. But he wasn't a father figure.

"The relationships that are really interesting are the ones between fathers and sons, like the one Louis Leakey had with his eldest son, Richard. God, they experienced it all! They went through distrust, public disagreement, and professional rivalry when Richard wanted to transform Kenya's National Museum into something akin to the Smithsonian. I'll tell you what, though, the best father-son relationship I know about was the one Dr. Bernhard Grzimek had with his two sons, Bernhard and Michael. Dr. Grzimek's the guy who offered to buy the Serengeti from the Tanzanian government so he could give the land back to the animals."

Everyone expresses astonishment, and Max, relishing his ability to hold an audience captive, continues. "Yeah, there was a movement among conservationists to get the Maasai and their cattle out of the area because they were encroaching on the natural wildlife habitat. The government wasn't acting forcefully in the matter because they were distracted with the Mau Mau problems, so officials decided to change the borders of the conservation area to make more room for the Maasai.

"There was a worldwide backlash and even some discussion of placing the Serengeti under the rule of the

United Nations rather than British administration. That's when Grzimek stepped in. His gig in life was protecting living species from extinction. His sons made films about African wildlife."

"So what happened?" everyone asks in chorus.

"Michael was killed when he took off from Ngorongoro on his way to Bangui to pick up Alan Root, the nature photographer who spent time with Dian Fossey. And Alan Root was once in the photographic safari business with Richard Leakey. Well, I guess that brings us full circle!"

Max savors another sip of wine and then changes the direction of the conversation. "Peter, how'd you get along with your father? Did he ever hit you?"

"Hit me? No, he wasn't around enough. The poor bastard was too busy schlepping Fuller Brush products door to door. Even when he was home, though, my mother wore the pants in our family. The dominant male figure in my life was my dad's boss. He was shrewd about money and broads. I'll share some of his philosophy with you guys later."

"Share it with them now, Peter," Sarah suggests, the liquor in her speaking, for she already knows the philosophy.

"Yeah, let's have it." It's Thad, hoping to glean insight with which to further postpone a commitment to Julia.

Peter proceeds. "Oh, he'd say 'Only tell a broad you love her if you want to sleep with her.' He had some fantastic-looking broads, but he'd date several at a time. When I asked him why, he said, 'For every beautiful woman, there's a guy tired of fucking her.' In other words, keep more than one broad around."

Sarah shudders, for although she encouraged Peter, this is becoming too much. "Okay, I think they've got the drift of it."

"Just one more thing, Peter. How do you feel about marriage?"

"I think, Thad, if you get married, you're crazy. Anyway, getting back to my family life, I used to pull a lot of crap, like taking money, ditching school, going to the track, and forging my report cards." Peter says it as if his behavior was commonplace.

Sarah thinks of Peter's mother, the person she holds responsible for his inability to intimately connect with women. She relentlessly nagged him rather than nurtured him through childhood—a peculiar strategy for a Jewish mother raising her firstborn son, but she was stubborn and sure of herself. A quiet resolve nested within Peter's indomitable spirit. He forged a singular determination to be a success, its measure defined in dollars.

Although Peter's family enjoyed a comfortable suburban life, his father's income depended on his being away for long absences. When he was home, he capitulated to his wife on all matters.

If Peter's mother had not been born to wear the pants in their family, she would have insisted on putting them on anyway. Witnessing his parents, Peter decided he would never allow a woman to wear the trousers in his relationships.

"So that was it: ditch school, forge report cards, then go to Hollywood and became a top talent agent?" asks Max, laughing at the idea of Peter's success being summed up in so uncomplicated a fashion.

No, Sarah might have added, not so simple. His was more like the initial chapter in a stereotypical story, where the hero begins his career in the mailroom and works his way from the basement to the executive suites by compelling those in important positions to recognize his uncompromising drive, will to succeed, and unflagging determination. He intentionally cultivated an enigmatic persona. One moment he would appear calmly pensive and controlled. The next, he might explode into anger so disproportionate to the event that those witnessing his response would be grounded in wonder as to what had precipitated such a reaction.

Peter's pause causes Thad to take up the slack. "Things were sure different in my house. My height seemed to piss my dad off. He never adjusted to it, no pun intended. My mother got cancer when I was fourteen. We had to watch her be taped, tubed, clamped, and needled till she went. A lot of ladies started coming around with food right after. You know the saying, 'In the South, all you need for a funeral is a body and a casserole.'

"My father pretty much flipped out. He eventually sent me to a military academy where I finished high school. But, to his credit, he did pay for college. We're okay with each other these days, but only because I've made a lot of money, I'm independent, and he's right there in Atlanta with me."

At the word "independent," Julia looks away, gazing first at the table and then to Sarah. It is this mighty word that sticks in her craw. Sarah is empathetic to Julia, this woman who is so much a younger version of herself.

As Peter and Thad's stories unfold, a slightly competitive edge to the conversation develops, as if this is a contest to see who had it worse as a kid. Max, the competitor, is compelled to reveal what would otherwise remain untold. "Jesus, both of your childhoods were a piece of cake. We lived in Peterhead, on the northeast coast of Scotland. My father was just an ol' herring and cod fisherman, a lemming, following the tradition of his father and his father's father, who caught cod and ling. When he came home from a trip, he was cold, mad, half-crazy, and one drunk son of a bitch.

"He'd beat the shit out of me just in case I'd done something wrong while he was away. Then, when he was ready to leave, he'd smack me as hard as he could a couple of times so I wouldn't do anything while he was gone. I think I've got more damn scars from him than from the animal attacks I've had since coming to Africa.

"He was the meanest bastard I've ever met. He wasn't even a particularly good fisherman. If they had to lay guys off, he was the first one they'd let hang.

"You know, if it weren't for bad luck, that prick wouldn't have had any luck at all," says Max, without his customary Howdy Doody grin.

"Listen to me, my boy," says Peter with unpracticed gentleness, "it's not that easy to be a parent. Most of us fool ourselves into thinking we're trying hard to do the best job we can, but our kids seem to disagree. Mine had everything. I mean, shit, they tell me things I did when they were young and I swear I don't know what the hell they're talking about."

"Peter, it's not the same. My parents never gave me anything, and I doubt either one of them would dare to say they did their best, not with me around anyway."

"What about your mom and siblings?" Sarah asks.

"My mother was useless. She was so afraid of my father it paralyzed her. My sister and brother were much older and never around. No one stuck up for me but me. I got outta there though. When I was seventeen, I ran away from home. I haven't had any contact with them for over thirty years."

Peter sits a little straighter in his chair, narrows his eyes as if looking through the sighting device on a rifle, and in an authoritative voice asks, "Well, don't leave us hanging. Go on. What was your plan? How'd you get out of there? You're a long way from Scotland, and you don't look like you ever wore a kilt."

"Ever since I was in primary school, the Scotsman David Livingstone has been my hero, and I wanted to come to Africa like him. He was a missionary and a doctor. I wanted to be a zoologist. As a boy, I'd climb the cliffs along the beach and spot rare migrating birds at this popular estuary of the River Ythan. I could identify all of 'em.

"I got so good that I started guiding bird-watching tours. On one of them I met a professor of ornithology from University of Washington who was there with a group. He gave me his card. After he left, I shot rare specimens with my slingshot. I'd gut, cure, and salt 'em, then send 'em off to him with long, handwritten descriptions of the birds—what they ate, their habits, and anything else I could come up with.

"One day I zinged a little ringed plover, which is pretty rare. When I sent him off to the professor, it did the trick. He persuaded the university to give me financial help if I could just get out there.

"I bought a one-way ticket to New York, which was as far as I could afford to go. As soon as I got my passport, I left home, and I've never been back. When I got to New York, I did a lot of odd things, strange things, including some 'midnight requisitions,' if you know what I mean. A few weeks after I got there, I met two guys who were driving out to the Northwest. So the three of us started off."

Max had studied and worked odd jobs, including a variety of dangerous, high-paying ones like helicopter rescues in national parks. When he was ready to come to Kenya, he was granted a visa on the condition that he work two years as a volunteer teacher at Scott's Mission School.

Sarah and Julia do not attempt to best Max's story of parental abuse, deprivation, and hard work. In lieu of telling tales, they demand to hear more of his. This time, it is Julia who pushes Max further into his past.

"How'd you learn to fly? How'd you get your plane?"

"I wanted to fly my clients from camp to camp to save time. My clients photograph, or spot birds or game, and they're usually pretty well-off, so they don't mind the extra cost of the plane and fuel.

"On one of my safaris, about ten years ago, I had this rich Texas oil dude and his wife. I took real good care of them and they liked me a lot. We started talking about flying. He told me if I came to Texas, he'd put me up and his private pilot would teach me to fly. So I went. I spent four and a half weeks out there, heard hundreds of redneck jokes I committed to memory, learned to fly, got my license, and eventually went to England to buy my plane. I had it shipped over here. It's taken me seven years to pay it off, but now it's all mine."

"So now you have everything you want?" asks Julia.

"Hell, no. I need sophisticated camera equipment."

"You've already proven yourself to be as good as any of the best photographers of wildlife. What would you do with more expensive camera equipment?" Sarah wants to know.

"I'd be able to take the type of close-up professional shots that would make me as famous a photographer as Jonathan Scott, Brandon Howard, Claudio Tomatis, or Peter Beard. I'd do special-edition coffee-table books with text written from the unique vantage point of a safari guide."

Sarah has stopped listening. His story has evoked images in some corner of her mind. She thinks of his inert mother, staring into the cold Scottish fields with empty eyes. She pictures his father, stooped over with years and turmoil.

Max's sister and brother, so much older, were already a life removed from him when he departed Scotland. They never knew him when he was home and probably never cared much when he left. His sister and brother, Sarah speculates, had probably been conceived when his parents were young and idealistic. Max was born fifteen years later, by which time the grim, working-class reality of their life had taken over, replacing the happier people his parents might once have been.

So lost is Sarah amongst the pictures and thoughts in her head, she has failed to notice the cessation of conversation, the stillness and the sound of a tune in the air. Sarah is humming and mouthing words to "Danny Boy."

"Are you okay?" Max questions, then instructs, "Let's move outside so these guys can clean up in here. Sarah, be 'Mom' and lead the way?"

Walking from the meal tent to the fire located in the middle of camp, Max observes Sarah's shoeless feet.

"How many times do I need to tell you that you can't walk barefoot? God knows what you're liable to step on. If you get an acacia thorn in your foot, we'll have to Medivac you outta here. The only reason I've ever had to stop a safari was when someone stepped on an acacia thorn, and we had to get them to Nairobi."

Peter, overhearing, adds, "I've already told her to keep her shoes on and she won't listen. Maybe you'll have more luck than I have."

Pulling Sarah aside, Max whispers, "By the way, no massage tonight. I'm gonna gather up some of the slack in my correspondence line."

Sarah turns about, facing Max, and asks incredulously, "Do you know what you just called me?"

"I called you Sarah. What the hell do you think I called you?"

Sarah collapses in her bed, quickly losing track of the word "Mom." The next time Max refers to her as "Mom," she will not get it either. When she finally does, it will be too late.

CHAPTER 8

WAITING TO BE HEARD

The flat green walls of the room into which Sarah and Max had been ushered were unadorned, except for the requisite framed photograph of President Moi hanging in every public building.

How different this was from the quiet sanctuary of the Serengeti. Sarah remembered the Samburu cheetah its image of quiet assurance providing inspiration to hold herself together under round two of the relentless questioning of her inquisitor.

* * *

Today they are at Lewa Downs, 55,000 acres of real estate and wildlife conservancy dedicated to preserving twenty-two black rhinos and twenty white rhinos, located on the eastern end of the Laikipia Plateau in the lower northern hills of Mount Kenya. Foot-and-mouth disease, along with the great drought of the early 1980s, ravaged the land, transforming this once-profitable cattle ranch into its present eco-business enterprise. Now, the guests are one of several profit centers in this new dynamic, which integrates farming, conservation, and tourism.

They will be riding English as they venture into the game park. Sarah, in a semi-permanent state of confusion, announces, "I only ride Western or bareback. I'm a good rider, but I can't ride English." In her disturbed mind, English means sidesaddle.

"Good God, Sarah," chides Max. "We're not going to be holding an equestrian competition. We're just going out for a few hours to view game on horseback."

At the stables, Sarah is astonished to see five horses with English saddles. How could she have thought they would be riding sidesaddle? The effect of medication meant to ward off malaria, combined with her antidepressant, continues to take bites out of her mind.

Julia receives a lively mount responding to the name of Maude. Max selects Fire, acknowledging the mare as his favorite safari steed. Thad's horse is a grand animal reaching eighteen hands high and responds to the name Bachelor, though he has never courted anything more than an apple from a passing stable hand. Bertha, a docile creature promising a smooth, steady, dull ride, is relegated to Peter.

Sarah is assigned an animal resembling a donkey with its slow-moving manner and ignoble head. His body seems to drag, although it has not yet moved. Sarah feels ashamed to mount it. The horse is named Spirit, a characteristic so obviously absent from the animal's demeanor that he could only have been so named for the irony of it.

When the group moves out, Sarah is unable to keep up with the others, at least not without dismounting and walking at her own brisk pace. Her task is to maintain Spirit's hooves in a forward direction.

She remounts and they ride over grasslands sprawling unevenly upon volcanic soil. The open space is green, yellow, and beige, the colors of bamboo, red oat, and buffalo grasses. The flats are wooded with dry cedars and nine different acacia bush and tree species.

Thad falls back, unable to keep up with Julia and Max, whose horses prance amongst the giraffes in carefree interplay, passing within mere inches of one another. The giraffes make off at canter speed, their hooves pounding into the earth, the dust rising, but never high enough to obliterate the movement of legs sufficiently long to elevate bodies to soaring heights. Their heads move, then their necks, their torsos, and finally their rumps, in articulated movement across the horizon.

Max directs everyone's attention to a brightly feathered bird dressed in pale yellow and red, and makes the sound "too-de-doo." He gets a response in kind. "That's a red-and-yellow barbet. They sing in chorus with their own. I just tricked this one into thinking I was one of them! I've never met a bird I didn't want to coax into conversation!"

Two hours pass, witnessing animals from this elevated, close-up perspective, including a sleeping lion, an isolated male expelled from the pride.

At 9:00 AM, the group turns around and begins the relatively short ride back to Lewa. Sarah, because of the reversal of direction, is actually ahead of the group, but her lead disappears when Max stretches in his saddle and twists toward Julia.

"Hey, Julia! Wanna let these two broads run?"

"Sure. Why not? Are you ready?"

"Yeah. Let her out! I'll race you to the plane."

Max and his mount catapult forward at a full gallop, with Julia plunging into his trail of dust. They reach the airstrip where Max's plane is moored, a lone boat on a dry lake, then thunder down the stretch, their laughter cracking in the wind like a determined jockey's whip. Thad and Peter ease their horses into a rapid trot toward the barn, while Sarah dispiritedly pushes her failing Spirit until the horse senses home, the one destination for which he will let out his all.

* * *

The cottages at Lewa are a distinct break with the tent camp accommodations, pleasuring guests with homey appointments—a dressing table and chair, a ceiling fan, a complete bathroom with a lava stone sink and shower adorned by spigots through which flows luxurious hot and cold water. Sarah lingers endlessly under a steady stream of cleansing water plumbed from a nearby natural spring. She remains under this cascade, hoping it will both bathe and baptize her, for she longs to start over. The water flows through the drain, filters through gravel, and irrigates the trees. It is a cycle of life, and Sarah imagines she is somehow part of it.

"Sarah, I'm starving. I'm going to breakfast." Peter manages to slam the screen door as he departs.

In the solitude of a brief reprieve, Sarah walks through the effort of dressing in slow, dream-like steps.

She wants to continue to indulge in this respite from the chaos of her mind. But meals should not be missed.

Meals have come to define that brief period of equality amongst travelers. It is the time when an intelligent remark has a clear advantage over a brilliant sighting.

Breakfast is served in an arboretum looking out across an open gorge, accessible to guests, flies, children, and dogs alike.

"What do you guys want to do for the next few hours till we go out again this afternoon? There's a swimming pool and that great veranda with books and magazines. You can walk around the immediate area, look around the huts where the workers are weaving and the furniture's made, or just rest. Sarah, there's a gift store on the property. You're probably ready for some retail therapy."

Sarah imagines what it would be like to be in real therapy right now. She would describe this experience as both a dream and a nightmare, with the unfurling of so many images that the doctor would be confounded, but they would book another session, and although he would press her to make sense of it herself, she would cajole him until he interpreted events for her and her mind would be unburdened.

Peter, benefiting from a good night's sleep in conventional accommodations, intends to explore with his camera. Thad and Julia want to exercise to erode the extra pounds they insist they have gained.

"I want to work on my journal," Sarah indicates, to no one's surprise.

Max responds with uncharacteristic understanding. "Come with me. I'm going to give you my porch, away from everyone else, while I go to the pool. No one will find you or bother you, so you have no excuses not to write."

Sarah is surprised by Max's offer, but follows him to the simple hut designated for guides. He points to one of two chairs on the deck, directing her to sit down, then walks into his single room and empties the contents of his knapsack over the bed.

"I'm going to put earphones on you and you'll be able to listen to music. What do you like? Jazz? Show tunes? Classical?"

"Classical, please."

"Mozart's Sinfonia Concertante, de Falla's The Three-Cornered Hat, Tchaikovsky's Symphony No. 4, Bartok's Violin Concerto no. 2—"

"Do you have Beethoven's Fifth?"

"Yeah, of course," Max replies, sounding as if such music is standard safari equipment.

"I thought you believed in traveling light," Sarah chides.

He ignores her effort at repartee and inserts the cassette into the player, gently placing it between her legs. Sara tries to balance it on her lap, between her journal, assorted notes, and a variety of collected books.

"When I checked the headsets in my plane, I saw that you've already ruined the foam covering on my earphones with your lipstick. It's going to take me forever to replace it. So don't, I repeat, don't let this cassette player fall. I can't get another one out here. Okay?"

"That's reasonable. I even promise to protect it from marauding lions."

Max shakes his head, perplexed that Sarah cannot simply acknowledge his instructions without commenting. He returns to his bed, drops his pants, and with his backside clearly exposed, changes into swim trunks.

After he disappears, Sarah picks up her pen and writes a nonsense stream of consciousness:

Nature has the peculiar effect of ameliorating the aftertaste of even the most hard-boiled "bad egg." Just a few hours ago, I was cursing Max and the horse he had me ride in on. However, he has now transformed himself into a helpful unicorn, prancing about my ballpoint "Space Pen," encouraging me to write. He is complicated. I like complicated.

Before she can continue this spontaneous tribute, her pen slackens and her mind is no longer in charge.

To Sarah, it is as if the next moment, Max is behind her. A full hour has passed. He stands with his hands on her shoulders, awakening her with a light touch. He reaches over her, his thumbs and fingers massaging her taut muscles. The feel of him upon her bare shoulders is unexpectedly sensual and unnerving, a forgotten pleasure.

"What are you doing?"

"Giving you a massage. Why? Are you rejecting me?"

"It's not that. It's just that this might really appear inappropriate: you giving me a massage, out here in full daylight."

"To whom?"

"To anybody passing by, of course."

"We're not exactly on Main Street, USA, Sarah."

Sarah thinks of Peter walking about the premises with his camera, trying to gain a special shot. "Well, Peter wouldn't appreciate this scene."

"So you are rejecting me! Why don't you just go now so I can get dressed for lunch? Give me the cassette player before you let it fall. You've already bent the right earphone when your head dropped," Max concludes sarcastically.

"You banish me with one hand and admonish me with the other. You're ambidextrous! I fell asleep. I guess my body needed that more than it needed to write. You shouldn't have spoiled me with a soft chair and good music. Better a bed of nails and solitary confinement."

He stares at her, perplexed. "Why can't you talk straight like a normal person? I can never understand you."

"It's not been my experience that the so-called 'normal' people do talk straight. I think I do talk straight. You're just not listening."

Max is not up to this, so Sarah slips off through the brush to let him bare his backside.

Peter is cleaning up in the room and, when he is ready, he and Sarah walk together, holding hands, past other cottages and across a wild lawn through the arched doorway of the dining arboretum. Sarah cannot understand why Peter has taken her hand. Are they a couple again, with all that that implies? Or, as is so often the case, is this just for appearances?

Max's group is again seated at the baronial table along with other guides and their individual safari groups.

The proprietors of Lewa Downs, a husband-and-wife team, attempt to engage the various guests in conversation, but in between explaining the origin of the dishes, the hostess's energies are deflected by children, nannies, and dogs, whose good-natured begging becomes intrusive.

The host's conversation with his guests is more labored than it is with the guides, whom he tells of the leopards being reintroduced into the wild, the elephants and the wires erected to keep them from off-limit areas, as well as a full complement of issues that have either progressed or regressed since each of their last visits. Guests pay the small price of listening rather than participating.

"We've been asked to 'retire' to another location. Follow me," Max announces, waving his group into formation behind him with a grandiose gesture.

Two wood posts at the entrance of a generous open porch support the weight of the patio's roof. Plain wood beams cross the ceiling upon which rests a tightly woven mat made of local sisal to form a conventional thatched roof, the hat upon this traditional East African home.

A long cabinet fashioned from enormous split logs provides the room's focal point. On top of its smooth surface sit coffee, tea, white cups, and saucers. Within its shelves are assorted books on Africa, animals, plants, and birds. To the right of the massive piece of furniture is a large round table with one leaf down, on top of which rests a plain pitcher filled with a miniature field of wildflowers.

Towards the far end of the buffet is an old upright piano, and Sarah becomes fixed on what she is certain are the grinning ivory teeth sneering at her. She thinks maybe life is black and white, and wrong and right are easily discernible, just like the keys. She seeks to know of the black-and-white keys of the piano what is wrong and what is right when it comes to memorializing a memory.

Peter's prerogative is to shoot photos on the safari of gnarled, fallen trees, signifying the falling of giants, the wrath of nature or, perhaps, nothing at all. He captures animals in a range of behaviors within the circle of his lens. One hears, "Steady, steady, freeze," and then *click, click, click*. The vehicle moves forward or backward as the driver maneuvers to allow them another shot, a better shot, a shot from a different angle or vantage point.

Not only are concessions made to provide opportunities for the hundreds of pictures taken, Sarah considers, but Max also relays a myriad of instructions to the two photographers in his charge. There are even humorous occasions when Max tells Peter to remove his lens cap, and they both laugh in the way men often do after one catches the other doing something ridiculous.

Why can't I keep my journal as full of words as their cameras are of pictures? she asks herself as she closes the piano, abruptly wiping the smirk off its face.

Several spotted morning warblers wearing cinnamon-red feathers sneak onto the cabinet, stealing small granules of sugar. No one on the patio but Sarah witnesses their petty theft.

It is one of those rare spaces of silence when the monologue of the safari guide is temporarily suspended, creating a void like the emptiness of a schoolroom after class has been dismissed. Max, usually indefatigable, stretches out on a sheepskin- and leather-covered sofa reading an outdated issue of *Pilot Magazine*. Sarah is on the adjacent smaller couch, which is covered with a handmade slipcover. On the table to Sarah's left is a strong cup of Kenyan coffee topped with whole milk and fizzing with eight tablets of Sharper's sweetener. Sarah stares, for this fascinates her, as she vividly imagines she is watching a microcosm of world trade. On the other side of this table sits Peter, puffing away contentedly on one of the Cuban Romeo y Julieta cigars Sarah bought for him at Davidoff's in London, prior to leaving for Africa.

At 3:30 PM, Max gauges the limited amount of sleep he can enjoy before the scheduled game drive. Sarah watches him as he rolls over on his unaltered side and wonders if he does so because it hurts to lie on a body missing part of itself.

Above Max's head birds come and go, alighting just long enough to chirp a few bars, then fly away when he does not reply. Sarah thinks of Max's various references to all of the ornithological tours he has conducted and imagines they are each submitting theories to him for his critique. The birds' dissertations will have to be heard by Max another day.

At four o'clock, Max's internal alarm sounds. "Okay. Let's hit it. I'll meet you guys out in front in ten minutes."

* * *

This afternoon the driver, Mungari, is not available. The Lewa team is shorthanded.

"Thad, you're going to be our driver this afternoon."

Max's directive is not questioned. Thad jumps into position with his customary "I'm up for anything" bounce.

The land is scorched a dried yellow, yet still provides a temporary home for huge ostriches that strut about, their large backsides looking like the plumed hat worn by Audrey Hepburn in *My Fair Lady*.

"Those pretty ones are the males. The females are plain. No frills."

Thad brings the vehicle to a stop, asking, "Permission to take a piss?"

"Permission granted, but give me your camera, with the brochure this time, so I can figure this baby out."

Max studies the instructions intensely, and within only seconds, announces, "Okay, I've got it now."

There is movement in the low growth several feet ahead. A family of warthogs is eating seed pods and flowers. Both dad and mom resemble eighteenth-century English colonels with heavy eyebrows and upturned handlebar mustaches. The babies high-step around them like small attachés.

A Verreaux's eagle-owl spreads its wings and allows something to drop. Max jumps out of the vehicle, picks up the fallen wad containing pieces of legs, ribs, a jawbone, teeth, and a section of the backbone and quills. He reads the parts like an ancient Delphic oracle. "This was a porcupine. It was regurgitated by the owl to clear its throat."

Max catches the distant sight of a rhino. "Hey! A white rhino! Thad, pedal to the metal and cross the bridge. Hang a left so we're off the road. Avoid the trees and the aardvark holes.

"As you can see, this guy isn't really white. They're called white because the natives were trying to say 'wide mouth.' White rhino is just a distortion of the word 'weit.' These are more docile than black rhinos, but they're about twice the weight."

Max directs Thad to stop and turns to Peter. "Get out and shoot at eye level."

"Are you serious?" Peter demands, convinced that Max must be kidding.

"Yeah! What's two and a half tons of rhino to a guy like you?" Max asks, his seriousness mixing with sheer delight as he scrambles to the ground. The rhino steps about in circles, his breath like smoke in the late-afternoon air.

"No way. You've got to be fucking crazy," Peter declares.

"Before he charges we can make all the noise we want and wave our hands. The bluffing will stop the rhino and buy us a little time." Not receiving the enthusiastic response he had hoped for, Max mumbles in resignation, "Give me your camera. I'll take the picture."

The vehicle is separated from a potential rhino charge by a narrow ditch. Max scrambles under the Land Rover, positioning his body so that only his head and arms extend beyond its scant protection. Flat on his stomach, he shoots rapidly while Peter and Thad stare at him incredulously.

Click. Click. Click.

Thad starts out of the vehicle. "I'll shoot with you."

"No. Sorry about that. The driver never leaves his position. Give me your camera too."

Max holds one camera, then the second, and finally his own. "Shit, it's times like this that I really need professional camera equipment."

He takes vertical shots and horizontal shots. He brackets up and brackets down. He moves on his belly, sliding closer, daring the moving, armored creature to charge him while he shoots off clips of film as if they were live ammo.

Max returns the cameras to the men, takes the binoculars, and spots a mother and baby in a clearing. "Thad, hit the accelerator. Go, go, go, before they take off!"

He directs Thad until the Land Rover is positioned on the same side of the ditch as the mother and baby. "Try going fifteen feet to the left . . . a little more. Peter's blocked out. Okay, that'll do. Perfect. Just perfect."

These instructions suggest that everyone will shoot from the vehicle. This, however, is not the plan.

"Peter, this time you're coming with me. Look, Bwana, you wanted great pictures. You're paying for great pictures. I'm gonna get you great pictures! Get out now! Stay close to the Land Rover. In fact, put your entire body under it except the parts you need to operate the camera. I'm going to get the kid to look at us straight on."

Peter is on safari with Max in charge. Sarah is amazed as she watches her husband surrender control in increments so small he appears unaware of it.

Max calls to the baby until it gives him a perfect mug shot. "I'll be damned. I just shot my first photograph of a baby white rhino. Boy, I'm hot today!"

Then, on a more authoritative note, he instructs, "Bwana, move away as fast as you can if the rhino charges."

"Max, my son, if that rhino charges, there's no fucking way I'm going to be able to move."

Max stands up and leans against the rear grill, body, hands, and camera steady in the face of the rhino's approaching horn.

Click. Click. Click.

"Well, you've got bigger cajones than I do, amigo," Peter confesses with increased respect for Max's confidence, as great in the bush as Peter's was in his world of business.

The baby male, three months old, lumbers awkwardly at Max and Peter, stopping before he is a foot away from his mother. His pouting mouth forms a classic bullying expression while he makes hard thudding sounds and romps about in tight semicircles. Max feigns a cartoon rhino voice, asking, "Hey, who's charging who here?"

Like musical chairs, both people and animals slide into different positions, until the rhinos are on the right and slightly behind the vehicle, yet well within shooting distance. The baby begins to nurse, tilting forward. Then, before the cameras can capture the feeding, he stops, turns one hundred and eighty degrees, walks around the back of his mother, and poses with the knees of his two front legs knocking together. He steps forward feigning boldness, then backs into her, making certain his security fortress is still there. A classic case of a kid hanging tough as long as Mom is there to reinforce him, thinks Sarah. Finally, his attention span wandering, he lays down behind his fiercest protector.

Max, having resumed a position inside the vehicle just long enough to devour another of Sarah's dwindling supply of PowerBars, jumps out again, but not before wiping his hand on the sleeve of the thermal underwear top she is forced to wear in lieu of her brighter-colored shirts. He relishes the PowerBar, smacking his lips as he chews the last bite. His only acknowledgment that they have been provided by Sarah is when he asks her where they were purchased. He will ask future clients to bring him a supply of PowerBars along with the baby bottles and nipples he requests for nursing abandoned animals in protective sanctuaries.

"Let's try to see them blink. Start the car and move slowly forward." The vehicle stalls. "Keep it going, don't stop."

A slight lurch forward but no ground is gained. They are stuck in a morass of mud.

"Okay, everyone out. Peter, move into the driver's seat. This is going to be a bitch. Thad, go find a long log, preferably split. First, grab the wench and lift the jack from the front grill. Julia, you're going to have to put your shoulder to the wheel, so to speak. And Sarah, you're barefoot again, goddamn it. Just stay where you are."

Max studies a localized spot beneath the tires and the path of debris ahead. "We're stuck in black cotton soil!"

Thad starts out of the car, extending his hand to Julia for balance. They hold on to each other in a brief, transitory touch. Then Thad's fingers lose their traction on Julia's. He moves to the side of the road and begins to pick up boulders, one at a time, tossing them with the ease of dribbling basketballs. Max rolls several, finally clearing a few feet of passage. Peter exits to help push as Thad jumps back into the driver's position and throttles forward over the pieces of wood placed under the front wheel.

"Okay. Everyone back in. Start her up fast. Watch out, Thad. Move slowly. Head to twelve o'clock. No, stop. Sorry. Didn't see those electric elephant wires."

Max spits out commands as he directs Thad. Then, changing his tone, he points to an old bull elephant, remarking, "Oh, look! There's Omar. Turn right. No, left."

The vehicle swerves and misses the wires.

"Sorry for the curve ball, Thad. Go right up to the chain at Park Headquarters. Look to the left, there's a road. Okay, straight ahead. It's rough going, so pick your way. Zebras! Stop, Thad! Quick, quick, quick, before they move."

Max imitates their inhaling and exhaling snorting sound, emulating the zebra alarm call. They respond by looking up and moving, thereby providing the best angle.

"Anytime you can shoot uphill at a mammal, or down at a bird, take the damn shot; it's much more interesting. Just keep shooting, and don't worry about how much film you're going through. It'll be worth it to get one great shot. That was a common Burchell's zebra. The difference between the commons and the Grévy's is the direction of their stripes. Commons go from vertical to horizontal."

A zebra with its baby stands at the edge of a high plateau. She is one of many who has wandered a short way from the line. At first, her eyes are fixed to a spot on the ground. Then she glances up and meets Sarah's gaze.

Standing on the seat, Max thunders, "Okay, Thad, let's move out. I want you to cover some distance. Turn right here. Too slow. Gun it for Christ's sake or we'll stall. Go straight. Stop!"

Max springs out of the Land Rover in a motion so fluidly abrupt that its passengers are dazed. He grabs his jacket from the rear seat, then plunges it down on the ground, as if swatting at an oncoming hornet. He bends down and returns, excitement thick in his voice. "This, my friends, is a puff adder. The deadliest snake around. I know you've been dying to see one. Well, here it is! Notice how I hold it so it can't bite me. I realize you guys don't want to lose me till the end of the safari." Max is lost in his own laughter.

Though lethal, the snake does not look nearly as menacing as its reputation. It is deep brown, and shades of pale tan punctuate the skin, with inverted arrows patterning its short, fat body. Its snout-shaped mouth sits below beaded, intimidating eyes accentuated by arched bands of white scales, overarched by dark-colored eyebrow scales.

"Okay," Peter exhorts, "now that we've seen a puff adder, I think I speak for all of us when I say, let the motherfucker go!"

Max winds up his arm and throws the serpent like a softball. It lands several feet way. As soon as he has catapulted himself back inside the vehicle, Thad presses hard on the accelerator, moving a safe distance from the killer reptile.

"Thad, go another thirty feet, turn into the small clearing behind those jagged rocks, and bring 'er to a stop."

By the time the vehicle comes to a rest, even Thad appears shaken by the proximity to rhinos, road ruts, black cotton soil, boulders, a lethal snake, and unfamiliar territory.

When Max speaks again, everyone aboard braces for what's next. "Okay," Max laughs as Thad pulls up to a precipice overlooking Lewa's great expanse. "Let's pull out the ice chest and liquor. That was nip and tuck. It's time for a 'Sundowner.' Remember the guys back home who said an African sunset would make you cry? Well, get out the tissues. It's crying time again!" He sings the last line imitating Ray Charles, and Sarah is, once again, captivated by Max's charm, this time manifesting itself in music.

The sun begins its retreat. Colors blaze in bold, erratic ripple formations across a sky that might be mistaken for a smoky battlefield, the hot-pink residue of fire powder fighting fiercely with white clouds marching over blue.

Within an hour, crickets sound out the cadence of day's end. Those animals previously operating under the sun now surrender to those that do so under the stars. Creatures of the night begin to take their place upon the savanna's graying carpet. Hyenas, jackals, porcupines, mongooses, lions, genets, and bats all sound out their respective notes as the evening's melody begins.

Everyone is lying down on blankets in their private observatory looking up at black velvet with intricate cutouts of stars and galaxies, each illuminated from behind, each shining with the brightness of its own spectacular silvery backlight.

"You probably already know the sun's really a main-sequence star," says Max. "And there's Venus, the second-brightest object in the sky 'cause of its reflective atmosphere. Jupiter's actually the largest planet in the solar system, one of four gas planets. It's 317.938 times the mass of Earth. But one of the most spectacular sights you guys get to see is that baby, the Southern Cross! See the magnificent star grouping? It looks like you could almost draw a horizontal line from one to another and then a second line, to intersect it vertically. It's one of the most beautiful patterns of stars in this hemisphere, even though it's the smallest constellation in the sky.

"Over there are the Clouds of Magellan, named by you-know-who around 1520. Just think: you're looking

170,000 years back in time because every light up there takes tens of thousands of years to reach us.

"Those galaxies really stand out with this full moon. No binoculars or telescopes required tonight. Here's a little question for you from the Scottish poet Thomas Seget: 'Columbus gave man lands to conquer by bloodshed; Galileo new worlds harmful to none.' Which is the better thought?"

"I'm not touching that one, Max," says Peter. "I don't think we'd be here tonight if there hadn't been a shitload of bloodshed. This would be just a land of tribes fighting each other for land. Where would we be if they hadn't shed blood in America? The damn British would probably still have us under their thumb. And don't even get me started on what would have happened in World Wars I and II if blood hadn't been shed. I think the question is one for the poets, not for us conquerors."

Max's body is close to Sarah's, his hand over her arm as he points out a particular pattern within the Milky Way, lifting her arm up, opening her hand, and pointing her index finger in the distant vicinity of its location. "It's starting to get pretty cold out here. Anyone want another cover?"

No one does, but he puts a third blanket over himself and Sarah anyway, then moves in closer so that their bare skin touches at the arms and again below their shorts, his left leg against her right. Max's calculated move to be close to her is exhilarating, yet confusing. She wonders if this is another aspect of his unique tease.

Directing the group's attention to a termite mound, he asks, "What do termites eat?"

"Wood?"

"Yeah, wood."

"Yes, definitely wood."

"No. Fungus. They burrow down till they find water, then they bring it up to the wood or grass they've collected and wet it to create fungus. That big mound you see over there is actually much larger under the surface than aboveground. Okay, that's enough information for today. We're heading back to Lewa."

Within the vehicle, Thad is assigned a position beside Julia in the rear seat. Peter is directed to the middle row, and Sarah is eased into the passenger side of the front. Max assumes the wheel.

"Oh shit," he murmurs as he looks about the front seat.

"What's the matter?" Sarah asks.

"I've lost my compass."

"Well, what a coincidence. I've lost my bearings."

"I just don't understand you," he says, his voice suddenly upbeat as he holds the compass he has just discovered under the passenger seat.

He starts the engine, rolls forward, then stops a few feet down the trail. From somewhere under the driver's seat he pulls out a floodlight and slaps it on the exterior roof, moves to the front grill, opens the hood, and connects the wires running from the light to the engine. The road is washed in light for several feet ahead. On either side hang night's dark curtains. Occasionally, a pair of orange-red or green eyes peers out through the fabric, belonging to bush babies, aardvarks, caracals, and mongooses. Max identifies them, describing their habits as if he were sitting around a campfire talking of his fraternity brothers.

Though the jackets and sweaters are still in the rear behind the backseat, Sarah feels warm with wonder.

"Are you okay?" Max asks.

"Absolutely."

"Good," he says, dragging the word out like a slow pull on a glass of Scotch.

In this moment, Sarah thinks the sky holds the blessings of stars belonging to the churches of the universe. In this moment, Sarah and Max are singing from the same hymnbook.

And for this moment, she forgets the other moments. Max smiles. She feels healed.

CHAPTER 9

KISMET

"Sit there." A mass of a man pointed to two chairs angled towards each other, facing a desk that his abundant stomach threatened to storm. His neck could not be contained within his collar and overflowed in two unstructured folds. His face superseded in size that of any in the room. It was, Sarah considered, too preposterous to produce the respect intended by the position of rank affixed to it. Sarah immediately thought of him as "The Bigger Man."

His words passed through a large space between two long-neglected front teeth. Other teeth could not be accounted for, though in total, they were enough to enable the clear delivery of his command to be seated.

* * *

Sarah wakes, midway through a journey in which she struggles to balance the emotional pain inflicted by

Max and Peter, with the ecstasy derived simply from being in East Africa.

By now, most vestiges of the polite behavior exhibited early on have evaporated, self-restraint sucked out by a seething sun, manners dehydrated. Peter, Thad, and Max have relaxed into individual stages of coarseness and machismo. They speak openly of bodily functions. Tongues are free to employ an abundance of four-letter words as if they were mere punctuation marks.

The group's compatibilities have stretched to minimize any potential troubles, not unlike the yellow-brown savanna camouflaging the spots of a leopard. The cat cannot remain covered indefinitely. Eventually, it will move in response to some instinct or necessity, and for a moment, the animal is exposed. Similarly, everyday life in close proximity to one another causes a sharpness in definition, and behaviors no longer automatically blend into the overall adventure.

Max always operates with an immediate goal. He must strike a hit with a sighting, a story, an anecdote, or a spellbinding experience. He must arrange the camp, the day's rides, and see to his foursome. On the first day, there was a sense that one was at the beginning, but Max's realization of the safari coming closer to ending, Sarah believes, is a shadow on the day; to be at the end is to be at the beginning of his being alone again. Max is no stranger to being alone, but he never really gets substantially better at it, she imagines. He needs an audience. That much she is sure of.

With the exception of the "Sundowner" the night before, the tenuous thread seems to have frayed entirely between Sarah and Max. The tautness in her relationship with Peter is palpable. He appears to be oblivious to Max's flirtatious behavior toward her. Neither is he moved to intercede when Max's comments come out as a string of slashing remarks. Sarah waits for Peter to sit in the saddle of the white horse, but he is riding his camera and cannot change mounts.

Other dynamics are at play. For one, the elements of basic primal fear are all about. In the evening come the shriek of hyenas, the tenor voice of the lion, the tread of elephants near camp.

Peter appears anxious whenever he perceives the approach of seemingly insignificant occurrences: running out of shampoo or toothpaste, losing his comb or precision mustache scissors, or lending Sarah his sweatshirt; he does not want to risk being without it should the weather turn cold.

Then there is the matter of photographs. If Peter is to capture animals acting out natural behaviors in split seconds, instant reactions and immediate adjustments to the camera's settings are required. Sometimes the subject of the picture runs out of the frame. In this environment of no second chances, a perfectionist is under relentless self-imposed pressure.

And there is something more. Peter is forming a bond with Max, differing from Peter's other personal relationships by the degree of genuine affection he exhibits for him. Max good-naturedly calls Peter "Bwana," master, and Peter uses terms such as "my son" or "my boy" for Max. Sometimes their rapport appears to be based on two kindred spirits, while other times it resembles compatriots battling a common enemy, occasionally joined by Thad when he feels a need to reinfuse his manhood and distance himself from Julia.

Sarah does not know what the dynamic between Peter and Max means. Even if she finds herself able to draw a conclusion, it is overturned the next second, as her mind roller-coasters up and down.

Max is consistent in his dissatisfaction with Sarah's behavior: her writing and her shoelessness. She is in a constant state of hyper-reaction and overstimulation, which she attributes to the captivating East African environment. Still, many of Max's remarks sting her with the whip of his tongue. His mouth, Sarah has decided, works like a sickle, cutting down her ideas and points of view, yet all the while bringing her under his spell. His use of her emotions makes Sarah angry, and yet it causes her to laugh in a way that feels delicious and that she wants to savor. He is complicated and, when she is not looking for emotional shelter, Sarah enjoys trying to understand his quixotic nature, while somewhere within her, she inexplicably awaits another possible round of flirtation.

Peter has essentially granted Max the right to treat her with the same disrespect he himself has so openly displayed. Sarah has failed to set boundaries out here with Max. She realizes she should have set them years ago with Peter. She could not then and she cannot now. If she set boundaries and they were crossed, she would have to tell the transgressor to leave, and maybe he would. Better, she believed, to bear the indignities and keep the man, regardless of which side of the line he was on.

Sarah sometimes has bouts of dry and wet heaves not only related to medication but to the emotional upheaval of her interactions with Max and Peter. Today is a Lariam day, so there will certainly be another hour's worth of nausea, one of the medication's more immediate side effects.

Originally brought along for the purpose of chronicling brief notes during the trip, her notebook has unexpectedly become a lightning rod of multisensory impressions. She fills pages with quotes, titles of songs, and long, vivid descriptions. Too many observations, however, are unrecorded.

Sarah never expected to be swept away into this other state of being, someone who is still outwardly her, but who, on the inside, is altogether another person, a person who has become confusing as well as infuriating to Peter and Max. Her mind darts into the past while she wrestles with it to remain in the present. This is a challenge she encounters particularly around Julia and Thad, for they are echoes of her and Peter, and Sarah and Peter are now but shadows of them.

Still everyone goes on, playing his or her way through the safari's itinerary. Today it calls for them to travel where relatively few visitors to Kenya have gone before: a small cabin called Rutundu, approximately 11,500 feet up Mount Kenya. Accessible but remote, Lake Alice, a pristine body of water, is the magnet drawing them there. This day has been specifically requested by Peter so that he will have the exclusive bragging rights amongst his friends for having fly-fished in the wet bosom of the mountain.

It is from this Lewa Downs enclave of home-cooked meals, varied books and magazines, and cocktails served while sitting atop boulders and observing vibrant sunsets that Max and his group will shortly take leave for the Mount Kenya Safari Club. There, Max's plane will be refueled and, due to the need to lighten the weight of the plane, the travelers will split up and depart in two separate waves to their destination.

A second pilot will fly Sarah and Julia to the Rutundu landing strip; they will depart first. The pilot has but a single pass at setting down safely, a fact so often emphasized it begins to sound like the one chance to prove one's manhood. Max will fly Thad and Peter in his plane within an hour of the initial departure.

* * *

At the Mount Kenya Safari Club, Max introduces Damian, a middle-aged Australian who arrived in Kenya five years ago anticipating he would earn a better living than he was able to in his own country. In East Africa, he works steadily, flying visitors to remote camps, lodges, and fishing lakes.

He offers his bear-claw hand to assist Julia and Sarah aboard his four-passenger plane. Assured that they are balanced, he secures their safety belts and earphones, inviting them to "Help yourselves to some lollies. I just received 'em from my mum back home."

Julia, sitting in the copilot's seat, filled with girlish fascination over Damian's rugged good looks and Aussie accent, plies him with questions, then basks in the timbre of his voice. His aura of masculinity reassures them while they gain altitude and fly towards the formidable glacier-streaked twin peaks of Mount Kenya.

Rutundu sits alone upon arid, undecorated elevation. Sighting it, Damian circles the small brown log cabin and a second, smaller replica, dropping low like a showman tipping his hat to a beautiful woman. He stops answering questions in order to concentrate on the approach pattern that will allow him to set the plane down on the short swath ahead.

The engine is throttled back, the brakes gently but firmly applied, and, as Damian lands, he engineers his own congratulations. "Look at the nose of the aircraft hovering above the very end of the runway, will ya? Not an inch to spare! Well done, I'd say."

Max has assured Sarah and Julia that two Maasai attendants will greet them when they land. They are to help carry the prepackaged food on board the plane to the cabin, food for the next three meals. They are also to handle the personal belongings and, most importantly, they will guide Sarah and Julia for the forty-five-minute hike to the Rutundu dwelling.

There they are, the two Maasai attendants who themselves reach to the sky with their long, athletic legs and shoeless feet. Half of their sleek torsos are exposed while the other half is swathed in vivid crimson cloth tied at the top of their shoulders. Bangle ornaments hanging from artificially shaped ears reflect glancing rays of sun and accent their gleaming heads.

They are agitated, rapidly delivering a message in Swahili, and direct their attention entirely to the pilot. Damian tenses, preparing for his response. His composure finally erupts into a hot flash of anger, banishing the previous gentlemanly veneer.

Damian's changed demeanor provokes Julia to ask, "What's the matter? What are they saying?"

Looking squarely at Julia, pulling off his outback hat and waving it about in syncopation with his words, he proclaims, "Look, sweetheart, that damn Howard's got himself stranded here with three gals. His car won't start, and these here blokes want me to wait for 'em and his group. These 'artists,' they're all alike, wanting everyone to jump every time they need something. What a country! He expects me to fly 'em outta here."

"Well, why not? Can't you wait for them if they're stranded?" asks Julia, arms akimbo.

"No! I'm not gonna wait for them, for Christ's sake! There are other people I'm supposed ta pick up. If he wanted a ride, he shoulda been here, on the damn runway."

"But you only just buzzed the cabin. How could they be here already? Can't you give them a few minutes?" Sarah implores.

"No. I told ya, there are other things I gotta do."

He kicks out words in Swahili to the two Maasai. Moving quickly as he reaches under the plane, he disposes of all remnants of Sarah and Julia, including food and belongings, as if in a race against confronting the would-be hitchhikers. Unburdened by passengers or remorse, he seals himself into his cockpit, maneuvers one hundred and eighty degrees, and taxis to the end of the runway, using every getaway inch of it as he takes off into the wind.

Julia, standing with her hands on her hips, declares, "What a bastard!"

"I agree, but we have other problems. Those guys have taken our purses and disappeared. We'll have to manage by ourselves and we've no idea where we're going."

"What are we going to do?" asks Julia. "We can't carry all this."

"Let's take our personal things and as many of the boxes of food as possible. We'll leave everything else for the guys to carry when they land," Sarah suggests.

"Okay. They're gonna be mad because we left it, but I don't know what else to do."

Gathering what they can, Sarah and Julia tread the length of the runway, each of them looking off to either side, searching for signs of a trail. Within a few moments, Julia locates an obscure white rock to the left of the landing strip, confidently declaring it to be the marker for their intended path.

They are hot, hungry, and tired, their strength sapped by uncontrollable fits of laughter. Their remaining energy is deployed in the careful execution of small, calculated steps along a barely discernible trail that periodically gives way to undergrowth, erosion, and roots.

At every opportunity, Julia looks back at Sarah. "Just follow me. I can read trails. Thad and I hike all the time. Don't worry. I mean, are you worried, Sarah?"

"No, absolutely not. On the contrary, I'm enjoying the absurdity of all this. Think about it. Here we are, having just flown for twenty-five minutes with a charming pilot suffering from a split personality disorder, to be met by two Maasai who show no concern for us, and who have taken our purses. We're trying to walk along a path that is so obscure it's not even a path until you, Julia, say it's a path!"

Gazing down, Julia contemplates where next to step, when two blond-haired, fair-skinned young women of about eighteen are seen coming up the trail. They are each wearing heavy jackets and carrying backpacks, looking upset and disheveled. They stop, and one of them asks in a singsong Swedish accent, "Was that your plane that took off?"

"Yes," Sarah tells them. "It did take off, despite our efforts to convince the pilot to wait for you."

Furious, the girls spin around and head back down the trail. Sarah and Julia resume picking their way along, pushing aside branches, stepping over endless clusters of dirt, to once again find themselves confronted by two figures.

One, a man, is enormous, appearing all the more sizable for wearing a padded flannel-lined jacket worn over a bulky sweater. The intense heat and exertion has flushed his skin. The sun has streaked his light brown hair, much overdue for a cut, which falls in waves over his left eye. His right hand is bound with soiled white gauze that is unraveling just beneath the thumb. Scars radiate out, traversing his index and middle finger.

The young woman at his side appears to be the same age as the two who departed minutes earlier. She too is bundled in a jacket. Her skin and hair so resemble that of the man she stands beside, they might be related. They differ in the coloration of their eyes, for his are the vibrant color of aquamarine while hers are paler and framed with wire glasses. She could easily have just emerged from a campus library if not for the raw landscape of Mount Kenya.

"Well, it appears we've missed the plane," he states matter-of-factly in a baritone voice and British accent. What a charming way to express the obvious, thinks Sarah.

Sarah apologizes to him as if she could have influenced Damian's decision. "We really tried to persuade him to wait, but he took off in a huff. Apparently he had an appointment to pick up another party."

The man flashes a roguish smile and Sarah takes the measure of his merriment, calculating quickly, like a human abacus. How can this be? He's stranded in this isolated place with three very unhappy young women. His plans for today are completely disrupted and he's probably without contingency arrangements. His car is inoperable, and he must be hundreds of miles from help. But somehow, in his world, all is okay. In his world, he's going to work it out. What must it be like, this "okay world"?

Sarah suddenly wants desperately to enter this "okay world," to experience what it is like for things gone wrong not to be treated and reacted to as if they were utter disasters that had to be attributable to someone.

The man from the "okay world" turns to retrace his steps, looking back over his shoulder. "Well, then, we shall just have to make do."

His strides leave the young woman attempting to keep up.

Sarah can only wonder why his leaving feels so like the sun setting too fast at the end of the day, running off with its warmth and energy. He has left, and somehow, she feels, he has taken a part of her heart with him.

CHAPTER 10

REMEMBER

Sarah and Max assumed seats facing the most recent official to confront them. But he did not speak. Instead, "The Big Man" crossed from the rear of the room, causing the two seated prisoners to turn from the desk of "The Bigger Man" and confront the redeveloping tirade.

"Tell us of your relationship with him," he said, looking at Sarah, his finger jabbing at Max.

* * *

Opening the front door, Sarah and Julia tentatively enter, and are greeted by a pervasive quiet within the primitive log cabin known as Rutundu. The two Maasai attendants are not to be found. The girls seen on the trail have vanished. The man with unruly hair and sparkling eyes has disappeared, but there is a distinct scent of his body musk. Not the sweat of labor, but the sweet, natural odor of a man bereft of cologne, aftershave, or even deodorant. It is the pheromones of the man from the "okay world," his personal smell print.

Sarah and Julia stand alone in the stubborn silence. They open a second door and look in. There is a sink and counter, cupboards filled with scant supplies of essential nonperishables—soap, matches, candles, plates—and several large hurricane lanterns.

In the main area, a third door can be seen, differentiated from the other logs of the cabin only by handle and hinges. On the other side, an average-sized room holds a four-poster double bed and a bunk, each draped with heavy quilts. Within this bedroom is a spacious bathroom with a functioning toilet, a sink offering hot and cold water, and an incongruously oversized tub, as if made to fit the man seen earlier on the trail.

Julia surveys the setting. "He's kidding, right? Max doesn't really expect us to all sleep together."

"Julia, be a sport. It's the kind of arrangement that will make for a good story over dinner back home. It's only for one night. Why don't we think of it as a big slumber party? "

As they walk out onto the porch, a much smaller cabin replicating the one they have just explored can be seen atop a small knoll a short distance off. Sarah gently leads Julia by the arm down the steps and up an incline to the secondary log structure.

The bungalow is furnished like the other, with a bed and two sets of bunks.

"You and Thad take this cabin, Julia. It'll be quiet and romantic, and you two can have some privacy."

"Oh, thank you. You can't imagine how happy I am."

Sarah teases, "Julia, your feelings are not entirely lost on me. I can still manage to remember the drumbeat of my own youth."

After Sarah has spoken, she wonders what character she is portraying. The response is not really her, but that of someone she must have read about. Sarah frequently relishes becoming the character of the last book she has read, acting out their personalities. She has been Dagny Taggart after reading *Atlas Shrugged*, both Dominique and Howard Roark after *The Fountainhead*, Anna Karenina, Napoleon Bonaparte's Josephine, Petruccio's Kate, the Madwoman of Chaillot, Cleopatra, Candide's Cunegonde, and even Peter the Great and Catherine. Friends would ask her, "Who are you today, Sarah?"

"Wouldn't you rather stay here?"

"No. You take this cabin. I'm certain you'll make far better use of it."

Filled with elation, Julia dashes back to salvage her few possessions. Sarah too eventually returns to the main house, envying Julia the evening.

The atmosphere is different here from anywhere else. It is cold yet comforting, solemn and silent. Sarah anticipates the shattering of the fragile picture. She takes in this small, rustic environment, with its simple floor plan. There is a picnic table with a bench on either side for eating, and a bar in the form of a modest wood hutch protecting glasses and a limited but adequate supply of alcohol and assorted bottles of soda. Supplemental sleeping is provided by additional bunk beds. To be warmed, one approaches the stone fireplace directly, standing on its narrow hearth, or sits upon either the antiquated couch or one of two overstuffed chairs.

Suddenly, the heavy front door is thrown open, revealing the men, carrying all that Sarah and Julia left behind. The two Maasai attendants appear from behind the second door, coming in from that sliver of space that is more pantry than kitchen. When Julia walks back in, it is as if all the actors have been summoned, and the director, Max, is about to call "Action."

"God, you guys, you're not going to believe it!" Max exclaims in a voice full of excitement. "I couldn't have arranged this for all the tea in Kenya. It's just unreal. Unfucking real."

His high-wattage excitement continues. "Do you know what's going on? Do you have any idea? The guy who's stranded here is Brandon Howard, the famous wildlife photographer. He's the one who shoots those unbelievable photos of animal behavior no one else can get. It's like he's got a sixth sense about where he needs to be. His car won't start and he needs to be at the Mount Kenya Safari Club by two thirty this afternoon for a speech he's giving to a bunch of journalists, so I gotta fly him there.

"When I come back, we're going to hike to Lake Alice and fish. Brandon and his group are gonna spend the night with us and, as of now, we don't have enough food. We're not going to have a lot of time either, guys. We'll have to be back before nightfall. We can't be on the mountain after dark or it's curtains.

"I'm really sorry we can't go fishing sooner, Peter, but Brandon asked me for this favor and I've got to do it. That's just the way things work out here. We all barter favors."

Favors. Chits passed back and forth, stocked up, then exchanged for survival. Although East Africa is made up of independent people, all eventually rely on others to get through. Now Brandon Howard will owe Max a favor.

Starting out the door, Max winds up his directions, speaking authoritatively over his shoulder. "You guys grab a sandwich and I'll be back in forty-five minutes."

An hour later, Max returns, and Peter, foreseeing Sarah's inability to complete the arduous walk, abandons his commitment to Lake Alice, announcing, "I think I'll stay here and fish this closer lake," referring to Lake Rutundu, situated within viewing distance of the cabin. "Sarah, do you want to come with me?"

Sarah, not realizing Peter has sacrificed the trip to the lake for her benefit, declines. "No thanks. I want to hike with them."

"There are two old bamboo rods hanging on the front porch, Peter. I have some leader and tippet material. You'll have to rig up something. You can use flies from my tackle box. I did bring one complete fly rod, but I've gotta use it," Max explains, pointing quickly to the articles through the window and flicking his eyes from one item to another. "They'll row you around the lake so you can cast," he says, referring to the Maasai. "There's a small pram, but it'll be big enough for the three of you. I'm sure there's an oar or two. Are you okay with this?"

Peter reaffirms his decision, retreating to the porch to inspect the rods.

Max excuses himself, returning with an empty one-gallon plastic container. He takes out his knife and cuts the bottom, and then he unscrews the cap ever so slightly. "Hey, Peter, wait up. Take this with you in case you have to take a piss. I know you're concerned about the environment."

Max nods for the remaining three to follow, and throwing wide the door, begins the march, retracing the course taken earlier in the day. Whereas originally the final fifteen minutes of the walk to the cabin had been achieved easily enough, this time the hikers attack the same trail in steep strides. Sarah is the last in line, struggling to keep up. Discreetly, she begins taking off articles of expendable clothing, hoping no one will notice her difficulties.

They are within a few steps of the runway. A short walk across places them at the entangled trailhead leading along a torturous path to Lake Alice. Max readies a small machete and cuts a passage through the impeding overgrowth. He delivers several blows to the vegetation. Unexpectedly, he spins about. "Sarah, you can't go any further. You won't be able to keep up, and we don't have time to wait for you. You're gonna have to return to the cabin. I shouldn't have allowed you to come with us."

Then why did you? I'm standing behind Julia, so how do you know I'm out of breath? What kind of a monster are you, with eyes in the back of your head? These are Sarah's silent questions.

Thad looks straight ahead, busying himself with sips from his water bottle to keep his eyes averted from Sarah's. Julia's expression cannot hide her anger at Max for his behavior.

There is nothing for Sarah to do but turn around. She executes her retreat slowly down the twice-traversed trail, occasionally bending to pick up articles of her clothing along the way.

Within the cabin, the light has waned, casting a dark mood that punctuates Sarah's isolation. The silence appears contemptuous of her inability to know precisely what to do.

Taking advantage of the bathroom sink and tub before everyone returns, Sarah washes up and applies fresh makeup. These simple, yet gratifying tasks assume a special pleasure. A comb run through hair now so short it could not possibly make a difference feels decadent. She had cut her long hair before the safari, concerned that a bad hair day might cause her to hold people up. What a different perspective, Sarah realizes, then and now. A bad hair day! That is the worst problem I foresaw!

Everyone will be dirty. They will clean up hurriedly, probably not even changing their clothes. She will be clean, freshly dressed, rested, and thereby at an advantage. Then she realizes how pathetic it is to try to steal a yard here, a yard there.

Now, at 3:00 PM, it will be just over two hours before all parties return, time that can be used for a nap. Sarah makes her way to the lower berth of a bunk and sinks down, slipping under the first two covers. Depression immobilizes her as if she has been nailed to the mattress. Only her thoughts roam freely. How did she come to this weak and overwrought condition? A prevailing contradiction has taken hold that she cannot divest herself of. She loves this country, but everything about this safari, which began with such certain promise, threatens to crush her under the weight of things gone wrong. Of Peter gone wrong. Of Max gone wrong. And, it would seem, of Sarah gone wrong.

Her thoughts journey back in time. Ten years ago to the day, she took twenty Placidyl and thirty Valium before slashing the tendons of both wrists. Sarah is a medical miracle. How proud Peter was when the doctors had quizzed her, trying to determine the extent to which her brains might have been scrambled, and she managed to answer those ridiculous algebra questions correctly. Sarah knew it was a moment he felt love; the next moment was one in which he stopped loving her, for he could not again take the emotional risk.

CHAPTER 11

GENETIC IMPRINT

Sarah considered how best to answer the question of her relationship with Max. "He was my safari guide," she said without flinching.

Looking at Max, "The Big Man" insisted on checking every detail of his deflated prisoner before resuming.

"Where did you take her on safari?"

Max sighed deeply and began to explain, only to be interrupted.

"I demand to know more. Something must have happened between you two. No one would take the risk of coming here for you unless you became something to each other. What was your relationship with her?"

* * *

Moment by moment, the light grows grayer. The girls encountered earlier on the road are outside the cabin, too timid to enter. Max, Thad, and Julia have not yet returned. Peter is just now making his way up the steps with the two Maasai.

"I only caught one lousy trout. Those idiots just kept rowing around in circles. They couldn't follow my directions. They don't speak a goddamn word of English. And as if that wasn't enough, I pissed all over myself! There was a hole in the container Max gave me. What are you doing in bed? Why aren't you with the others?"

"Max didn't think I could make it. He sent me back once we reached the landing strip."

"I knew it! That's exactly why I stayed behind and asked if you wanted to fish with me. You're in no shape for that kind of a hike. You just broke your fucking leg eight months ago for Christ's sake, and you're overweight. Thad and Julia are much younger than you and they're in shape. They hike all the time."

"You know, Peter, if you and Max felt I couldn't make the trip, it would've been helpful to tell me before I hiked forty-five minutes for nothing."

"It wasn't for nothing. You needed a walk. You needed to get some exercise."

With lead weighing down her limbs, Sarah rises from the rumpled bed. She restores it to its homespun look, and withdraws to the main room. The two Maasai, witnessing Sarah's unsuccessful attempts to create a fire, relieve her of her effort.

"Girls, you must come inside now. It's too cold to stay out, and we have a fire," Sarah insists to the girls outside.

The tall girl with dark hair answers with some degree of resolution. "Thank you, but we'll stay out here and wait for my father."

"Come in and share the fire with me. I'd like to interview you for my journal."

"Well then, all right. We'll come in."

They all huddle down on the hearth, and Sarah flips ceremoniously through her remaining empty pages.

"What's the journal about?" asks the brown-haired girl, acting as spokesperson.

"I'm trying to chronicle everything we see and do, and write something about the lives of the people we meet, especially those we encounter unexpectedly."

There are small giggles of approval.

"Who wants to start?" Sarah asks.

"Oh, I'll begin," volunteers the girl with brown hair. "Well, my name is Ella and these are my friends Nancy and Annie," she says, first pointing to the blond girl, and then to a younger girl with hair the color of chalk.

"We're here with my father. We've been traveling around with him a bit because I'm taking a gap year. I'll be going to Nepal to work on an environmental project. There'll be two months of training in Nepal to become socialized, then I'll be looking at various environmental issues."

Sarah's pen advances across the page, writing in half words and abbreviated sentences.

"This project is part of 'Students Partnership Worldwide.' It's based in London where I've just finished school, and I've been chosen to participate. There are three of us going to Nepal actually, and one is going to Tanzania."

The other girls have heard the story before, but it suits them to remain warm and listen. Ella is filling in some details when Sarah looks at the space between the still-parted curtains, seeing only the blackest night beyond the panes of glass. Where are they? Sarah wonders. Max said everyone had to be in the cabin by dark. Before Sarah's thoughts become words, the three march triumphantly into the cabin.

"We didn't catch anything," Max laments. "We're counting on you, Peter. What about it, did you get the big one on?"

"Just one, not even big enough to make fish stock."

Max, Thad, and Julia burst out laughing as they unroll their jackets, inside of which are three six- to eight-pound rainbow trout wrapped in newspaper.

"Christ, if I'd known you caught fish that size, I woulda let mine go. Son of a bitch!"

"Gee, Peter, we didn't exactly know how to get the message to you!"

"Okay, okay. How about if I atone for my poor fishing by making you a drink?"

Peter busies himself with mixing drinks. Max is in the kitchen pantry cleaning the catch and instructing the Maasai how to prepare it, while Thad and Julia slump heavily down on the couch to catch their breath from laughter and the fast-paced hike back to the cabin.

"I'm interviewing the girls," Sarah says, and introduces everyone. She is about to ask Ella to continue when the door is hurled open and a bracing wind blasts through the cabin. Everything comes to a halt as the force enters, creating a thunderclap just inside the cabin's entrance. The explosion is Brandon Howard.

"By God, it's damn cold out there! Hello, everyone! Someone flew me back and I've been hiking in the dark to get here."

Brandon stands loosely, at ease with himself. He removes his jacket with one hand, gesturing a bandaged greeting with the other. He looks at Sarah, trying to place her, not recognizing her from the encounter on the trail hours earlier. She was a mess then. Now she is not.

"Didn't we recently meet?"

"Not formally. My name is Sarah."

Max introduces everyone else.

Peter offers to make Brandon a drink, but Brandon moves knowingly to the separate parts of the cabin, collecting a glass and the ingredients for his drink from different niches. While he does so, Sarah forces herself to turn back to his daughter.

"My father is a very well-known photographer. He's done lots and lots of books and exhibits. He's always quite busy, and we're just now getting to spend a little time together because I've been living with my mother and going to school in England since they separated. Father also does some lecturing, but only in very special circumstances, like this afternoon."

"Okay, everyone, let's sit down for dinner." Max is back at the helm.

The table is covered with a red-checkered tablecloth. A lantern spotlights dark purple beet soup served in large pottery coffee mugs. Bottles of South African and French wine appear from one bag of Max's culinary packages prepared for him by his cook in Nairobi.

"Brandon," Max begins a toast, "here's to an absolutely unbelievable chance encounter with someone

I've always wanted to meet. We're going to celebrate this good fortune with a pretty decent meal, including the fresh trout we caught at Lake Alice."

Max is as radiant as a man can permit himself to be. He leans forward to watch Brandon and grasp his every word, struggling to keep his enthusiasm in check.

Brandon explains that the lake is stocked, then digresses to how things run in Kenya, as if it is a natural progression everyone should easily follow.

Sarah too leans forward, her gaze fixed on the far right of the table. Brandon, she realizes, is blessed with superior good looks, his comfortable style suggesting he has enjoyed his advantageous appearance from an early age. Though soiled and exhausted, his sophistication is unaffected. He is a man of the world who walks through life with an ease bordering on sheer indifference. Sarah suspects that underneath this persona he is a calculating creature, for no career can depend on the vagaries of luck alone. Her own experience in the business world has taught her that much.

Sarah is undeniably fascinated with him and, when coupled with the extraordinary circumstances of his being here, the compulsion to write once again overwhelms her. She reaches for her journal from beneath the table and registers pieces of Brandon's speech, which he underscores with his long arms. "As whites are replaced and blacks take over, the judiciary will become more lenient," Sarah catches him saying.

Magic pervades this evening. Nothing like this will ever occur again, not even in her fondest recollections or most vivid dreams. And so she writes:

Candles and hurricane lamps flicker brightly upon the rough-hewn logs of the cabin sheltering us this night. Residual light illuminates the functional interior and provides a glow, highlighting the intrigue of the activity within. Two dark, elongated Maasai, cloaked in blood-red shukas, move rhythmically toward the fireplace, throwing shadows on surfaces as they kneel before the coals to cook each course of our evening's meal. Like lanky puppets, they approach our table, ebony arms extended in a gigantic vertical reach of service. Taut faces display thick lips, which curve slightly upward in visible satisfaction of their culinary efforts.

Piercing the fragility of this primitive scene, Max leans in front of Peter and angrily whispers another of his terse directives. "Stop writing! Put away that damn journal. Do you realize who's talking? Participate, for Christ's sake."

Peter sighs, not reproaching Max even now. Ella's eyes widen in astonishment at Max's rudeness. For Sarah, there is paralysis. What an improbable place for a second nervous breakdown, she thinks to herself.

The journal in her lap lies open, its purple page dissected into two halves, the comments of Brandon reserved for one side, and Sarah's description of the evening on the other.

It is imperative to hold myself together, she counsels herself. She shuts the diary, placing it at her feet, and grinds it with her heel into the cold floor.

At the far end of the table, Brandon skips neither a beat nor an English-accented word. He remains engaged in an animated description of his life and the politics of Kenya. He has not, Sarah believes, witnessed her numbing humiliation.

All the while, outside the cabin, a cold wind blows across the high desert, ruffling everything in its path. Blow as it will, its gusts are incapable of rearranging the stars embedded in the African sky. Despite the swells of anger rising within her, Sarah studies the tribal tableau from her seat at the makeshift dinner table. She is swept up into ancestral déjà vu as her mind wanders.

This is our cave, she imagines. Over there, the flints that provide the light, and there, the fire for heating our food and providing our warmth. In the corner, standing tall, are the hunter-gatherers who have prepared our evening meal. And here am I, on safari, experiencing this magical, exquisite night, over eleven thousand feet up Mount Kenya.

Glancing again at Brandon, who is still telling stories of politics, photographs, and narrow escapes, she wonders: Why does this all feel so absolutely familiar, so comfortable, so natural?

Then Sarah remembers a brilliantly insightful two-word phrase she once read by Dr. Richard Leakey: "Genetic imprint." And in a rare moment of certainty and equanimity, she realizes, Oh, yes. Of course. I am home.

CHAPTER 12

THE STAND-UP MAN

As the question was asked, Sarah crossed her legs, relaxed, and smiled openly at the thought of the nimble Max trying to define a relationship that would satisfy the man waving his arms about. He must, thought Sarah, try to represent it as normal, yet no normal woman would be sitting here under these circumstances.

"The Bigger Man" folded his hands together, creating a picture of patience that contrasted vividly with the fever pitch of the man talking, striding, and waving his arms about hysterically.

* * *

Throughout the meal, Max adds several postscripts to his initial toast, as if by the volume of his words, he might mirror Brandon or compete for a speck of the admiration he receives. "A health to the man on the trail tonight; may his grub hold out; may his dogs keep their legs; may his matches never misfire. Those are perfect words, I think, for this evening, courtesy of Jack London."

Dinner is an unexpected harvest. The meal has been innovatively conjured up using a combination of canned goods, freshly caught fish, the addition of water to dried gravies in foil packets, and, of course, specially prepared dishes by Mary, Max's cook.

Brandon eats like a man breaking a fast and drinks with the thirst of a parched desert receiving the season's first rain. His dynamic presentation about everything Kenyan continues, including its policies, its conservation efforts, tourism, agriculture, imports, and exports. He opines, answers questions, toasts, and thanks everyone profusely for their hospitality. Max hangs on Brandon's every word. Sarah is spellbound, never having met anyone from "the okay world," and never having experienced the hypnotic effect of someone whose voice gives a verbal serenade while describing so many different subjects.

"Gawd, what a day," Brandon concludes. "I was up at five thirty this morning trying to start the van and, of course, I haven't the faintest bloody idea what's gone wrong. I'll have to get my mechanic up here tomorrow to take a look at it. He'll manage to sort it all out with the proper spanner."

The Maasai begin to clear the table. Max asks the two attendants to bring coffee, tea, hot milk, and sugar. Brandon directs them in Swahili to move the requested beverages to a position at the end of the long table, closer to the fire.

The girls huddle together on the sooty hearth, sipping hot tea and yielding the couch to Thad, Julia, and Peter. Each of them imbibe strong coffee mellowed by cognac. Brandon is in constant motion, acting with all the familiarity of a lord moving about his favorite manor. Sarah sits tentatively atop the arm of one of the old chairs.

"You seem to know where everything is around here," Thad comments.

"I should hope so. I use it quite often. The whole cabin was constructed elsewhere—at Lewa, actually. Every piece was numbered and then moved up here to be assembled just as it was originally built."

Overshadowing everything, Sarah takes note, is Brandon's ebullience, which openly challenges any of the day's events to bedevil his good humor. This is a quality unknown to Sarah in any man before tonight. A quality drawing her closer to him. And closer still.

Max stands with his coffee cup in one hand, waving it slightly as he talks. "What happened to your hand?"

"It was grazed by a charging rhino of all things! I was trying for a particularly close shot. Damn unfortunate, but it's just one of many near disasters. No real harm done."

"Where would you like to travel to next, Brandon?" Peter wants to know, intrigued by this man of high profile who appears impervious to fear.

"Well, actually, I would love to travel amongst the Tuareg nomads, with two thousand camels crossing the Sahara. They fight their way through the borders, you know. They're smugglers. They smuggle mirra, a sap from trees for making incense. They're beautiful people, actually. Imagine it! Three to four hundred camel trains at a time moving across the desert. One would negotiate their way through the entire experience. It tests a man, it really does. I'd drink my camel's milk and sleep on the ground. It would be absolutely marvelous, I think."

He looks off into the fire. Brandon's interest no longer can be sustained by entertaining the group. He glances about, as if bored with questions he has so often been asked, not wanting to go into the realm of his fame and notoriety, and perhaps hoping to circumvent curiosity about his techniques for acquiring the more controversial animal photos he has captured.

Sarah senses his restlessness, understanding him as she had once so profoundly understood Peter. Brandon must hold others spellbound, and then his audience must know the precise moment to let him go, lest they lose him altogether.

Brandon studies Sarah, and after some reflection, roars out in alarm over the fact that she is not drinking something warm. He pours a cup of tea and hands it to her. The cup dances nervously upon the saucer, evidence of her shaking hands. "Now Sarah, come over here to the table. I'm going to give you an interview, because I noticed you were asked to put your notepad down during dinner."

There is stillness, interrupted only by the sound of Sarah's ceramic cup jumping slightly off the saucer. In this small spark of time, something is transmitted by Brandon to those in the room, and whatever it is, Sarah realizes, it is a turning point in her favor. "Oh no, that's all right. I'm sure you're exhausted. You've been up since the crack of dawn—"

"Nonsense. Up you go," he demands, reaching out to her until she is standing. He removes the tea cup from Sarah's grip and sets it down, then leads her a few steps to the table as if it is she who is made of ceramic.

They straddle the bench, facing each other, close enough to talk softly. Sarah listens intently to the deafening silence.

"Well, have at it," Brandon directs her.

Sarah shakes from her cropped hair to her hiking boots. Her pen bobs about between her thumb and forefinger without the requisite tension to write. "I don't think I can do this right now."

"I'm sure it's been a bit brutal, but if I talk, will you calm down and write?"

"Yes. I think I can do that much."

"Okay," he begins, as if he has just convinced a fan to purchase one of his pricier photographs, "then let's have a go. Where do you want to start? I can talk about anything."

"Start wherever you're most comfortable. I suppose I'd like to know about Kenya, and for right now, about something other than the animals. Oh God, I'm sorry. That's your business, photographing animals."

"Don't give it a thought. First, I want to tell you about the land, because it's fundamental to understanding everything else. Kenyatta, our first president, set up a system to change the tribal land rights into a constitutional entitlement, giving farmers title to the land. This provided them with collateral to borrow against, to develop their crops. The residents of the country became participants instead of spectators."

Brandon continues talking excitedly, but Sarah ceases to write. Rather than recording his words, she allows them to soothe her.

Unexpectedly, he changes course, asking, "Why did you cut your hair, my dear? I imagine you with long hair, pulled straight back. What made you decide to wear it short?"

Sarah is baffled by the jump from land to hair. "For the safari. But how could you possibly know how I used to wear my hair?"

"I've wonderful intuitive senses. I'm seldom off the mark. I shall tell you the most astonishing stories of my intuition someday. How are you doing? Okay?"

"Yes. I'm fine," Sarah is able to say with a rediscovered steadiness.

"Atta girl. Deep breath now. Here we go. The collateral makes Kenya more independent and therefore, less desirous of being drawn into political experiments like the rest of Africa. Our people don't want change."

"Excuse me, Brandon, but they must want some political reform. I mean the corruption, the—"

"Ah. I'm speaking of general stability."

"So, the cost of general stability is general corruption?"

"Corruption is everywhere, my dear. Here, regrettably, it is tolerated. There are many more pressing, fundamental matters."

He is infectious, and although he skips from subject to subject, it all makes sense to Sarah in some strange, African, Brandon Howard way. And the fact that she can follow along and banter back is a wonderful blessing.

"We need to adjust the economy and the politics so there is no subsidy. Now, at the end of the cold war, third-world countries such as ours are expected to follow the reforms dictated to us. It's often like dreadful experiments suggested by people who haven't the faintest notion of what they're bloody doing."

Sarah resumes sharing Brandon with her journal. "Slow down!" she pleads, trying to ensure that not a word runs off the catch basin of her page.

"Would you believe some of my ancestors were missionaries involved in releasing slaves into the free society? I think I've actually assimilated these goals. Yes, I believe you could say that of me!"

He appears more mischievous than missionary by the lantern's twinkling light reflected in his eyes. Sarah becomes momentarily lost until she forces herself to form words. "Photography and missionary work don't appear to be very compatible, Brandon."

"It's not entirely separate. My earliest days were spent taking sensational pictures of wrongdoings in our game parks and selling them to any newspaper I could. My missionary work with a camera was all about getting the exact shot that would speak volumes to the people reading the paper or looking at the photograph. The point was to touch the viewers' values sufficiently to encourage conservation wherever we could."

He has great zeal, not unlike a missionary assigned to make at least one new convert this evening, Sarah concludes.

"Yes, I've very recently become interested in people's values, or lack of them." From Sarah's declaration hang all the intended overtones of sarcasm.

Brandon leans in closer to Sarah, whispering, "Well, it's absolutely apparent that you should be, Sarah. How have you tolerated this abominable behavior? You've become a bird with a broken wing. You once soared. Now you have fallen and you're struggling, unable to fly until that wing is mended."

"I haven't even considered not tolerating it," Sarah confides.

"That's a mistake, a terrible, unbearable mistake. Why do you think people in Africa are tolerant of a military regime?" Brandon asks, eyebrows high under disheveled hair.

Sarah ventures, "I suppose because of the way they were raised, fearing their father, especially in regard to that moment that, I suspect, they think about for most of their adolescent life: circumcision and the boy's possible inability to hide his pain."

"Yes! Well done! The children are accustomed to harshness. Harshness is acceptable. Did you realize your father has the right to kill you if the family is stigmatized at circumcision? Consider how very powerful the psychology of it all is! This explains a lot of what happens in the political process. They think of their leaders as their father!"

Max has had enough of Sarah engaging Brandon. He stands, cupping his hands to his mouth in a gesture reminiscent of a call to an animal he desires to charm.

"We've got to figure out the sleeping arrangements and get to bed. It's going to be a long day tomorrow."

"Oh God," Brandon sighs dramatically. "He needs to be thwarted a bit. Ask me a question, preferably one that will get a rise out of me. Go on, have at it!"

"Okay, okay. Umm, how does it feel to be one of the world's foremost and wealthiest nature photographers?"

He throws his head back and laughs. "My dear girl," he says, in a charming, slightly reprimanding voice, "I am by no means wealthy, for my spending is always outrageously out of control. I never tire of being famous, so long as it is not brought directly to my attention when I am trying desperately to blend in. Like tonight."

"It was a ridiculous question, wasn't it?"

"No, just a bit naïve. I see Max will have the final word. I think he's insisting on lights-out. But I have so much more to tell you. Your journal is really quite barren."

"Well, have at it, Brandon."

"How old are you?"

"Old enough."

"I think you should call it halftime, take a seat on the bench, and think things out before going back into the game."

Sarah nods, although not quite understanding, certain it will come when she is free to consider his words and his slow, deliberate way of delivering them.

"Brandon, did you know we might have gone to Lamu, or Lake Victoria, but we chose Rutundu instead?" Sarah asks.

"Never underestimate fate. Remember, there are no coincidences."

Of course, Sarah does remember. There are no coincidences.

* * *

Max intends to sleep in one of the bunk beds in the room assigned to Sarah and Peter, who will sleep in the high, king-size bed laden down with coverlets and sheepskins. Nancy and Annie will sleep in the smaller cabin and, when informed that Julia and Thad are also sleeping there, they shrug their shoulders. In a brief, nonverbal exchange between Julia and Sarah, it is understood that the two girls have just erased Julia's special time with Thad. The couple walks in defeated steps across the room and through the front door.

Although there is a set of bunks in the common living area, Brandon volunteers to sleep on the floor with Ella, near the fire. As Peter and Max retreat into the bedroom, Sarah remains to watch as the two Maasai pile sheepskins over father and daughter, then walk toward the front door to remove coats and jackets from pegs, throwing them atop the bodies as if to layer Brandon and Ella in additional warmth. Finally, the candles are extinguished and the Maasai depart. Sarah has no further excuse for loitering and, un-riveting her eyes from Brandon, she opens the door to the room in which she will spend the night with her husband and her safari guide, who has arranged to sleep but a few feet away.

As she enters the room, Max unexpectedly grabs her with one hand, pressing his other hand over her mouth. He leads her to his bed, pulling Sarah down next to him.

"What the hell are you doing?" she whispers in a small voice directly into his ear.

"I'm freezing cold. Stay here till I warm up."

"Max, my husband is right over there. Are you out of your mind?"

"Listen. He's already snoring. We have some unfinished business."

"Yes. We do. Thanks for reminding me. I want to know the answer to the question I asked you that night in your tent. What's causing you to be uptight? Your muscles were so clenched, it was all I could do to make a dent in them. What's going on?"

"If I tell you, will you stay here awhile?"

"I want to hear the story. I'll stay for that."

Initially she is ambivalent about being so close to Max. The proper thing to do would be to crawl into bed with Peter, but he is asleep, and his reaction would be one of annoyance if she wakes him. The truly improper thing to do, the thing she really wants to do, is to lie down with Brandon, an impossible thought considering his daughter is at his side; besides, she's had no indication that her presence next to him would be welcome. Sarah aches to be with Brandon and to abandon herself to him regardless of the consequences. But Max wants her next to him, and for now, she is content to be at his side, for there is a hole so large in her that the unkindness he exhibited earlier in the evening falls right through. She settles in, resting her head on his arm.

"I'm getting screwed, really screwed, and it could cost me everything I've worked for. I took on two German business partners about a year and a half ago. They were supposed to pour some capital into my business that would've allowed me to hire other people and train them before they're turned out with tourists. I could have marketed safaris in other cities besides Atlanta. I could have bought the camera equipment I need. It won't get better for me as a guide, but I could be famous and wealthy as a photographer.

"About ten months ago, I told my partners that my work permit and residency visa were about to expire. I was booked up with nonstop back-to-back safaris, so they told me they'd take care of it. Every week I'd check with them, and each time I did, they'd assure me it was being handled.

"Within the last thirty days, I found out they hadn't done a thing, so I hired my own lawyer. Two days before picking you guys up, I realized my so-called partners had paid off my lawyer. Paid him *not* to get my papers updated and to see that my permit and visa were *not* renewed!

"I hired another lawyer immediately, but I've only got about two weeks left before my papers expire. If this one can't go higher up the ladder than the bureaucrats who were paid off by my first lawyer, I'm going to get thrown out of this country. Everything I've worked for, down the shit hole."

"I don't get it," Sarah says. "Why would they want to destroy you?"

"Because when your paperwork has expired, some guys come to the door. They don't say, 'Hi, we're Mr. So-and-So, and we're here to inform you that you have a few days to get your affairs in order.' No. They throw you into the jail at Nyayo House, your worst nightmare come true. I'd rather die than be stuck in that hellhole. Everything I own would be confiscated. I'd lose my plane, my camera equipment, my photographs and negatives, my ability to earn a living, and my reputation. My so-called partners would get all my assets, including my future safari business, without having to buy me out. Get it now?"

"What excuse are they using for this?"

"They say I am not reporting my tips to them. It's ridiculous, but there's no way to prove it, 'cause usually the tips I get from clients are in cash. They think I've been withholding a lot of the money. It can add up for sure, but that's not the problem; it's just the excuse they've latched onto. It's all bullshit. They want to see me expelled from the country. They want everything I've worked for.

"I've been told by other guides and pilots that this lawyer I have now is the best. He works very quietly. I keep paying money that's supposedly going for bribes to the top guys at Nyayo House, but I don't really know for sure. Anyway, it's not like I've got a lot of choices."

"God, Max, how do you go on, acting as if everything is okay, being funny, taking care of all of us?"

"Because, Sarah, it's my job. I'm not like you. I don't have the luxury of letting my emotions show. If I did, there'd be consequences."

"You don't know a thing about the consequences I've had to pay for not showing my emotions. If I permitted myself the luxury of exposing how I've felt on this trip, I'd have taken your goddamn head off tonight. Instead, I kept my mouth shut. But I'm about one hangnail away from going over the edge, and if I do, there's going to be a big, ugly splash of emotions. So why don't you let up on me just a bit?"

"Jesus," Max sighs, "let's cue up the orchestra."

"Maybe you do belong in Nyayo House."

"I'd survive, but you'd never make it. Anyway, if you've felt so abused, why didn't you just raise your hand or something to give me a sign?"

"If I had to raise my hand to deflect your every insult, I'd have carpal tunnel syndrome by now."

Peter makes a sound, breathing the way one does when surfacing from a deep sleep. Sarah jumps out of Max's bed abruptly, landing at Peter's side in one fluid motion. He grabs Sarah, holding on with an unnaturally strong clench, as if to grip her tightly enough to set it all right. "I'm freezing. Get over here. I can't sleep it's so fucking cold."

For the remaining hours of that evening, Sarah is caught in the vice of a man so frigid he cannot relinquish her. She contemplates on the one hand the fact of her entrapped embrace, and on the other, the cold facts told to her by the man in the bed a few feet away.

Transcending these considerations is a more provocative thought. It is one of the stand-up man, lying down by the fire with Ella at his side, his arm around her lovingly, for the single purpose of keeping her warm and letting her know that despite the mishaps of the day, everything is okay.

CHAPTER 13

A GREAT LEAP FORWARD

"I was a private safari guide for her and her husband for two and a half weeks. That's all," Max offered in a measured voice.

"You are lying," thundered *"The Big Man,"* his arms jutting straight in front of him, as if they would find the truth. He crossed the room again, folded his arms, and stopped in front of Sarah.

"What did he speak to you of on this 'safari'?"

"Of the animals, how they are either the hunters or the hunted, their habits, their . . ." Sarah tried to explain.

"Why do you call this business a 'safari'? Where does this word come from?" he asked Sarah.

Put off guard, she answered, *"I thought 'safari' was your word, a word that came from here!"*

"You are wrong. We have no such word."

"Well, you ought to tell that to the whole damn tourism industry. A lot of printed material out there calls what I just did a safari."

* * *

The magical time at Rutundu will soon be over. Signs of its premature ending permeate the room along with the day's first filaments of light. People are afoot. The door to the large bedroom and the communal loo (as it is referred to by Brandon and his group) has opened and closed twice within the last half hour, which means Brandon and Ella are up. Earlier furtive sounds in the bathroom could be heard, including a short burst of shower water. That would have been Max.

Peter waits for the opportune moment, after the third closing of the door, to vault from the bed, claiming the bathroom as his. Sarah contemplates the choice of remaining alone in the chilly room or, despite her disheveled condition, getting up and taking her chances by the fire, the smoky invitation of which is delivered through the door.

"Ah, there you are!" Brandon greets her, his voice carrying across the room. "Are you ready for a cup of coffee?"

"Only if you don't look at me."

Brandon laughs easily, erasing Sarah's self-consciousness. Max, unable to resist the opportunity, approaches to survey the damage. Smudges of makeup not washed off last night blotch her face, and her short hair stands upright. Max shakes his head. "Well, aren't we a sight for sore eyes. That's what I love about being out here: there's no pretentiousness. It's really just a level playing field."

"Here's your coffee," says Brandon. "And I promise I'm not looking at you, but if you want to continue our discussion from last night, I'll be happy to oblige you. In the meantime, I'm going out to have another look at the van."

"Sarah, you can use the bathroom now, but there's no more hot water. I didn't even have enough for myself." It's Peter's first announcement of the morning.

Sarah applies cold water and soap to dissolve the residue of the last fifteen hours. She scrubs and polishes herself, succeeding in producing an altered face. This is the best she has looked, the best she has felt. And this is the first morning since Samburu that the relentless dry heaves have not racked her.

Sarah decides not to take her medication. Any realization that one does not eliminate a daily regimen of medication is absent. She cannot imagine negative consequences. She perceives herself to have permanently become a resident of "the okay world."

Sarah sits on the steps of the porch, barefoot, caressed by the early-morning breeze. "Brandon, did you figure out the problem with the van now that you've had a good night's sleep?"

"I can't actually find anything mechanical. Damn curiosity, you know?"

"If the problem isn't mechanical, what could it be?" Sarah asks.

"I think it's simply destiny!" Brandon responds.

His answer is either the glib comeback of his easy banter, or he too has read *West with the Night*, in which

Beryl Markham conjures up a similar statement made about Tom Campbell Black, a man fixing his car along the road, the man who will teach her to fly and become one of her many lovers. But right now, Brandon's banter is being directed to Sarah, and that counts for a great deal. "And now it's your destiny to tell me more, as you promised you would."

Sarah writes as Brandon speaks, but his dialogue stops when the aroma of food reaches them. Breakfast is served outside, and everyone is summoned by Max to assemble around a table made of the same rough logs as the cabin itself. The meal is uncomplicated, consisting only of porridge, eggs, and toast.

"I simply loathe porridge," Brandon announces, making even this statement sound fascinating. "I certainly had my fill of this stuff at the British boarding school I attended, a place I left early in the game to return to Kenya to learn to speak Swahili fluently. And so I did. When I call someone in Parliament for a favor, they think I am a black Kenyan, one of their peers!"

"I'm flying Brandon down to the Mount Kenya Safari Club," announces Max. "Then I'll be back for the girls. Julia and Thad, you'll be next. And finally Peter, you and Sarah will follow them to the airstrip about forty-five minutes later and I'll pick you up. I want you waiting for me on the runway. Okay, guys, let's motor!"

"Wait!" Brandon demands. "When will you be back in Nairobi? I should like to say good-bye only then."

"We'll be there in five days, but I can't give you any particular time. Thad and Julia will be leaving for Atlanta that night, and the next day I'm taking Sarah and Peter to Tanzania and the Ngorongoro Crater."

Max communicates the logistics in a hurried manner, as though hoping to discourage Brandon from attempting a rendezvous.

"Good-bye, Brandon. Thank you for the interview."

"Well then, I'll see you in Nairobi. I've a few more stories for your journal."

"Probably not, but we have each other's address. I hope if I write to you, you will write back."

"It's bloody hard for me to write, Sarah. I think the chances are better I shall catch up with you."

They pose for pictures and extract promises from Ella that she will write from Katmandu to let Sarah and Peter know if she's planting trees or building fireplaces.

Before scattering, Brandon extends his arms in a reach that is exactly Sarah's size. It lasts only a moment.

Sarah is unclear about a lot of things right now, except for the recognition of his kindness as a form of therapy, offered by one who grasped more in a few moments of observation than an entire phalanx of psychiatrists.

"Good-bye," says Brandon.

"Good-bye," Sarah responds.

* * *

In the cabin, Sarah walks about in circles. By the side of the couch, a pink baseball hat with a khaki visor stops her like a flag waving down a racecar for a pit stop.

She wonders if it's Julia's. I'd better take it, she decides. If it's not hers, it belongs to one of the girls. If not one of the girls, then it's Brandon's. No, his hair would never fit under this cap. He'd never wear a . . . Stop! Stop fretting over the hat, for God's sake. It's time to hike to the airstrip with Peter.

Sarah and Peter are going to pick up Thad and Julia at the Mount Kenya Safari Club and then make their way to Island Camp in the district of Baringo Springs.

* * *

Max's plane lands later in the day, just outside the village of Kampi Ya Samaki in Nakuru. The group rides along a dusty, brittle road bisecting a group of three-walled structures on one side from another set of similar shops and dwellings on the other side.

Villagers rush the vehicle. Their bodies are clothed in a minimum of frayed vestments encrusted with fine dust from the slow wheels of the van clawing into their midst.

"*Nilikwambia kwa sitokupa kitu cho chote hapo awali na nikakufamisha kwamba hakuna kuomba pesa kwa wateja wangu. Kwa hivyo kaa kando na gari langu hivi sasa.*" ("We do not intend to give you anything. I have told you before, there is to be no begging for money from my clients. Move away from this vehicle right now.") Max spitballs orders at the solicitors in the authoritative voice of one whose mission it is to protect his charges.

He does not entirely dispel the group. His warning does, however, appear to dilute the numbers who beg, somewhat easing the passage to the edge of Lake Baringo, where a water taxi sits in wait. Its outboard motor makes a sound as methodical as a metronome while it sends small ripples through the brackish passageway. It is about to make one of several trips back and forth between the camp and the village.

In a confined but conspicuous area where the land draws down to the shore, expectant vendors stand beside improvised stalls laden with leather goods and wooden and soapstone carvings. They smile, entreating the travelers to purchase their wares.

"I want to get one of those purses," Julia declares excitedly. "That one is exactly what I've been looking for. I didn't have a chance to get one in Nairobi."

"No. Get in the boat. We're not buying anything." Max is quick to derail Julia, demanding that the riverbank salesmen not be encouraged. His instructions are so firmly delivered, one would think she had committed an egregious breach of etiquette.

Thad is entirely preoccupied with the business of unpacking the van and loading the boat, oblivious to the fact he might have intervened on Julia's behalf.

Julia sits by Sarah, who motions her closer and pulls out the pink baseball cap from her carry-on, asking, "Julia, is this yours?"

"Oh my God! Thank you so much. Stick it back down there. Don't tell Thad. He'd kill me if I'd lost his hat. He can lose my stuff, but I can't lose his."

"Julia, don't you know, that's rule number three hundred and seventy-six?"

"Yeah, part B." She shrugs, resigned to the imbalance of rules. She and Sarah don't speak often, but when they do, they are immediately at the core of what they want to share.

Muddied water below the craft has turned to the consistency of black syrup, looking as if it might harbor things both living and dead. The motor purrs and licks at the liquid, the craft moving at an even speed across the water to Baringo Springs Island Camp.

Gliding horizontally several feet from the group is an elongated, narrow craft resembling a leaf blown down on the water. It carries a young man whose long, muscular legs are bent at the knees, compressing him while his vessel appears to drift. His upper arms display the perfect symmetry of a sculptured body; his hands paddle forward in a smooth slide across the lake.

"That's a fisherman in a *piroguo*, from the village behind Island Camp. The villagers fish for their food. No cattle herding to speak of here."

A sound like that of a gull spills from the throat of a large bird, its head crested in white, wearing the color upon its round, inflated chest like feathered armor.

"That's a fish eagle," Max points out and, as he does so, the bird engages its sizeable brown wingspan to soar and then dive, fracturing the aquatic plane in an instant and securing a fish that had surfaced just seconds before. He removes the still-flapping feast from water to air in the tongs of its beak. "Half-collared kingfisher," says Max, pointing his finger to the color of blue reaching from bill to tail along a bird's back, gradually meeting up with a peach underbelly. "And that guy's a jacana." The comic little bird is set upon tall, spindly legs with disproportionately long webbed toes that provide running traction along the reed beds.

"You know what they say about guys with big feet," Julia whispers to Sarah. She is out of her slump, the purse temporarily forgotten.

Two bold hippo craniums surface, breaking the water, and their eyes shift, appraising the six morsels afloat a boat-shaped plate set before them. Their bulging eyes protrude from sockets situated beneath stern, bony brows, reflecting curiosity. They track their potential targets with a steady look. Their frames remain submerged, the actual size of danger hidden below.

"Get used to them, because tomorrow we're going waterskiing. Don't worry, they're herbivores."

Max is dead serious, and Sarah wonders why they would waterski with hippos, for she has read that they cause more deaths than puff adders.

"I can't waterski," Julia announces. "The last couple of times I tried, I couldn't even get up. I'll just watch. Anyway, I heard hippos can overturn boats and crush them with their jaws."

"No voyeurs allowed on my safaris," chides Max.

"Julia, we've got to do this. How many times do you get to go waterskiing in a lake with hippos? It's gonna be great. You'll just try it, that's all." Thad is again abundantly ready for whatever the safari serves him, exclaiming to Max, "Count us in!"

"I've never waterskied," Sarah confesses. "But I'll try."

Peter offers to photograph everyone's efforts.

As soon as the motor stops, powerful arms pull the women up and out of the rocking craft to a stony path inclining up toward a thatched opening anchored by a counter with an engraved sign: REGISTRATION.

The tents at Island Camp are comparatively luxurious, resting on slabs that extend approximately five feet beyond the canvas, allowing for a porch, upon which two wooden chairs and a table invite the guests to relax and enjoy the view. It is a place, Sarah imagines, to sit and talk, perhaps to sip a drink loaded with a healthy shot of strong rum. A place to share stories and impressions. She and Peter, she realizes, will not sit in these seats.

After the porters have consigned the individuals to their destination, the travelers are warned to keep the tents zipped. This time there are not only monkeys to contend with but, due to the proximity to water, mosquitoes as well.

"Sarah, test the zipper so you'll know which direction it goes."

Sarah bends down to find the small metal pull. She cannot get the zipper to connect.

"You better try this thing, Peter. I don't think it works."

"Go get one of those geniuses to fix it immediately. I refuse to move from this tent until it's fixed."

The accommodations are connected by a system of rock-hard footpaths spotted with acacia thorns, all of which eventually lead to the dock below or the dining room above. Sarah walks barefoot up a slight grade, finding her way to a cavernous deck, the bar's breezy lounge, and the anteroom to a restaurant without walls. She looks at her feet and fears she will be chastised, then wonders why she cannot force herself to obey Max's rules.

Max is thumbing through a dog-eared, out-of-date *National Geographic*, pacing the length of the bar.

"Max, Peter said to have you send someone to our tent because we can't get the flap to zip. He says he's not moving till it's fixed."

His blue eyes light up. "Well, that solves that particular problem, doesn't it?"

"No, actually, it's just creating a new one. I think we need to send someone down there."

"Okay. I'll get someone to take care of it. By the way, I need a haircut. You want to do that for me before or after lunch?"

He takes for granted that Sarah will cut his hair. There is no reservation in his voice and no hesitation in his question. He knows Sarah just as he knows the animal behaviors he so capably describes.

"After lunch. I have to find my scissors and razor," Sarah explains.

"I'm glad you have your own stuff. I don't want you using my razors; they're for shaving. They're the only ones I like and they're impossible to get out here. Okay, come up for lunch as soon as the tent is fixed. I'll be waiting. I'm also waiting for you to put on your shoes," he states in a voice of exhausted resignation.

* * *

Sarah has two pairs of steel scissors with her, a medium pair and a small, blunt-nosed pair. She has also brought along a straight razor, like the one she once used to cut both her wrists. Peter no longer allows her to cut his hair. Since the time Sarah tried to obliterate herself, she has recovered sufficiently to again be trusted with sharp objects. She can cut anyone's hair except Peter's.

Sarah arranges her limited arsenal outside Max's tent and waits as he leisurely removes his shirt and settles into a chair with his cassette player and headset. Exercising great care for proper placement, he fits the earphones to the exact position required for optimum listening. Sarah has complete access to his scalp and neck.

"I usually run in about every three weeks to see the woman who cuts my hair. I've just been too damn busy with these lawyers, what with trying to fix my work permit and renewals and keep my ass out of Nyayo House."

"How much do you want me to take off?"

The thought of cutting his hair begins to intimidate her, for it is impossibly thick and falls perfectly into place however he tosses his head. Sarah is not professionally trained to cut hair, a fact that has never before stopped her from taking scissors and razor to a willing subject.

"Take off as much as you want, I don't care."

"How about an inch?"

"No, I won't be able to get another haircut for at least a month. Take off an inch and a half or more."

Max closes his eyes, appearing relaxed. Slivers of sun filter through the leaves, creating lacy patterns of light on his freckled upturned face. Only his lips move. "You wanted to ask me questions to fill in the blanks of your journal. Now's as good a time as any."

Sarah thought he had drifted away, but, she realizes, he is here under her scissors, making her crazy. She has asked him often before today for information, clarification, but he repeatedly denied her. Now, when he knows it is not possible for her to take advantage of it, he is offering her help.

There is a long pause. Before she can respond, he speaks again. "What's the matter? Can't you cut and talk at the same time?"

"I can't. Max, I don't remember what I need to ask you right now. I don't have my journal. Besides, I really can't talk and cut. You wouldn't want me to make a mistake, would you? I've got to concentrate when I have a razor in my hand."

"Don't say I didn't try to help you. I'm trying to give you the chance to ask questions, and you won't take advantage of it. Suit yourself." Within a few seconds, he has transported himself into a trance, relaxed and unmoving.

Her approach is to gather small parcels of hair between her forefinger and middle finger, holding each batch up, then cut it at a thirty-degree angle, taking off the top, letting it fall down against the last-clipped section and correcting miscalculations. Max's troublesome forelocks mock her. They have been shorn so perfectly that even at their present length she is challenged by the quality of the previous cut.

The ritual begins again, with Sarah increasingly cautious as she tries to decode the pattern her predecessor used with such successful results. She steps back to study the problem, then sits down, examining the contour of Max's hair.

Max's meditation is unexpectedly over. "What's taking so damn long? Whenever I get my hair cut, I give the stylist only fifteen minutes. That's all."

"I didn't realize there was a time limit here."

"There's always a limit. Time's up. Give me the scissors. I'll finish it."

He pulls the scissors from Sarah's grasp and enters the tent, stopping before the bathroom mirror to study the result of her effort. He directs the tips of the scissors straight down in quick, efficient clips, then randomly repeats the movement at adjacent spots, finishing the job in less than sixty seconds.

Sarah is in awe. Oh, that's how it's done. She would never have thought of cutting his hair that way.

He cleans the sink with meticulous precision, as if calculating that each hair lost from his head should now be accounted for in the trash. A confirmed bachelor, Sarah acknowledges.

"Thanks anyway," he allows, just like Peter, speaking in a tone that for Sarah carries with it the deadly implicit message: "You didn't do it right. You've failed me." Who else did that? Someone. Someone she could never please.

"I'm going out. I'll see you at dinner."

Sarah returns to her tent and gathers her journal and several books. Peter lies on the bed, eyes sealed. She is uncertain if he is simply trying to avoid her or if he is asleep. "Peter, I'll be in the area by the bar. I'm going to read and do some writing."

Peter's breathing is even, noiseless; he does not acknowledge her. Assuming Peter is asleep, she departs, careful to draw the zipper's set of spiraling metal teeth together, ensuring he is sealed in against both monkeys and mosquitoes.

It is late in the afternoon, the sun declining by degrees. Couples stroll past Sarah or take seats and order drinks, crunching on nuts, popcorn, or potato chips, enjoying the coolness offered by the vanishing sun.

* * *

Tonight's menu tempts guests with cream of vegetable soup, baked aubergines, either grilled fillet steak served with pepper sauce or pan-fried Nile perch with tartar sauce, Pont-Neuf potatoes, and pineapple surprise. Sarah elects to forgo dinner. As Max passes by, she informs him of her decision. He shakes his head to let her know she upsets him, reinforced by the fact she is again without shoes; prickly acacia thorns lie about like active grenades in a harmless-looking minefield.

During the dinner period, a shy but concerned waiter inquires if Sarah would like something to drink and a few "bitings." He brings her a small plate of assorted finger foods and glances over his shoulder as she writes random observations. He is between serving in the dining room and his clean-up responsibilities. Later, after his shift, he insists on sharing with her the story of his community, wanting to contribute to her journal.

"In the seventeenth century," he begins, "Lake Baringo started as a swamp, due to the sinking and folding of the land formation of the Rift Valley. The swamp continued to come up because of heavy rains. As the water increased, the community living here found themselves on an island, for water had surrounded them. They had to invent an object to cross the lake. They joined some rafters and made a boat called Ambatch.

"This Ambatch was used to transport sheep, goats, and cows to the mainland, because here at the island, water had covered the grazing land. The community had to practice fishing using their clothes as nets. They later made hooks by using the brass ornaments worn by the wives on their hands and legs.

"These tribes are religious people, for they pray to their God the Creator, called Enkai. When they experience drought for a long period of time, women are sent to pray to God asking for rain to enable their families and their few cattle to get green pastures. During all of those days, they are not allowed to have sex with their husbands or their boyfriends, because they should be clean, not to annoy their God."

Sarah sits on a deep, low-lying chair, with her new friend, Luke, and books purchased at the gift shops of the Aberdare Country Club, Lewa Downs, and, a few hours earlier, here at Baringo Springs. The weight of her duffel bag has increased by several pounds, a problem that must be rectified before departure, the day after tomorrow. With the success of today's bounty, which includes *The Scramble for Africa* by Thomas Pakenham, *The Great War in Africa* by Byron Farwell, *Facing Mount Kenya* by Jomo Kenyatta, *Origins* by Richard Leakey and Roger Lewin, and a small handbook on bird life in East Africa, Sarah decides to jettison personal cargo to right the weight. Old friends will have to be discarded; it is a time for making new ones, rearranging priorities. Jewelry, clothes, makeup—some of each must be sacrificed. It is a prescient sign.

The bar is deserted. Luke bows and departs.

She feels herself surrendering to the grasp of Kenya, its people, and their uncomplicated pattern of life. Her love affair with this quixotic land takes yet another leap forward into the unknown.

CHAPTER 14

THE MAASAI MARA MAZE

Sarah attempted to define "safari" as a trip or a journey, not certain if "The Big Man" was really ignorant or just baiting her. Max attempted to instruct her under his breath. The sounds he made were a harsh, muted admonishment, the exact words of which she could not distinguish.

"Speak up, Max," Sarah advised. "There's nothing to hide."

Had "The Big Man" seen the look in Max's eyes when Sarah spoke, he might have satisfied himself that there were no feelings between them at this moment, except the mutual contempt in which they held each other.

"Tell me, what do you think of East Africa after this safari of yours?"

This question Sarah found to be the single most difficult of all, for how could she quiet this storm of a man long enough to explain the transition that had occurred in her and what she now believed? How could she make him understand how her thoughts had been altered, shaped, and refined— not so much by Max, but, as she believed, by nature itself?

* * *

Max, Sarah, Peter, Thad, and Julia arrive at their final camp by the first light. Their flight takes them from Baringo Springs to the Maasai Mara, along the early edge of a day designed for the wings of a small plane. This morning there is crisp visibility, a trace of thermals along the route, and yet, just enough wind to push the plane without rocking it about.

For Sarah, it is hard to distinguish which observations are most intensely felt, the beauty of the Maasai Mara or the fact that today is the last day of the safari in Kenya with Julia and Thad. She and Peter are going on to Tanzania, to Tarangire National Park and the Ngorongoro Crater. But there will only be the three of them, gone for four days, and then the whole damn trip will come to an end, and life will never again be the same. That is how Sarah sees it.

This trip, Sarah considers, has fundamentally changed her. She has never kept a journal before, but now she cannot put it down. She has never considered the universe, yet now, when her mind is not racing, she tries to identify her place in it.

Sarah has traveled extensively with Peter to the hotels of cities and towns: Capri's Quisisana, Paris's Hotel Bristol, Madrid's Ritz, Venice's Gritti Palace, Portofino's

Splendido, Positano's San Pietro, and so on. But those sights, captured in Nikon or Canon boxes and caught on film, then printed and pressed into scores of albums, cannot rival the images that impress themselves on her mind. She is her own camera, set on automatic, shooting day and night, her journal acting as her film, yet capturing only a fragment of this new world she has discovered.

She has visited major citadels of art in foreign cities, museums memorializing artists in remote villages where they lived, painted, occasionally went insane, and died. She has gazed at the munificent treasures of the renowned palaces of England, France, Italy, and Russia, but the gold and gilt, the acrylics, oils, watercolors, charcoals, glass, and clay cannot compare to this place. All lack the luster necessary to outshine the sun on the savanna, the bullion breast of the spectacled weaver bird, the 18 karat fleck in the eye of the cheetah, the burnished lion's mane, the yellows of the golden shower tree and frangipani flowers.

The colors brushed, stroked, or thrown on canvas by the hands of artists are works of dilettantes when hung against Kenya's treasures.

The great, thousand-year-old baobabs—tall, broken, bending, snarled, wicked, wayward, and uprooted—mock the strokes of charcoal against paper in their sanitized museum environments. The stars fixed across the galaxy wink at the objets d'art blown of glass, as both move around intense orbs spitting fire. And the clay of pottery, however expertly thrown, is no better than the clay beneath Sarah's feet.

But it is knowing that her feelings for Kenya, its people, its flora and fauna, will be relegated to the vulnerabilities of a fading memory that is most difficult for Sarah to accept. She wants the sights and smells and cacophony of serenading sounds to go on playing, but she knows that in four days this song will be over.

Sarah extracts her sunglasses from their case, inscribed with the haunting words "Fight Fury with Knowledge." "Well, I'd like to," she broods. "Thanks for the message."

She has not been able to truly elaborate on the reactions of her five senses or the new ones she has developed. She has stumbled around her blotchy notebook, the back of napkins and scraps of paper, each time writing in furtive strokes. But always waiting for the inevitable reprimand.

Sarah puts on her sunglasses to cover her tears. It's a good thing, she acknowledges, that it's so damn hot that tears can pass for sweat, if anyone were to be looking.

Today Max will decide if he is going to take them to Tanzania as originally planned, or substitute another "very competent guide" to take his place. "Sarah," he had said last night in his tent, as she sat on the floor, her back against his cot, "I can't risk going into Tanzania. My work permit and residency visa are going to expire the day we land in Nairobi. I'd be okay flying out again, but the authorities would sure as hell be waiting to arrest me when we come back from Tanzania. I can't chance it. I can't ever wind up at Nyayo House. I'll get someone to go with you who I personally guarantee will do a great job."

"Max, you could guarantee us Jesus Christ himself and it wouldn't convince Peter. There's no way he'll go on without you. Either we go with you, or we don't go at all."

"What difference does it make?"

"Peter wants what he paid for, what he's become accustomed to. That means he expects you to remain with us. God, he almost lost it completely when you left us the first night of the safari. If you're worried about flying, why not get a vehicle and we can drive? They would be expecting you at the airport, not the border, I assume."

Max had sat up in bed, looking somewhat shocked that he had not thought of this simple alternative. "Yeah! I could hire a driver. The cost would be about the same as the cost of flying my plane. That might work. Let me think about it. I have to consider the risks involved if I go that route. I'll let you know tomorrow."

This is the day Max will tell Sarah of his decision. For now, it is the moment of the Maasai Mara, that great expanse that adjoins the Serengeti in the northern part of the Tanzania ecosystem, extending over eleven thousand square miles. It is defined not so much by the cartographer as by the migratory range of the wildebeest and zebra, moving north about mid-July, returning south in October.

William left the park early this morning, calling on the radiophone as he departed to tell Max of a cheetah sighting. He then asked for Francis and told him where to pick up the cat's tracks.

This is the last day of the cheetah. This is not that first virginal feeling of the unknown. Now there is the anticipation of renewing an acquaintance, of wondering which behaviors will be exhibited and what additional knowledge will be gained.

As they enter the reserve, they see a topi male along with his harem and several delicate young topi on the road ahead, bucking at one another like notes of a song rising and then colliding.

Max halts the vehicle. "That shrill crying sound is the guinea fowl warning his neighbors of a predator's approach."

Peter spots a cheetah. It is not the one identified by William. She is old. Her eyes flash the hardened look of a successful hunter as she heads towards steadfast gazelles.

"Why the hell aren't they moving? The cheetah's moving," observes Peter.

Max looks through the binoculars. "Never mind that. See if you can frame the scene with the large topi to the left and the large acacia to the right."

An open-back white truck pulls up. Three slate-colored men sit tightly against one another. Max tells them emphatically not to get out. "We're looking at a cheetah," he yells.

They have not seen it. They pull around and one man steps out. Paying no heed to Max's admonishment, he saunters to the vehicle and places a large metal gas container on the hood.

"Take that damn thing away! We don't need any gasoline!" Max shouts at the culprit. "The old gas scam," he says as he jumps from the hatch and runs the can back, slamming it down in the open bed of the truck. He returns and pulls himself into the Land Rover.

The man has stumbled on his way back to the truck. He gets up, dusts off his pant legs, and they drive in a straight line, away from the cat lying but a few feet away.

Sarah shares the hatch space with Max, which he considers to be acceptable only if she stops moving her legs and remains still. Sarah has been sitting for an interminable length of time with legs folded in the lotus position. She now manages, without being detected, to unfold them so that they are straight out, over the hood latch. Her bottom is buttressed against one part of the horizontal frame while her heels touch the opposite side. From this vantage point, she can see warthogs disappearing into empty holes like transients moving in and out of vacant garrets.

"Beryl Markham," Max begins, "or whoever wrote 'her' book, had the definition of a warthog down perfectly: 'He is the peasant of the plains; the drab and dowdy digger in the earth.'

"See those jackals stopped up ahead, on the road? They look as if they're saying, 'Hey! We have to walk and those guys get to ride!'"

Sarah observes that, indeed, they do appear to be glancing at them with a sense of righteous indignation.

Gazing across the vastness of the immediate Mara, Sarah gives thanks for all that she is not doing. She is not replying to the phone or to the endless list of questions that confronts her daily from Peter: if she has fulfilled his directives that she get this or that fixed, if she has made arrangements with friends for dinner, if she has called his parents. The wonder is that her only task right now is not to do anything. Specifically, not to do anything that will disturb the cheetah.

But questions are endemic to her relationships and, out of nowhere, Peter wants to know how many spaces they have available back home to display his photographs.

Sarah juts her head forward in the direction of the second seat to answer his question. "I don't know." Sarah has just moved.

"Sarah, I told you not to move," Max chides.

Sarah begins to feel singled out again, but stops herself. She will not surrender here, she vows, reminding herself that in the big scheme of things, Max's comments mean nothing.

Remembering the lesson of the first cheetah, Sarah contemplates the possibility of becoming as unconcerned about her image as the Samburu cheetah was when she went for the African hare instead of the Grant's gazelle. She had not appeared less noble in her carriage and self-assuredness. The cat's reaction was automatic, with no long face or head hung low.

Max looks at Sarah, who is reddening and starting to fidget. "Do you have something to cover that yellow band across the top of your bathing suit? You're attracting too much attention, and I don't just mean from the animals. You should have brought clothes that cover your arms and your chest."

Max waits for a response, and Sarah, having nothing else to put on, braces to take the blame for not wearing the khaki shirt on his back.

A safari van can be seen in the distance, pausing as if to evaluate the best direction to take. The driver spots Max and turns the steering wheel.

"Don't look at the cheetah. Take out your binoculars and look away from the cheetah into the open savanna at nothing at all. We're going to fool them."

Then he entertains an even better idea. "Let's really fake them out. Get your cameras ready and point them over here, away from the cheetah. Now, act as if you're taking a shot."

Peter and Thad join the joke, positioning their props, while Sarah diverts her hands to her face to cover her laughter.

The oncoming driver inches so close his open pores can be seen emitting beads of sweat. Close enough to allow scrutiny of his tooth-decayed smile. "Where's the cheetah?"

There is a burst of Swahili from Max.

"What happened?" asks Peter.

"I told him that I'd tell him where the cheetah is if he would just take a few pictures and then back off."

"And he wouldn't agree?"

"It's not that he wouldn't agree. He wouldn't commit."

Max is on display. Funny. Quixotic. Superior. Max.

* * *

"We're going to have a picnic lunch al fresco, a moveable feast," Max says, delighting his group.

"Like the book by Hemingway, *A Moveable Feast*?" Sarah asks, trying to calm her excitement.

"Yeah, like that."

Sarah assumes she is "in."

"Okay, name the city in the story," Max directs her.

Damn! It's not over, Sarah realizes, as she berates herself for breaking the First Rule: never assume anything.

Keep going, stay in the game, she tells herself. "Paris," she responds.

"Good."

Sarah relaxes, again too soon.

Max continues, "Now, who were his companions while he was in Paris?"

How the hell do I know who his companions were? she asks of no one. She thought Hemingway was a loner.

What were the rules of the game? The rules and the stakes were constantly changing, but someone had to lose. In all the years of her marriage, Sarah has learned she can grab a momentary advantage by throwing the bully temporarily off balance. She would dare to introduce her own rules. She would simply collect herself and authoritatively announce her own New Rule, with all the bravado she could muster. The New Rule needed to be delivered as if it were really okay to have one's very own rules in someone else's game.

She states with forced conviction, "Okay, okay, I don't know who Hemingway was with in Paris, so here's the deal: number one, I get five guesses, and two, I get thirty minutes."

"Fine, fine." Max sounds bored, as if he knows she is going to lose and does not want to wait the thirty minutes to announce her defeat.

"Dos Passos," Sarah offers, shocked she can even remember this author's name.

"No."

Over the next thirty minutes, Sarah guesses four other male authors she believes could have been in Paris with Hemingway. Each time she is wrong.

Max laughs. "Gertrude Stein."

The non-zero-sum game is over and the day has just begun.

* * *

Max locates a grove of trees with a wide blanket of grass, and they stop for lunch. From the rear of the Land Rover, Thad passes Max the ice chest, and he opens it to discover an assortment of fresh and leftover food that he spreads out upon the tailgate.

Max extracts garlic salami, traditional safari pickles, sweet gherkins, hot English mustard, smoked fish, fried chicken, hard-boiled eggs, thick slices of homemade bread, small red cold potatoes, hot tomato chutney, and a plastic container of fruits and vegetables.

"What are you supposed to do with this eggplant?" asks Peter with genuine confusion.

Max doubles over with the abandon of a child, exclaiming through his fits of laughter, "Well, I'd try assuming it's an avocado and work off that premise!"

Max tastes everything, heartily recommending what he samples and handing tidbits to Julia, Thad, and Peter. He makes himself a sandwich of sliced potato, avocado, apple, and mustard between two slices of day-old bread. He takes a bite, and with a full mouth, suggests, "Sarah, why don't you play Mom and help everyone with lunch?"

Max picks up a small jar of tomato chutney. "Speaking of eggplant, did you know that the tomato's siblings include tobacco, potatoes, eggplant, and red pepper? I have a great recipe for this stuff. I use ginger, black mustard seeds, chili pepper, and fresh coriander. I love coriander. I use it with cardamom when I make mashed potatoes, too."

"God, Max, I don't know if I'll be able to cook again. I don't think I'd want to try making a meal for you."

"Don't be silly, Julia. I think your cooking's great. Don't stop cooking," Thad pleads.

"Did you get that in your notes, Sarah, about the mashed potatoes with cardamom and coriander?" Peter asks.

"Uh-huh. It sounds, um, interesting." Sarah waits hopefully for Peter's acknowledgment of her own culinary skills.

Max picks up a slice of lemon covering the cut fruit and sucks it hard, using his tongue to wipe the acid from his teeth. He picks up a second piece and repeats the ritual with the sourness reflected only slightly in his expression. Julia, curious about this activity, asks, "What are you doing that for?"

"One of my countrymen, the Scottish doctor James Lind, told the captains of vessels in the British Navy to provide citrus fruits for the crews to avoid scurvy. Speaking of interesting food facts, what is the perfect food?"

"Honey?"

"Nope. The perfect food is blood."

Just then, a topi comes forward with his mother to have a better look. Peter reaches for his camera.

"Open it up to 2.8. Try shooting at eye level. Sarah, get out of the way. Move over here, Sarah. Shoot him now, Peter."

Max has his right arm braced on the driver's right shoulder, and one hand on the camera. "Freeze." He takes one shot, then another. "He's just six months old." He is as certain as if he were holding the topi's birth certificate.

Following lunch, Thad and Julia stroll around; they are to stay within earshot. Max lies down, his back and head slightly inclined on a mound of grass covered with dirt, twigs, leaves, and assorted pellets of animal spoor, arranged about him helter-skelter. Peter smokes a small

Partagas cigar, his back resting against the inverted draining Coleman ice chest. Sarah makes notes about the taste of Sparletta, a ginger-flavored beverage produced by the omnipresent, global, and maybe even intergalactic folks at Coca-Cola.

* * *

Max arises and spots something in a tree a few feet away. "Peter, get under there with your camera. I'm going to make that little monkey up there jump from one tree to the other so you can take a picture, okay? Aim your camera up."

Max approaches the living prop that nature has provided for his next antic. After giving it a cursory appraisal, he shimmies up with the agility of a primate. There is a thrashing sound as Max shakes a branch, accompanied by a loud primal scream. Not a small monkey, but a screeching baboon falls from the tree, yelling and baring conical teeth when it lands at Peter's feet. The yellow-brown baboon jumps as if she might attack. The Canon falls, useless, and above the noises created by both Peter and the angry, fearful baboon is the sound of Max laughing.

"How do you like Vera, Peter? Isn't she something?"

"You son of a bitch! You scared the living shit out of me."

Peter loves a good laugh, but rarely at his own expense. Max has instigated a small cruelty by bending nature to his will, for Vera represents man's fear of something falling, which he spoke of the first night at dinner. Peter is not as indulgent a subject as Sarah, and by the sound of his epigrams, Sarah is certain that Max will not pick him again as a target anytime soon.

* * *

It is time to begin the journey to the special place Max has been alluding to all day. On the way, he spots a Thomson's gazelle with its tail held high, running like a moving target across a video screen. "Boy, he's sure strutting it. My theory is that his high visibility is to warn the others. But he's cool, 'cause at the same time, he's saying to the predator: 'I see you. You see me. I'm in great shape, so let's just forget it!'"

Everyone nods in agreement, as if they too are capable of comprehending the private language of fauna.

Max takes the binoculars and, leaning against the truck, tries to see what predator caused the topi to flee. The predator, if there was one in the vicinity, manages to evade detection. When Max realizes he is coming up empty, he slams the vehicle with his open fist. "We're outta here."

The sky is a thin line stretching against the blue, looking like a place where the world ends, a place where one has to get out and decide what to do about it. It is an escarpment from which the group will be able to view a large convocation of hippos.

"Okay, guys, let's get out. This is Rhino Ridge."

Sarah reaches for her shoes, assuming they are in the car. She has left them at the lunch spot. She waits for everyone to unload, then lingers awhile so the others can get ahead, following behind them at a safe distance, hoping her shoeless feet will not be detected.

When Sarah catches up, she stops a few feet away from the others, on a wide ledge high above the murky Mara's waters. As others observe and photograph, she ducks down and begins to take in the many hippo heads from her separate vantage point. Their heads are too numerous for her to count, though she attempts repeatedly to do so, thinking this to be a matter of urgent interest to her journal. The faces of several hippos slowly surface. Pairs of big ears twitch, and then small slanting eyes look about suspiciously. Sarah's trance is heightened as still more of their girth is revealed. Enormous snouts drip the water runoff over the beasts' muscular lips and then back into its muddy source. In a few instances, the backs and rumps break through, revealing their glistening hide, so strong that natives used to cut strips of it to make whips for thrashing their fellow blacks, beating them into submission during slave raids.

The hippos bump into each other as if playing a contact sport, but as Max said at Lake Baringo, "When they lumber out of the water, they go their separate ways to forage." In the water, their proximity insulates the young calves from crocodiles and from those in the group straining over the cliff to catch sight of them.

Sarah is still squatting, sitting on her heels and writing, when she looks up to see Max standing over her.

"Hippos' main enemies are crocodiles and lions. My enemies are people on my safaris who don't pay attention to my instructions."

Sarah assumes he is shaking his head over the fact that she is at her journal. It could be worse, she realizes. He hasn't yet observed that she is barefoot.

Close at hand, there is a beautiful orange flower with a black dot in its center.

"What is this?" Sarah asks, hoping to deflect his attention from her feet.

"It's a black-eyed Susan. I think I'll rename it the 'black-eyed Sarah' because you may actually get a black eye before this trip is over."

"Are you kidding me?" Sarah asks, gullible and surprised.

Max has discovered her bare feet. "Are you kidding *me*?"

There is no longer any point in trying to hide the fact that she is without shoes. Max looks down, shaking his head. Heavy locks of hair fall on his face. He uses his fingers as a comb, raking it back, after which it falls into his eyes again.

* * *

Late afternoon pushes Francis to drive fast, racing the sun. From afar, the destination looks like a string of rounded, hunchback hills. It is a place where a pride of cats nap on the scorched earth. It is undulating ground, layered with a coalition of lions, lionesses, and cubs.

Francis nuzzles the Land Rover in amongst them. They accept the vehicle with a slight upward glance, so habituated are they to the purrs of motors and widened eyes of tourists.

The heat has lazed them into lethargy, emphasized by their incessant yawning, lying on one side and then the other as they shift their weight from right to left, showing off the black leathery pads of their paws.

To the side of the vehicle, the heads of two males rise several inches as they sniff a breeze and expand their jaws. A third lion forms a perfect triangle with the other two, offering an interesting composition for a shot. Peter fires his camera but misses the first few yawns. Finally, one of the lions looks directly at him and slowly stretches its jaws, gradually extending them to their full expanse. Max gives voice to what the king of the pride might be thinking. "Okay, mister, if you want a great shot, let's give this yawn thing one more try!" Then Max instructs, "Focus on the one to your left, not the one moving toward him. They'll probably butt heads."

They do butt. The heads touch, then their entire bodies connect.

"Lions need more contact than other cats—Peter, use your 200-400 mm lens and open up to F3.5 to decrease your depth of field. No point in getting good depth of field if it's out of focus. Shoot at two thousandth of a second; that'll freeze the action. You need more light at this time of day. Is three hundred too much power for the composition? I had to change lenses."

The lion on the left gets up to stretch, then disappears into the red oat grass growing all around where the scattered members of the pride have tucked in.

"If you look at the left male, he has a whisker spot pattern of two, four, three, four on the left. On the right, it's one over the third and one over the fourth. There are two nicks in his left ear at twelve thirty and three o'clock. He's only got two whiskers in the top row.

"You won't believe this, but when a new male comes into the pride and displaces the old male, he'll usually kill the cubs. Why? Because they want the home-field advantage. They want the other guy's kids killed so the cubs he'll be defending will be his own. Sometimes the females of the pride won't allow it, so we don't know who these cubs belong to. They might not be his. On the other hand, if a female has just one cub, she'll kill it. It's just not worth it to her."

Over an hour passes observing the lions. It is 6:05 PM and there is one other party in the area. Two people occupy the front compartment of a Mitsubishi jeep. The other vehicles and tourists have been departing like the tick-tocks of a clock. Having taken their pictures, they are now returning to the lodge for cocktails at sunset.

The sun goes down as if being swallowed by the sky. The quiet is such that only Max's voice and those of some secretary birds, with their three-inch head quills, can be heard until the notes of night fill the air. A persistent breeze washes clean air down the dust-caked nostrils of the viewers. The lions patiently wait in the continuing onset of dark for the most propitious time to hunt. The sound of protruding zoom lenses emanates from the Mitsubishi.

A cub slaps his mother across her face with a sliver of dark tree bark. Another cub sits on hind paws, balanced by a front paw on his mom's head. When they tire of teasing her, they scamper off and nuzzle into the side of dad, a magnificent specimen who permits them to listen to the beat of his heart. The man in the Mitsubishi has it all in frame.

Click. Click. Click.

Cubs tumble over the larger cats like unruly kids climbing atop living room furniture.

Click. Click. Click.

"That fellow's Jonathon Scott, the famous wildlife photographer! Look at the size of those lenses. Now, that's the kind of equipment I need." Max turns to Julia. "Stop working on your nails. You need to watch these guys."

Max has spoken, and Julia puts away the red and silver Swiss Army knife she has been using for her bush manicure. Sarah motions her up on the hatch and there they sit, suppressing their smiles.

Max has avoided meeting Sarah's eyes since discovering her bare feet earlier in the day. In fact, he has not been able to spare a thimbleful of goodwill all afternoon. Now it is so dark, Sarah cannot see him as he continues ignoring her.

As they make their way back to camp, Sarah's face is streaked with tears born of a stinging wind and the stinging realization that tomorrow they will be in Nairobi. She wants nothing more than to clean it all from her mind. The thought of returning home is unbearable, excruciating in a way she has never experienced. She does not feel that she can return home; she no longer feels that she belongs anywhere but here. She believes this without any knowledge of what is yet in store for her.

The cadence of a hyena pack provides an appropriate distraction. Visible by the light of the moon, they appear like spotted devils recently escaped from hell. They are a cabal of cackling scavengers, their teeth bared while they prowl in packs for the blood-coated garbage of the land. When one or more of the slightly humpbacked animals momentarily leaves the group, it does so with a sneer and the cadence of a convict dragging a ball and chain. Every now and again, one of them turns to look at the spectators with the empty black sockets of a creature bereft of its soul.

* * *

Once Sarah hears the attendants say "Water ready," she removes her clothes and showers. After cleaning up and drying off, she ties a sarong around her and moves purposefully outside to wash her face in the bowl of fresh water. As she unzips the entrance flap, she notices Max walking by. He stops, moves his hand below the inside rim of the washbasin, and drops something into the water. He knows Sarah is standing there, less than a foot away. He walks on toward the camp's fire to have drinks with Peter and Thad, glancing back to give her the information she has been waiting for since the previous evening: "I've decided to take you to Tanzania."

Sarah looks in the ceramic circle to discover what has been relinquished. It is a black-eyed Susan. Sarah suspects this means they are friends for the evening.

CHAPTER 15

THE LAST WATERING HOLE

"Your husband was with you. Where is he now?"

"He left to go home. I decided to stay on for a few extra weeks."

"When did he leave?"

"October 12."

"The Big Man" pressed on. "You were to leave at that time as well?" he asked, one chess move ahead of Sarah.

"Yes. That was the original plan," she responded, not realizing she was about to be checkmated.

"I see. Give me your passport and visa."

Sarah, unaware of the implication of his request, plunged into her purse and found her passport.

He flipped through the pages ceremoniously, strode past Max, and dropped the paperwork on "the Bigger Man's" desk.

"She's in Kenya illegally. Her visa expired October 12!"

* * *

While kneeling in front of the cold porcelain toilet, Sarah cannot avoid hearing the theories of Max and Peter as to why she is retching.

"Must have been the plane ride. Now that I think about it, maybe she couldn't take those loops outside of Nairobi. And traffic was pretty heavy getting here from the airport. It might have been the diesel fumes that got to her."

"No, no, no. Here, Max, step outside a minute. . . ."

Peter and Max talk in voices of secrets right below the window of the bathroom.

". . . very emotional. I just asked her to get the suitcase we left here before starting the safari. I also asked her to lay out some clothes for me and get the laundry taken care of. Anyway, we'll be over in a few minutes."

"Okay, 'cause everyone's waiting for you guys, and Thad and Julia are starving. Oh, can I come in and use your phone? I've gotta get a hold of my lawyer."

"Yeah. Sure."

Max passes through, glancing at Sarah on the bathroom floor. Peter closes the door behind him and stands looking down at his wife. "Sarah, you need to get cleaned up so we can have lunch."

"I can't get up right now. You don't need me to eat. Go ahead without me, please."

"Just throw some cold water on your face. You'll be fine."

"Thanks, Peter. I left this room number in case my lawyer tries to get me," Max calls out as he exits.

Sarah uses a towel hanging from the glass door of the tub to pull herself up and pat her face dry.

"Now you're going to have to get more clean towels for me," Peter dictates in mounting frustration. "And I'm still waiting to find out what your plans are for the laundry."

"I have no immediate plans for the laundry."

"Well, you'd better do something. There are a ton of dirty clothes here."

Sarah flings the towel around her neck in a gesture Sarah Bernhardt might have affected. Picking up the laundry bag and slinging it over her shoulder, she passes through the Norfolk's lobby and ends her march at the Lord Delamere Terrace Restaurant, not twenty feet away from where, under very different circumstances, Theodore Roosevelt set out for a big-game safari with five hundred porters, each carrying a sixty-pound head load.

"Good God. What on earth is that towel and laundry bag for?" Max asks in exasperation.

"Peter wants fresh towels and the laundry done. You want me at the table to order lunch. So here I am."

Julia's head swivels toward Sarah, the currency of silent thoughts exchanged. Thad grabs a menu, into which he manages to bury his entire head. And, like the last line in a drawn-out joke, in comes Peter, looking bewildered at the sight of Sarah with the terry-cloth towel and laundry bag, each of which represent more signs of her unraveling mind.

"What the hell is going on?" Max asks of Peter.

"Damn if I know," Peter mumbles, pantomiming his frustration with rolling eyes and hands thrown high.

"Pizza. Just cheese and tomato sauce," Sarah whispers to the waiter.

"Peter, now here's the game plan for tomorrow. William will drive us to the border of Kenya and Tanzania. We'll get our passports stamped and the visas checked. Another driver will take us into Tanzania."

"I assumed we'd be flying in," Peter manages through clenched lips. He has no tolerance for unauthorized changes or adjustments.

"Change of plans, Peter. Don't worry."

"Driving in Tanzania, Max? Isn't that dangerous? Won't there be a chance for problems if we do that?"

"If so, we'll drive off that bridge when we come to it!" Max laughs. "Sarah, there's something you have to get today. You too, Julia. You gals have gotta get a tanzanite stone before you leave. You can buy just the stone if you want and then have it put in a setting back home. I buy a few and resell 'em every time I go back to Atlanta. They're really hot right now."

"We don't need a tanzanite, to tell you the truth," Thad emphasizes while Julia looks as if she might be persuaded to need one. Thad's gift to Julia is the safari. His next gift will be a saddle for her birthday, and from the discussion between them, there appears to be no room between the trip and the saddle for a stone.

Peter is in no mood to buy jewelry or anything else for Sarah, and if he were, it wouldn't be in a foreign country without reliable means to authenticate the quality of the stone.

"Max, I don't need more jewelry, and I don't feel like going anywhere. I just want to lie down."

"I know what women want, and you guys can't resist jewelry. We'll stop at the store so you can at least look at these babies, and then I'm going to take you over to the marketplace to look at art."

"Really, I . . ."

Traffic is noisy and bites at the atmosphere like a mad dog, but the bark of midday congestion is interrupted with the screech of a vehicle abruptly pitching to a halt. Sarah cannot react to the cacophony. Her eyes remain glued to the pizza.

"I've managed to catch up with you after all!" The man who "has managed" is Brandon Howard, who leans against the hot brick wall separating the terrace from the sidewalk.

"Max, how are you?" Brandon asks. "Peter, Thad, Julia, how are you?" With each inquiry, his demeanor belies the very interest he feigns.

"Great."

"Fine, fine."

"Couldn't be better."

Just how Brandon had found them is the question on everyone's mind. Except Sarah's. She does not care how he has found them, for she is a void waiting to be filled with the emotions she experienced at Rutundu.

"Sarah, you don't appear to be well. How are you? Not good, I suppose?"

Sarah looks at him, the intoxication of this reality enveloping her. Her nerves are stilled and the frenzy of her brain is suddenly tranquilized.

"I think you need a hug." It is not so much a statement of fact as of defiance for anyone who might think otherwise or attempt to intervene. Almost aloud she wonders if angels really drive vans. If they use body language suggesting that they are holding the stem of a glass, about to toast you with a martini fielding one small pearl onion.

Sarah's chair tap dances back a few steps while she looks everyone deliberately in the eye.

"You look like you really do need a hug." He gestures for her to meet him in front of the hotel entrance.

"There," he says, giving her a big embrace. "Tell me, was that sufficient?"

"Not really."

"Ah. Well, come sit with me in the bar. I have more to share with you. I don't believe I've told the story of my dreadful fears."

"No. I think I'd remember if you had. But I have to go with the others to look at tanzanite stones and African bric-a-brac."

"Then let's meet for cocktails at four this afternoon. You really must hear this story."

"Brandon, I've a question for you. You can't possibly be . . . you know, flirting?"

His head is pulled back by the force of his laughter. "Heavens no! I decided several years ago never again to attempt to seduce a married woman. It's far too complicated. Not to mention the sheer indignity of it."

"Then you're not attracted to me?"

"Well, when I came upon you on the trail to Rutundu, I did say to myself, 'Damn fine-looking woman.' When I realized you were married, though, that finished me off."

"Why exactly are you here then?"

"You need me right now. You won't make it much further without knowing that someone cares. Right now, I am that someone. And I intend to remain that someone until you don't have any further use for me."

Sarah cannot imagine when that time might come.

"Why do you care about a complete stranger?"

"We're kindred spirits. We've both had nervous breakdowns. And, dear lady, you are on the verge of yet another."

It was, she realizes, his marvelous instincts, just as he had boasted at Rutundu. So Sarah does not bother to ask how Brandon could know about that part of her past.

* * *

Inside the jewelry shop, Thad and Julia browse amongst the stones.

Max looks casually at the store manager. "Can I borrow your phone, Sandra? I'm trying to make contact with my lawyer." He moves around the counter, then dials a memorized number with indifference to his group's interest in the tanzanite gems.

Peter settles into a stiff leather chair in the corner and looks through the viewfinder of his camera. He is the first to witness Julia fixing upon a tanzanite stone set in a contemporary gold design.

A second woman appears in order to entice Sarah. She points to several luminous stones, emphasizing a loose emerald-cut one of electric blue.

Sarah thinks she knows why they are really here—the commission Max will no doubt receive—and she believes it will all be so much easier if she plays this hand. She slips her Platinum American Express card across the counter and whispers, "Just charge me for the stone and don't say anything. It's a surprise."

The woman acknowledges the message with a slight bow of her head and disappears into another room behind the counter to write up the transaction and, for all Sarah knows, to switch the stone. Returning within seconds, she palms the credit card slip. Sarah signs, and they exchange the tanzanite for the paper.

Sarah tucks the small velvet pouch into her bra, to be given to Max as unceremoniously as possible whenever the right moment comes along.

"Julia, you can have either the ring or the saddle."

"I guess I'd rather have the saddle." Julia sounds like she has almost managed to convince herself.

"Okay, you guys. Now we're off to the marketplace." When Max opens the door of the vehicle he has commandeered for the afternoon, Sarah makes an unpremeditated decision to defy him. She darts through the afternoon traffic to a taxi stopped at the light a few feet away. From the safety of this metal fort, she sticks her neck out of the open window. "I'll see you back at the hotel. I'm going to an interview."

"Sarah, I told you we're supposed to stay together, damn it." A dragnet of noise covering the Nairobi street smothers Max's voice.

It is a quarter to four by the time Sarah arrives at the hotel. There is nothing cool about her as she runs to the room, sweat pouring off her face and neck and from under her armpits, taking with it salt, leaving neurotransmitters in her brain unable to conduct the stuff of sanity.

She washes her body with water from the sink, spilling everywhere, then pulls on a black T-shirt and a silk skirt with a subtle snakeskin pattern. It swirls around her, a size or two too large, Sarah notices, and she feels embarrassed by her appearance.

"I waited for you. You're ten minutes late, you know, but I waited. What would you like to drink? I'm having a vodka."

"Then I'd like a vodka. And a cigarette. Do you smoke?"

"No. I stopped the day my sister died."

They sit down next to each other on a wicker sofa in The Lord Delamere Bar. Sarah tries to explain, "I don't smoke, actually, but I just need a cigarette right now. Do you mind?"

"Heavens no. I'd never try to influence or change you. Not in any way. It's a must that you remain just as you are. You're quite crazy and I like that about you."

He juts out his chin in the direction of a waiter and beckons him with his palm down. In a voice that travels from deep in his chest, Brandon orders a drink and a pack of cigarettes, both of which arrive without the usual delay endemic to service in Kenya.

"Very impressive. Now, let's see if I can light this goddamn thing." Sarah's hand jumps, skips. The flame never has a chance. She withdraws the cigarette from her mouth and attempts to hand it to Brandon. "Could you please light this for me?"

"No. I won't put one of those foul things in my mouth anymore, but I'll tell you what to do. Put your head into my hands. This will get the bloody job done!"

His hands are pulled in close to his torso as he strikes a match. The cigarette clenched between Sarah's lips jumps down and kisses the waving flame at the end of the match. Ignition.

She inhales her cigarette and sips her drink. But unconsciously, Sarah's drink mysteriously finds its way over to the glass side table, and the Marlboro dies within seconds of impacting the ashtray.

Brandon shares his story with Sarah. He was apparently "to the manor born" and afraid of everything, a fact that shamed his father, a high-ranking official in the colonial government. When Brandon was seven, an underling of his father's gave him a camera. He was a very competent photographer, and managed to develop in Brandon a keen interest in taking pictures. His parents, encouraged, asked the trusted mentor to organize a safari, taking Brandon, his camera, and all the film they could carry.

Sarah floats as she listens to him confide in her, as if she is the first woman to have ever heard his story.

The safari transformed Brandon's life, for there was no animal that he did not attempt to photograph. Even after dark, he would spend hours outside in the hopes that something wild would come charging through camp, giving him a chance to shoot it before the camp guards chased it away.

From then on, he went constantly into the bush to test his mettle, continuing to raise the bar. Before long, there was no thought of fear, only the picture he desired to capture.

The lesson he learned and wants to share with Sarah is that "Fear can be tamed. One can get beyond even the most stagnating, intimidating, and paralyzing fear, once you take the first step."

Sarah sweeps through every corner of her mind, trying to associate Brandon's words with her own condition, a condition so obvious that this renowned photographer has taken his time to share his story.

"We're over there having a drink. Why don't you join us?" Max, appearing eager to interrupt, points to a table in the far corner.

"Actually, I've a few more things to tell Sarah. Perhaps in a bit."

Thirty minutes later, Max returns. "We'd like to invite you and your lady friend to join us for dinner tonight. You can go with us, or meet us at the Carnivore. You know where it is?"

"Yes, of course. I spoke there just last night. Got terribly ill, as a matter of fact, but it was probably the heat and exhaustion. I'll meet you there. I need to take a shower and check with Adele."

Adele? It is a name with a question mark for Sarah.

Brandon explains, "My last wife and I have been apart for several years. I've just begun to see my children again. I'm only now becoming reacquainted with them. Being at Rutundu with Ella was a step across that bridge."

He now lives with a woman he has known for thirty years, Adele. He became attracted to her because she was a bird with a broken wing, and he has the habit, Sarah is learning, of fixing broken-winged women.

". . . And now, she's dying of leukemia. Damn shame, you know."

* * *

"Let's have you be Mom again tonight and sit at the head. I'll sit next to you. When Brandon and Adele arrive, we'll put them down there," Max says, pointing at the far end of the table. "You guys move up here," he orders Peter, Julia, and Thad.

The first round of drinks has been drained when Brandon arrives, unaccompanied. His body hulks above those seated, his face and eyes overflowing with grins, his black shirt patterned with colorful palm trees that sway as he moves. He has showered and shaved. His long hair, still wet, lies neatly in place. "I'm sorry. Adele couldn't make it tonight. She thanks you profusely, but she wasn't up to it. Max, move down one seat please, and I'll sit here, next to Sarah."

Sarah looks apprehensively across the table at Peter, but he is throwing down one vodka and about to order another.

Brandon boyishly surveys the thick grove of trees displayed across his chest and, looking down at Sarah, asks, "What do you think of my shirt?"

"I think you clean up real nice."

Roasted zebra, eland, ostrich, and crocodile on long Maasai swords dulled by grease are served by waiters who almost impale the cast-iron plates as they present one selection after another.

"I'll just have chicken, please," Sarah says.

Each time a skewer is presented, it bears another animal, an animal that, on safari, had been seen grazing, playing, running, killing, or being killed. All are willing to taste the game except Sarah. Even Brandon encourages her: "You should taste everything. Taste life, Sarah."

The chicken finally arrives, disjointed pieces on a large white porcelain circle. Sarah eats, trying to ignore her fear of going on to Tanzania tomorrow without Thad and Julia, to face who knows what, alone with Max and Peter.

"Well, I'm going to grab a taxi for Thad and Julia. I'm sure they don't want to miss that plane. Peter, Sarah, I'll see you outside. Brandon, very nice spending time with you."

"Yes, yes. Thanks again for flying me out of Rutundu, and if you ever need a favor, Max, you've got my card."

"Julia, good-bye," Sarah says, reaching up to give Julia a kiss and realizing how much she has come to like this woman. She wonders if the promise they've made to get together later this year to compare photographs will actually come about.

"It was great to be with you, but I'm worried about you. You're going to be all by yourself. Please give me a call when you're back."

"I'll give you a call when we return to Nairobi," Sarah pledges, grateful for Julia's genuine concern.

"You probably won't have time to, Sarah. We're going to be stretched for time all the way. You can call Julia when you get back home."

Brandon reaches for Sarah, but Max steps between them. Turning toward Brandon, hoping no one else will hear, he says, "You know, I may actually give you a ring.

I'm having some problems that you might be able to help me and my lawyer straighten out."

Angrily, Sarah faces Max, taking from her bra the velvet pouch and extracting the exquisite stone. She rolls back the fingers of his flat, sardine-tin hand, and presses the jewel into his palm. "Here. Sell it to some fool in Atlanta. Now you have the kickback from the store plus the value of the tanzanite. This should help you pay your lawyer or bribe the bureaucrats." There is a look of surprise on Max's face and Sarah does not know if it is because she has guessed his game or because it is the first time she has asserted herself.

"It's Tanzania, is it?" At Sarah's side, Brandon again makes himself part of the conversation. "Well, off you go then. I shall see you back in Nairobi. Oh, and Sarah, if you're going to Gibb's Farm, please look up Margaret Gibb and tell her something sincere and wonderful from me. She's a good friend."

The departing hug is not, in fact, the last emotional watering hole. It embraces Sarah for five days, until they meet again.

When she does see Brandon next, she learns of a resort called Hemingway's, which will lead to her discovery of a home his youngest daughter affectionately refers to as "the little duckling house." It sits about fifty feet back from the high-water mark of the Indian Ocean, just beyond a juggernaut protruding majestically from below tiny pearls of alabaster sand, reaching for the sky.

CHAPTER 16

TARANGIRIE

"The Bigger Man" unfolded his hands, repositioning them on Sarah's limp visa. He looked at her with the full knowledge that he held her in check.

"We can detain you here," he informed her, waving her visa in the air as if it were an origami bird.

Then he looked at Max, inquiring in the same tone of voice, "And you, do you have family?" He was toying with Max, implying that there might be a reason to notify relatives of his plight.

Yes, Sarah remembered, Max had family, but they would be as useless to him as his absent cronies and invisible lawyer.

* * *

"That's sensational. Really, a once-in-a-lifetime experience." It is William's affirmation of the extraordinary happenstance of the encounter with Brandon Howard. Max is gushing with the wonder of it all as he and William load bags into the jeep parked in front of the Norfolk Hotel.

William is driving Sarah, Peter, and Max to the Kenyan-Tanzanian border. There, a Tanzanian driver will transport them to their destinations.

Max surrenders the front seat to Sarah and joins Peter in the back. "You know, he's got quite an amazing reputation. He is so extraordinarily patient that he often lives in his van and then manages to capture a unique presentation of his subject."

William's excitement is as unrestrained. "Have you seen his photographs? He's really rather creative. But he's quite infamous as well. He will stop at nothing to get a sensational shot. And he employs an African artist for a mere pittance to draw depictions of tribal life into some unobstructed portion of the picture. It is a bit galling that the poor artist makes so little for his work. Is Brandon still married? I suspect he's not; his lifestyle is quite unorthodox."

"He's not with his wife," Sarah answers. "There is someone in his life, but she's quite sick, and—"

Max's tongue lashes out to snap off the end of her sentence. "Okay, Sarah. This is getting ridiculous. You sound like some Hollywood gossip columnist. Let's get off this subject, shall we?"

Sarah and William stare straight ahead, not daring to look at each other. They remain silent until William stops several feet from the thickly dusted block structure where passports are inspected and visas are issued. This is Namanga, the border post between Kenya and Tanzania.

"The other vehicle and driver should be just over there, on the other side," William motions.

"Peter, you and Sarah go in and fill out the routine paperwork. I'll be here transferring the bags."

No one notices that as Sarah and Peter turn away, Max hits the floorboards of the jeep. William rolls the vehicle across the border, wearing an implacable expression as he steps out to present his impeccable credentials. Kenya has a treaty with Tanzania, making Max persona non grata here as well. William has tossed the dice and won.

"Where are you going in Tanzania? How long will you remain? Where will you be staying?" asks one of three bureaucrats, staring offensively at Peter.

Peter turns to Sarah. "I'm not exactly sure. Where is Max when you need him? Goddamn it!"

Sarah answers the man's questions, referring to her daily itinerary and pays for the Tanzanian visas.

When they walk from the din of authority into the blinding sunlight, they strain to see the vehicle.

"Hey, guys. Over here!" Max calls out from inside a drab green Land Rover parked on the Tanzanian side of the border. "This is Godfrey. He'll be our guide from now until we meet up with our next driver when we return. William is off to practice fishing in an important fishing tournament in Watamu, so he can't pick us up on our way back."

Godfrey is a compact man of medium height. Although he acknowledges the introduction, he is reserved, rigid, and careful. There is a dignified air about him and seriousness in the set of his jaw. If there was once a sparkle in his eyes, life has long since snuffed it out.

Godfrey is precisely the type of person who would usually challenge Sarah. She would attempt to coax him into conversation, hoping to gain some small congeniality as a reward for her effort. She would wrestle with him till she won a smile. She might still try, she decides, but not now. Perhaps later.

For several hours, they drive through dust, stopping only to eat their midday meal. By nine that evening, they have each slipped away into sleep, serenaded by hyenas sending up high-pitched voices to a moon shrouded in ghostly clouds.

* * *

Here, in the Tarangire National Park, lying to the south of the southern Maasailand, the air is crisp, the world at dawn dimly lit. Max stands on the rear seat of the safari vehicle, his head reaching upward through the open hatch, silhouetting him against the faint blue sky of an emerging dawn.

He wears the same shorts of the last two weeks, sandals crafted from the remnants of discarded rubber tires, and a fleece sweatshirt emblazoned with a small embroidered logo of a mongoose, the moniker of his company.

There is a tin army cup that Max methodically moves up to his mouth with his right hand, then down to warm the left. After a swallow, he bellows over his steaming mug to his captive audience, "We got fire in the belly. Let's go."

Sarah has no idea what this expression means. Perhaps it's a reference to the hot coffee he gulps down in between surveying the surroundings, issuing orders, and licking the thin black brew from the top of his lip.

Climbing over the first and second seat, Sarah withdraws the thermos and pours herself a full cup of "fire in the belly," then scrambles back to her position beside Godfrey.

Peter, bundled in a lightweight green jacket, manages to say, "This is great, really great," expressing his enthusiasm for the early-morning photographic outing, despite the unabated and telling chattering of his teeth.

Oblivious to the cold, Sarah is wearing only shorts and a T-shirt, as if being here is fuel enough.

She logs into her journal.

It's 6:30 AM. We are the first people to be out of the lodge and on the road . . . but then, with Max, we are always the first on the road.

Today's early start is driven by the intention to capture a majestic Tanzanian sunrise.

With ears and nose pointed forward, Max leans comfortably against the open hatch, strained in his alertness like an animal on a strong scent. His body arches upward as his eyes fix on the subject in the sky. He narrowly misses grandstanding the event itself, as he draws a deep breath and pronounces, "Look, sunrise over the acacia grove."

The sun peeks expectantly over the horizon, stretching skyward.

"Peter, use the cloud line on top and the grass line below to frame your picture. People forget that with a long lens, you can concentrate on an interesting spot. Listen up, use your telephoto lens."

Peter, his confidence briefly undermined, hands the Canon to Max. "Okay, you take it, Max. This is terrific. You can get each of those great trees. Take a look at that."

Max looks through the lens. "Oh, that's good. You can put both trees in the same frame." He returns the camera firmly into Peter's tentative hands, demanding, "Take the baobab and frame your picture, keeping the larger tree to the left."

Click. Click. Click.

Max glances a few degrees right, spots a herd of Grant's gazelles in various shades of tan, then brings his early-morning class to attention. "The gazelles here are not as dark as those in the Maasai Mara because these fields are lighter and they need to camouflage with their surroundings."

Max looks past the gazelles. "There's a wildebeest. During the migration, zebras migrate first, eating and trampling the high grasses. The wildebeest goes second, foraging and beating the grasses down. The Thomson's gazelles come third, and they're able to exist off the new small grass that has sprung up. That wildebeest is not exactly a migration, just a lone straggler."

"You mean a poor man's migration?" asks Peter.

"Yeah, that's it, a poor man's migration!" Max nods in approval of Peter's sense of humor. "It's more efficient for animals that migrate to do so than it is for them to remain in a specific area and forage for diminishing food."

The wildebeest's skull, shrouded in mist, a goatee protrusion at its chin, suggests the long angular face of a Chinese elder about to point a bony finger and deliver a proverb of ancient wisdom. But in fact, the wildebeest's behavior is neurotic as it thrusts its head from side to side and takes a series of indecisive steps.

"Well, you wouldn't know it from this guy, but the Serengeti is one of the last substantial gathering places of animals on earth. It's a pretty poor commentary on man's sensitivity to the animal kingdom."

Repositioning his binoculars, Max sites lionesses with cubs. "They're very far away."

"What's very far away?" Sarah asks.

"Lionesses and cubs."

Sarah is astonished by Max's uncanny ability to spot life lurking within the confines of camouflage. Godfrey, too, sees cubs being carried by a lioness. Peter sees nothing for several minutes and clenches his binoculars tightly.

Seeing the lionesses is understandably difficult. The problem results from nature's purposeful handiwork, for the very same spinning wheel that produced the golden color of the Serengeti has spun the lionesses' gold coloring.

To assist Peter in locating the camouflaged lion, Max lines up two large, distant trees as reference points. "Okay, Peter, see those baobab trees? Move your eye to the right and back to the first dark patch of grass."

Peter sees the darker area of grass, but not the lionesses, even as Max announces, ". . . there are six, seven, or eight cubs! Maybe more."

Godfrey provides an alternate count. "I think six cubs. Yes, there are six cubs."

"Invalidating his count," Max stresses, "No there are actually no more than eight."

Now the sky bursts with the anticipated brilliant yellows and oranges of sunrise, a spectacle so dramatic that it momentarily diverts attention from the pride.

Priorities are reshuffled by Max as he swiftly secures his camera, deftly making adjustments to the settings.

Click. Click. Click.

Despite the certainty that she will again be taken to task, Sarah is hard at her journal. With pen and paper fully engaging her, Sarah extends her arm to Godfrey. "Here, use my binoculars, they're very powerful." She will see his smile yet.

She hands Godfrey her glasses, making the transfer just as Max grabs Sarah's intended offer of friendship. "No. Don't do that. I'll give him my Zeiss binoculars. They're better than yours."

Godfrey stands close to Max. They speak intently in Swahili. The word *simba* is repeated for emphasis.

Godfrey climbs back in the car and grasps the steering wheel, still skeptical of the count. The engine turns over and Godfrey, on his own initiative, begins steering the car toward the pride as Max grabs back his binoculars.

Max trains his binoculars away from the cats and their offspring. "Large male lion dragging a wildebeest, moving from three thirty to five o'clock, one hundred yards."

Max is furious with himself for not sighting the kill. He acts quickly to make up the missed step. "We'll see the lion bring home dinner to Mom and the kids. Don't worry, we're still in good shape."

Agitated, Max hastily grabs Godfrey's collar, directing him to turn left, off the road, toward the lion, which is dragging the wildebeest away from the scene of the attack, a short distance across the veldt, and home.

Godfrey's expression is one of utter confusion. He reacts to Max's rapid-fire directions, while at the same time processing multiple concerns, one of which, Sarah suspects, is that it is against the National Park rules to turn off the road, according to all the posted signs. A guide could have his license pulled. A driver could be banished from the park.

Who, Sarah wonders, would take the bullet: Max or Godfrey?

Max's orders become torrential, splashing over Godfrey's better judgment. Max has a simple and straightforward modus operandi: either drivers follow his orders or he will hijack the wheel.

In the spirit of this understanding, Godfrey turns the Land Rover into the direction of Max's pointed finger just as a large, bearded wildebeest crosses the road. Max pushes the same outstretched finger just used on Godfrey deep into Sarah's shoulder, causing her pen to jump across the page. "You're going to miss this. Stop writing and look!"

Sarah's eyes have been darting between the wildebeests crossing the road and her description of them on her pad.

"No, look to your far right. See the babies?"

Sarah drops her pen obediently.

One wildebeest flits off randomly, leaving trailing numbers of his kin. Membership in the herd is a chaotic affair, with individual ungulates bolting about in random quirky movements.

"Oh well," Max shrugs, "what do you expect? He's only playing with one horn!"

Sure enough, the renegade wildebeest is missing one of his horns. Max has noticed the single protrusion and instantly parlayed it into another of his observations with a comic kick.

The vehicle spurts further forward until, for no apparent reason, Max commands it to stop, asking Peter, "Care to join me?"

"No. I'm okay for now."

Max advances alone to the front right headlight. His arms and hands are now invisible. He is relieving himself. This ordinary act represents the first image Sarah has had of him since the safari began in which his head is bowed low; the first time his hands are not pointing out something, or cupped to his mouth emulating an animal vocalization. For this moment, Max is an uncomplicated creature of nature.

Rolling onward to the kill, Max commands "Stop now," without taking his eyes off the focus of his attention, while Godfrey pulls up parallel to the conquering lion, the fallen beast, the hungry cubs, and the stalwart lionesses that Max refers to collectively as Mom.

Lions no longer can make a first impression. Sarah and Peter have viewed many by now. No lion, however, is ever like the last lion, no behavior repeated. And so the spectacle begins anew. The male lion's massive claws cleave through the wildebeest flesh like a butcher tearing away superfluous parts of an animal he carves into prime cuts of meat. Flesh falls, muscle sinews unwind like yarn from a skein of wool, enormous pointed teeth hack at bones, and now and again the lion's tongue wanders about, mopping up his stained face. He is the true Lord of the Manor, regally focused on his agenda, and undisturbed by the rabble. The lion slowly raises his massive head. Its noble face is smeared with the crimson emblem of his successful hunt.

Ultimately his feeding frenzy slackens. When he is satiated, he moves back and allows the females to enter the large red banquet hall. The lionesses behave fastidiously, somehow managing not to soil either their smocks of golden fur or their demeanor of noblesse oblige. And yet the unmistakable traces of carnage linger around their jaws, lest anyone observing forget that they sit before the royalty of carnivores.

When it is the cubs' turn to eat, they come falling and rising, like miniature waves of fur, tumbling over one another, stepping into the carcass itself. Blood drips from their small tongues. Each of the cubs has a medallion of the meal somewhere upon its tiny body.

The vultures gather, some by air, some appearing to arrive by land. Hyenas, growling hideously, move on to the stage. The sound of death amplifies with each additional animal of prey, as if new sections are being added to an orchestra ready to perform a funeral dirge.

It is 7:55 AM, time to depart to the main road, the lodge, and breakfast. Six rolls of pictures have been shot using two separate cameras, and such productivity gives rise to abundant appetites. Even Godfrey smiles—if somewhat guardedly—at the idea of returning for a hearty breakfast.

Heading back, Max entertains with an animated lecture on the art of replicating bird and animal sounds. After performing examples of assorted indigenous sounds, he confesses, "My favorite animal vocalization is the elephant."

He is in luck. Standing directly in front of him is a herd of eight pachyderms, including three young elephants skipping along, unfettered for now by the worldly concerns of water, foraging, or future survival.

Max cups his hands and communes with them. They respond by stopping in their formidable tracks, turning to face him full on. The smallest of the elephants juts forward capriciously, reaching out for the tail of his older brother, while grinning in childish delight at his own silly antics. The young tyke whimsically wraps the tail of his larger playmate around his short trunk, creating a distinctly elephantine knot.

Sarah desperately wants Peter to take this particular shot. "Oh, take a picture of that!" she implores, pointing to the two elephants joined together.

"No, I've got enough elephants."

Bullying the audience into taking his small, comic being more seriously, the youngster makes a charge toward the vehicle, then stops abruptly in his tracks, looking around to see if one of his older kin will back him up. The large matriarch responds to his invitation and, within seconds, both animals lumber in Max's direction, unaware that he will not be intimidated.

Devoid of fear, Max explains to Godfrey, "I want you to start the engine and drive forward slowly. Go straight at them."

Godfrey sighs in resignation, confronting the elephants with the Land Rover, the sight of which causes them to turn abruptly, cowering from the advancing vehicle.

"Okay, we're outta here," Max announces, turning to take a parting picture of his own.

Earlier, during this morning's game drive, they had spotted the skull of a Cape buffalo. Despite being on a course back to the lodge, Peter now wants to photograph it. Max looks at his watch, then, making another effort to comply with Peter's requests, directs Godfrey, "Go near the far bank of the river."

The once-magnificent specimen of a Cape buffalo had been killed or had died nearby, its calcified remains placed by human hands on a termite mound to serve as a directional marker. It now lies near a large, old baobab tree believed to be, Max confides, "a sanctuary for ghosts and spirits."

The proud head has been reduced to a white bleached skull, pockmarked by two sunken, empty sockets where alert, active eyes resided in life. Max surmises, "They like to drink often and they get a kick out of wallowing in the water, so they stay close to the river when they're here. He was probably with the bulk of wildlife moving east across the boundaries of the park, along their traditional migration routes, searching for food and water. He might have been stampeded, which is kinda weird when you realize that the Cape buffalo is considered the most feared animal of the big five."

Protruding out of the flawless, bossed horns that stand fully erect are dark, stringy tentacles, hanging vertically like hundreds of earrings.

"Hey, Sarah," Max says, interrupting her writing, "those droppings are living larvae. Blowflies lay eggs, and the larvae live inside the skull and horns, eating out whatever it's attached to. Moths do the same thing, living inside the bone, emerging as caterpillars, extracting the inner stuff, then turning into moths and flying away. Okay, guys, let's go eat," he roars over the engine.

As they head back to the lodge for breakfast, Sarah tries to erase Max's description in order to regain her appetite, which is now as dead as the late, great Cape buffalo.

CHAPTER 17

BACK AT THE LODGE

Max responded respectfully that he had no family to speak of. Sarah looked defiantly at "The Big Man" as he took back the visa from "The Bigger Man." He held it in one hand, allowing his fingers to shuffle through its pages. He tapped it against the inside of his other hand in a rhythm that might have been in keeping with the many thoughts passing through his head. Finally, he spoke.

"Yes, we could keep you here . . . perhaps indefinitely. What would you think?" he asked Sarah with unrestrained superiority.

"Take your best shot," she answered sarcastically.

"You are provoking me! You show me no respect. I do not understand this."

Max's head hung down, resting on his chest. Each time Sarah spoke, he lifted it, and in so doing, displayed the worry lines of a man twice his age.

* * *

It is now almost 8:30 AM and Max, Sarah, Peter, and Godfrey have been in the game park for over two hours. Predictably, their return coincides with the serving of breakfast.

Meals continue to define the structure imposed by Max. There is not only order in eating regularly, but the nourishment required to maintain an unflagging set of demands on oneself and on others.

Max suggests washing in the restrooms off the lobby rather than spending unnecessary time returning to the tents to clean up. Sarah performs a cursory rinsing of her hands, then, sitting upon the bathroom's sink counter, places her feet in the porcelain basin and attacks them with soap. Once again, she has been barefoot all morning, her urge to remain free of shoes inexplicable to all, including herself. She wonders if it is the confinement that she cannot tolerate, like a Geisha whose feet have been bound for too long.

As she observes her boyish appearance in the small mirror, she thinks of Kafka's Gregor Samsa. At any moment, she expects to be on her back, struggling to right herself, only to realize she, like Gregor, has become a beetle. Transfixed by the face in the mirror, she does not recognize who she is anymore. Sarah questions the image. Who is this specter looking at me, as if we should recognize each other, as if we have something in common, and worse, as if we are one?

The sink is filthy. Darting from the bathroom, she takes a half-empty can of Ajax from an open supply closet, thinking, what a coincidence! Ajax, the fleet-footed

Greek hero in the Trojan War who killed himself because the armor of Achilles was awarded to Odysseus. Sarah wishes she had Peter's armor, Max's armor. Any armor.

She walks briskly to the breakfast table, her journal under her arm. Surely, she assumes, there will be yet another remark about her writing at inopportune moments. Sarah can hear it now: "My God, she's crazy. She even takes notes in the can!"

But Peter and Max are already in the buffet line, well past the trays of boxed cereal, pastries, and sliced fruit. Safe from their scrutiny, Sarah slides the notebook onto the seat next to her.

The buffet tables snake around an enormous dining area within the open-sided lodge, the expansive roof of which covers the lobby, the restaurant, the kitchen, a bar, and an outdoor patio; it is an architectural element designed to minimize the effects of wind and rain.

As she turns in the direction of the buffet, she sees a lady parading about in jewelry and resort clothing, from somewhere in the Deep South, as best Sarah can determine from her loud, distinctive drawl. The overweight woman is a creature unlike any seen thus far, like an animal that has strayed into the wrong ecosystem. She is far from home and out of place.

The tourist has caught Sarah's attention simply for that reason, because she epitomizes the type of person a guide would loathe to have on safari, the sort that is talked about after the group departs, at a time when guides get together and compare notes over drinks.

Sarah stares at the woman's head, on top of which she imagines she sees bushy, dandelions after they have gone to seed. The strands form no specific style, blowing as dictated by the breeze.

Later that afternoon, Sarah sees the woman again as she walks from her tent to the pool. The woman asks pleasantly of Sarah, "Where did you get that sarong? It's perfect."

As she draws closer, Sarah assesses her tinted cheeks, which complete her peach palate. She considers the woman, thinking, perhaps, with this coordinated peach coloration, she might be from Georgia. That's it! She's a Georgia peach.

The thought of Max taking a delicious bite out of her, and then viciously spitting her out, completes Sarah's imagery. It is not that Sarah really wants to think about what Max would have done with her had she been on his safari—just that the Georgia peach is a useful reference point. I am not so insufferable, Sarah affirms to herself. After all, I've been a pretty good sport. I've cut my hair; I never ask the vehicle to stop so I can relieve myself; I don't take long to get ready; I try to make conversation. I'm okay, Sarah repeats to herself.

The Georgia peach and Sarah reach the pool and separate. As the woman walks towards her friends, Sarah notices that she is wearing sandals. Perhaps I am wrong, Sarah considers. Conceivably, Max would prefer having her on this safari.

The pool and patio are overrun with a great many foreigners and Americans. They create population density in blue water, juxtaposed against the parched saffron yellow of the Tarangire background. People in these numbers have not been observed since beginning the safari, and its effect is disquieting. The disproportionate number of animals to people has come to feel natural. It has become Sarah's new comfort zone. This crowd belongs to a former reality, the one she had escaped from and would soon be called upon to rejoin.

Sarah seeks out a table so she can write. There is only one available, adjacent to Max, who lies on a lounge reading. His presence surprises her; she cannot comprehend why he withdraws here, amongst this herd of loud, stampeding tourists.

He is oblivious to everyone, including Sarah. He has successfully escaped into his book, *The Man and His Art*, a biography of Brandon Howard.

"Well, well, well, Max. Where did you get that book? You didn't have it in Nairobi, before we left for Tanzania." Sarah is impressed that he has managed to acquire the book. Now he will have more facts, the better to embellish the story of meeting Brandon. The tale will be entertainingly told, she knows. How she would love to be a fly on the tent when he tells of it!

Max does not answer; he does not even look up.

Sarah pulls a chair up to Max, neither expecting an invitation nor anticipating his approval. "I have an idea for your book, Max." Without thought of logistics or consequences, she adds, "I have decided that I will buy you the camera equipment you need."

Max looks at her for only a moment, his face briefly registering disbelief. Then he continues to read, making it clear he does not intend to make further eye contact.

"I'm listening," he says, not taking his eyes from the book, but not turning the page, either.

He's doing this on purpose, to make me furious, Sarah decides. This is exactly what Peter does when I'm talking to him. He continues to be engaged in what he is doing, and assures me he is listening, but he won't look at me, won't engage in what I am trying to communicate.

"It's a peculiar problem that I have, Max, but I prefer to talk to people when they're looking at me."

"You think that's your peculiar problem? If you've got an idea, why don't you write it out and, if I have time, I'll look it over tonight?"

Sarah drops several notebook pages onto his chest. She has already written out her ideas. The first page provides a brief introduction to her background, intended to establish her credentials for the ideas that follow. The next two pages suggest how the photographs in his book should be multicaptioned to appeal to a broad audience.

Max places the paperwork under the lounge. "I'll look at it later," Max states offhandedly, finally turning the page of his book.

Sarah stares at him, struggling with another of his rebuffs. It does not occur to her to stop trying to please Max, nor does she consider that he is the hired hand and that she has paid a great deal for this trip and has the right to be treated with the same respect he would give any other client. She returns to her table, struck down by Max and the merciless sun.

It is this very sun, Sarah remembers, that Winston Churchill, while undersecretary of state for the colonies, feared would affect the nervous system and the brain. Debility, nervous breakdowns, even plain irritability were dangers from such heat and altitude, as were mood swings from elation to depression.

Winston, Sarah confirms, you called that one correctly!

This sun is now a punishing force, eventually picking off each tourist, sending them into one spin of relief or the other—a cool drink, a refreshing dip in the pool, a retreat to shade.

The heat overtakes Sarah. She pushes herself away from the table and plunges into the pool, experiencing instant gratification.

Six hours later, towel, candles, and matches in hand, with nothing more than a sarong around her body, Sarah makes her way back to the pool and lights a shrine of thin, wavering wicks under a sky gorged with now-familiar stars. She sits down on the edge of the pool, unties her sarong, and immerses herself, oblivious to the fact that the lodge's guests and personnel are yards away. It is a feeling of weightlessness, of complete hedonism and utter tranquility, a rite of restoration.

Without warning, emerging somewhere out of the darkness, a native waiter balancing a small empty tray appears at the edge of the pool, a black man against black sky, with only an outline to define him.

He kneels down, flashing a slow, friendly smile, never once allowing his eyes to wander past the waterline that meets the top of Sarah's breasts. "Can I get anything for you, Madam?"

"No thank you. I don't care for anything."

He bows his head, turns on his heels, and softly disappears toward the lights of the bar.

She begins again to savor the taste of being alone.

Then, from the edge of darkness, there is another sound. It is Max's voice, mimicking, "You look like you don't care for or about anything."

His eyes are on her just as they had been on the lion earlier in the morning. It is clear that for her and for the lion, escape is not possible.

A smile of guile, his gaze locked to hers. Then he walks away towards the full moon, creating another of his mysteries. Sarah feels disappointed, for she thought he might slip into the pool with her, dive to the bottom holding his breath and then climb out, pick up his clothes, and walk back into the dark. It would be a tease worthy of him.

The candles on the tables surrounding the pool have burned low. They flicker, like flagmen on a runway, waving her to take off. She pulls herself out of the water and up on the deck of the pool, where she wraps her sarong around her. Reflecting on what has just occurred, she decides to visit Max's tent, the last one in the row of canvas, stopping first at the bar to order two glasses of Harvey's Bristol Cream.

On the way to his green canvas chamber, illuminated by a small hurricane lamp burning atop a table on his front porch, Sarah pauses to watch mongooses clamoring in the open spaces between the tents. There, amongst the shadows, the capricious rodent-like mammals romp and cavort without inhibition. They are in a domain now considered to belong to the tourists, yet they are everywhere, behaving as if the rising moon is there to illuminate their parade.

Like the playful, mischievous mongoose, Max has been liberated by the dark, hiding in the shadows beyond the pool, playing in places he was not meant to be. Now Sarah will ask him why.

Reaching his tent, she softly whispers his name over the sounds of his heavy breathing. There is no response, and she edges closer to the zipped flap that serves as his front door. "Max?" His response is to snore even louder.

Yes, Sarah muses, it appears all God's creatures are playing tonight, liberated by the forgiving dark.

Sarah gulps down the cream sherry and counts eight tents back in the direction she came, unzipping the flap and making her way in quietly to the canvas lodging she shares with Peter.

Inside, Peter snores lightly, peacefully, and other than the rhythm of his breathing, the only sounds heard are hyenas braying at the moon. It is the background lullaby of predators.

* * *

The next morning, Peter reaches for his toothbrush. It is gone. "Sarah, what the hell did you do with my toothbrush? Can't you leave my things alone?"

"I didn't touch your toothbrush. I've got my own," cries Sarah, distraught that Peter would start on her first thing in the morning.

"Christ Almighty," Max, standing at the entrance to the tent, blurts out. "What's the matter now?"

"My damn toothbrush is missing. This is just ridiculous. It was here on the window ledge. I know I put it there after I used it last night."

Max steps into the tent to investigate the windowsill, now the scene of the toothbrush heist. He shakes his head from left to right, then walks outside to the back of the tent. He returns with a gnarled red toothbrush in his hand. "The theft was committed by a mongoose. See those markings? Little mongoose teeth. You can get a new one at the souvenir store."

Max exits the tent, his steps slower and more deliberate than two weeks ago.

"Peter, do you want me to walk over and get you a toothbrush?" asks Sarah, still willing to indulge him.

"No. I'll get it."

At breakfast, Max picks up the dying conversation with more mongoose facts. "You probably won't believe this, but hyenas are closer to the mongoose than to a dog. When they're young, the males and females both have penises and . . ."

"Mongoose females have penises?" Sarah inquires.

"No. Hyenas. That's why they were once thought to be hermaphrodites."

"What else? What about mongoose?" Sarah asks with awakening fascination.

"They're masters at exploiting chaos."

When Sarah and Peter arrive at the reception area to settle the bill in preparation for departure, Max pulls a brand new red toothbrush from his back pocket.

"Thanks, Max," Peter says heartily, slapping the guide on the back. "That's great."

"Hey, no problem. Us guys gotta stick together!"

CHAPTER 18

GIBB'S FARM

"The Big Man" had not elicited a fragment of fear from Sarah, and this fact was destroying him.

"Why are you not afraid of me?" "The Big Man" demanded to know.

"Because," Sarah began, "you're going to do as you please anyway. You are trying to frighten me, you won't allow me to finish my explanations, you continue to . . ."

"Explain then. Explain why you have come for this man."

"Because he is an American citizen. His lawyer is not here, and there's no one else. He has no family."

Sarah heard a lighter snap and turned back to the desk to see "The Bigger Man" start a cigarette. In a Pavlovian response, she took out one of her

*own and leaned across the desk as if it were a
demilitarized safety zone.*

*"Can I have a light?" She did not ask permission
to smoke. She simply took her right to do so for
granted.*

*As "The Bigger Man" flicked his plastic Bic in front
of her, Sarah found her eyes meeting his. The
flame wavered just enough for her to realize his
hand was unsteady. Perhaps her situation was less
precarious than it appeared. It never occurred to
her that anger shook inside him, reverberating to
his hand.*

*Sarah was in unknown territory. Her steps needed
to be measured carefully, cautiously, but she was
utterly incapable of making any such judgment. At
this moment, if ignorance was not bliss, then at
least it served as a source of confidence.*

* * *

The sights on the way to Gibb's Farm preoccupy the
travelers. On the left side of the road, a child rides
an ox. On the right, a small boy sits upon the wood plank
seat of a cart with two diesel drums as wheels, and an ox
serving as the engine.

Ahead, one woman appears in a field of red and
green flax, a blue swatch of cloth tied around her head.
She bends down, forcing her bottom up into the air while
grasping at the grass. A large circle on the sarong over her

rump gives her backside the appearance of an archery target. Other targets rise from the grass, each a colorful, different pattern covering round bottoms. Women are at work in the field.

Before long, the three stop at Gibb's Farm for lunch. It is an intimate hotel, an enchanting oasis. Eliminate Abercrombie and Kent, et al, and maybe even a romantic place . . . bungalow #4, perhaps, Sarah imagines.

This stop, however, has been selected for lunch rather than romance. Max and his reduced entourage are en route to the Ngorongoro Crater.

Faces and clothes are dusted with a fine film of sienna-colored powder flying up from the roughshod road traveled from Tarangire, which has elevated the party seventeen hundred meters, providing access to an enchanting enclave located at the edge of civilization's most dramatic and extensive trail, the Great Rift Valley.

From this vantage point, Sarah sees a vast symmetry of agricultural land supporting a cornucopia of maize, beans, barley, and, in a good year, the most profitable crop of all, coffee.

Lush red soil covers the immediate grounds. It contrasts starkly against brilliant displays of flowers and assorted vegetation in exaggerated shades of green. Walking through it provides the illusion of an imaginative garden hologram.

Inside the whitewashed walls of the main house, everything is orderly, polished, and perfectly presented. The waiters are attentive, and the winding buffet displays selections that attest to the deft hand of the chef. Travelers circle the many tables making selections. Margaret Gibb's influence is everywhere.

After lunch, Max offers Peter options, including the opportunity to take some photographs, smoke a cigar, or relax before continuing. Peter elects to take a few color shots and finish the roll currently inside Sarah's Pentax camera.

"When you're finished taking photographs," says Sarah, "I'd like to put in a new roll and shoot it all right here, in this place."

Tacitly, Peter acknowledges her request.

While Peter is occupied shooting off the remaining film, which Sarah estimates to be six to ten shots, she scouts the store for a book about Gibb's Farm. Perhaps there is a Gibb's Farm cookbook.

There is neither a book about Gibb's Farm nor a cookbook, not even a brochure. She purchases two postcards and sets out to explore the property's charms.

Infused with the prospect of photographing her discoveries, she returns to the outdoor dining table, finding Peter comfortably lounging in a lawn chair, a cigar in one hand and a cup of coffee in the other.

"Did you shoot off the film yet?" Sarah inquires.

"No, not yet. Why? Do you want to take some pictures?"

Her reply is controlled and measured. "Yes, Peter! Of course. I want to shoot my own roll. I've selected my shots and I don't want them to get mixed up with yours."

Peter assures her he has only snapped pictures of a few flowers and that she can use the remaining film.

"If I can't shoot a new roll with my own camera, I guess I'll shoot off whatever you've got left. But do we have time?"

He responds with equivocation, "No. Well, yes, probably. I'm sure we do, but frankly, I'd just as soon get moving to the crater and not waste more time here."

"Okay. Never mind then about my taking pictures. I'll take them somewhere else." She is shaking. She can take them "somewhere else," of course. But damn it, Sarah screams silently, "somewhere else" is not here. And, "somewhere else" doesn't have the secret little pathways I've discovered, with configurations of fallen flowers strewn upon cayenne-colored soil, or specially shaped rock formations, or trees stooping down to personally greet you with their outstretched arms.

"Somewhere else" doesn't have the irregular steps with a tiny, crooked "Private" sign that leads to the rear of the main house where there is nothing to be seen but laundry hanging on a line to dry. What do they say about a clothesline of laundry? Oh, yes, she thinks, it's "the international flag."

She is filled with disdain that this trite, overused description comes to her mind. She must really be sinking, and much lower than she had imagined. She conjures up survival stories in which a person, isolated and without provisions, attempts to hang on, recognizing all the signs of life-threatening deterioration, and realizing that such signs, if they intensify, spell certain doom.

So here is her sign of deterioration. She is experiencing her mind reacting to the sculpted beauty around her with stale, overused imagery. Imagery that is not the slightest bit clever.

Yes, she concludes, I am definitely slipping.

Sarah's attention snaps back to the present. She looks at Peter still puffing deeply, rolling smoke from the end of his Davidoff cigar. The cigar scent passes under her own nostrils, and, in response, she reaches for a cigarette. She is bereft of both cigarettes and matches. Not one cigarette. Why? Because several days ago, she had lit one, taken two drags, and then extinguished it in deference to Max, who objected to her smoking. She wrote "last cig" on it along with the date. She intends to give it to Max as one of many mementos to be presented to him when they depart.

Fuck it, Sarah decides. Who cares if I have a cigarette? It will just be one more annoying thing that I apparently continue to do.

Pushing herself up from the low-lying chair, she returns to the main house, purchases a pack of cigarettes, negotiates for a match, returns to the lawn, and lights up, drawing in the filtered nicotine.

When Max returns, he remarks, "Oh, I thought you'd given up smoking. Somehow I had a feeling you wouldn't."

"You know, Max, it's funny, and almost unbelievable, but I am human. Sometimes I slip. Perhaps I'll try again to stop smoking."

"Was it a serious effort or were you just playing?"

Max's sarcasm lodges in the pit of her knotted stomach, and it is worse than the smoke burning in her lungs.

Peter continues to puff on his cigar, enjoying his coffee.

God, this must be great sport for them, Sarah assumes. The hunt, the chase, the cornering, the kill. She is now the only woman, since Julia departed.

She suddenly remembers Brandon. Oh God! Brandon asked her to introduce herself to Margaret Gibb, and she has made no effort to do so. "I must talk to her, to Margaret."

Max shrugs and walks away in an attempt to find her, returning within seconds. "She's gone for the day."

Sarah searches within her purse, digging about furiously, and extracts a bent postcard. She initiates a message, falters, throws it away, retrieves the second card, more wrinkled than the first, and begins anew:

Dear Margaret,

I've recently met a man who is a good friend of yours, Brandon Howard. He wishes me to tell you "Hello" from him, and to let you know that he hopes to see you soon.

Sincerely,

Sarah, Brandon's new acquaintance

Sarah is unclear as to whether she is remotely close to representing what Brandon would have said.

Max takes the postcard from her and delivers it to someone who will see to it that Margaret receives it.

He walks back briskly, pulling up on the waistband of his Levi's, then struts toward the vehicle, voicing his now familiar call to action: "We're outta here, you guys."

Sarah indulges in a slight grin. For someone with a PhD in Zoology, Max does not appear to recognize the simple fact that she is a woman.

Within Sarah there is a rising elation as she contemplates the next stop, Ngorongoro Crater, a location near where Louis and Mary Leakey believed it may all have officially begun: human life, crude tools, flints, the first small flickers, spirits moving onward, thinking, feeling, maybe even laughing, touching.

Now Sarah, too, runs toward the vehicle, passing Max and Peter, her arm waving them to follow. "Hey, you guys, let's go!"

CHAPTER 19

NGORONGORO

At some point, Joseph had slipped into the room. He stood upright against the open door-jamb. All present awaited the show. Joseph tried to engage eye contact with Cecil in order that he might read some sign or prognosticate events. Cecil revealed nothing of his thoughts or his earlier sparks of spirit.

The room had become a stage; the actors, by turn, upstaging one another. The audience was audible at appropriate cues.

But there was no playbill, no designation of scenes. There had never been a production such as this, for the action was new, unfolding by consequence of one caustic remark, question, or response.

This was great theatre, but it was not play. For Sarah, there was only a grit that she had reclaimed in the last week; a grit she had lost during the safari, no vestige of which had been accessible to her . . . not even the memory that she had ever possessed such a quality.

* * *

Sarah sits in the rear of the vehicle, her back supported by duffel bags. Peter and Max huddle in the middle seat, swapping stories about initiation into their shared world of photography.

"After we got married, Sarah decided I should have some hobbies to take my mind off work and help get me into things I could do in retirement. So, about fifteen years before I actually left work, she bought me my first Canon and hired a professional photographer to spend the day with me, teaching me to use the goddamn thing."

"The guy kept putting his arm around Peter, and it made him so nervous that when he left, Peter told me to take the camera back and sell it for ten cents on the dollar!" Sarah laughs.

"Did you?" Max asks, always curious about how the rich indulge themselves.

"No. I just left the camera on the coffee table and, little by little, he began fidgeting with it."

"How'd you know he'd take the bait?"

"I had excellent intuition then," Sarah replies.

Peter looks past Max to the tangled vines that presage the crater.

Signs stand around the curves of the road. "Bumps ahead," Max calls out each time he sees one, followed by, "Yeehaw!" as if he is riding a bucking bronco up the side of the great crater's wall.

"I learned to be a photographer in Washington when I met an old man on campus called 'the Master,'" Max explains. "I followed him around every chance I got. He'd give me pointers, but mostly, I'd watch him and ask questions. He taught me a few simple premises and I managed to absorb everything he said and did. Just kept tagging after him till I got the hang of it."

"Of taking pictures?"

"No, of course not. Of being a photographer. Anyone can take pictures."

"Well, you obviously have a natural ability."

"I have something better, Peter. I have a passion!"

"It translates."

"Yeah, my wisdom's my current wealth, but my talent as a photographer is my annuity for the future."

"Annuity?" asks Peter.

"Money to retire, when I stop doing this safari stuff. Look at me. How much longer can I do it?" Max asks, his eyes roaming over his scars. "Anyway, I don't know if the Kenyan government is gonna continue to let noncitizens work as guides. They could restrict this job to Kenyans only. I want to be ready for whatever happens."

"Son, you're always going to land on your feet."

"I want more than a safe landing. I want my shot, no pun intended. I want to create photography books and let them produce income."

"Is that a possibility?" Peter asks pragmatically.

"Like I said, if I can get the camera and lenses I need, and not get kicked out of the country . . ."

"What are you talking about?"

"Oh nothing, just seeing if you're paying attention."

"Max, my boy, I'm all ears."

Peter's concern for Max, and his willingness to listen to him, follow his instructions, and surrender to him in simple, successive stages, are Max's grandest trophies thus far on the safari. But Max does not realize this, Sarah guesses. He probably thinks his greatest accomplishment is securing her promise to get him the camera and lenses he needs. Hell, that's just money, she thinks. What he's got from Peter can't be bought.

* * *

Millions of green fingers reach out to one another, Sarah writes. *The vine hand-holding starts at the ground and continues to the sky, grasping, climbing, and draping between and over bushes and trees, the leafy tops of which canopy into a great, green revival tent eclipsing the sky. A breeze begins singing "Amazing Grace."*

On the last note of the hymn, the tent is yanked away and we find ourselves looking down into the magnificent caldera of the Ngorongoro Crater. The scene is enough to make one want to pray. "Thank you, Lord, for . . ." What would be said? There are no earthly words for this heavenly sight.

Here before them lies, arguably, the eighth natural wonder of the world—a volcano that once burned and belched, exhausting itself until there was a great abundance of ashes. Gases filled the vast chamber for two and a half million years, and then sparked into an explosion of such ferocity that it blew off the volcano's upper peak and reverberated through the vast plains between Lake Victoria and the Indian Ocean.

The implosion formed a cavern. Vegetation prospered in the volcanic soil, and a parade of herbivores traveled the steep slopes to find paradise, their predators following close behind.

A separate climate created by the sheer size of the crater walls came to be, creating a Garden of Eden and an ecosystem. Nature reinvented itself to a more useful purpose, for here, almost all species indigenous to East Africa could be found in one place, including human life, as Mary Leakey discovered when she found the Zinjanthropus skull at Olduvai Gorge, just a day's walk from the crater.

* * *

"I'm going to breakfast. It's six o'clock. I'll meet you in the dining room," Sarah calls to Peter as she skips out of the room. When she reaches the bat-cave-dark dining room, she hears Max yelling at the kitchen help.

"Where is the manager? Didn't anyone tell you we were supposed to have a portion of the buffet set up so we could eat and get out of here? Coffee was supposed to be ordered for five thirty this morning. What's going on?" Max is out of control.

"Can I help?" Sarah asks as he brushes past her, shaking his head.

"Yeah. Get into the kitchen and grab some coffee cups and bowls for cereal. Set them up at a table in the lobby."

Peter has trailed in and taken a seat at a table on the fringe of the dining room where there is a modicum of light seeping through from the kitchen.

Sarah runs into the kitchen and pulls three coffee cups, saucers, and bowls from the large aluminum baskets. As she rushes out, she trips on the lace of her untied hiking boot, falling on her left side. Her bad knee crumples under her and the ceramics crack into hundreds of chalk-white splinters scattered over the black slate floor.

Max looks down at her. Without registering a single expression, he asks, "Are you okay?"

"I'm fine."

"Go sit down," he instructs. "I'll get the stuff myself."

Sarah takes the chair next to Peter, a few feet from where she somersaulted. "I just fell and broke the dishes I was carrying. Didn't you hear it?"

"Yeah. I also heard you say you were okay."

She waits for Max to bring breakfast to her, silent as she thinks about the word "okay," and remembering the man she had attributed it to, Brandon Howard.

Cereal, chased down by scalding coffee, fills empty stomachs, consumed at a rate to make up lost time and meet Max's timetable. But Max is dismissive of the waiting vehicle, yielding instead to his overpowering need to hunt down the manager. Finding him, he attacks the man for not following through on his breakfast instructions, and then double checks that lunch has been packed. Max delivers his sobering opinion of the service in front of a skeletal early-morning staff, then saunters to the vehicle parked in front of the Sopa Lodge and climbs aboard.

Descending into the crater's open mouth, Max, Sarah, and Peter are driven first toward shale ledges crowned with waving grasses of yellow. Plateauing mountains rest in the distance, framed by the arc of the crater. Standing green water is freckled with lily pads, and taupe-colored flat stones slightly break the water's surface, gradually revealing their true hippo identity.

Confident cow egrets perched on ebony stalks walk atop the hippos' slippery backs, appearing like bird-gods walking on water. All the while, the black-beaked ibis birds wait for the hippos to roll over so they may feed on the leeches stuck to their slimy bellies.

Flamingos shimmer through oscillating waves of heat, a pink mirage for the viewer's eyes. European white storks scout for grasshopper tidbits. Tawny eagles survey the habitat for jackal leftovers. Green-feathered bee-eater birds perch on an overhead branch awaiting their insect lunch. Secretary birds nest in the top of a shorn tree readying to hunt, a feat performed on foot.

Strutting about in the most dramatic attire of all is a male kori bustard, a bird with a neck of white fluffy plumage plumped out and falling to its chest. He stands a proud three feet tall as he booms out a call. The ruff at his neck and the song in his throat are for the females he seeks to attract in his march to mate.

A few wildebeests, Don Quixote-like with their gaunt faces and sparse goatees, scramble about as if attacking imaginary windmills. They blurt rather than sing to their Dulcineas.

It is a day full of gazelles, buffalos, lions, black rhinos, and other beasts that make the crater their home. They are captured on film by Peter and explained in words by Max. After a long day, it is dusk, that scrim between light and dark, draws its line between sky and earth, sending the spectators back to the lodge.

* * *

In the evening, Sarah settles into a plush chair by the expansive curved window of the Sopa Lodge lounge. She has purchased stationery that depicts a zebra, and is captioned "The African Horse." She writes a note to her brother, Daniel, describing her enchantment with East Africa.

While flipping through the ragged pages of her telephone and address list, she realizes her brother has moved to Las Vegas sometime during her trip. She does not know where he is.

What disturbs her is not so much his relocation, but the realization that he will no longer be an hour and a half away from her home. Close enough to take her to lunch and make her laugh with his deftly executed one-liners.

She is down to her last reserves, and somehow, this new reality is tearing her to shreds. She starts toward the bathroom to be consoled by Kleenex and cold water when Max and Peter strut into the lounge.

"Where are you going?" Max wants to know.

"I need to excuse myself for a minute. I'll be right back. Peter, could you please order me a stiff drink?"

"Oh God, what's the problem now?"

"Nothing. It's just that I was trying to send a note to my brother and I remembered that he's gone."

"What do you mean 'gone'? Gone means dead. Is he dead, Sarah?" Max demands.

"No, he's not dead. I mean he's gone to Vegas."

"That doesn't make him 'gone.' Dead makes him gone," Max continues to taunt.

"Yeah, Sarah, if you feel so bad, why don't you go over there to the pay phone and just call him?" Peter asks, thinking he is being helpful.

"You don't understand. I don't know where he is. I don't know what his phone number is."

"So what? We're going home the day after tomorrow and you can figure out how to reach him then." This is logic in the face of emotion, a strategy that is too late to help Sarah.

"Excuse me." Sarah rushes to the bathroom, shaking and undone.

When she returns to the lounge, Peter and Max remain standing, ready to pursue the fact that her brother is not gone in the literal sense.

"I don't want to hear any more about it," Sarah pleads. "He's not 'gone.' I get it."

"Well, what do you want, Sarah?" asks Peter.

Sarah responds in a voice of uncharacteristic calmness, with an answer that surprises even her. "I want to stay on in Kenya for two more weeks. I want to organize my notes and try to finish the journal."

"That's completely ridiculous. You can finish it at home," Peter insists.

"No, I can't. I—"

"Yeah, you can," Max agrees. "Hemingway wrote after he left Cuba and won the Pulitzer Prize."

"I can't do that. I need to be here. I can't ever get anything done at home. I always have to do something for you, Peter, your kids, the house, my parents. There's no time left for me. Besides, if it's so easy to get what we wanted at home, why did we even come? We could have gone to the zoo and you could have taken your wildlife pictures there. You know it's not the same." Sarah's voice escalates, as if becoming louder will better prove her point. She sees that she has the attention of some in the bar. Peter will not tolerate humiliation.

"Do what you want, I don't give a shit."

"Really? Can I stay? Without your being mad?"

Sarah takes a deep breath, intending to continue, when Max stands with his face uncomfortably close to hers. "You got what you want. Now, for Christ's sake, drop it already."

The confusion Sarah feels leaves her no choice but to follow Max's advice.

Peter advances to the bar, orders three drinks, and gradually lowers himself to the middle cushion of a plush couch, helpless and uncharacteristically confused. Max slides down next to him and gives him a piece of paper filled with questions he has written on Sopa Lodge stationery. It is a personal photo exam he has written out for Peter.

"Okay, Peter. I want to see how many of my photography lessons you've retained. I've put together this little quiz. You get twenty minutes to complete it!" Max remains close and watches as Peter reviews the questionnaire.

Max has provided a space in the upper right-hand corner for a name, and underneath, sufficient room for a grade. The instructions read: *Answer all questions or NO dinner. Test consists of multiple choice, true/false, and one question requiring a written response.*

Peter inhales deeply and smiles as he reviews the challenge. When he is finished, Max grabs the paper, emblazons 100 percent across the top, slaps Peter on the shoulder, and gushes, "Hey, old man, you get to eat dinner. Let's go. I'm starving."

I'm going to stay. I'm going to stay. I'm going to stay, Sarah repeats to herself, as if it were a chant.

During dinner, Max explains how he has come to know so much about wine and why such knowledge is critical to his ability to be a well-rounded host on safaris.

"Max, that reminds me. What was the name of the wine we had at Rutundu? I want to include that in my notes about the dinner."

"I don't know." Max returns his attention to Peter.

"Enough about wine. Peter, in the gift shop, I bought you Jonathan Scott's book, *Kingdom of Lions*, and when we have our midday break tomorrow, I'm gonna go through the book with you and comment on every photograph so you can get an idea of the difference between a good picture and a mediocre picture."

Max holds up the book with a handsome lion staring out from the cover. On the bottom of the book is a quote from the BBC Wildlife: "His best book of all."

Once in the privacy of their room, Peter vents his disbelief to Sarah. "You're not serious about staying here, are you? That was just . . ."

"I'm dead serious, Peter. I want to finish this journal. If I had been able to write during the last two and a half weeks, I wouldn't have to stay. You have already agreed to it. You said it would be okay. Don't go back on your word now."

"Stay, then," Peter allows, full of renewed anger.

* * *

Just after noon, Max directs the driver to a camp-like setting, with firepits, spigots of water dripping into concrete basins, and Goliath trees held aloft by serious root systems that have poked up above the ground, gnarling over each other like inflamed joints on an arthritic hand. After consuming a picnic lunch packed by the lodge, Max throws down a tarp under the thick branches of a great-grandfather of a tree.

"Lie down here, Peter. I want to go through this Jonathan Scott book with you."

Sarah stands at the outskirts of the tarp, watching the two figures lying on their stomachs and flipping through pages of *Kingdom of Lions*, while Max critiques each photograph in terms of the subject, focus, light, and composition. She wanders off a short distance from them, finds a remote concrete basin with flowing water, and washes off the morning dirt. When she walks back, the scene has changed. The book is spread-eagled on the ground. The two men are snoring lightly, Max resting on his right arm, Peter on his left.

Sarah stares at the scene, which scratches insistently at her mind like a cat on a screen door. What is it? she wonders. They look so much like . . . like . . . like a father and son!

Click. Click. Click.

The realization of what this represents struggles forward from the back of her mind, then expands into confirmation.

Peter is the dad. Max, the son. And I'm the mom, the figure that failed them both. Mom, the object of their lifelong derision and contempt.

Click. Click. Click.

On the last day of the safari, Sarah believes she understands the underlying dynamics.

Click.

CHAPTER 20

ONE DEPARTURE

"I understand you are a friend of President Clinton," "The Bigger Man" said with a challenging overtone. *"You think your president can help you? He has no jurisdiction here. What do you think he can do?"*

"The Bigger Man" pushed the phone across the desk to Sarah.

"Please. Contact him if you wish to do so."

Sarah's bluff was being called. To sustain credibility, Sarah pushed the phone right back and made a correction to the story she had contrived.

"Did you hear me say I was a friend of President Clinton? No, what I said is that I have friends at the World Bank. My contacts are with the World Bank."

An awkward silence replaced every person's bravado. The World Bank was another matter.

This was an organization Kenya could not afford to offend.

* * *

A t the Norfolk Hotel, Peter is in a state of high-pitched tension. He is returning to California and Sarah is not going with him. He did not allow himself to believe she would stay. She had not believed she would stay. But stay she would.

On the ride back from Ngorongoro, Max even offered to help Sarah with her journal. He mentioned several people he would introduce her to, but only on the condition that she tone herself down. "I mean, you can't just barge in and start asking people a lot of direct questions," he had said. "You have to be subtle. And you should be careful about what you wear."

"Okay, okay, Max. I did manage to survive in a pretty competitive business environment for almost twenty years, so I think I'll be able to handle myself."

Max had exhaled deeply, feeling that despite her rejection of it, she required his constant vigilance.

* * *

"You're really not coming back home with me?"

"What part of 'no' do you not understand?" Sarah tears up her airline ticket to prove her dusted-off resolve.

"I want you to call the travel agent and confirm I am in first class. After you do that, lay out my clothes and give me Valium, some sleeping pills, and the key to the house."

"Why do you need the key? The housekeeper is there to let you in."

"Don't question me. Just give it to me. I'm not taking any chances. I'm going to take a shower. You can have one after dinner," Peter declares. "I'm leaving everything here except my camera equipment. I don't want to be bothered with luggage. Just bring it all with you when you come back."

While Peter is in the shower, Sarah notices the amber light on the phone flashing with a persistence she is anxious to quell. When she retrieves the message, she learns that Ella has called and left a phone number. Sarah dials it and hears the girl's upbeat voice at the other end. "Are you still going to be here tomorrow? Can you have lunch? I'll be in town to get my passport and I'd like to treat you." She will meet Sarah in the Terrace Dining Room of the Norfolk Hotel. Her father is coming along. Sarah is ebullient. She is going to see Brandon.

In the far corner of the room, Peter creates a pile of dirty slacks, shorts, shirts, socks, tennis shoes, and hiking boots. Sprawled across the bed are the clothes to be worn this evening. On a table by the door is his camera case, the x-ray-proof bags of film, the list of things he must do at the airport, his wallet, the airline ticket, and the house key. Sarah cannot know these are the tools that will make him self-sufficient, giving him a sense of independence he will later learn to enjoy. If Peter does not need Sarah to arrange for the luggage to be loaded in the vehicle and direct it to go to the airport, to have the bags checked in and secure a boarding pass—in short, to handle things and make arrangements—then what, in fact, is it that Peter needs Sarah for? She cannot foresee that these things alone are what he needs from her. Everything else, he can get elsewhere.

Dinner at the Terrace Restaurant proceeds in stony silence, heavy with the nervous anticipation of a departure from one life and the reentry to another. The atmosphere is so stilted even Max cannot find it within himself to produce a joke or fascinating story. He has all but punched his time card.

Sarah is anxious for the last hour to sprint and cross the finish line so she may claim the victory of rest, relief, and a long bath. Peter is already home mentally. Africa is behind him, and the sooner this becomes reality, the more relieved he will be. Max's responsibilities have wound down to watching the time and putting Peter in the cab at the appointed hour.

Three men dressed in business attire walk through the Terrace Restaurant pushing a wheelchair in which sits a deformed female child of about ten years of age. The chair is equipped with both hand and feet restraints. The girl's body is contorted, all control having been lost to the illness that has ravaged her torso and limbs. Her eyes are sunken, her complexion sallow. Her hair is parted in the middle and held to her head with a metal barrette affixed to each side. She smiles, revealing both an overbite and a mouth of metal: one more restraint.

Music marches in from the lobby, and at the sound, the girl's grin widens into flamboyant aluminum joy. Enter twenty-three somber men, their hats held fast by straps affixed beneath their chins, each wearing white shirts tucked into black pants that taper downwards to black-and-white spats. This is the Third Battalion Royal Gurkha Rifles sounding out the British National Anthem from drums and bagpipes in an emotional final performance capping off over 180 years of ferocious fighting. The caged girl is, unequivocally, the happiest person in the restaurant.

"Max, where do you think I should go for some peace and quiet to organize my notes and get some writing done?"

"Go to the Mount Kenya Safari Club. You can wear all your fancy clothes there."

Sarah wonders what he is talking about, for she has nothing except dirty laundry and one skirt that no longer fits her. Why, she considers, is he still doing this? Which leads her to wonder, does he think Peter will give him a bigger tip if he manages to insult her one more time? I have the tip, you idiot, not Peter, she almost vocalizes. Peter doesn't even want to give you a tip.

"I don't have any 'fancy clothes.' I asked you about a quiet place to write, not where I could conduct a fashion show."

Once Peter is secure in the taxi, Sarah reaffirms her decision to remain, believing that when she sees him again, everything will be all right. Peter will be fine, Sarah thinks, trying to convince herself.

Max turns to Sarah, rubbing his eyes and face with one sun-spotted hand. "I guess you're not going to get me the camera equipment. You're just going to sit around trying to write up your notes, right?"

"I don't go back on my promises. And I am capable of doing both. You greatly underestimate me." And it was so. She was unable to go back on a quick promise and incapable of judging when she should do just such a thing.

"Can I come tomorrow to go over the list?"

"It's not necessary. You've talked about it so much over the last two and a half weeks that I already have the information written down. You see, my pen and journal did come in handy!" She speaks the words as if she has won rather than Max, for there is a new euphoria settling over her; whatever vestige of caution remained in the confines of her behavior had left along with Peter in the departed taxi.

* * *

The wand has been waved and everything is transformed. Sarah is in her bath. Peter is boarding his plane holding only his ticket and his camera equipment. Max is on his motorcycle dodging near misses, speeding towards home and the first night of sleep in over two and a half weeks without the weight of concern that comes with attending to the needs of others.

Sarah gingerly climbs from the filthy water, grabs a towel, and suddenly remembers she should call the travel agent in California, who is also her cousin, to confirm Peter is in first class and to change her ticket.

"How was the safari?" Nikki wants to know.

Before her mouth can form words, tears flow uncontrollably. All the tension she has endured is released in the wet, salty downflow.

"That good, huh? I'm just kidding. Are you okay?"

Sarah describes the safari, not in its physical aspects, but in psychological terms. Her speech runs faster, words trip over words, sentences fall on top of one another. The effect is incoherence.

"Do you want me to come and get you, Sarah?"

"I don't think so. I'm sorry. I think I just need some rest and a few days to put this experience behind me. Do you have a phone number for Daniel?"

"No, but I can make some calls and get back to you."

Sarah empties her duffel bag and then the large suitcase stored at the Norfolk during the safari. The shirts go in one pile, the pants in another. She continues to shuffle the clothes in and out of heaps, replicating the same inability to focus as she had ten years earlier when she had suffered a nervous breakdown.

It's happening again, Sarah fears. No. She won't let it.

* * *

At 4:00 AM, Sarah awakes, the earlier fears diminished. Within the hour, Sarah's brother is on the phone asking about the safari and listening to the same outburst as Nikki had endured. The first description hours earlier does nothing to dilute the trauma that accompanies the retelling. "I need a favor," Sarah sobs.

Daniel forces one syllable through clenched teeth: "What?"

"I want you to buy some camera equipment for me. I have the information on everything I need, but you may have to go to a couple of different stores to get it."

"Wait. Stop. You're supposed to be home today. Who is this stuff for?"

"I'm staying here in Nairobi for two more weeks. I'll explain later. Get a pen and let me give you this information."

Instinctively her brother realizes something is wrong. Sarah doesn't know her f-stop from her camera speed. Why would she want expensive, sophisticated camera gear? "Who is this for?"

"Max."

"For the guide who just took you through hell?"

"Yes."

"Do you want to explain why you want to reward him with thousands of dollars' worth of camera equipment?"

"I don't think I can make you understand. I just believe he might change if he got a break, and he's definitely got the talent. I want to be the person who proves him wrong about not trusting someone who makes a promise. Especially me. And I did make him a promise that I would get the camera equipment for him. I want you to bring it to me personally because I've been told there can be problems at customs unless someone carries it into the country as their own possession."

"I can't have this discussion."

"Why not?"

"You're crazy."

"Please don't make me call someone else to help me."

Daniel says he'll think about it and then calls Nikki back. How had Sarah sounded to her? Does she think there is a problem? Yes. Nikki is certain something is wrong.

After putting the phone down, Sarah climbs beneath the covers again. In the silence, a rush of feelings threatens her solitude. This is the struggle to maintain safety in a sea of chaos.

Later, Sarah rises from her brief nap and sets herself the task of organizing her books by category on the balcony, a job she wants to finish before lunch. Photography books, animal behavior books, novels, autobiographies, books containing facts about Kenya and Tanzania, brochures and pamphlets. They fall naturally into categories at first, but will not stay fixed. As if performing a ritual, she moves them from one stack to another, deliberating on each to determine if a book that displays an animal belongs to the Photography group or the Animal Behavior group. This is primate tasking gone wildly wrong.

* * *

"Where do you think I should go this weekend to get out of the city and write?" Sarah asks of Brandon and Ella over lunch.

"Go to Hemingway's in Watamu. It's about eight hours from here, but you can probably fly down. If not, the hotel can hire you a driver. Are you on your own now? Are you finished with Max?" Brandon asks.

"Absolutely. I'm a free agent!" Sarah exclaims. "And I have something for each of you." Sarah has two small, pale-blue boxes from Smythson of London. The first she gives to Ella. It is an alphabetical diary for recording memorable places. Under "R," Sarah has filled in Rutundu, and the date of their meeting. Brandon's pocket diary is for recording wines. "I wanted to put in the name of the wines we had at Rutundu, but when I asked Max, he came down with a sudden case of amnesia. Perhaps, if you remember them, you can enter their names. I just recall that one was a French wine and the other was South African."

The gifts are acknowledged with expressions of gratitude and surprise. Their delight adds another layer of gaiety to a lunch already filled with smiles and, between Sarah and Brandon, she imagines, telegraphed thoughts.

Hemingway's it is, Sarah decides.

CHAPTER 21

HEMINGWAY'S

There was silence as "The Bigger Man" and Sarah looked at each other, neither one able to access the other's thoughts. They had reached an impasse.

"Get them both out of here. Have her visa extended for another five days. Finish what you came for and leave." This was intended for Sarah.

"The Big Man" wanted to add his chastisement. "You better hope that I am not at customs if you ever try to enter this country again."

Unless he gets demoted, Sarah wondered, how would he be at customs? Better not even ask.

"This one," "The Bigger Man" said, pointing to Max, "must appear tomorrow morning in the courthouse for a hearing with the magistrate. Take him away and process the paperwork."

* * *

I t is Friday morning and Sarah is at Hemingway's, a haunt of its namesake during the days Ernest Hemingway relished being strapped into a fishing chair, eager to land a hard-fighting marlin. This beach resort sits on the coast of Africa, the part called Watamu, one of many remote and idyllic oceanfront villages in southern Kenya.

Sarah sits alone, outdoors, at Hemingway's Bar, adjacent to a pool clearly designated FOR ADULTS ONLY, in audible contradiction to the high-pitched sounds of children.

Barefooted black nannies, capped with bright cotton scarves tied about their heads, wearing simple blouses and skirts of variegated colors and prints, hover in close proximity to their small charges, resembling bees buzzing around their hive.

In contrast, the pool designated FOR CHILDREN is vacant and hushed, a sign that everyone is on vacation, and no one intends to observe the rules.

Yesterday Sarah had been in the congested, diesel-scented city of Nairobi. Today, she is in a Hemingwayesque paradise, a spot of heightened beauty where the author may have sought refuge from the depths of his recurring depressions.

Sarah rethinks the circumstances under which she is here. She had first placed a call to Peter to determine if he had arrived home safely. She had managed to work out the time difference but woke him up nevertheless from an uncustomary noonday nap. He had been irritated and instructed her to "Fax me from now on."

Sarah was incredulous. "Fax you? I'm not going to send faxes to my husband, for Christ's sake. I can call you back later."

"Don't bother!" Peter had hung up the phone.

Sarah could not understand his anger, although she might have if she had been capable of reason. Instead, she became furious, dialed the transportation desk in the hotel, and made arrangements to leave for Hemingway's the following morning. She had arrived last evening following a ten-hour ride from Nairobi, a trip the travel manager at the Norfolk Hotel had assured her would take six to seven hours.

Her driver appeared to have stepped off an illustrated page of the New Testament, a black St. Christopher whom Sarah fancied was the very patron saint of travel itself. He was grizzled but still managed to smile profusely. His hair lay flat on his predominately bald scalp, and what little there was shone a luminous silver gray, to match his scrappy beard. His chest puffed with pride, but why, Sarah did not know, for upon introducing himself at the hotel, he opened the door of the well-traveled white van, announcing, "I must stop for gas. I am so sorry not to be ready."

Why hadn't he anticipated this before picking me up? Sarah thought, becoming irate at his negligence.

As if reading her thoughts, the driver volunteered a laborious explanation, the effect of which put Sarah into a trance. Her soft suitcase became a pillow and she nestled into it, her last image being that of her driver plunging the nozzle of a gas hose underneath the van.

When she awoke, ten hours had elapsed. It was pitch black, and hotel porters emptying the van flanked her on either side.

The lobby of Hemingway's received her with its large and lazy space. Comfortably decorated, the veranda was spotted with oversized furniture in soft, muted colors under a domed thatched roof. It all summoned up a casual, open-air environment, cooled at night by a feisty ocean breeze.

Catherine, the assistant manager, presented herself as if she were Sarah's welcome gift. She perched atop the floor like a bird, checking everything in her immediate domain with conspicuous energy while directing the driver, the porters, and the desk attendants. Leading Sarah gently by the arm, she accompanied her to her room, a sizable space with three beds. Sarah's mind simply concluded that this room was intended for a ménage-a-trois. Ah, I've thought of sex. A good sign, she conceded.

"Sarah, come to the dining room and eat, before the buffet is taken away," Catherine instructed.

Not having eaten in over ten hours, Sarah realized she was hungrier than she had been in the last three weeks. This, she thought, is the second good sign.

Cold vegetables and hot entrees of broiled chicken, Chinese beef, Moroccan lamb, rice, and bread were piled on Sarah's plate by men attired in white double-buttoned shirts. Each smiled generously, either genuinely glad to see her, or happily contemplating the conclusion of their shift.

Sarah chose a table and unabashedly attacked the meal. This is when she noticed Catherine eating dinner alone, at a table directly across from hers. In a move much out of character, Sarah picked up her plate and invited herself to join Catherine, who easily accepted the gesture, chatting freely and at great length.

"I live close to here, in a place called Malindi. But when I work late, I stay here. I take care of my sister's three daughters because she died. I pay for them, for their school and their clothes. I'm not married, and who cares anyway? I make the money."

Sarah began to cough uncontrollably and the conversation halted. Catherine waited for a break in the rasping, then chided Sarah when she lit a cigarette. "Sarah, why do you smoke with such a cough?"

Sarah snuffed out the cigarette and bid Catherine good night, promising to have a drink with her the following day.

Returning to her room, Sarah stepped over the disarray of books, stripped off her clothes, and released the mosquito netting from above the bed. She found a small card placed upon the pillow with words by Shelley: "In the first sweet sleep of night . . ." She dropped hard upon the tightly sheeted mattress and fell into that very first sweet sleep.

* * *

Nine hours later, Sarah opens her eyes, eager to see where she is. Nothing prepares her for the exterior of Hemingway's. Palm trees sway to a silent rhythm, fine alabaster sand sparkles, magnificent craggy rock formations intermittently interrupting its glow, an azure sea lapping the shore. Now, Sarah too is part of the tableau.

She walks toward the ocean, stepping onto the thick blanket of ultrafine sand into the sea until the water reaches her waist. Swept up in the spell, Sarah swims toward deeper shoals while gentle seaweed rhythmically caresses her limbs.

Back on shore, two jubilant young black men of about eighteen greet her. Without any words of explanation, they begin to sing an infectious song of welcome as they dance beside her, musically accompanying Sarah back to the hotel.

Jambo, Jambo Bwana
Habari gani, Mzuri sana
Wageni, Mwakaribishwa
Kenya Yetu Hakuna Matata!

They skip about in rhythm to their music, sometimes straying a few feet ahead, then falling back, one on either side of Sarah. They twice repeat the spirited chorus of their anthem:

Kenya inchi nzuri
Hakuna Matata
Nchi yenye amani.
Hakuna Matata
Inchi Ya Kupendenza
Hakuna Matata
Jambo nyote
Hakuna Matata

At the beach entrance to Hemingway's, they bid Sarah good day and disappear.

Detouring around the pool to her room, Sarah gathers her writing material, then makes her way to the end stool at the bar.

Here she is now, arranging two chairs as a fortress, ordering a Tom Collins, and savoring the freedom of uncensored activity. She begins to write:

My bare feet are stretched out in front of me, a welcome reminder that it is now acceptable to be shoeless. On my lap is the tablet of writing paper purchased on the run while at the Tarangire Safari Lodge, so long ago it has already become another life.

Fanning the air is a northeasterly wind I have been told is called the Kaskai, which blows through from late October to Easter. The Kusi is the cooler and stronger southeasterly wind, which stirs between mid-March and November. I feel that as the winds shift, they are reminding me: so will your life.

In this setting, with its refreshing breeze, there is an abundance of gemstone blue. It embraces the adult pool, filled with turquoise, warmed by the equatorial sun. It is but one dot, connecting to the dots of the turquoise sky, and then to the vast expanse of dense turquoise water flowing to the skyline. This is the Indian Ocean.

Sarah stares, transfixed by the hues, then breaks her gaze and looks at a couple sitting a short distance away. A deeply browned, well-preserved man of about sixty is engaged in impressing a far younger companion. Sarah overhears him speaking eloquently as he describes the vista. "These are the waters charted in Ptolemy's *Geography*. Think of it! The liquid treasure chest that yielded Cleopatra's pearls, one of her many tools of seduction."

He smiles lasciviously and places his hand over the girl's, using words calculated to bring her under his spell. Sarah takes down his every line. "And this is the very ocean of that cruel slave trade that carried some fifty million Africans away from their homes over a period of four hundred years. Even before the time of Christ, these waters provided the highway for trading nations . . . the Persians, the Chinese, the Malaysians. And this mixture of people eventually produced Kiswahili, a language from Bantu tribal grammar and words from the Arabic, Persian, Hindu, and other Indian Ocean languages."

Sarah is decidedly more interested in the seducer's story than is his companion. The young woman looks with vacant fascination into his eyes, reflecting the impression he has made by the weight of his words rather than their substance.

As they depart hand in hand, Sarah catches the faraway sight of a gigantic hook used to weigh sport fish after they have been caught, reminding her of the fishing tournament being held this weekend. This is the time of the Malindi Festival, an international tournament conducted annually for over forty-five years, the very one William had to practice for when he left them at the Tanzanian border. He might be out there now, in the "Rips," an area over ten miles off the coast, where undersea shelving and tidal movements create up-currents and turbulence, all of which make for a better chance of catching the billfish when they are running through. Or he might be one of the figures Sarah can barely make out, bringing in his catch, hoping it will register sufficient pounds to win the sizeable glass trophy.

Sarah contemplates more of this ocean, remembering that it reaches far, far beyond the horizon, stretching straight across to Indonesia, with Asia and India lying to the northeast, and Australia to the southeast. Where could it take me? she almost asks aloud.

This turquoise tranquility is devastatingly hypnotic, and were it not for a few undulating white caps beyond the reef to break the continuum, Sarah would be writing in her sleep.

Is writing in one's sleep as potentially dangerous as sleepwalking? Sarah does not know. She only knows of one person who has walked in his sleep: her brother, when he was young. This nightly wandering was, she always believed, a subconscious desire to get away from their dysfunctional family life. But her brother is far away, and now he too has joined those who are angry at her aberrant behavior.

Although fighting an undertow of sleepiness, her pen moves ahead, becoming a small sailing vessel carried along a course determined not by the captain, but by the wind.

Perhaps I should conduct my own experiment and write while dozing? Sarah asks herself, concluding: I think not.

No, she does not want to experiment with writing in her sleep. It could be dangerous, and she is completely alone. Yes, I am alone, she realizes. But for the first time since the safari began, I feel both alone and completely, utterly safe.

* * *

In the gift shop, Sarah settles on two disposable cameras, a pair of sunglasses, a straw hat, and four kangas—pieces of colorful cloth to wrap around the body. She has already collected every book displayed.

Her hands too full, the cameras drop. When she lowers herself to retrieve them, she becomes unbalanced and falls on the floor, then struggles unsuccessfully to put things in order. From this ungainly position, she hears a familiar voice wrapping itself around a single word: "Hello!" The voice belongs to Brandon Howard. He is here, looking down at her, somewhat amused by her startled reaction and by the fumbling manner of Sarah's attempts to regain her composure. Bent over in laughter, Brandon still manages to appear larger than life, a solid lighthouse, his smile a beacon guiding one into the "okay world."

She manages to quip, "Dr. Livingstone, I presume?" as if she has found him rather than him locating her; as if they were in Ujiji where Henry Stanley discovered the good doctor, instead of the gift shop at Hemingway's.

"Come, come. I want to speak with you," he implores her, effortlessly lifting Sarah to her feet.

His foot beats impatiently while a cashier tallies her purchases. They move from the store to the lobby; the chairs are taken. They move outside where the heat is overpowering. They stride past the pool to the bar, but children are squealing over their attempt to talk.

"Let's go to my room, Brandon, we can talk there."

He follows Sarah to her quarters with its three beds, which the maids have swathed in mosquito netting. She unfastens the protective mesh of two adjacent beds. Sarah and Brandon sit, facing each other, while Sarah anxiously drums what remains of her fingernails on the night table. The thought crosses her mind that he might move beside her, put his arms around her here in private as he had done in public, and let that embrace take them where she felt they both wanted to go.

"Look," Brandon begins, "I have my youngest daughter, Victoria, with me, and three of her girlfriends. This is the first time I've had Victoria for the weekend in—oh, I don't know—ages, I suppose. She's been living with her mother. The few times she's come to visit, I'm afraid I've been absorbed with Adele and her wretched illness. I don't want to botch this, so will you help me out? Will you join us for lunch?"

"Yes, of course," Sarah replies, struggling to right her disappointed façade. "Bring them here for lunch. There's plenty to keep them busy. They can go snorkeling right out front. There's a reef, and—"

"No, no need. I'm going to take them snorkeling now, in front of my house, just down the beach from here. I have a boat and I shall row them myself."

Having delivered his message, he leaps up, announcing as he reaches the doorway, "I'll bring them back with me for lunch. I don't know what time we shall be here but I'll find you. I've done it more than once, you know!"

The room is bereft of its previous force and all too conspicuously quiet. Staring at the sight of the two beds, Sarah's memory rolls back approximately forty years to when her mother had informed her and her siblings of their father's suicide. She admonishes herself to snap out of it, for her father is dead and she is suddenly alive.

To clear her head, she envisions Brandon rowing four teenagers atop the Indian Ocean.

Four teenagers and Brandon, the rower! What an appetite they will have! Quick! Call to reserve a table for lunch. And, despite Brandon's comment, make arrangements for them to go snorkeling again, but here, at the hotel. And perhaps a massage for Brandon and her!

The quiet is fractured by a series of successive knocks on the door. It is Catherine. Like a bouncy and diligent bird, she is here to personally deliver a notice of eviction. "My dear, you are not ready yet, and so I will help you myself. You know, the Malindi Festival fishing competition is this weekend, and already there are people here for your room. You must come with me to a smaller one. The three fishermen, they will have this one. You remember, I told you about it already?"

Sarah has about forty minutes to make her move. Anger and frustration join as one—her new two-headed monster companion. Somehow, she thinks, I must stop moving about, stop packing and unpacking.

Once in her new, smaller room, Sarah finds it manageable and less formidable than the one recently vacated. This room is substantially smaller and has two single beds. It represents a standard of sufficiency without excess.

* * *

Shortly past one in the afternoon, there is a hard thump at the door. Sarah is layering a white cotton pant and jacket outfit over her bathing suit. Brandon's fist upon the door has caused it to blast open, just as it had at Rutundu. "You see, I've found you again!"

Brandon stands in the doorframe, looking as if he is holding it up. He is sunburned and disheveled, his hair longer than ever, making Sarah think that he might accept a haircut from her. She congratulates herself for bringing along her scissors.

"I thought I locked that door."

"You can't lock it, and there's no need to around here. The girls are in the pool. Shall I make some lunch arrangements?" Brandon questions, looking eager to take charge.

"I have already. Give me just a minute. I'll meet you over at the table set for six."

"Very good, but make it appear as if you've just happened to run into me. I'm afraid I've spotted a friend of Adele having lunch and I don't want anything to be misconstrued."

Sarah hates deceptions, even the small ones, and she regrets that Brandon has asked her to perform one. To hell with it, she decides, forgoing the thought of any feigned surprise at encountering Brandon.

Minutes behind Brandon, Sarah arrives with her overloaded purse, journal, Pentax, two just-purchased disposable cameras, and a large straw hat. Brandon waves his arms about, signaling the girls out of the water. They join him one by one until there are four teenagers, each extending a dripping hand to Sarah.

The first girl is as thin as a reed. Her hand is flat and her fingers long and delicate. Sarah shakes her hand softly out of fear of knocking her over. This gimlet girl is Brandon's youngest daughter, thirteen-year-old Victoria.

The next hand is pink with new sunburn from the morning's ride to the reef. The hand comes with perfectly proportioned fingers and buffed nails. This hand belongs to Lauren.

After Lauren, there is a tiny, elf-like hand, which belongs to a small girl with deep olive skin, dark hair, and eyes bright with the wisdom of an old soul. Sarah remembers her as Jewish Myra. This is to differentiate her from the fourth teenager, also named Myra, who is Swedish.

Brandon instructs each of them to sit down, but his orders do not translate into obedience, for the girls are still exasperated from their eight-hour drive from Nairobi the previous afternoon and the prospect of reliving it tomorrow. They fidget about the table until his third command hits its mark.

The orders are noted and the waiter dispatched with a vigorous appeal from the girls to "Hurry, hurry, we're all just absolutely starving to death."

It is the sort of over-exaggeration at which thirteen-year-olds are particularly adroit.

"Father, you should have a hat. You've got this terrible sunburn going and you never wear a hat." It is Victoria, straining into womanhood, as she looks after her father.

"Here, Victoria, take this. Perhaps he'd like it better if you'd decorate it for him." Sarah gives Victoria the straw hat she purchased earlier, along with her arsenal of lipstick, eyebrow pencil, and pens, all of which make for a moment of great sport at Brandon's expense. The hat is not Brandon's style, but after Victoria has personally decorated it with small drawings of frivolity, he graciously submits to wearing it. He does not look at all silly, and Sarah understands that this is a moment of bonding in which he revels in being the object of his daughter's deliberate attentions.

The problem of how to entertain the girls for the period of time it will take for the hamburgers and fries to appear is another matter. As the girls' expressions become ever more somber, Sarah has an idea inspired by the two disposable underwater cameras purchased earlier.

"Okay, ladies, listen up! We're going to have a contest, a photo contest. We'll divide you into two teams so each of you has a partner. Both teams will have one camera. We're going to agree on four categories for which your team can win a prize, so if you take this seriously, then everyone should win. You're also going to help me decide what the prizes will be. Okay?"

Victoria teams up with Lauren, leaving the two Myras to form the competing team.

"I think the first category should be for 'Originality.' Do you agree?" Sarah asks, looking around at the faces, each of which wears some show of budding interest.

"Well, yes. But precisely how would you define 'originality'?" Victoria asks.

"Um, I think we could say it is a special, different way of looking at something everyone else sees as ordinary."

"You mean, seeing something and making it look like something else?"

"Yes, like taking a picture of something and presenting it in a way most people wouldn't see."

"Oh, we get it."

Victoria approaches Sarah at the end of the table and requests the camera she and Lauren will use. She examines the mechanism, then confers with her partner. Lauren stands up, walks a short distance to the sand, makes a single deep footprint, and stands back for Victoria to take the picture.

"Excellent! How about if we finish deciding on the categories, because you each only have twenty-five pictures. In your case, Victoria and Lauren, twenty-four."

Jewish Myra wants a category for "Most Beautiful," which is so appropriate coming from her rosebud lips that it is immediately written down as the next category without need for an explanation.

"Most Unusual," suggests the second Myra, and this, it is decided, will be defined as "a snapshot of something that cannot be posed, but must be taken of an existing sight or item."

By the time the food arrives, all the categories have been defined and the prizes of the contest noted in Sarah's journal.

"I know you already went scuba diving this morning, but I've arranged for you girls to go out on the hotel's scuba-dive boat this afternoon, and—"

"Father, I want you to come too. Will you?"

Brandon looks first at Victoria and then at Sarah, who realizes she has only booked space for the four girls, never considering that Brandon might want to join them. Sarah had, in fact, booked them both for a massage.

"Your father can go with you, but you all must be down by the dock in about thirty minutes, so let's finish up here."

Later, Sarah and Brandon herd the girls to the edge of the water where each person on the afternoon scuba boat is fitted with goggles, snorkels, and fins. Those remaining behind are expected to help push the craft into the water. As Sarah begins to shove the boat off, the girls suddenly realize she does not intend to join them.

"No, Sarah! You must come along too! Come on, jump! Jump!"

"I can't. I haven't paid, and—"

All those outstretched hands she had shaken earlier, along with Brandon's, now extend over the boat to hoist her up and over the side, dragging her camera and wet sisal purse along for the ride.

"I'm going to have to be the group photographer. I don't have a mask or a snorkel." Sarah positions herself on the flat overhead plywood top of the boat, a vantage point that will enable her to catch each of the snorkelers as they flip over the side and emerge from the water.

The boat rocks through the water to a point almost beyond the sight of the hotel. Here it stops and offloads its passengers above multitudes of fish colored with scales of bold blues, lacquer greens, striking oranges, sunburst yellows, and lipstick pinks. The ocean is teeming with life in shapes, sizes, and patterns that dazzle the goggled eyes.

Within forty-five minutes, everyone is back on board and ready to return to shore. Bodies are counted, gear collected, and the motor jiggled to a start.

"Will you join us for drinks tonight at my house?" Brandon wants to know.

"I'm not sure. I think we ought to put this to a vote. Girls?"

"Yes, do come."

"All right, I'll come. Where is your house?"

"It's the little duckling house down the beach," Victoria states in a matter-of-fact manner, causing Sarah to wonder if this is a destination she is expected to know.

Brandon gives directions in kilometers, using local landmarks along the beach. Sarah's mind spins. Aside from not understanding the conversion of kilometers into miles, she knows nothing of these reference points.

"No, no, no, Father. Sarah, just walk to the very large rock, and beyond it is the little duckling house. But it is set back from the sand, so we shall make something to mark where you should turn in."

"I'm going to put two very large bamboo poles in the sand," Brandon offers. "One here, and one like this." He makes the mark of an X in the sand.

"Just tell me this: How long will it take me to walk from the hotel? I want to know what time to leave in order to be at your place by . . ."

"Come at five thirty, or whenever you can get there. Whenever you like. As a matter of fact, come as soon as possible."

"Well, now that we've nailed the time down, let me go take a shower and change. Then I'll start walking down the beach. But there is one condition. You'll all come back to the hotel later and have dinner as my guests."

A consensus votes yes, and Brandon, nodding in approval, corrals his group, steering them toward the parking lot. Sarah makes her way back to her room. Exhilarated by the memory of the day behind her, she is excessively joyful at the contemplation of the evening ahead.

* * *

The day's high temperature lingers into the late afternoon. Moist from the heat, Sarah selects a kanga with colors to match her bathing suit and wraps the cloth around her waist. She leaves the room carrying a large basket stocked with reading glasses, sunglasses, camera and film, chocolates for the girls, a wildly tropical shirt for Brandon purchased from the hotel souvenir store, a bottle of chilled Moët & Chandon, and one crystal fluted glass etched with the likeness of a zebra baring firm buttocks to whomever holds the glass.

Sarah's walk is difficult, for the basket is heavy; there is no way to divide the contents and equalize the weight. She stops frequently. In order to stay cool, she walks into the ocean, allowing the water to swirl around her calves. She is confident she will be able to sight the bamboo signposts from the water. The rock finally looms ahead, acting as a mirage hovering just beyond her reach. Eventually, she arrives at the landmark. But Victoria's reference to it as a "big rock" was an injustice to the great protrusion that thrusts itself up through the sand. Thousands of caverns pit its face. The hardened sediment twists and turns as it claws its ascent to the sky.

It is another of nature's profound handouts, and the defining marker of Brandon's home. However, she cannot find the bamboo poles.

She wanders well beyond the rock, her head bowed and as close to the sand as her five-foot-six-inch frame will allow. She turns around and retraces her steps, going past the rock in the direction of the hotel. Set back on a thicket of twisted mangroves, Sarah sees a lavish dwelling far from the sea. Walking up a slope overgrown with a thick spread of green and fuchsia land cover, she discovers ground scrub tearing furiously at her feet. Her toes react with an acid stinging sensation and a purple swelling. A black man walks toward her, appearing alarmed at her invasion of the property he is employed to protect. The look on his face is menacing or questioning, Sarah cannot be sure which.

"I am looking for Brandon Howard's house," Sarah explains in a voice filled with hope.

The man, a guard, smiles eagerly. He knows the house. He offers to guide her there. Thank God. Oh, thank God, Sarah whispers under her breath.

No more than ten minutes pass before the two Myras, along with Lauren and Victoria, rush Sarah, shouting their laughter through the air. Sarah expresses her appreciation to the guard, giving him several shillings and shaking his hand.

Snuggled up against the berm of Brandon's home, set a far distance from the ocean, are two enormous bamboo poles, crossed in the sign of an X. Sarah had missed it altogether.

"There you are," Brandon booms. "We didn't think you'd make it. I was quite concerned. Just about to go looking for you, actually."

"I've been walking for over an hour. I couldn't see the poles."

"Well, they're quite obviously here!"

There is nothing to do but laugh, for indeed, it would be difficult to find two bamboo poles larger than those that mark the entrance to Brandon's dwelling.

"Come with us. We'll show you the little duckling house."

Sarah follows Victoria inside, with Brandon flanking the rear, a Tusker beer in one hand and the failed bamboo poles in the other.

As Sarah crosses the entrance, she is engulfed with tender affection for Victoria and her characterization of the home. It is obvious that Brandon's youngest daughter refers to this as the little duckling house because the only material encapsulating the structure and defining the perimeter walls is mesh chicken wire. Brandon apparently could not afford to finish the house properly. It is just as he had explained to her at Rutundu: always pressing needs and never enough money.

"What have you got in that monstrous basket?" Brandon insists on knowing, his eyes as wide as the children's.

"This is for you and the others," Sarah explains as she passes the chocolates to Victoria.

"And this is for you," she says, passing the flowered shirt to Brandon. He holds it up and appraises the size.

"And this, this is for me and anyone else who wants a sip."

Sarah hands Brandon the bottle of now-warm champagne. He flourishes its opening, sending the cork off into some corner of the dining area. Sarah retrieves the elongated glass from her basket and takes the first sip, Brandon the second.

"May we each have a sip, Sarah? Just one sip?"

"Yes. Just one sip each." Sarah makes the allowance without consulting Brandon. As he does not move to stop her, she gives her glass first to Victoria, who after a ladylike sip, passes it on to the other girls. Even Lauren, the least emotional of the teenagers, demonstrates excitement at her turn at the flute, which, until this moment, she had seen only as a glamorous prop in a foreign film.

Sarah and Brandon take the champagne to one of many sandy knolls situated between the chicken-wire house and the tide. The girls follow, and Sarah wonders if Victoria is trying to chaperone her father. She does not want to let him out of her sight, perhaps afraid of sharing his attention after the time that has come between them.

"Father, I want to go into town for dinner. Can't we go to that little place we always used to go to?"

Sarah had already invited them to the hotel for dinner and had made reservations. I'm going to stay out of it, Sarah decides. I'm going to take a swim and cool off and, perhaps, make my swollen feet feel better.

When Sarah returns to the sandy knoll, she realizes Brandon and the girls have returned to the little duckling house, and so she follows the direction of the light.

"Well, we've decided to go to dinner in town, Sarah. Does this suit you?"

Feeling drained from the sun, the walk, the water, and her stinging feet, Sarah realizes that she must lie down. "I'd rather remain here and rest. You all go and have a great time. Just wake me up when you get back."

Brandon looks at her, confused and hurt, and Sarah wonders if he thinks she is angry because the plans have been changed.

"Where can I lie down?"

As if feeling contrite for having taken over, Victoria offers Sarah the couch in the large space in which they are presently standing. As she reclines, Brandon strides to his bedroom, removes one of the heavy woven throws, and places it over her. Sarah's eyes close immediately, and she hears only a few words before she falls into a pit of sleep.

Sometime that evening before everyone returns, Sarah awakes briefly and realizes she is wearing soaking-wet clothes. She removes her bathing suit and sarong, drops it on the floor beside her, and rolls herself up several times in the rough blanket. As she drifts back to sleep, she thinks of Cleopatra coiling herself in a carpet and is somewhere in Egypt waiting to meet Mark Antony when she hears Brandon tentatively call her name.

Sarah struggles to wake. Brandon tries to help Sarah sit up, and when he cannot move her, asks if she would like to remain the night.

"No, thank you anyway. But I shall need a lift back to the hotel. My clothes were wet, so I took them off, and now I'm afraid I have to keep this blanket on me until we get back to my room."

Brandon picks up her fallen things as well as her basket and assures the girls he will return shortly. Then he helps Sarah hobble barefoot to the van.

Sarah kicks her hotel door open, just as Brandon had done that afternoon. She makes her way to the bed, eases in, pulls the covers back over her, and wrestles off the blanket. "Here, take this."

"I would like to stay awhile, but the girls are waiting up for me. I hate to leave you, poor thing. Are your feet still bothering you terribly? Should I call for someone?"

"Please ask at the front desk if they have a doctor on site. That would be helpful."

"What are your plans for tomorrow?"

"I think I'll make arrangements to leave tomorrow. I want to go back to Nairobi."

"Possibly we could give you a lift. We shall be departing tomorrow as well."

I'll be damned if I'm going to be relegated to the backseat, Sarah decides. I can't begrudge Victoria her desire to hang on to her father. I understand all too well.

Sarah's feet continue to burn, and before long, she is out of bed and sitting on the bathroom counter with cold water washing over them. She has not dressed, and so is taken by surprise when she turns to face a person standing in the doorway.

"Hellllllloooooo! I am Nurse McGraw. What seems to be the problem?"

The tall, large-boned nurse has a husky voice, coming from somewhere deep and passing through smoke-scarred lungs. The face is tanned into fine crepe-paper lines. Although she is a woman, her femininity has long ago deserted her, leaving the caricature of a male in its place.

Sarah, startled by her presence, is momentarily unmindful of the fact that she is undressed. But when she looks into the mirror, she rushes from the bathroom to find a kanga.

"Let me see your feet. Oh, I know what you've been up to. You've been out in the foliage without your shoes. You have a rather nasty burn, but it should be better tomorrow. I'll sit here on the other bed while you go to sleep."

"No, that won't be necessary. I appreciate it, but I feel much better now."

"I insist. If I get tired, I'll just lie down. Don't worry about me."

There is something about this person that unnerves Sarah. Maybe it is her questionable sexual orientation or her attitude of one who expects to call the shots, but either way, Sarah fears Nurse McGraw actually wants to spend the night. "I wouldn't be able to sleep if you were here. If you go and let me sleep, I promise to see you in the morning."

"You do? You promise?"

"Absolutely."

As Sarah is being driven back to Nairobi the following day, she tries to remember if she has ever broken a promise before, and concludes that not visiting Nurse McGraw this morning is her first such transgression.

CHAPTER 22

MARY-ANN OF CARGO WINDS

"Can I get my wallet and things back?" asked Max.

They were directed out of the office and departed without looking back.

"You will leave now." It was "The Big Man" dismissing Sarah in the hallway, pointing to the stairs. He pushed Max into the very next office, the office of the man with the French fries, the office next to Cecil's.

"No. I want to stay with Max." She entered the office and almost sat down.

"Sarah, I'm telling you to leave this to me now."

"You cannot come in here." The still somewhat inebriated man pushed her back into the hallway.

"Okay. I'll be waiting outside."

For the first time in hours, Sarah felt free to use the restroom.

Sarah and Joseph waited outside the door where Max was being informed about his hearing the next day while his file was being reviewed again and updated.

"The Big Man" walked up and down the stairs on the pretense of seeing how the meeting was going, talking to other bureaucrats, and executing meaningless acts that took him near Sarah. On one of these occasions, she confronted him. She advanced her hand in an attempt to shake his.

"Now that this is over, I'd like to apologize for my behavior. I just felt that I couldn't get anyone to help me."

This was her characteristic "get 'em to like you at all costs" compulsivity.

* * *

A fax awaits Sarah upon her return from Hemingway's. The camera equipment and other packages have arrived, but they would now have to clear customs. She falls into bed cursing her brother for not bringing them to her personally. Her anger dissipates, however, when she realizes that he had at least agreed to purchase the items.

The message from customs has extinguished any possibility of sleep. She lies in bed, trying to block out the tormenting sounds of wooden crates filled with glass bottles of Coca-Cola, Sprite, and Fanta Orange crashing into one another as they are unloaded behind her room from a never-ending procession of trucks.

Hundreds of clamoring cases are being disgorged by noisy warehouse men operating as if oblivious to the guests of the Norfolk Hotel backed up against the alley.

I must change hotels tomorrow or, if I haven't already, I'll surely go mad, Sarah decides.

In an effort to fall asleep, Sarah recalls today's unproductive events. This was to have been a particularly special day, one filled with the satisfaction of taking possession of packages sent to her from the United States.

It is Tuesday, and although the packages arrived yesterday, Monday was a public holiday. Sarah's cargo contains the camera, lenses, camera case, and film for Max, as well as an assortment of lightweight summer clothes for her.

Max called this morning to check on the status of his gift, and to again reaffirm his doubt that he would ever enjoy the use of the camera and lenses. His psychology worked. His pathetic lack of faith triggered the desired effect of redoubling Sarah's resolve, and she again assured him with great bravado that she could manage anything, including keeping her promise. "Max, I told you, you will have the equipment. For God's sake! It's been acquired. It's been paid for. It's been sent. It's here. I couldn't get it out of customs on a holiday. You know, you are so stuck in your lack of faith, you wouldn't know your angel if she flew into the engine of your plane. Call me tomorrow."

Max could not just say good-bye. "Nothing's ever worked out for me and it's hard to believe this will be any different."

As his self-appointed angel, Sarah responded, "Ye of little faith, it's your script. Rewrite it."

"After I get the stuff."

Sarah's confident position with Max, in some part, was based on the call that preceded his. Brandon had phoned last night to check on her, to let her know he was leaving Tuesday morning to go to Mombasa on business, and that he would clear her packages through customs while at the airport, prior to his departure.

He assured her that he was familiar with customs, their officials, and their modus operandi, so Sarah had no doubt that Brandon's promise to her and her promise to Max would be fulfilled. Max would be a new, different person.

It was 10:00 AM when she reached for the phone and learned that the complications endemic to life in Africa would spare neither her, Max, nor Brandon.

"Sarah, Brandon here. Look, my dear, we've got a bit of a problem. We can't get your things out of customs unless you are willing to pay some sort of tax on them, or a bond, which will be roughly the equivalent of the value of the packages. Or, you can pay a bribe. You'll probably not see the money again. Or, there's another way out. You can come down here, board a plane for London, say, and return with the equipment, bringing it with you into the country. What will it be?"

None of the suggested options made sense to Sarah, as she had already paid for the contents and considered their original price the termination of her financial obligation.

She had sighed audibly for Brandon's benefit, then vowed she would not surrender to the very practices everyone in Kenya she had spoken with said must change. "No. I won't agree to any of those options. You go catch your plane before you miss it. I'll handle this in my own way," she assured him.

"Oh gawd, Sarah, please don't do anything until I come back tomorrow."

"I won't do anything too outrageous." Her assurance sounded hollow, but it was respectably delivered.

As Brandon and Sarah disengaged the phone, it began to ring. One call followed another, each initiated by someone who, aware of the packages at customs, offered their help for a fee. Every clearing agent working the beat had been wired into the arrival of Sarah's goods, and each of them would be honored to assist her.

Only a single call was generated by a female clearing agent: Mary-Ann of Cargo Winds. Sarah chose her for the task, believing that as the only woman in this competitive field, she would work more conscientiously than the others.

Shortly after their verbal arrangement, Mary-Ann sent her assistant to the hotel with explicit instructions to have Sarah sign documents authorizing her to be the representative in this matter.

Mary-Ann's assistant was young and painfully shy, with a barely audible voice that compelled Sarah to lean forward each time she spoke. Her eyes expanded and contracted as she reacted to the conversation. They experienced some serious difficulties understanding each other, but this worked to Sarah's advantage.

When the assistant handed Sarah the standard agreement, she reviewed it quickly, concluding that she could not sign it, as it relinquished too much control to the proxy, Mary-Ann, who Sarah had yet to meet. Instead, Sarah had an idea she believed would perfectly reflect her position and achieve the desired results. It would represent the high road, while blasting the establishment into surrendering her property to the agent.

Sarah drafted a letter for the head of customs, to be delivered by the young woman who stood patiently at attention in front of her, not comprehending what was being done, but relying entirely on her misperception that Sarah did. The secretary of the manager of the Norfolk Hotel reluctantly typed the letter in final form.

Sarah's defiant letter was two pages long. It strongly challenged them about holding her things, emphatically letting the recipient know that under no circumstances would any money be paid to retrieve what was already hers, things she had paid for with money earned by the sweat of her brow over the last eighteen years.

Sarah would be happy, she informed them, to pay the published tariff for receipt of the goods, but nothing more, and certainly nothing that would go into someone's back pocket.

The assistant read the letter, and with her enormous expressive eyes, projected the fear she contemplated at the thought of placing this communication in the hands of the appropriate authorities. She wanted to check with her boss, Mary-Ann, but Sarah prevailed upon her to leave immediately for the airport, lest they lose another day.

Sarah tried to give her some encouraging words, to the effect that she was just the messenger, and messengers don't get shot. The unfamiliar expression only served to exacerbate the poor girl's confusion. Although Sarah's words provided her none of the intended consolation, she took her leave.

Predictably, the reaction at customs was explosive, as Sarah later learned from Mary-Ann. It is not acceptable to make reference to bribes or other forms of extortion in writing. These things happened, of course, but one did not talk about them directly, and to write explicitly about bribery was unthinkable.

Apparently there had been a fierce scene, as officials reacted to the letter, taking it all out on the assistant, who found herself unable to respond and was compelled to track down her boss, Mary-Ann.

Mary-Ann finally appeared herself at customs, took additional verbal blows, retrieved the letter, and assured the officials present at the scene that no other copies had been circulated.

When Mary-Ann called from the lobby, requesting Sarah's approval to come to her room, Sarah naively expected the agent to arrive with all the packages. Instead, Mary-Ann approached cautiously, bringing with her nothing but a briefcase.

Around thirty, tall and slender, Mary-Ann wore a smile that was, under the circumstances, more an article of business than a reflection of her current state of mind. Sarah's heart skipped with a beat of compassion for her. She noticed that the agent had put herself together in such a manner as to maximize the dignity of her appearance, but without makeup, accessories, or unnecessary accouterments.

Here she is, Sarah considered, in need of business, and she is compelled to chastise her client during their first encounter. Tough assignment by anyone's standards.

"You can accomplish nothing in the way you have acted," Mary-Ann began. "You created a big scene. It was really very bad. Now, we will have to start from nothing all over again. If you will do just as I say, I can get your packages. It will take several days."

Sarah allowed Mary-Ann to debrief. Then Sarah smiled at her, forcing her to make a slight upward change in the direction of her lips. Each of them reflected for a moment on the unspoken terms of this small smile summit. The result was mutual disarmament. The accord acknowledged, they were able to move forward.

All these events were sufficiently exhausting to erase the last of Sarah's ability to stay awake. She slept for four hours.

* * *

Sarah does nothing in the following days to interfere with Mary-Ann's activities on her behalf. Her only efforts are to leave messages for Max assuring him that there is, indeed, a Santa Claus, regardless of how many times he and all his damn reindeer had been delinquent at Christmas or had defecated on Max's perfectly mowed lawn.

A week later, after patient negotiations with customs, Mary-Ann delivers Sarah's packages just as promised. Sarah insists that she remain while everything is opened and checked to be certain nothing is missing or broken.

After this exercise has been completed and Sarah is about to pay the female clearing agent, Mary-Ann sheds long-contained tears. "Can I speak to you of a need I have?" This woman who has displayed such composure is now in the throes of a problem that has unwound her.

"I would like to borrow five hundred dollars from you. With it, I will buy a computer and that will help my business. If I can do this, I can leave my husband."

She is an earnest, hardworking woman and Sarah is moved to help her.

She learns that wives have very few rights in Kenya, and that even if beaten, as Mary-Ann has been, they are expected to remain with their spouses. If they leave, their children must stay with the father.

Mary-Ann departs with the five hundred dollars, and Sarah conceives of a plan to help women suffering from the same fate as the customs agent. She will create a nonprofit on a grand scale. It will have several objectives, each dealing with one problem or another that Sarah has observed during her stay.

The East African Development Organization, the intended name of her company, will be a major undertaking, but in her elevated mood, she feels equal to the challenge.

CHAPTER 23

ABERDARE, AGAIN

"I will not shake your hand," "The Big Man" snorted. "You should not have meddled in our affairs. Your actions were disruptive. It would be a very good thing for you to leave this place at once."

His contorted face made it clear that Sarah could not charm him. She had offended him and his system of conducting his affairs. There was no present remedy. It was not the method of legitimate business she had offended, but rather the conventional conduct of the unspoken ways to finesse wrongful procedures. Sarah, however, did not understand. The suave know the number of shillings. The more sophisticated know how long to wait before the money is proffered . . . the correct way to do the incorrect thing.

Every movement Sarah exhibited was a voice over the loudspeaker proclaiming that she was bungling the job.

In this sense, Max had been right. She was endangering him.

"Joseph, I've got to eat. I'm going to the Intercontinental Hotel for some food. Please bring Max over as soon as he gets out of there."

* * *

One thing is certain. Sarah has to change hotels. She cannot listen to soft drink bottles being shuffled from the truck to the warehouse one more night. She also realizes that the minibar service attendant has no intention of observing the "Do Not Disturb" sign hanging on the outside patio door or Sarah's repeated entreaties for him to go away. He will continue to appear once to review the minibar status and a second time to bring the necessary replacements. He will then be followed sometime later by his supervisor, who will check out the accomplishments of his underling; he will be as indifferent to her pleas for peace. The cumulative effect of these interruptions is, Sarah believes, pushing her towards a state of extreme nervousness, not grasping that she is actually falling over the precipice of sanity.

And so it is this state of continuous noise, interruptions, and the foreboding dark atmosphere of the room that accounts for her walking several blocks to the Nairobi Safari Club Hotel at eight o'clock this morning. As she opens the door of her room, she picks up the morning paper and reads the headlines of men performing ignoble atrocities on fellow human beings, occasionally a tourist. She is numb to the otherwise fearful black ink.

She enters the handsome, wood-detailed lobby, inspects the commanding dining room, and knows that she must move into this hotel immediately. With this resolution, she confronts a dainty young man at the front desk. "I'd like to see your best suite, please."

He smiles infectiously, every tooth and almost every molar revealed. He nods and takes a large stick with its dangling key from a rack at the end of the counter. "Please, follow me."

They ride the elevator to the top floor, turn right, and enter the largest suite Sarah has ever beheld. The suite is a rectangle, the length of which is almost entirely glass. The long windows rise up from the floor, stopping just below the ceiling. Rich blue satin blackout drapes are drawn at both sides of the room. The far left portion of the suite is a sitting area defined by a stiff couch. Perpendicular to the couch on one side is an armchair, across from which is a television console. A coffee table servicing the seating area is crowned with a display of pale silk flowers.

In the far right portion of the space there is a round English dining table surrounded by six magnificent antique chairs backed and cushioned with the same blue satin of the curtains.

To the right of the entry door, where Sarah stands, is a guest bathroom. Also on this side of the room is a five-foot bar with stools on one side, a counter, drawers, refrigerator, and shelves on the other.

Beyond the main room is the bedroom, itself the size of a small apartment. There is another wall of windows, a California king-size bed, an antique writing desk, and an oversized armoire. Off the bedroom is a smaller pantry-like area of drawers and closet space, leading to a spectacular bathroom with two porcelain sinks, a separate shower, and a grand oval tub set upon a marble platform two steps up from the marble floor. The towel rack is four feet from the tub, but slipping, Sarah feels, would be a small price to pay for the luxury of this suite.

"I'll take it."

Back in the lobby, Sarah reaches across the desk and asks the still-smiling youth about the cost.

"Normally it is $265, but you look like you need the suite very badly," says the youth, appraising her disheveled appearance. "I think things have not gone well for you here in Nairobi, so I will see if I may offer it to you at $215 per night. Would that be all right?"

"Yes. It would be very all right."

The gentleman disappears into the back room and returns promptly. "The manager is in agreement with me, and you will pay just $215 per night."

Sarah thinks to look at his name badge. "Moses," she smiles at him, "somehow, I think you've led me to this place! I am now staying at the Norfolk. I'll pack my things and be back in just a few hours."

At the hotel, Max is in the courtyard, walking towards her room.

"Max! What are you doing here?"

"I'm going out on safari later this afternoon and I need to use your room to call my lawyer. I've got a few things to do in town, so I am going to tell him to call you."

"Call me? But I'm going to be changing hotels and—"

"It's okay, he's going to call back this morning."

"Why are you involving me? What's his name?"

"He goes by Patel, but that's not his real name. No one knows his real name."

"What am I supposed to do if he calls?"

"Find out what's going on about extending my work permit and residency visa. I've got to know exactly what's been done. And I need him to give me back my passport and the other papers I gave him."

Max has stampeded Sarah with instructions, after which he turns around walking toward her room.

"What time will you be back?" she asks.

"How should I know?" he responds, indignant at her attempt to pin him down.

In her dark room at the Norfolk Hotel, there are clothes scattered everywhere. The only sign of organization is the pile of clothing Peter left for Sarah to handle. On top of the pile, she has placed a postcard depicting a vulture. She plans to leave the clothes where they are, inviting the minibar attendant and his supervisor to help themselves.

The most intimidating aspect of the dishevelment is the far-reaching sprawl of Sarah's growing book collection. It is as if the big books have spawned middle-sized books, which have reproduced smaller books, while even the smaller books have given birth to pamphlets and brochures.

Around lunchtime, Max returns to check on whether the lawyer has called. Soon after, Brandon drops by on his way out of town. "How is Sarah?" he wants to know, and, "Do you have anything to eat?"

Sarah points to her last remaining PowerBar and he waves it off as if the name alone makes his consideration of it impossible.

The lawyer has not called. Sarah says she is fine, while continuously coughing and sweating. She orders lunch from room service without consulting anyone.

"I don't know, Max. This is a bloody tough one. Who are you working with?" Brandon asks.

"I've hired a guy named Patel. He's trying to get to Onduko. That's all I know."

"Well, Onduko's the man all right. But there are hundreds, thousands of Patels. Which one is he?"

"I don't know his first name, but he's my best shot right now. My ex-partners can reach all the other lawyers and they're bribable, I am told. This Patel can't be bribed; that's also what I've been told. I mean, he'll bribe others, yeah, but he won't take a bribe."

"Ah Max, I hope you have that on good authority. Well, I don't think I should step in right now then. I'd let this fellow see what he can do first. You don't want too many hands in the game. Let me know, though, if he doesn't come through. I still owe you a favor."

"Thanks. I'll give you a call if he can't wind things up."

"Well, I'm off, then. Good luck. Sarah, let me know if that doctor I contacted for you fails to call. He's very good and your cough is getting much worse. You've managed to make me worry about you. He should come to the hotel to see you. That's the message I left for him. Usually you have to go to the hospital to see a doctor, but I don't think you're up for that. I must go now. I'm driving. I'll just take lunch with me if you don't mind."

"Here, take this bottled water with you."

"How did you know I would be driving across the desert, my dear?"

"My intuition is improving," Sarah banters back.

"I'll call you if I can when I get there. There's no phone, but I'll figure it out somehow."

"You conduct business with international clients and you have no phone?"

"It keeps me from being bloody bothered when I'm working. I enjoy the solitude."

After Brandon leaves, Max says, "Sarah, I'm leaving too. Here's a number to reach Patel. Keep calling him. He doesn't have a secretary or a recorder. If he doesn't answer, start calling this number after four thirty this afternoon. It's not his home number. It's the number of a friend. You call the friend and tell him you need to get in touch with Patel, and then the guy will send one of his kids to go get him. Patel has to walk from his house to the friend's, and it should take him about forty-five minutes to call back, so you'll have to stay by the phone."

"This guy you're entrusting your life with doesn't return phone calls? He has no receptionist, machine, or home phone? Can't we just bang out a message on a drum or send smoke signals?"

"This isn't funny, Sarah. He's the only one that can help. Brandon didn't offer to help, he—"

"No, no. He said to wait to see what your lawyer has done. He didn't say he would not or could not help. He just doesn't want efforts to overlap. I was only trying to add a little levity here. You're not the only one with problems. I'm sick, in case you haven't noticed. You said you'd help me meet people so I could interview them for my journal, and you've done nothing. I've got all this to pack, and—"

"Yeah, but your life isn't at stake."

"So I have to be bleeding from the ears for any sympathy?"

"I've got to go. I hope you feel better," Max manages, holding up his hand not in farewell, but in a motion indicating he has heard enough.

Sarah, oblivious to the time difference between Kenya and California, places a call to Peter to let him know she is changing hotels. "Peter, I'm going to move to a different hotel. This one is dreadful; compared to the Nairobi Safari Club, and the price is about the same. Max should never have put us here."

At some point, Peter hangs up. Sarah talks right through the click, recognizing the sound in retrospect once she realizes there is no one on the other end.

She attempts to make sense of it: It's not a broken connection. Or maybe it is . . . a broken connection between us. I'll call him again later, she decides.

The next call is to the front desk. Sarah notifies them of her departure and requests a final bill and twelve boxes for packing. Hours later she is still packing, and by all appearances, has made only moderate progress.

"I'm not going to do this in an orderly way anymore," she informs the remaining books and clothes as she begins to stuff things randomly into the last of the containers.

Two bellmen, each equipped with a dolly, arrive and Sarah leaves them debating as to the best method of stacking the boxes and whether they should make one trip or two.

"I'd like to check out," she informs the cashier. "I need you to add fifty dollars to the bill so I'll have money to tip the porters and for the taxi." Sarah reviews the bill, discovering over $5,000 in telephone charges alone.

"No. We cannot do that. No money can be added on."

It is now close to 7:00 PM, beyond the end of the day and Sarah's remaining patience.

Travelers jam into the close quarters of the lobby, filling its tight space with far-ranging complaints. For the most part, they are returning from safari and releasing the accumulated stress of maintaining socially acceptable behavior within their group. The voices of one couple rise above the rest, forcing Sarah to increase her decibel level to be certain the clerk checking her out can hear her. "I want to speak to the manager," she yells, adding such a maelstrom of expletives that the manager quickly authorizes the additional charge to Sarah's bill, apologizes, and sends a third porter to expedite the removal of her things.

* * *

"I'm sorry to be so late, Moses. It took me hours to pack."

Moses has remained on duty. He remains smiling. But this time, there is an expression of surprise as he watches the boxes being discharged from the two taxis. "You can go to your room now. I will take care of this. I will send something very nice for you to enjoy."

Sarah fondles the smooth wood stick connected to the key, which will open a new door to what she believes will be the remaining week of her stay in Kenya. She reaches the entrance and notices the engraved room name: Aberdare Suite. The Aberdares, where her trip began over three and a half weeks ago.

Within fifteen minutes, the doorbell rings. A waiter bears a tray of fresh fruit, cheese, and a bouquet splashed with colorful flowers.

My God, she rejoices. I really am starting over.

CHAPTER 24

STRANGERS IN THE NIGHT

The Intercontinental Hotel sat across the street from Nyayo House on the Uhuru Highway. Sarah selected a table on the cusp of the dining area yet still in the lobby. From here, she could order, watch for Max, and listen to the piano player just coming on duty. She ordered three hamburgers and was not at all disturbed by the incongruity of American music and junk food so many miles from home.

The food arrived, as did Max and Joseph. Max was grumbling to Joseph, who said nothing, marching onward toward Sarah and the hamburgers.

Max reached the table, took off the aluminum plate coverings, grabbed a hamburger from one of the plates, and spun around toward the front door. "I gotta get outta here. Let's go."

Sarah and Joseph reached for their food and followed Max's march. Once outside, Max realized he had no idea where he was going.

"Joseph's car is over there," Sarah pointed.

Joseph paid the attendant a princely sum for the long hours the car had been in his care. Sarah pushed past Max into the front seat, forcing him into the back.

From the moment they pulled into the street, Max raved to Joseph in Swahili. He was loud, he was mad, and his mouth was at full speed.

* * *

"**J**oseph, you work for me, not him. I only want you speaking in English, goddamn it. I'm the one paying you," Sarah instructs as her driver negotiates traffic.

Max, in the backseat, continues to speak in Swahili.

"Don't answer him until you've told me what he's saying." It is Sarah's turn to be angry now, so long suppressed it springs out of her like a bat screeching its way from the dark of her throat.

"Madam, he is saying that you did things wrong, that you made things bad for him. He is very angry."

"Tell him—"

"I told him that you did the best you could. That you did not do so badly and that it was what was in your heart that is important, not your words."

"This is bullshit, Sarah. You fucked everything up. I told you to get out of there. Now I'm expected to go to court tomorrow—"

"As opposed to what, Max? As opposed to an indefinite stay at your favorite vacation site, Nyayo House? Where do you want to be let off?"

"I can't go anywhere. I'm going to your hotel with you."

"No, you're not. Joseph, take him back to Wilson Airport. I'll walk back to the damn hotel." Sarah jumps out of the car and slams the door violently before stepping into the chaos of Nairobi's five-thirty evening traffic. She darts in front of an oncoming pack of cars, over a crumbled line, the remnants of a once freshly painted lane, and reaches the decaying sidewalk. She recognizes familiar landmarks and realizes that she is in front of her own hotel. The drama drained from her act of defiance, she stamps out her fury by climbing the steps to the entrance.

Max struts one step behind, close enough to follow her into the elevator.

Numb to the impact of his accusations, Sarah heads for the privacy of the master bath to clean off every remnant of Nyayo House and the day's ordeal. She turns on the water, gauging the minutes it will take to fill the tub. In the living room, Max and Joseph are again engaged in an exchange of excited Swahili.

"Joseph, I told you not to speak to him except in English. What are you saying?"

"I am telling him, Madam, that you did all you could do. You did not know that only a bribe was necessary to get him out. You did not understand the custom."

"The custom? The custom? Why in hell didn't you tell me of the custom? Why did I go through all that if a bribe would have solved the problem?"

"It was too late. You went too far, Madam. It could have been handled in the beginning, but you were too loud, too disrespectful, too . . ."

"Never mind. I get the picture. Joseph, please, you can go home now. I don't need you anymore tonight."

"I will be back at nine tomorrow morning."

"The bathwater!" Sarah reaches the tub as the water begins to pour onto the marble floor. She lets out enough to displace her weight, and climbs into the tepid bath with its flat bubbles.

Max struts in, surveying the bathroom as if it were a newly established campsite. His eyes evaluate the two sinks, the plush towels, the separate shower, and finally, the tub. He unbuttons his shirt, throws it on the floor, and then adds his belt, Levi's, boxer shorts, socks, and safari boots, making a neat pile of sweaty clothes.

Before Sarah can react, Max stands exposed on the platform of the tub, climbs in opposite her, takes the soap from her hand, and starts lathering himself.

If there had been sexual tension during the safari and the days after, here, Sarah understands, is the opportunity for expression and relief. They are alone, physically exposed, and submerged in luxurious privacy. But she cannot reach out to him; it is too late. She cannot feel what might be felt; in its place is only the realization that she is the stronger of the two, for she sees him for who he is: defeated, afraid, soaking wet.

"I only needed to bribe those guys, Sarah. That's all they wanted."

"Did you have the money to bribe them?"

"No."

"Then what in the hell did you intend to do? I couldn't have given you any money, even if I'd understood how things were to be handled."

"I've got to get money for tomorrow. They expect to be bribed before I go to court. That's the deal."

"And where do you suppose you're going to get it?" Sarah asks, already anticipating the next assault on her purse strings.

Max looks at her; although his face is speechless, the very emptiness of it is the answer.

"How much do they figure your ass is worth?"

"I don't know exactly. Probably $2,500."

Sarah covers herself in a terry-cloth robe and is walking carefully on the slippery floor to the phone hanging adjacent to the bathroom's towel bar when it suddenly rings of its own accord. Moses is calling from the front desk.

"Hello. I want to know that you are all right, and may I send you something special? I have flowers for you." He is voicing his nightly consideration for Sarah's well-being, as he has done since her arrival.

"Moses, I appreciate your offer, but what I really need is for you to send up the cashier again. I want to withdraw some more money from my account."

"You will have it, then. I will find him for you, and he will be up shortly."

"Thank you, Moses."

Fifteen minutes later, Sarah confronts the cashier in the living room, only to be informed that she cannot draw another cent from her account. "Why not? It's my money, and my credit on the card is unlimited."

"It is our strict policy. You have already overdrawn your limit."

"I knew this wasn't going to work out," Max despairs, looking about the room as if it might be hiding someone else who could provide the money.

"How were you going to get the money?" Sarah asks, repeating her earlier question, this time with a strong measure of irritation.

"I was going to borrow it from a couple of friends. But it's too late for that now. It's all over. If you hadn't—"

"Oh God, don't start that again. Do you think I'm finished?"

"Don't you get it, Sarah? It's over!"

"Don't you get it, Max? It's never over! It's never, ever over."

Sarah dials Joseph at his home. "What time do the currency exchanges at the airport close?"

"Not until midnight, Madam."

"Then please come over immediately. I need you to take me to the airport."

"I can be there in fifteen minutes."

And so he is. It is 11:15 PM when Sarah leaves, Max still standing in the bedroom doorway, the towel riding his hips.

Sarah and Joseph reach the airport in fifteen minutes, allowing just enough time to retrieve $1,500 from American Express and $1,000 from her Citibank Visa card. The night's work is done.

In the Aberdare Suite, Max sits in the large chair facing the television, flipping between CNN, the BBC, and two local Nairobi stations. Coming through the door, Sarah offers, "I'll pay you $2,500 to stop channel surfing."

Max stares at the money and plucks it from her hand. He counts the bills as if he is dealing a hand of cards, first wetting his index finger and then pushing one bill against the other. "This'll work," he announces.

This must be my karma, Sarah muses. I make things look too easy.

"I'm starving. Do you want anything to eat?" Sarah inquires, flush with her victory.

"No. I've lost my appetite," Max responds, as though Sarah might be responsible for his condition.

Sarah orders a large pizza from room service and lies down upon the couch, fading away within seconds. Over an hour later she opens her eyes to see pieces of crust lying atop a plate on the room service tray. Max has eaten everything. "Great. Thanks for waking me up. Look, Max, I'm going to sleep. You can have the bed and I'll sleep on the couch." Sarah walks to the bedroom and removes the heavy satin spread from the bed, dragging it behind her back to the living room.

Only minutes pass before the next crisis. Max cannot sleep. "It's too cold," he yells plaintively from the other room. "It's freezing in here and there aren't any extra blankets."

Then Max is standing over her, eyeing the spread and Sarah, realizing there is only one solution, says, "Look, the only way we're both going to be warm is by sharing the bed and the spread." They walk back to the bedroom. "There are two mattresses," she points out. "That's your mattress, this is mine. Each mattress defines our individual sides of the bed. Don't cross this line."

Sarah puts two of the four pillows down the center of the bed, then adds, "Please don't hog the cover and don't talk to me."

Sarah is on her back. Nothing can be heard except each of their sighs as they release the day. The pillows start to move, and soon, Max's fingers are lying atop Sarah's left hand, resting there. Tremulous, tentative.

"What the hell are you doing?" Sarah asks, her voice soft but hoarse.

"Touching you."

"Why?" It is the one question Sarah is certain she does not know the answer to.

"I like touching."

"You do?" Sarah's surprise surpasses all tiredness.

"I didn't get touched at all as a kid, except of course when I was being hit . . . close encounters of the wrong kind. My dad and mom never touched each other. No one in our family did. Maybe it's a Scottish thing. Anyway, affection was in very short supply. Do you mind? My touching you?"

How to answer? How to suspend the hostility? How to keep the fragile sliver of his humanness from slipping between the crack separating the two mattresses? How to keep him on his side?

"No, I guess not. Roll over."

Max obeys and Sarah cuddles up to his back, puts her arm around him, and they both fall into a sleep that is deep and palliative.

* * *

In the morning, Sarah is first to rise, for Max is still under the spell of a dream revealed in the rapid flutter of his pale lashes. She looks at the upright toilet seat, smiles as she puts it down, and dresses for the day ahead. She removes herself from the bathroom to the living room, where she orders breakfast for two, then places a Sinatra tape, *Strangers in the Night*, into the Sony tape recorder she had sent Joseph to purchase on a day she needed to keep him busy.

Max walks stiffly into the living room with a gruffness that erases any softness revealed the previous night. He is Max again. "Will you turn that damn stuff off?" he demands.

"No," Sarah responds, adjusting the sound down so low that she can barely hear it. "I have something for you that might improve your disposition." She leaves the music and visits the bedroom closet to fetch the camera and accessories.

First she brings in the Nikon F4 camera, then the 80-200 lens, then the 300 mm and the 400 mm. Finally, she retrieves the Penguin case and one hundred rolls of professional film.

Max assesses each piece, employing every tool of his practiced control to conceal his disbelief. He does not appear to be pleased or grateful, Sarah notices. Rather, there is a boyish fascination about him as he examines the metal box and the cylindrical lenses. He runs his hand slowly over the Penguin case, his fingers measuring off its size. His eyes calculate the number of rolls of film until his mouth forms the words "One hundred." He catches himself, and swallows the three syllables. "This isn't the model I asked for, and this case is way too big."

"Max, this model has replaced the F3, which is no longer made, and this case is the smallest size that will hold this equipment and your other lenses. Did you forget about them?"

"Oh, yeah. Well, don't think I'm not grateful, because I am. It's just that . . ."

"It's just that you have a very unusual way of expressing your gratitude?" Sarah finishes his sentence, thinking how like Peter he is when receiving a gift.

"I guess I really didn't expect it. Listen, I have to go to court and then I'll be back to pick this up. Will you be here?"

"It depends on what time you return. I'm going to run some errands and do some research. I'll be back around three this afternoon. Will you be back by then?"

"Yeah, I should be but give me an extra key just in case."

"Before I leave, I need a favor from you. When I was at Hemingway's, I had Brandon's daughter and her three friends take some pictures while we were there. It was for a photography competition I put together. They were promised prizes. I need to get the decision of the winners over with so I can give them their awards. You are the real photographer, so take a look at the shots and write on the back which is the winner in each of these categories, okay?" Sarah writes "Most Original," "Most Creative," "Most Beautiful," "Most Unusual."

"Oh, one more thing. I'm planning a dinner party at Mr. Lee's Chinese Restaurant for next week. I am inviting William, and Brandon's ex-wife and kids, maybe Brandon, and several other people I've met. Would you like to come?"

Sarah has asked a question to which the only possible answer could be no. Max refuses to socialize with people he does not know, who he cannot in some measure control, who might judge him, who might talk about him.

"Maybe. I'll see how I feel and how this court thing goes."

"You mean this bribe thing, don't you?"

Sarah gathers her things and leans down to mockingly kiss Max on the forehead in a gesture imitating a wife leaving her husband for the day. "Good-bye, dear. See you later."

"Stop that shit, will you?" Max's disdain is as thick as the breakfast jam with which he is lathering his toast.

* * *

In the afternoon Sarah returns, bursting with amazing accounts of her day. Max is not there. The camera equipment has been removed. There is no note. On her desk are five photographs separated from the approximately fifty Sarah had given him earlier. She turns them over. The first is the single footprint Lauren made in the sand, the first picture taken at Hemingway's while the contest categories were being decided upon. Because there is no other footprint beside it, Lauren managed to create the illusion of a foot hovering above the ground in solitary isolation. Victoria had taken the picture, awarded by Max "Most Creative."

She is definitely Brandon's daughter, Sarah realizes.

The second photograph is of two teenagers holding hands underwater, heads covered with scuba masks. Their feet dance on the ocean's floor while fish approach as if to ask for the next dance. This Max has awarded "Most Original."

Max has marked another picture "Funny," with the words "Great shot!" embellishing his judgment. This was not one of the agreed-upon categories. In this scene, one of the girls underwater is looking wide-eyed at a single striped fish that had broken loose from its school, approaching her with the very same wide-eyed fascination with which she viewed it.

"Most Beautiful" was awarded to Jewish Myra, sitting atop the bold sediment structure, looking out contemplatively at the waves breaking in front of her fairy fortress.

Sarah finds a picture of herself sitting on top of the scuba boat, her legs encircling the large basket-purse that she had used to balance a writing tablet. In her right hand is a pen aimed at her journal. Her feet are bare. The wind has styled her short black hair to stand upright against the background of a translucent floating cloud. On the back Max has written, "Still Writing. Still Barefoot."

She puts the pictures on a corner of the desk, turns on the Sony player, and returns to Sinatra. "Strangers in the night, two lonely people . . ."

* * *

At around 9:00 PM, Moses calls. "There is a man here to see you. I do not know him. All he will tell me is his name, which is George. He wants to speak to you. Do you wish to talk to him?"

"Please, Moses, put him on the phone."

"No, he is saying he wants to talk to you personally. He wants to be in front of you."

"Well, I can't come down; I'm not properly dressed. Have him come up to the suite." She does not pause to contemplate the impropriety or possible danger, for she is operating as if she is beyond ordinary rules.

"But Madam, he is a black man."

"Oh Moses, for heaven's sake! Don't be so—so—I don't know, so colonial! I don't care what color he is!"

"I will send him up then, because you say so. But I will call you before I am off-duty."

"As you wish, Moses."

George appears at Sarah's door infused with an obvious gravitas. He respectfully accepts the invitation to enter the suite, hesitating as if he thinks the meeting should take place in the hallway. Such are the normal considerations of a black man entering the room of a white woman.

"Who are you and what do you want at this hour of the night?" Sarah feels certain his presence has something to do with Max's disappearance.

"My name is George. That is not my real name, but the one you can call me so you will remember it. I work in Nairobi as an independent reporter for the *Daily Nation* and *The Standard*. In addition to stories of interest in Kenya, I also gather information from Tanzania and other countries of interest to our readers. I wanted to know if you require any assistance, any personal help, or if there is anything you wanted to know. I am available to help you, and it would be my pleasure to do so."

"I don't understand. Why would you make this offer? How do you even know about me?"

"Nairobi is very small when it comes to interesting news. It is even smaller for a reporter whose trade is information."

"What makes my being here so interesting that my presence is considered 'news'?"

"Yesterday you became news. Not news for a press story, but news for those who are part of the network of people who talk amongst themselves. Your actions at Nyayo House were such that people talked quite a bit. It is known that you are here, that you have a forceful way, and that, Madam, you are rich."

"How does anyone know about my finances?"

"You gave the hotel a $25,000 deposit. That is unusual, even for an American."

"Oh God, now what? Am I some sort of target?"

"Not necessarily, but there are some who might wish to take advantage of you. I only wanted to introduce myself and let you know I am available to help you if you wish me to do so. I have lived in Kenya all my life. My parents worked for men who served in the colonial government, so I am well acquainted with many people, as well as how things operate here, which is certainly different from other places. And I am very well educated."

"I would like to talk to you about some ideas I have about a foundation I would like to create, but I am so tired now, I don't think it would be productive. Could we meet tomorrow evening, or sometime soon? You could join me for dinner."

"Yes, but if you do not mind, it would be better to stay here. Privacy is important. You should try not to attract any more attention than you already have."

CHAPTER 25

THE COBRA AND THE CLAN

S arah's clothes have been reduced to a pile of dirty laundry. Before the last shirt and pair of slacks meet their inevitable fate, she wanders into the lobby to ask Moses for directions to the closest women's clothing store.

"The Grand Regency Hotel, mezzanine level, I believe."

Although she has been warned countless times not to walk through the streets by herself, not to wear jewelry or anything that would draw attention to her, she struts like a storm trooper towards her destination in heels and gold earrings. Her swagger is formidable and no one dares to approach her, not the beggars who usually approach anyone on the mere chance of improving their odds, not the street-smart hijinkers, nor those willing to offer any service—from a man hawking a taxi ride to a woman offering the sale of her baby for the equivalent of twenty US dollars. Oblivious to the danger about her, Sarah reaches the Grand Regency, a monolithic structure of marble, mirrors, and mass, all made accessible through revolving doors reigned over by a sky-high doorman named Samson.

Following a circuitous route taking her past the lobby, up to the mezzanine, and to the rear of the hotel, she discovers, tucked in among other small, elegant shops, a storefront showcasing trendy women's clothing from Europe.

Sarah selects a skirt and matching blouse, two pairs of slacks, and several tops, and because she has lost more weight, all one size below the size ten she had been upon originally arriving in Nairobi. Too tired to try anything on, she simply hands the clothing to the salesperson, whose slow-witted gaze begins to infuriate Sarah.

Minutes accumulate as the girl repeatedly and unsuccessfully attempts to calculate the sum of the price tags. Sarah's nerve endings crackle as if they are a system of disconnected live wires. "I really can't wait here another minute," she declares impatiently. "I'm staying at the Nairobi Safari Club Hotel. You can figure out what I owe you and bring the clothes to me after you get off work."

Later that evening, the phone rings, awakening Sarah from a deep sleep that has left her soaking wet in the air-conditioned room. Her moist palms reach for the phone.

"Excuse me. I am in the lobby and I have the clothes you purchased in my store this afternoon. I am the owner, Nasir. I would like to bring them up to you, if it is convenient."

"Yes. Of course. I am in the Aberdare Suite." When Sarah opens the door, she discovers a trim, thin man in a well-fitting Italian suit. He is an Indian of the lightest caste. His skin looks buffed and his bald head is a shiny, oiled surface, glowing like a crystal ball. He smiles and reveals a perfect set of teeth inside a Cheshire cat grin.

But his eyes are indiscernible, reflecting nothing and everything.

"I must apologize about the inconvenience you have suffered at the hands of my salesperson. She is too slow. I have known this, of course. I mean to be rid of her, but it is quite difficult to find adequate help these days. No one wants to work. Nevertheless, she is slow, too slow."

"That's all right, so long as I have the clothes now. I've been on safari and I'm staying for another week or two. I have nothing clean," Sarah explains, as if the idea of laundering the many articles in her growing accumulation of discarded clothes has not occurred to her. As if she owes him an explanation.

"Oh, a safari! How delightful. Did you enjoy your adventure?" His smile stretches his lips backwards. He leans forward. He reacts with an interest that implies he has never been in such close proximity to anyone who actually visited the game parks of his country.

"Yes. And no. It's a long story, but there were parts of it that were exhilarating and others that were taxing," Sarah tries to explain, so delighted is she to have someone interested in her adventure; so manic that her words cascade over each other. "It was an amazing time in many ways, and I never expect to experience anything like it again. I have a great deal to do to record my thoughts about it all. This is why I am still here in Nairobi." Sarah is coughing up her explanation, her voice all but spent.

"Ah, I see. I think you are sick as well. Isn't it so?"

"I'm sick, but I can't get a doctor to come to the hotel and I've been warned about going to the . . ."

"Hospital? Yes, it is true. You would not want to go to our hospital, although it is much better than we are given credit for. Those of us who live here believe that Americans must have such hospitals as we could not imagine and that you would be unhappy with our facilities and our doctors. Never mind. I have a doctor friend. If I may use your phone?"

"Of course, please."

Words are spoken in the enchanting Punjabi of Kenyan Asians.

"He will come in an hour or so, after he has finished his rounds at the hospital. He is one of the best medical men in our mosque, and we are very close. He is the doctor of my wife and our three children. But he also has a reputation here. It is a good thing, isn't it?"

"Yes, a very good thing. Would you like a glass of wine?" Sarah asks, forgetting the Muslim admonishment against alcohol.

"Please," Nasir replies, his oath of abstinence put aside. "So, you are alone, and sick. How unfortunate. You must meet my wife, Shelley. We will come and check on you tomorrow, if that is all right."

Sarah will later learn how well-versed Nasir is in picking up the inadvertent cries for help of his next target. He guesses the great cost of staying in such a suite. He regards Sarah's jewelry. He has had her sign a credit card form for over $600 in clothes without a breakdown of the items. The wine is expensive. He is particularly astute these days because Nasir has been waiting for someone to come to him in answer to his prayers, and he has been praying quite a great deal lately.

"Yes. Actually, I'd like some company. Come after work and I'll order room service. We can have dinner together here, in the suite."

"I must leave now. This is my home number. You must have my friend call me after he has checked you and determined your condition. He will make a prescription and I will pick it up for you and drop it by tomorrow on my way to work, Inshallah."

"Inshallah," God willing. Nasir has tried everything else in the last year. Now he is depending on God.

Nasir, the smile still frozen on his face, departs with a sure-footed gait and the barely concealed excitement of having befriended a lone, rich American woman in need of his help. She has fallen at his feet like fish thrown to a stray cat. He can only imagine the chits he will earn from both the doctor and from Sarah. The doctor will be in his debt for such a referral. Sarah will be beholden to him for arranging a personal medical visit, unattainable before his arrival. So a chit is passed, one is now owed, and Sarah is in the system: the system of survival in East Africa.

Dr. Dogra's arrival heralds the first in a series of checkups by a dedicated physician whose examination suggests to him that Sarah's condition is a severe form of bronchitis, for which he prescribes medication he calls into a pharmacy. He is reticent to write out a bill, and finally Sarah produces a traveler's check for one hundred dollars, causing the good physician to acknowledge the check with a profusion of gratitude and surprise. He looks at the amount, appearing dazzled by the fee his after-hours visit has secured. The money accepted, he departs with humble bows, promising in a low, respectful voice to return in a few days to evaluate her condition.

The next night, Nasir calls from the lobby, announcing his arrival and requesting permission to come up to Sarah's suite. When the door is opened, Sarah greets him like an old friend, and his wife, Shelley, embraces her with the happiness of possibly having known her in a previous life.

Sarah notices Nasir is again dressed in a contemporary Italian suit, while Shelley is dressed less fashionably. His gray shoes are new or recently shined and match his jacket and pants; hers are well-worn black pumps. Nasir's tie is contemporary, but Shelley's dress is out of style by five years or more. His nails are manicured; her polish is chipped. His skin resonates with health, as if he may have had a shave finished off with a moist, hot towel before arriving; her makeup was applied in the early morning and never touched up during the day. Her skin color is two shades darker than Nasir's. Nasir represents the store's flashy front window, while Shelley symbolizes the operational back office.

Shelley's elastic expressions jump about, telegraphing a reaction of delightful surprise to each utterance made by either her husband or Sarah. It is more difficult to access Nasir's thoughts, for his smile is an indelible ink mark on the expansive parchment paper of his face.

Sarah coaxes dinner selections from each of them, dials room service, and places an order to the voice on the other end, whose standard response upon picking up the line is, "What do you want?"

"I want to order room service, naturally!"

"Tell us about your safari," Shelley implores, her eyes enlarging under long, thick massacred lashes.

"It was very much an adventure and a time to learn about people as well as animals. But it is difficult for me to talk at this point; my voice is almost gone. I'd like to learn about you. How is it that you live in Kenya?"

Shelley, in the deference that is her nature, yields to her husband. Nasir is the spokesperson. "My grandfather came to Kenya at the turn of the century, brought here from India by the British to help protect the men working on the rail line from Mombasa to Lake Victoria from the man-eating lions.

"Each night the lions attacked a different tent, and so, my grandfather was thinking that in time, he should do something else for a living.

"Nairobi was the highland center for the railroad, and because he was educated, he stayed on afterwards and started a clothing store. My father later took it over and made it a profitable business with imported contemporary clothes for the politicians. He befriended them and did special favors for them. Now I run the store and provide the politicians with business suits and French dresses for their mistresses.

"The educated Indian population here has worked very hard, and we have made money in the retail trade and finances, so we are resented by the Kenyans. We do what we must to gain what we can gain; that is our politics."

After dinner, as Nasir and his wife leave, they elicit a promise that Sarah will be their guest on Sunday for brunch. "We will go to the Muthaiga Country Club. You will learn all about it. This is a good idea, Shelley, isn't it?"

"Yes, it is, and we shall have a splendid meal. It is a very good idea he has," Shelley assures Sarah.

They leave, and soon the dishes, scraped of every morsel of food, follow them on a rolling table down the corridor.

* * *

On Sunday morning, just at the appointed time, Nasir calls Sarah from the lobby on his cell phone. Shelley is circling the street, there being no parking available anywhere. She stops the car and waves when she sees her husband escorting Sarah through the revolving hotel doors.

As Sarah looks at the latest-model silver Mercedes, she notices Shelley hastening out of the driver's seat and into the back where she attempts to crowd herself in amongst three children, ages twelve, five, and three.

"You can't all squeeze in back there. Come sit on my lap," Sarah insists, addressing the little female member of Nasir's clan. The children, with their wide eyes, appear innocent of sin. It is as if Nasir might have brought them along to indemnify himself from any suspicions of his motives.

A tiny girl with olive skin and black oval eyes scampers from her seat and pounces onto Sarah's lap, squealing with runaway joy. Sarah finds herself holding a lively bundle of squirming limbs. The name of Sarah's newly discovered treasure is Alicia, the middle child.

The eldest boy is Munir, and the baby, who can't look up for the weight of his lashes, is Ali. Ali is in a state of perpetual motion, trying desperately to break out of his shy demeanor.

Munir talks to Sarah from the rear of the car, the last word of each sentence ending in a high note so that each statement sounds like a question. He inquires if Sarah has seen elephants and tigers on her safari, what America is like, and why she is still here.

Munir does not realize tigers do not exist in Kenya. He has never seen an elephant. Sarah tries to grasp the fact that a child of Indian heritage has never viewed an elephant, an incongruity she finds distressing.

* * *

Dressed in a green denim Chanel suit sent to her by her Hispanic housekeeper in Southern California (who had misunderstood her request for "summer clothes" as one for "sophisticated clothes"), Sarah believes being with Nasir and his family is part of the great adventure her life has now become. Every turn of events, in Sarah's mind, has come to take on grandiose proportions. Her excitement today cannot be contained, for they will have brunch at the famed Muthaiga Club, a place she has read a great deal about. It feels like a very natural direction for her to be heading.

The Muthaiga Club, between Muthaiga Road and Serengeti Avenue, looms in front of them. The architecture is classic British colonial, splendidly restored to its 1912 authenticity. If every city and town has a favorite place to meet, this was once such a spot in Nairobi. Here, wealthy colonial settlers, the early politicians, white businessmen, landlords, the most famous safari leaders, and racehorse owners and trainers gathered, talked, brokered deals, and began to formulate the shape of a new colony.

Upon arrival, Nasir attempts to clarify his identity with the maître d', a pompous man who neither recognizes him nor the arrangements. Nasir has asked a favor of someone who is a member of the club, thereby claiming or surrendering a chit. The favor, though granted, has not yet been processed by the man who bars the entrance.

After Nasir directs Shelley to make multiple phone calls, one of which connects to someone she has her husband speak with, they are seated at two adjacent tables, which serves to separate the adults from the children.

The confusion leaves Nasir without the Cheshire cat grin.

To Sarah, the slight inconvenience is of little consequence, for this club has a rich and raunchy past, a place once filled with legendary characters who lived sensational moments strutting across its historic diorama. In Sarah's increasingly delusional mind, visiting the Muthaiga Club is part of her destiny. She senses she has been here in another lifetime. She cannot tell if this is the residue of reincarnation or a result of too many readings of *White Mischief*, the book by James Fox about one of Kenya's most famous unsolved crimes, containing within its pages many characters who frequented the club.

Here once sat Sarah's favorite character, Beryl Markham, who, before becoming a record-breaking aviatrix, was the first woman in the male-dominated field of horse racing to receive a trainer's license for her work with thoroughbreds. This remarkable woman held court and talked of working and winning horses, which jockey was best suited to which steed, and what sums of money should be laid down in favor of a sound bet. Later, when Beryl's hunger for speed and adventure accelerated, she transferred it from horses to airplanes. A cottage at the Muthaiga Club served as her home base and lover's den.

These walls, perhaps more than any others, had witnessed Beryl's numerous flirtations and rendezvous, including her most meaningful and cherished affair with the remarkable safari guide Denys Finch Hatton, whom she is said to have charmed away from Karen Blixen. Within this privileged fortress, they celebrated what was to be their last evening together, for two nights before his fatal crash, Beryl and Denys had dined at this club, discussing the possibility of flying to the coast the following day. Stubborn as she was, Beryl was persuaded by her mentor to stay on the ground, a decision that saved her life.

After the meal, the children insist, "Sarah, you must come back to our house and see all the puppies!"

"The puppies?"

"No!" Nasir exclaims, his voice higher than usual.

"Yes! Yes! Yes!" the children insist. "Come and see our puppies."

Between Sarah's enthusiasm and his children's clamor, Nasir can only look to Shelley for help in avoiding a visit to his home, which is the single outward manifestation of his decayed financial situation. Shelley votes with the children. He is finally forced to explain.

"We have eight guard dogs, and all have had a litter within a week of each other, so there are many, too many to feed. Two of the bitches have no milk to nurse their pups, so I do not know what will become of them, isn't it so, Shelley?" asks Nasir in his characteristic way of ending a statement by asking Shelley to validate it.

"Yes, it is very sad to see them. You must also forgive our home. It is badly in need of repair, but we are renting, and because of circumstance, we are unable to fix anything right now."

The cat is out of the bag.

* * *

The glittering Mercedes passes through Muthaiga Estates, a splendid section of town encompassing the embassies of Colombia, Saudi Arabia, Kuwait, and Romania. The countries' flags salute the car and its group of rowdy passengers.

Midway along this street, the car turns in to a compound. An armed caretaker steps out from the small guardhouse adjacent to the swinging wrought iron gate at the entrance of the driveway. The Mercedes crawls along the gravel until reaching a large, circular turnaround where it stops in front of a derelict house.

"Let me show you inside," offers Nasir as graciously as possible considering his embarrassment, while Shelley shushes the children and herds them into the house.

They enter a foyer, small in comparison to the size of the estate, and there, waiting to greet his son and daughter-in-law, is the dark-skinned and wrinkled senior Nasir along with his aged wife. Nasir's mother, bent, toothless, with her hair pulled back into a thick salt-and-pepper braid draping down her spiny back, lifts small bony arms and hands in salutation to her family and their guest.

"My parents live with me. It is our custom to care for our parents, and since I am the eldest, it is I who has them. I have siblings, but they do nothing. It is all on me."

Sarah is taken on a tour of what was once a grand, palatial estate, but which now has fallen into a coma with an inadequate life-support system. Disintegration drips in varying degrees from the curtains, couches, mantels, and gardens. A strong layer of age has settled over the last coat of paint. Badly spotted white couches are clustered randomly in the cavernous living room, and everywhere is the unpleasant odor of old things, discarded things, things no longer viable.

In the kitchen, carved chairs sit incongruously around an oval Formica table, sufficiently large to seat Nasir's entire clan and the few guests they might still occasionally invite over.

Hanging over each fireplace is a large gilt-framed oil portrait of the Aga Khan, which looks down on this homely decay.

Apparently Nasir and his family have fallen on hard times. Their embarrassment is palpable to Sarah, as they escort her from one area to another, each room eliciting an explanation for its present condition.

"These parquet floors are wonderful, and the other woodwork is magnificent," Sarah offers, attempting to exaggerate small, salvageable vestiges of the home's former respectability.

"Ah, yes. It was once very beautiful, but it is no longer possible to maintain it. The expense. The expense is too great now. Isn't it, Shelley?"

"I would love to see the puppies. Where are they?" Sarah asks, using the sound of nearby yelping as her excuse to exit the house, staking her escape on the eight litters of underfed Alsatian dogs.

"Oh my God, they're so scrawny!" Sarah exclaims, taken aback at the sight of fur hanging in loose folds from the hungry hounds in an outdoor pen. These dogs of wolf-like breed are a most bedraggled representation of their kind.

"Look at these four. They won't make it, I am quite certain. The mother is too weak to compete for the little food we can spare for them, so she cannot suckle her pups," Shelley explains.

"Let me take these four to the hotel and feed them."

"How can you do such a thing? Dogs are not permitted, and anyway, listen to the great noise they make."

"I will be able to sneak them in if you have a box or a basket. Just give me enough food to fill their little bellies until I can get them past the lobby and into my suite. If I feed them regularly, they won't continue to cry."

"Well, there is one problem. Munir has it in his head to take them to school to sell them—"

"He can't possibly sell these puppies; they're too sick and ridiculous looking. Let me fatten them up, at least. Then, if he wants to, he can have these back to sell."

* * *

Once Sarah is at the hotel, she dials the reception desk and asks for Moses, who agrees to come up right away, sensing a problem with one of his longest-staying, highest-tipping guests. He arrives, assesses the situation, and looks for guidance from Sarah, for now he is her accomplice and, having broken the hotel rules, there remains only the question of how to mitigate the damages.

"Can you manage to keep housekeeping out of here from now on? I don't even want them coming to the door. Tell them I have leprosy or something. And I shall need scraps of food every day to add to what I order from room service. I'll need a lot of old newspaper, and . . ."

Moses, in a small effort to reprimand Sarah, decides to forgo the gift he customarily sends to her each night. "Yes, I see that you will need my help. I will get everything. But there will be no flowers for you."

By the third day, Sara rents the room adjoining her suite for the puppies. There she bathes them, feeds them, and allows them to sleep. They are permitted to leave their room and come into the Aberdare Suite only to play and to be shown off to special visitors.

CHAPTER 26

MISSING

Not long after Sarah returns to her hotel room, the phone rings. "Max did not show up for his hearing in the magistrates' court. He was last seen with you. Where is he now?" It is Cecil, the smartly-suited politician who had assured her of his help with Max.

Sarah retraces the day at Nyayo in her mind. She had initially left without Max, for he had been detained. She had waited for him across the street, at the Intercontinental Hotel, where he and Joseph had joined her. They had grabbed lunch on the go. Max had probably been followed.

"I don't know. The last time I saw him was Thursday, and I assumed he was going to be in court for his trial Friday morning. That's what he told me," she said, neglecting to add that she had armed him with money for his bribe and that they had spent the night together.

"You are to let me know immediately if you hear from him. He has greatly compromised his situation. It now appears as if he has fled, a serious offense, as you can imagine."

Sarah reaches for the various scraps of paper that substitute for an address book and begins calling anyone who might have contact with Max. Eric, William, Damian, his housekeeper. Anyone. Even Patel. Regardless of who answers the phone, she leaves the same urgent message: "You must tell Max I have the sales receipt for his camera equipment and that I am leaving Nairobi. He needs to get in touch with me so I can give him the paperwork. Otherwise he's going to have a problem with the warranty."

Although no one quite understands why Sarah should have the receipt to Max's possessions, they agree to pass on the message.

Many hours pass while Sarah washes the puppies in the bathtub of the adjoining room. She photographs them against backdrops such as high-heeled shoes, rolls of film, and various other objects to demonstrate their size. She then shoots pictures of them on pillows, contrasting their scrawny black-brown bodies with the pale blue silk, until they collapse into one solid mass, their four protruding noses raised just high enough to catch and expel small, panting breaths.

The phone rings. It is Max. The confidence of being one step ahead of everyone else has returned to his voice. "Hi. What's up? Why the all-points bulletin?"

"'What's up?' Where are you? Why didn't you show up for your hearing?"

"There's no way in hell I was going to put myself at their mercy, even with a bribe. I still don't have my visa or work permit, so in their eyes, nothing's changed. Hey, what about the sales receipt and warranty paperwork for the camera? I'd like to get that stuff."

"I'm sure you would. Where are you?"

"You don't need to know that. This line is probably tapped anyway, something you might want to keep in mind."

"What in the hell was the money I gave you for if you didn't use it to pay a bribe or your fine?"

"It was a loan."

"That's certainly not the way you characterized it when you had me running all over town."

"That was your choice. I just said it couldn't be done, you couldn't raise the cash. I only gave you a challenge. It was your idea to prove me wrong."

"So that's it? You're gone, and I'm left here to answer questions whenever Cecil calls, like he did this morning?"

"You don't know anything."

"I do know something. You're an ass," Sarah thunders as she slams the phone down.

Sarah considers the possibilities. If anyone was listening to that conversation, they now realize she's assisted in the escape of a fugitive. She wonders what she will be charged with first—inadvertently helping Max, or harboring four puppies in violation of hotel policy.

Sarah tries to determine which person got the message to Max. He must be in contact with one of the people she phoned. One of them has managed to reach him and convey her message. There was a significant amount of static on the line, suggesting that Max might be in some distant place, far out of town. He would have needed the help of someone who had not been identified in Nairobi so that the authorities would be unable to make a connection. This eliminated Eric and the housekeeper. She remembers a crackling noise over the line when Damian had called her back after receiving her message. Damian, the Australian pilot who had flown her to Rutundu. No one in Nairobi had seen them together.

Max is gone, possibly for good. Brandon has disappeared into the bush, calling Sarah several times while she is out and leaving messages empty of substance, each one differing from the others only by the time of his call. ("Hello, Sarah. Brandon here. It's about 5:30 PM and I'm sorry to have missed you. I am thinking of you and trying desperately to check in on you, which is quite a difficult matter. In any event, I hope you are feeling better and I shall try to ring you up again.") Peter will not talk to her. The only people in her life are Nasir and his family. The only comfort, the four puppies.

All of this does nothing to diminish her exalted perception of her existence in Nairobi, however, for the smallest positive occurrences override any challenge.

Always an incessant itch is the dilemma that she must go home to face Peter, albeit there is the parallel refusal of her doctor to allow her to fly back alone . . . a fact that is not as troublesome to Sarah as it should be.

* * *

Time passes with little in the way of a pattern except the drinking of as much Aqua-Nova water as Sarah can tolerate, and tea with hot milk and honey, and the constant replacement of Philips light bulbs and the useless Bic pens she must dispose of as she writes.

Philips light bulbs, each packaged in a royal blue and white box, are brought to the Aberdare Suite daily. They are hurried in to replace dysfunctional spheres of glass in side table lamps, standing lamps, and the overhead lighting in every socket of the suite. Bic pens, Sarah learns to her great frustration, are as incapable of delivering their purpose as are the Gillette razors made by the same company. Be it lights, pens, or razors, merchandise sent to third-world countries is third rate.

On one such routine day, Sarah punches in the international access code, followed by her area code and home phone number. Seconds plod along until the connection is made. Most of her calls outside the country do not go through, and if they do, it is a gift one does not take for granted.

"Hello." It is Peter, sounding out the greeting as if he were saying, "Hell. Ohhhh . . ."

"Peter, it's Sarah. I—"

"What now?" he asks, the question resounding with intimidation.

"For once, will you please not hang up?" Sarah pleads. "Why are you so mad? I've told you that I am sick and unable to come home. The doctor has told me that I cannot risk flying until he feels it is safe for me to travel. He doesn't want me in an airplane while I've got this thing, whatever it is that I've got."

"Sarah, why don't you pull your head out of your ass. When you do get back, I'll certainly let you know why I'm so mad, if you haven't figured it out by then."

Peter slams the phone down and the connection is abruptly broken.

In time, Sarah contemplates, surely his anger will dissipate. Yet there have been so many occasions when his hostility has mushroomed and he has carried it around, raising it for her to see just when she thinks he has abandoned it. She knows that if she returns home, it will be such a time.

Sarah's legs tremble, slamming against one another, though she is sitting down. Her hands move about without heeding her instructions to stop. Inside her chest, her heart threatens to burst through. I can't go home, Sarah suddenly realizes. I cannot face one more scream, one more session of hostility, one more reproach, one more finger pointed in disapproval. I cannot look at those eyes burning with anger or rolling with revulsion. I won't plead my case one more time. I am no longer able to search for common understanding or sympathy. I really just cannot do it one more time. I can't. I won't.

Sarah picks up the phone and places a person-to-person call to her lawyer in Los Angeles. His secretary, moved by the urgency of a call from halfway around the world, promises that she will have "Mr. A" call back as soon as she can reach him.

Sarah is at a crowded intersection of emotions. There are tears, but there is relief. Sorrow brakes when confronted by a sense that she will never again be intimidated by anyone; in that realization is the green light for self-empowerment.

CHAPTER 27

SECRETS

Nasir has become an integral part of Sarah's day. There is no end to the acts he volunteers to perform, for he is always insistently helpful. This is how it comes about that Nasir begins looking for a home for Sarah.

"You cannot go on living in this hotel. It is always too cold for you and, never mind that, it is too expensive. For what you are spending, you could be in a wonderful place of your own. I can find out about renting something, perhaps in the embassy area, Inshallah."

To Sarah, this appears to be a very practical idea. She would have ample space for her art, her books, and, of course, the four puppies. And why not? She can never return home. Regardless of the daunting newspaper headlines emblazoned on the front page of the paper pushed under her door every morning heralding the dangers of life here, nothing rivals Sarah's fear of the consequences of taking legal steps to officially end her relationship with Peter.

"All right. Look for a house that is spacious, with many rooms. I intend to have friends visiting me."

Nasir's network, though somewhat weaker than years ago, for lack of consistent gifts and entertaining, can still be effective if Sarah's shillings are to be made available. Soon information about a fifteen-room manor is brought to his attention. "It is in perfect condition. The former director of the Criminal Investigation Department built it for his wife, but she wanted to live elsewhere. Everything is custom built, with the best money can buy, and the home is filled with new furnishings from around the world. What a showplace it is!"

* * *

Nasir has one hand on the wheel of his Mercedes; the other grasps his cell phone. "The owner will be late, but we can go in and look around for ourselves. He has left instructions with his guards."

It is a home well worth guarding. Although Sarah has no conception of what a Kenyan-style mansion would look like, she knows a French Normandy estate when she sees one. "What is the Criminal Investigation Department?"

"It is the equivalent of the US FBI. Their people can be persuaded, with money, to criminalize a civil offense and continually harass someone who has committed a crime. It is often more efficient and effective to have someone from CID get involved than to go through normal legal channels."

"How does a public official afford to build a home like this? How does he afford to not live in it and build another one?"

"You see, in his position, he had many contacts, and he was able to do things for them. He is a friend of mine.

He once helped me go to the United States. He would also tell me to buy certain stocks. He had information."

"And what happened?"

"Unfortunately, it did not come about for me as well as it did for him. He knew when to buy, when to sell. I only knew what to buy."

"Did you lose a great deal?"

"Oh yes, indeed. A great deal. It is, in part, the reason for my current financial problems."

"And you bear no grudge for this man?"

"It is not prudent to hold a grudge against any man in the government here. It is sometimes less prudent to hold them against men no longer in politics, for one never knows what they may be doing or if they will again be in power."

Walking through room after lavish room, Sarah begins to justify the possibility of her renting a white elephant that she would neither be able to cool in summer, heat in times of cold, nor provide with adequate maintenance. The rooms are vast caverns, with ceilings in excess of twelve feet. The floors are either wood or stone. Ornate pieces of French and English furniture are forced into formal compatibility. Light fixtures, lamps, ceiling fans, and throw rugs abound. There are even throwbacks from another era: a masculine bar with stools, small feminine tables and chairs, a smoking room for the men, a parlor with card tables for the women, a fireplace in the kitchen, verandas both upstairs and down from which to view the Olympic-size swimming pool, and opulent gardens filled with statuary.

Along the garden's perimeter are dark beds filled with rainbows of flowers. Trees that matured many years ago are deeply rooted in a pattern that enhances the property with shade and serves as a visual barrier from the neighbors.

Sarah examines every room with a new respect for the Kenyan workman, the politician who can turn his government office to such an advantage, an unknown man who has never slept a night in a home that took five years to complete.

She slumps down in one of two living room couches. Nasir sits opposite her, cool and collected. They are waiting for the owner who, only upon his arrival, will tell them of the rental terms he would not reveal before meeting and interviewing her. Sarah's clothes are soaked with perspiration. The overpowering brown leather sofa dwarfs her. She struggles repeatedly to maintain a straight, upright position, but the dampness of her body and clothes causes her to drip downward. The comic act is repeated until it flips the circuit breaker of her mind and switches on a memory, reminiscent of another place, another time, another life.

The same involuntary sliding. The same as when she was in the hospital and the nurses put her in a chair by the window so the staff psychiatrist could interview her. She was wearing a hospital gown, open in the back. Peter was there, explaining that everything depended on answering the doctor in a certain way. He coached Sarah. If she said she wished that her suicide attempt had been successful, she would not be able to leave the hospital; she would be placed in a special ward. If she said she had made a terrible mistake and would never try to kill herself again, then she might be able to go home.

Sarah was determined to pass the test. She was going to lie like hell.

The psychiatrist came in and took a seat. He was positioned casually, as if it was easy to question someone who ten days earlier had been mysteriously able to slit her left wrist after cutting through the tendon of the right.

Sarah slouched too, but not out of nonchalance. Her bottom, wet with the dampness of the unbearable heat, simply could not remain secured to the base of the plastic chair. She continued to slide downward as the doctor asked one ridiculous question after another. She was barefoot and unable to gain traction on the floor. She could not take a shower, and her waist-length, blood-soaked hair had been piled high on her head and tied in a knot by a nurse. No one would dare take the chance of giving her a hairpin.

"Do you think you will ever try to kill yourself again, Sarah?" asked the expressionless man.

"No, Doctor. It was a terrible mistake." What in the hell, she wondered, did this idiot think she was going to say! Did he really believe that anyone who assaulted herself as thoroughly as she had wasn't serious about their intent? And what did he think happened in the last five days of consciousness to convince her that she had made a mistake? Did he think all the people poking her with needles, trying to find a vessel to yield blood, taking urine samples, watching her every move and analyzing each word, had somehow motivated her to lead a nondestructive life?

Sarah had been incensed at the sheer stupidity of the process and wondered why this jerk was not quizzing her on her reasons for trying to kill herself in such an extreme way. Now *that* would have been the question.

The owner of the house enters, trespassing over her thoughts of the past. Coming out of her reverie, Sarah implores the absentee owner to reduce the monthly rent from fifteen thousand dollars a month to ten thousand, since no one is living in the house anyway and she will bear the cost of maintaining it. She carefully constructs an image of being a responsible individual who will "honor" his home with her care for it. Her entreaties would be more effective if she could sit upright during her presentation, but she continues to slide down the couch. "I must go. I am sick. I can't stay here any longer."

Back in the car, she reprimands Nasir. "I can't go running around like this, looking at houses that I have no realistic chance of renting. Next time, be sure to look at the place yourself and determine what the rent will be. I don't want to go over $10,000 a month."

As a result of this chastisement, every one of the eight homes looked at over the next few days is exactly $10,000 per month.

* * *

Alarmingly, Sarah's dependence on Nasir continues to increase. He finds innumerable ways to make himself indispensable. He often brings Shelley and the children over to keep her company, has her clothes altered as she continues to drop weight, and personally delivers an assortment of magazines. At his direction, the doctor appears at least once every few days, always writing out another prescription, certain that he has finally managed the correct diagnosis. Nasir has also arranged for a veterinarian from his mosque to visit the hotel room and vaccinate the dogs. With money from Sarah, he has purchased ordinary dog food that she now mixes in with the food from room service, thereby weaning the dogs off their expensive diet.

To wean Sarah off the same cuisine day in and day out, Nasir has discovered a Chinese restaurant near the hotel where he picks up food at least twice a week. Sarah notices how Nasir initially avoids the pork dishes, but eventually allows his fork to wander, as if by its own accord, into the white cardboard boxes, finishing off the last remaining morsels of greasy meat as he utters through his mouthfuls something about "waste."

In light of not having found a proper residence, he continues to press her. "Sarah, you should move over to the Grand Regency. Shelley and I are working there in our shops every day. We could help you with whatever you need. It would be so easy for us all to be together. And the puppies are healthy enough now that I can take them home so that Munir can sell them at school."

* * *

The sales director of the Grand Regency meets Nasir, Shelley, and Sarah with practiced hospitality. The suite is a sprawling, well-appointed apartment. One walks through the door into an entry with a closet on the right and a guest bathroom on the left. Beyond the entry is a large living room filled entirely with English antiques and a muted Persian throw rug under an heirloom coffee table. There is a separate dining room with a handsome table seating ten, crowned with a crystal chandelier. Off the dining room is a small kitchen with a door leading out to the hallway, thus allowing staff to bring in room service items without passing through the living room.

The living room stretches into a sitting area with a television, and although one space runs into the next, they are differentiated by a change in the mood of the furniture, a less rigid sofa and plush high-backed chairs.

Nearby, a bronze gate encloses a room dedicated to a desk with accompanying stiff leather chairs in front and behind it, bookcases, and lamps that are more decorative than functional. There is no key with which to lock the gate enclosing the office, rendering it accessible to anyone with a curious nature.

The bedroom is not pretentious. It is tastefully appointed in peach and pastel blue. A hall of closets and built-in drawers separates the bedroom from the bathroom, which has two sinks, a bidet and toilet, a scale, and stairs leading up to a granite tub; midway up the wall is a shower hose that appears entirely impractical unless the shower is to be taken from a sitting position.

"How much is it?" Sarah asks after completing the guided tour.

"It is normally $1,000 a night, but because you are a friend of Nasir, I have received permission to charge you only $650 per night."

Sarah once more surrenders her American Express card with instructions to charge her account $25,000 and to have the desk notify her when the end of her deposit is in sight. She, Nasir, and Shelley sit down in the living room. Before long, a bottle of Moët & Chandon champagne, compliments of the director of sales, arrives with three flutes. They sip and celebrate, imbibing from the buds of the long-stemmed glasses.

"To another change!" Sarah sings out enthusiastically, raising her vessel and blocking out thoughts of packing and moving her increasing accumulations one more time.

"To another change!" parrots Nasir and his wife with an enthusiasm that cannot conceal their own changing fortunes.

* * *

By the time Sarah boxes all her belongings and moves to the Grand Regency, it is well after 11:00 at night. She wears a long gray silk shift, which has become visibly stained with perspiration. Without removing it, she lies on the bed and falls asleep.

When she awakes, she examines the twelve cardboard containers scattered throughout the suite. There is a sense she is being leered at through invisible eyes, as though the room has video cameras everywhere.

Starting with the bathroom, she realizes that no one could take a shower in the tub. Foreign dignitaries, she has been told, use this suite. For what? she wonders. She inspects the office, but again reaffirms that it is not functional. The only viable illumination comes from the sun, which provides good light in the morning, but will diminish as the sun moves throughout the day. The effect of the sun in the morning, however, is to render the office too hot to occupy. In the kitchen, she observes that there is no stove. The most troublesome aspect of the suite is the entry, for above it is a bank of high-wattage lights. The guest closet has a small stool in it, and there is a cutout from which the activity in the main room can be observed. It is obvious to Sarah that the lights are to illuminate the person entering the suite in order that they may be clearly identified on video.

Terrified, Sarah grabs the room key and rushes to the elevator, still wearing the gray satin shift creased with wrinkles. She has not washed her face nor fixed her hair. She is barefoot. When she steps in the glass elevator, she is in the company of one who has taken a great deal more care than she in preparing to go downstairs.

"Are you a guest in the hotel?" a stocky, handsome man in his forties asks her. He is wearing gray slacks and a burgundy blazer. He does not appear to be a businessman, but he is clearly not a tourist. Perhaps he's security.

"Yes, I'm a guest. Are you security?"

"Not exactly. I'm with a private security firm doing some business in Kenya."

"You are exactly who I need to speak to."

"Why is that?"

"I don't want to try to explain it. You must come with me to understand."

"Can I do this later? I'm on my way to a meeting and then I have appointments until around four this afternoon."

"Please come to my suite when you're done. I'm in the Presidential Suite. My name is Sarah."

He looks at her disheveled appearance. To enhance her credibility, she shows him her imposing key, on which the name of her suite is engraved.

When she reaches the lobby, she turns toward the back of the hotel and takes the escalator to the mezzanine, making her way to Nasir's store. "I need you both to come upstairs with me. You're not going to believe what I've discovered."

Nasir and Shelley follow Sarah to her suite. Once inside, she races around from room to room, talking so fast her small entourage has difficulty in keeping up with her. Finally, they settle in the living room.

"May I order some tea and croissants?" Nasir asks, the phone already in his hand.

"Yes, of course. I need several glasses of juice as well. I'm completely dehydrated."

The breakfast service is intolerably delayed, causing Nasir to berate the waiter in Swahili, then to call room service to repeat his admonishment. In a final thrust, he asks the operator to connect him with the director of sales, to whom he explains that service to the Presidential Suite must be on an immediate and preferential basis.

"What do you intend to do about your discovery?" Shelley asks, breathing reality into Sarah's suspicions.

"You won't believe this either," Sarah repeats, "but on my way down to get you, I met a man in the elevator with a private security company and he's coming over this afternoon to discuss the problem with me. It's probably his company that has installed all the equipment!"

Shelley's eyes widen. By now, she is beguiled by this American who attracts the people she needs at the moment she needs them, and who, at the same time, appears to avert danger while placing herself at its very epicenter. "Timing is again with her, isn't it?" she asks of her husband.

"Yes. You have done the right thing. Should we be here when he comes for this meeting with you?"

"Yes, of course."

* * *

Anthony, the man from the elevator, rings the bell of the suite at 4:30 PM with minimal explanation for being late. He is surprised to see Nasir and his wife. When he realizes that this is not to be a private meeting, he refrains from sitting down and suggests, "I'll come back later. I have another meeting across town in a little while and I don't think we'll have enough time to talk about your problem right now. I can be back here by seven thirty or eight tonight."

When he arrives that evening, Sarah has a bottle of champagne on ice along with several plates of hors d'oeuvres. She fills his glass and takes his hand, pulling him roughly around the suite, pointing out each of the suspicious points of interest, saving the entry hall and the closet for last. "Was your company hired to put all the video equipment in here?"

Anthony laughs. "I can absolutely guarantee you that there's not one recording device of any kind in this suite. I'll stake my life on it."

"How do you know that? Maybe your company didn't do the work, but that doesn't mean the equipment isn't here. There's no way to explain everything I showed you otherwise."

His laughter continues, not mocking her, but reflecting genuine pleasure in the answer he knows will quell her fears. "I'm telling you, there's no equipment in this suite or in any other suite of this hotel. Believe me."

"I don't even know you. Why should I believe you?"

"Because I'm the one who's going to install it next month!"

The humor hits Sarah in her face like a banana cream pie. Suddenly, she cannot help from laughing along with Anthony at the absurdity of her paranoia.

CHAPTER 28

THE LUO VILLAGE

George, now in the lobby of the Grand Regency, registers a distraught look over the fact that Sarah has changed hotels. "I was told by the doorman at the Nairobi Safari Club you left and might be staying at this hotel. Why did you move again? Did someone offend you?"

"Yes, but not until after I tried to check out. The cashiers couldn't seem to add up the bill. It was late and they were taking forever, so I told them to just bring the bill to me over here when they figured it out. The manager sent it over with a very rude cover letter that read as if I were attempting to skip town. It was quite stupid."

"May I speak with you?"

Because Sarah had not yet been able to fit him into her dinner schedule, she feels obliged to include him in her plans. "George, I am on my way to have brunch with a friend and his family. If you'd like to join us, take the elevator up to the pool deck and I'll meet you there."

"Yes. I would very much like to."

Sarah makes a round of introductions and George meets Nasir and his family with background music provided by a four-piece ensemble. The mid-morning is bright, the sounds alive, the buffet aromatic, the children hungry, and Nasir pleasant while registering this new person in Sarah's orbit.

When brunch ends and good-byes are bestowed, Sarah and George remove themselves some distance, to chairs under the shade of a pool umbrella.

"I want to ask you to check on the background of my driver, Joseph. I think there's a problem with him."

"What is it that concerns you?"

"The other night when I changed hotels, he was to have helped me with the packing and my move. Instead, he called at the last minute and said his cousin was going to take his place because he was feeling too sick to get out of bed. The next thing I know, this very well-dressed man showed up, who apparently couldn't speak English, although he managed to communicate the fact that he was on a two-week vacation from the Nairobi Post Office. He packaged up everything and brought me over here.

"Because it was almost midnight, I asked him to return the next day and we would figure out what I owed him. He arrived the following morning, immaculately dressed in an expensive business suit. When it came to discussing what amount he should be paid, his English improved immensely.

"I felt that he was not who he represented himself to be, so I called Nasir and asked him to come up to my suite. I assumed he would know how to handle this and be able to determine if the man was who he said he was.

"Nasir requested to see his identity card and his driver's license. The names on the two cards did not match one another, and neither name was the same as the one Joseph had originally given me. Nasir went to make a photocopy of the two cards, and while he was gone, I tried to question the man, who suddenly began speaking perfect English, doing so in a hostile voice, as if I had no right to interrogate him."

"It is not a problem for me to find out about him, Sarah, but it is definitely very curious. Do you have the photocopies?"

"Yes, in my purse. Here. There's something else I want to ask you about. I've met a man with a security firm doing business here in Kenya and elsewhere in Africa. I don't exactly know how to say this, but I believe it might be a Mafia-controlled company!

"Ordinarily I wouldn't care, but they have a contract with the American Embassy, which is curious enough, but I've recently represented myself as being attached to the Embassy, which might suggest that I'm involved with them in some way."

"Attached to the Embassy? You are referring to your statements at Nyayo House?"

"Yes, the statement I gave at Nyayo House. I did specify the Embassy, but now I am worried that they might identify me with the security firm. I don't suppose anyone really cares or would take the initiative to check out my story, but I feel a certain paranoia about potentially being identified with a Mafia company, if that is what it is."

"Well, you have certainly met a great many people during your relatively short stay here. I am afraid I must tell you yes, there is a Mafioso security network operating under the cover of Investigation Services International Limited. Their offices are about five blocks from here."

"Good God! Whom do they work for?"

"Among others, the local US Embassy, US government agencies, and various American and multinational non-governmental companies."

"Stop. I don't think I ought to know any more."

"What about the conversation we were to have had?"

"I think we should have that another time. But I would like to tell you quickly about an idea I have so that you can check out some things for me. The woman customs agent who was able to obtain my packages when they were being held up told me she wanted to buy a computer for her business, which she owns. She asked to borrow $500 and she had a pretty decent proposition for paying the money back. She was crying, which seemed peculiar because every time I was with her, she was very composed."

"What was it that made her cry?"

"Apparently, her husband beats her regularly, and several times she has run away to her mother's house. But each time, her mother sends her directly back home because she is supposed to be with her husband. That is her upbringing and mentality. Her mother tells her it is not right for a woman to leave her husband. She has two small children and, as she explained it, the children, by law, must remain with the father."

"And what has all this to do with your idea?"

"Well, I was thinking of establishing a nonprofit called the East African Development Organization. Its purpose would be to raise funds for several different activities. One function would be to provide a refuge for battered women, where they could come and receive help with their situation before making any final decisions about what they should do.

"This is sounding very ambitious."

"There's more. You ought to have some sort of training program for the young men who leave their villages and come to Nairobi to find work, only to discover there is no work to be had."

"How would you fund the organization? It would require a great deal of money."

"I would begin with my own money, then raise additional funds by finding an appropriate public speaker and giving presentations throughout the United States. With the money raised, my organization would buy stock in all the international companies dumping their substandard goods on Kenya and other third-world countries. As a stockholder, the East African Development Organization would apply pressure on these companies to stop providing products with little or no remaining shelf life. And, most importantly, pressure them into making donations to the organization in order to help the people they have been taking advantage of."

Sarah's words run red lights, streaking in a blur past George's ears. He no longer sits relaxed, one leg across the other. Instead he is on the edge of his chair, eyes straining to ascertain her sincerity.

"This is quite a large undertaking. What do you want me to do?"

"I wouldn't want to initiate programs that might overlap with any short- or long-term plans your President Moi might have in the works."

"Therefore?"

"Therefore, I would like to meet with him and discuss my ideas. I want to determine what he thinks. I want to do so as soon as possible, actually."

"You want an immediate meeting with the president of Kenya? Is that what you are asking for?"

"Yes, exactly."

"I see. Of course. I think I can first arrange a meeting between you and Mr. Kassin Owango, who is a long-time acquaintance of mine and a good friend of President Moi. He would listen to you, and it is he who would be in a position to arrange such a meeting. This is the manner in which it should be handled. However, before such a meeting, I believe it is crucial for you to visit a rural village. You must witness the problems firsthand. You may even change your agenda based on your visit. A short trip to my home, Gem Rae Village, would allow you to meet my people and to learn much. I could take you there. I would bring my family. This should be a priority."

"Well, I am not certain when I could make this visit . . ."

"We shall go sometime in the middle of next week."

"Fine. Then I shall wait to hear from you."

George rises, about to depart, when a phone is brought to Sarah by the maître d'.

"Hello, Brandon? We've finally connected. Yes, of course. When? Okay."

Sarah puts the phone down and addresses George. "Sorry. That was a friend of mine."

"Was that Brandon Howard?"

"Yes, it was. Why? Do you know him?"

"Of course. Everyone in Kenya knows him or knows of him. He is very famous outside of East Africa as well."

Sarah wants to invite George to sit back down so she can ask him any number of questions about Brandon that have occurred to her since their original meeting.

No. Too obvious. Too . . . well, just too damn obvious, that's all.

* * *

Sarah cannot go to George's village the following week. She is hesitant about leaving the luxury of her hotel while still manifesting the signs of an illness the doctor has been unable to accurately diagnose. Inevitably, however, she must give in to George's persistence, given his refusal to set up any meetings for the East African Development Organization until she personally visits his family and his village.

Today they will make their way to the Nyanza Province within the region of Lake Victoria.

An eight-passenger van and driver have been hired to convey Sarah, George, and his family over long, difficult roads. George's wife is Meresha. His daughters are Dorothy, six years old, and Sarah Frances, the youngest, recently christened with Sarah's first and middle names.

The journey begins early and will be tedious in the way travel can be when it is uninterrupted except to stop for necessary relief. First, George directs the driver into the heart of Nairobi to purchase drinks and snacks. Everyone has packed a small overnight bag, as the trip is approximately seven to eight hours each way; the group will spend the night in the village.

They are traveling to Gem Rae Village, the home of George and his family. George's entire clan—those that remain—occupy the land. Many have died of natural causes, but too many more have died of malaria or of mysterious causes that were never properly identified.

Sarah remembers little about George's previous description of the village except that it is inhabited by the Luo tribe, the second-largest tribe in Kenya.

"The British made Nyanza the home of the Luo tribe, which observed new ways of life, including the novel concepts of education, health care, and the usefulness of money."

As the van jerks over countless ruts, Sarah again listens and learns from George, scribbling on a pad that abruptly jumps with each erratic movement of the vehicle.

George sips his tepid orange drink and begins a long monologue about independence and the part his tribe played in achieving it, which Sarah discovers does little to break the tedium of reaching his village. It is an arduous undertaking made all the more so by the driver's insistence on taking a number of wrong turns, disregarding George's directions to the place where he was raised. They arrive about an hour and a half before dusk and are greeted by George's mother, Susana, an aged woman who has buried four of her children, each death etched forever in her sagging face. Any remnants of joy appear to reside with George and his family.

Susana encourages the group to come inside her home. They follow through the low doorway into a room with a few scattered chairs and two couches draped in crochet throws. A wooden armchair holds the skeleton-like frame of a once-healthy man, George's father, Nicanor Oyare Sonde. He is frail and in too much discomfort to do more than convey his greetings through groans. Although he retains some sight, his eyes have the vacancy of a blind man. He suffers from a combination of ills for which he is unable to receive treatment. Medical facilities are neither within his access nor his resources. On a table beside him sits a large basket with a frayed handle. The treasures within include a few pills garnered by George from a source here, a source there: an assortment of over-the-counter pain medications. The stash is a small and insufficient army against his suffering.

George's father had once been a traveling representative of a large pharmaceutical company. The irony that this man, who formerly earned a living purveying pills, is now unable to obtain any medical treatment sweeps over Sarah. She sits down and then wonders if she has violated any protocol. No one has told her what to do. In a moment, she is back on her feet. Susana is staging an event. When the attention of each person in her home is hers, a prayer is said thanking God for her family's safe journey to the village and welcoming a new member to their inner circle. Although the light is dimming, there is still time to make limited rounds about the village to visit a chosen few.

George urges Sarah out of his mother's home. She is wearing a dress and three-inch heels, an outfit so outlandishly inappropriate that she cannot help but interpret the villagers' benign smiles as contemptuous sneers.

George watches her step gingerly as they walk through the village, its streets potted with furrows and, to Sarah's chagrin, pockmarked with the detritus of its residents.

Most enclosures are made of cow dung and mud capped with corrugated tin roofs. Sarah will sleep in such a structure this night.

Sarah is introduced to a figure who, in contrast to his physical composure, is smartly dressed in a freshly pressed shirt and trousers held up by snappy, once-colorful suspenders. George informs Sarah that the man's clothes have been ironed using an old triangular-shaped iron filled with hot coals from a small, ever-burning fire on the ground nearby. Seeing the man's shirt and pants in sharp contrast to his backward surroundings, Sarah is rattled with a thought: if one could still be motivated to wash and care for one's clothes in the midst of squalor and poverty, what possibilities might exist, for it takes effort to put oneself together.

Sarah sees in an instant the various times she has had to force herself out of bed. To wash. To dress. To make up her face and do her hair. In periods when these efforts seemed impossible, she would drain her reserves before she left the house, before beginning the business of doing her job, dispatching people and memos, and making decisions that could cause her to lose her position.

Winston Churchill referred to his depression as the "black dog." Sarah thinks of her clinical depression as entering an unlit tunnel while driving a car. Once entering it, she still must remain functioning, alert, and at the wheel, but within her particular tunnel, there are no signs indicating how many miles till she reaches the exit and the light.

The man whose hand Sarah is shaking is Peter Ddulo. His shoes are covered with the brown powder of the unpaved road running from within the compound to the nearest town. He has walked several miles this morning for no purpose other than to buy a newspaper in order to stay abreast of world events. His interest in the world results from time spent in the United States during the turbulent 1960s.

Sarah questions how he came to be in her country.

George moves her beyond Peter's hearing, confiding, "Senator John Kennedy and a leading Kenyan politician from the Luo community launched the Student Airlift Program to enroll Kenyan students in American universities to supplement their education. A place at a university was found for his brother and for Peter.

"Peter got involved in heavy drinking and consorting with American women and was given a one-way ticket to return home. In early 1963 he was back on Kenyan soil and worked for the Kenyan government, carrying out official duties until his retirement in 1985."

Sarah pities him for the mistakes that cost him a chance to live in the country of his dreams. It always fascinates her that some people make one mistake that can alter their lives forever, while others make mistakes without apparent consequences.

* * *

There is no dinner bell, no phone going off to communicate the need to return to the home of George's parents. The sun has dropped the ball, night has picked it up, and it is time for the evening meal.

Dinner is served in layered courses, beginning with a flat, sweet, donut-like piece of bread. There is no dining table; everyone sits around a central low table in the one living space. Following each dish, hot water is brought to the table by Meresha for everyone to wash their hands.

It is late, and those who have traveled the long distance are as tired as those who have not. A place has been selected for her to sleep, a semipermanent home belonging to George's younger brother.

Sarah is led by George's sister to a hut where motions are made indicating that she is to undress and place her garments upon a wooden chair in the corner. Sarah, too spent to consider the implications, follows the instruction. George's sister leaves momentarily and returns with two plastic pans: one Sarah is to stand in, the other full of still-hot water she is to use for rinsing. She is handed soap and a threadbare towel. The woman removes herself to stand sentry outside. After glossing the soap over her body, Sarah sparingly applies the clean water for rinsing, then steps outside and slips into a pair of waiting rubber flip-flops.

Sarah then follows George's sister to a small structure surrounded by Euphorbia trees; there is a gate segregating the dirt path leading them there from the dirt porch. Inside, Sarah is surprised by a small colorful couch and coffee table. There are two metal-framed windows covered by mosquito netting and outlined with embroidered curtains. There is no bathroom within. The toilet is in a tiny enclosure approximately thirty feet from the hut. Having used it already, Sarah is vaguely aware of its location and intends to take advantage of the dark and the lack of audience as soon as George's sister discharges the last of her hospitality.

A second room embraces a bed and exposed mattress with several faded blankets piled up at its foot. The bed is swaddled in netting. The barren floor of the hut is hardened mud and dung, but the light is too dim for Sarah to fully appreciate its rustic ring.

When she feels as if she no longer is being watched, protected, or followed, she takes her lantern to the tin shed, then makes her way back, covers the barren mattress with one of the blankets, pulls another over her, secures the mosquito netting, and falls into a sleep so deep no dream dares to impose.

Hours later, giggling voices shake her awake. George's small daughters are standing as close to Sarah as possible without penetrating the netting. Dressed in the colorful pastel cotton outfits Sarah purchased for them in Nairobi, they appear to her like a vision of two bright Easter eggs boasting heart-shaped mouths. They are laughing at her laziness, for she has slept through the cock's crow, the sounds of the chickens, and the brash braying of the village's lone donkey. But their mission is serious and so Dorothy implores Sarah to get up.

The children insist on watching her prepare, and when Sarah takes out her lipstick, they demand that the same glossy substance be applied to their lips as well. They require powder and eye shadow before removing themselves to announce to their mother that their "auntie Sarah" will be ready for breakfast soon.

* * *

After consuming tea and freshly-made fried sweetbread, George wants Sarah to meet his other relatives. She loads her camera and they begin the rounds in some order of priority that appears to be predicated on age and seniority. Everyone knows that George and his family are in the village and that he has brought someone special. They each want their picture taken, sometimes with George, but more often alone, as if it will represent their individual survival. As Sarah positions herself to take the best shot within the confined spaces of the huts, she notices children pushing their faces through the windows. Sarah begins to photograph them, thinking that the composition will make for good images. After several shots, she asks, "George, why aren't these children in school? It's a school day, isn't it?"

"Yes, but they do not attend because they cannot afford the books. If a child does not have the required learning materials, they are sent home."

"I thought children were able to attend school at no charge up to a certain grade level."

"Oh no, that is a mistake. Once it was so. But now there is cost sharing in education and the health services. It is because the International Monetary Fund and the World Bank made adjustments that withdrew financial support for teaching and learning materials in schools. Parents were to pay for about sixty percent of maintaining and building classrooms and for providing the teaching materials, with the government paying for the balance. So enrollment in schools has decreased, and health has suffered. These children are here because they were sent home. Their parents cannot afford to buy them books."

"If they had the books today, could they return to school?" Sarah asks, her anger rising.

"Yes. They can go back as soon as they have the materials."

"George, I don't want to meet any more people. Please, let's go back to your parents' home and find your brother. He can gather the names of all the children in the village who do not have books. He can go to the school and have the teachers write down what they need next to their name, along with the cost. He is to come back here and I will give him the money. He can go into town, get the books, and—"

"Yes! And give them to the teachers."

"No. Absolutely not. He is to bring the books back here and we will see to it that they are put directly into the hands of the children. Their parents will be instructed that when their child is finished with the book, it is to go to another person in the village who needs it."

"Well, this will delay us in getting on the road, and we will not be in Nairobi until very late at night. This could be quite dangerous, for if we are on the road when it is dark, bandits can put strips of nails along our path. The tires puncture, and when the vehicle stops, you can be robbed."

"Then we shall be very late in getting back and it will be dangerous. We'll drive with our headlights on high beam. When we stop to get gas, we'll see if we can get an auxiliary light to put on top of the van. Regardless, George, these children will be in school tomorrow morning."

CHAPTER 29

FAR-FETCHED PLANS

"**S**o I think, if you are willing, I could book you as a speaker and we'd raise an enormous amount of money for the East African Development Organization," Sarah bubbles. "It would be wonderful publicity for you, and you'd have a chance to do something important for Kenya."

"How much of my time would be involved?" asks Brandon.

"I'm not sure yet, but let's assume four lectures each in New York, Chicago, Boston, Philadelphia, Atlanta, Miami, Dallas or Houston, Los Angeles, and San Francisco. Worst-case scenario is one lecture per day; that would be thirty-six days. If we allow three days for travel and rest per city, that's another twenty-seven days. So far, we're up to sixty-three days, maybe less if we can get this down to a science," Sarah calculates breathlessly.

"I can't see any way to donate so much of my time. It would simply be impossible. I'm always quite desperate for money, considering how fast I go through it. I still must earn a living, dreadful as that is."

"I realize that. The organization would hire you for $75,000 a year to provide the presentations, by which I mean a slide show and a lecture. That's . . . I don't know, I can't figure it out without a calculator, but it would be almost $2,000 a lecture. What do you think?"

"I think it would be necessary to give a great deal of consideration to the content of these so-called presentations. The thoughts I have may be very disturbing and controversial to audiences. My philosophical point of view about people versus the animals is the message I would want to get out there. The African people never took more than they required to eat, and they were in balance with their environment. But now many animals are in danger of extinction, and the diet of most East Africans is deficient in protein.

"The scarcity of animals has the same effect as any rare commodity: it generates a market, and in this case, the market is the tourist. I believe animals could be used to pay their own way, through the visitors who come to see them. I could go on and on about this method of conservation, but I presume you get the picture. Anyway, I'd like some time to reflect on it. Is there any particular rush?"

"Only if I get a meeting with the president."

"Are you likely to?"

"In all probability, yes. Do think about it. By the way, what did you want to talk to me about?"

"Sarah, I honestly have no bloody idea. I can't remember. You have rather unnerved me. And you've managed to make me famished."

Looking at the mess around her, Sarah notices a PowerBar. Although he had refused one the day of his visit to the Norfolk Hotel, she thrusts it forward. "Would you like a PowerBar?"

"Good God, no. I couldn't possibly eat anything with a name like that."

"Well, while you're here, I want to show you the winning pictures the girls took for our contest at Hemingway's." Sarah provides Brandon with the short stack of winning pictures.

"Don't keep me in suspense. Who has won?"

"Turn the pictures over. The winning name and category is written on the back."

As he does so, he realizes that his daughter, Victoria, has won in every category but one.

He spreads the images over the coffee table and reviews them thoughtfully for several minutes. "Do you think I'm capable of being worthy of her?" Brandon asks somewhat hopefully.

"Yes, I do. I think you are becoming a marvelous father, Brandon," Sarah assures him.

He smiles, encouraged. "Hopefully a better father than healer. Adele's condition is worsening. This is all so wretched. I can't bear it much longer."

"You should go now, to be with her."

"Yes. I need to compose myself before seeing her."

"Are you that attached?"

"Yes. No. I've only watched animals suffer. This experience is hardly usual for me. When it's my time, I want to die as I've lived—disgracefully!"

Sarah is certain she has found a soul mate in Brandon, who has delivered his declaration as convincingly as Oscar Wilde.

CHAPTER 30

AN ATTEMPTED KIDNAPPING

A force stronger than Sarah causes her to act in another reality, referred to as "abnormal" by those with whom she is in contact in the United States. She desires others to join her odyssey, and she conveys her message with a conviction that raises a loud alarm amongst her friends.

"Come to Kenya for Christmas!" Sarah implores at all hours of the day and night, sputtering out her sentence with a failing voice. The invitations are always met with the same incredulous silence.

"We'll all go on a safari together!"

If only she could take them to where she has been. They would understand her enthusiasm then. They would have to.

One day, a friend responds affirmatively. "Can I come for Thanksgiving instead?" It is Genya, a woman with whom Sarah has enjoyed a twenty-year friendship, the rare variety imbued with the implicit message that one will do anything for the other.

"Of course," Sarah responds, coughing the two words into the receiver. And with this answer, the events of the third phase of Sarah's saga are set in motion, unwittingly on Sarah's part, very deliberately on Genya's.

* * *

As Sarah will come to learn, Genya had called Sarah at home, anticipating her return from Kenya. After the preliminary hellos, Peter began ranting about his wife staying in Kenya to complete her journal, remarking, "She must think she's writing *War and Peace*." Not anxious to deal with Peter in his maddened state, Genya suggested that it might be better if they spoke later, and immediately called Sarah's brother, Daniel, to describe the conversation. She placed several follow-up calls, pleading with him to accompany her on the long trip, reminding him, "I'm seventy years old."

"Genya, she's out of her mind. We're not talking to each other at this point. She had me buy $17,000 worth of camera equipment and then got mad at me when I refused to take it to her personally! She's been calling me at all hours of the day and night and I can't understand a thing she's saying. She wakes me up, then starts talking a mile a minute. I can't keep up with her. I can't even hear her. I don't know if it's the connection or if she's lost her voice. She's either coughing or the phone lines are crackling. I don't know. I can't take it anymore."

* * *

"Sarah, your friend is coming for Thanksgiving. It's wonderful, isn't it, Nasir? She's arriving at seven? We will pick her up because we rise early to go to the mosque.

Anyway, it's too cold and damp in the morning, and you are too sick. So you can stay here and we will bring her." It is Shelley, again performing a service, smoothing the way, anticipating a need.

"And today the children will be here after school to see you. Munir has a school assignment to write a ghost story. He is excited to have you help him."

The children's almost daily visits to Sarah have become ritualized over the last few weeks. They want to be with her, to order ice cream and treats from room service and to watch television. Munir comes, gives Sarah a hug and kiss, then darts down the hall to the Regency Club and signs onto a computer screen where he checks stock prices. When his mother and father join Sarah at four thirty in the afternoon for tea in her suite, Munir quotes the closing price of his favorite stocks and communicates any significant news to have come across the wire service. He maintains meticulous notes in a small notebook and refers to them if he needs to connect a current news item to one in the past. He comments on stocks, which of them experience significant movements, either up or down. And always, he wants to buy, buy, buy. But never is there any money to do so.

* * *

Sarah, not suspecting the true nature of Genya's visit, begins work on an itinerary designed to enthrall her friend. First, Sarah decides, they will stay at the Grand Regency for two days, during which time Sarah can share her stories and Genya can rest. The third day, they will go to Giraffe Manor.

They will return to the hotel for one night and then fly to Mombasa to be picked up by shuttle and taken to Hemingway's. There, on the Indian Ocean, in the comfort of a resort Sarah is already familiar with, they will spend Thanksgiving.

Secure in the knowledge that this will be a most memorable experience for the both of them, Sarah initiates the calls and makes the necessary reservations.

Her suite is a scene of abandonment and large-scale disorder. This is the result, in part, of a nonstop spending spree: art, native handicrafts, jewelry, and Christmas presents for family and friends back home. Her library expands at a furious pace, with Sarah establishing categories for African art, rites and traditions, poetry, colonialism, and scientific writings on the origin of man.

The handicrafts and presents are displayed on the expansive dining room table and buffet. In the living room, sparkling gold, silver, and multicolored beads sprawl across the top of a cabinet encasing the safe in which the treasures properly belong.

The African art, including large baskets, rugs of all sizes and origin, carved Somalian milk containers made of wood, and gourds displaying animals etched into their exterior, has replaced most of the suite's décor.

With each purchase, an article that once made up a piece of a premeditated English motif is placed outside the suite to be picked up by a housekeeper and stored away for when the accommodation can be put back together. Even the master bedroom's soft satin spread is jettisoned for a tribal substitute (a harsh woven rug), without consideration for the fact that it causes Sarah to wake each night scratching and tearing at her skin.

These displacements cause the Presidential Suite to resemble the collision of two civilizations, the outward manifestation of Sarah's increasingly flamboyant personality.

Sarah delights in the eclectic world she has created. Brandon Howard heartily agrees with her, as his compliments made clear upon first inspecting her most recent accommodations.

This unsettled suite is where Shelley will bring Genya a few days hence.

* * *

On what has, with numerous delays, become the appointed day, the plane lands on time. Shelley and the children meet Genya. Finally, the doorbell rings. Though naturally inclined to embrace, Genya holds Sarah off, examining her leaner frame, her three-inch hair, and a subtle difference in her demeanor. Seeing each other again under such improbable circumstances, and so far from home at this nostalgic time of year, creates a burden of emotion that, even though shared by two, overtakes them both.

Shelley witnesses the reunion with pleasure, while the children act out their excitement at being included in yet another small adventure.

The doorbell rings again. It is Saturday morning. Who would be ringing my doorbell at this hour? Sarah wonders. She opens the door, and the reality of the person standing on the other side is at once too much and too unbelievable. Her legs buckle, causing her to almost fall towards the tall, lean, well-groomed figure that is her brother.

"Daniel! What are you doing here?" Sarah asks, reveling in the fact that he has surmounted judgment, anger, and eleven time zones to be standing there. "I can't believe this!"

"I wasn't sure how you'd feel about my coming after all the fighting we've been doing over the phone."

"Your coming says more than anything you've said to me before!" Sarah realizes it is the very first time they have genuinely hugged. In the past, it was simply a gesture used as one or another of them slid by the other's life.

"We would have been here yesterday, but . . ."

Genya and Daniel describe an ordeal so entangled in unfortunate circumstance, Sarah loses track. It is not yet 10:00 AM, but both travelers are drained.

"Go to your rooms, clean up, rest, and give me a call when you wake up. Then I'll tell you what I have planned," Sarah directs, realizing that she must backtrack and arrange for an additional room at both destinations as well as another airline ticket to Mombasa.

Genya is in the room directly adjacent to Sarah's suite, while Daniel, having made his arrangements at the last minute, is off by himself in a distant part of the hotel.

Twenty-five minutes later, Daniel sits beside his sister again, neither showered, rested, nor ready for lunch. "Sarah, you've put everyone through hell. There's something wrong with you, and someone's got to have the guts to tell you. No person in their right mind goes on a safari and then decides to stay and live in Africa. You just don't give up everything and everyone."

"What exactly is it that you think I am giving up? A wonderful relationship with my husband? You have witnessed it firsthand and know that Peter's treatment of me is dreadful at best. A meaningful, productive life? My life is doing Peter's bidding. A beautiful home filled with terrible memories of fights and humiliation? You, Daniel, above anyone else should understand that my life has been untenable."

"That's not the point. Whatever you're trying to find, you're going at it the wrong way, and now you've dragged Genya and me into it. We've come to take you home. I want you to know that's why we're really here." Daniel's voice, continuing to climb, reaches Genya in the next room.

"For God's sake, what's going on in here?" Genya asks, reentering Sarah's suite.

"I told her why we came. I told her she's out of her mind and we're here to take her home. I know I was supposed to wait, but I had to tell her now. I had to get it off my mind."

"Daniel, damn it, this isn't what we discussed. We said we'd come and be with her and try to understand her situation, and then persuade her to return with us."

Sarah's reply is calm. "I appreciate the both of you coming here. Give this place a chance. Let me try to explain what I want to do. See for yourself if I am not a happier person than I have ever been before. Then you can decide what you want to do about me."

Genya's hard stare provides Daniel with a series of instructions. It is time to leave. Depart immediately. Don't utter another word. Daniel obeys and retreats to Genya's room, and it is now Sarah's turn to hear her chastising

Daniel for shredding the plan they had constructed over the last seventy-two hours.

* * *

The conviction that one should forcibly take one's sister back to the United States is difficult to sustain while eating buttery croissants with a beautiful Rothschild's giraffe nuzzling your cheek through an open window. As Sarah observes her brother and the giraffe charm each other, she wonders if he might come to agree with her regarding this country. Certainly Genya's resistance is softening, or so it appears to the one who would have it be so.

Giraffe Manor is a small jewel of one hundred and twenty acres. When early owners, Jock Leslie-Melville and his wife, Betty, bought the house, they established the African Fund for Endangered Wildlife, subsequently relocating five baby Rothschild's to the manor's grounds.

Daisy, one of their earliest and most famous giraffes, as well as a favorite of the current owners, had drowned in a ditch the previous day. Daisy's tragic death affects the party's hosts as if they had lost their firstborn child, and the guests who have come to meet Daisy mourn as well.

Shelley is bringing her children to the manor the following day, and this alone helps to lift the fog of sadness. The children, upon hearing of Sarah's journey to the manor, had been quick to point out that the giraffe is yet another animal, along with the elephant, that has so far eluded them.

When the three youngsters tumble from the car into Sarah's outstretched arms, the children's bond with her is more obvious to Daniel and Genya. But for Alicia and Ali, one hand is as good as another to hold, and anyone's lap will do.

A private guide leads Sarah, Genya, Daniel, Shelley, and the children through the grounds. They feed the giraffes and witness resident warthogs shuffle about, tusks down, plowing the earth with an earnestness so convincing, each becomes almost a caricature of itself.

The children's departure is followed by a period of tranquil quiet and afternoon tea. Later, cocktails will be served, and after a decent interval, dinner will follow. Such civilized practices do not guarantee civilized behavior. After tea, Daniel asks Sarah to come to his room. He has something he wishes to share with her. "I want you to read this . . . if you have the guts to look at it."

"What is it?" Sarah asks, watching her brother take several Xeroxed papers from his suitcase.

"These are pages I copied from a psychology book. If you read them, you'll understand the problem everyone has with your behavior. These pages describe your condition."

"I don't have a 'condition.' There is absolutely nothing wrong with me. Maybe it's just been so long since you've seen me happy you don't recognize it."

"You're not happy, you're delirious," snaps Daniel, sufficiently loud for the sound to carry to Genya's bedroom at the far end of the manor hall.

Genya materializes, intervening again between protective brother and older sister. Weighing less than ninety-eight pounds, she is an unlikely referee. "Give them to me," she demands.

"Why don't you make her read it? Let her see what her problem is," Daniel suggests.

"This isn't the way to handle 'the problem.'"

The two interact as if speaking of an abstract concept, or of someone who isn't standing inches away. "Look, I have been through every mental condition imaginable. I don't need to read that article. I could probably have written it!" Sarah offers in her own defense.

Does the untrained, well-intended brother believe someone in a manic condition reading a detailed description of classic bipolar behavior could possess the capacity to recognize herself as being in a manic state? Apparently he does. What escapes a normal individual trying desperately to make contact with one who is not is that logic and reason are lacking in the undiagnosed, untreated patient.

Well, things will go better when we're all at Hemingway's, Sarah believes. Tonight, she is Scarlett O'Hara, with a fistful of dirt clinched in her hand. "I'll think about that tomorrow."

* * *

Just as she was the first time Sarah arrived, Catherine is at the entrance of Hemingway's, as if she has been waiting in the same place for Sarah's return. "This time I insist that you, your friend, and your brother go out tomorrow evening on the dhow with me. I will not let you miss this experience again, Sarah. It is a most pleasant way to spend the evening and watch the sunset. We shall have cocktails and some bitings with us."

"Tomorrow we Americans celebrate Thanksgiving, but since there is no such holiday here, we have a date." As has become customary recently, Sarah speaks for everyone. The energy driving Sarah's words, spoken at an abnormally accelerated speed, effectively preempts anyone else from participating in the decision.

The group's luggage is eventually sorted out, permitting each to settle into their separate rooms. They agree to meet within the hour in order for Sarah to show them around. When they reconvene, she walks them through the hotel like a museum docent, explaining the resort's background, Ernest Hemingway's visits, the fishing tournaments, and Brandon's "little duckling house" just down the beach.

"I need a drink," Daniel announces in desperation. The ease with which his sister is moving about is unsettling to him. It is bad enough she is mentally and physically sick, but to participate in this ride through her new world is only taking him and Genya further from their mark. Each movement Daniel takes in lockstep with Sarah is a step away from the course he has set.

It is particularly troubling to him when he thinks he may just understand some of what Sarah has been feeling about Kenya and its people. When he finds himself gazing at the alabaster silk sand, the settled ocean, and hypnotic palm trees, he must bring himself back on point. If he meets a congenial person, engages them in an enjoyable conversation and learns something about the local customs, he catches himself. He takes photographs, just like a person on holiday. When he remembers his true purpose, the camera is sheathed and he returns to his work of being serious and determined.

Daniel's job is to be angry. His mission is one of figuring out how to bag his sister and bring her home. It is not one of reclining atop the carpeted deck of the antique dhow, propped up with colorful pillows, sailing along the coast of the Indian Ocean. He should not be enjoying Catherine and the crew singing melodious native songs while the sun throws itself a farewell party, decorating the sky with hot-pink confetti.

He should not, but he is.

Giving up one's plans seems increasingly unavoidable, for ultimately, there is something infectious about this place. The issue becomes: How seriously is one contaminated?

Following the ride in the dhow, Sarah, Genya, and Daniel enjoy an ersatz Thanksgiving with a candlelight dinner outside Hemingway's Bar.

"I'm getting an after-dinner drink. Do you want anything?" asks Daniel.

Sarah desires only to sit outside the bar, gazing at the stars. Genya, drained by the sun, tension, and even the enjoyable aspects of the day, declines, wishing to retire for the evening.

This time the fight begins a few moments after Daniel's return to Sarah's side. It is as empty of substance as the argument at Giraffe Manor. The only difference this time is that when Daniel stands over Sarah, pointing his finger in her face, raising his voice, the bartender abandons his station, stands between sister and brother, and asks Sarah, "Are you all right? Do you want any help?"

"No, I'm fine. We're just having a rather spirited discussion. Daniel, I can't do this. I am not going to argue with you. I don't understand why you are mad at me."

Daniel's display of anger has no impact on Sarah. By now, Sarah's mood, elevated and expansive, her self-esteem inflated, her need for sleep decreased, the rapidity of her words rushing headlong into sentences, are amongst the classic signs of a manic episode. Daniel and Genya recognize her behavior as excessive, but neither Daniel's hammer nor Genya's glove are sufficiently effective to subdue her.

Worse, the contagious nature of her euphoria captivates others, pulling them into her thrall: Brandon, his children, Moses, George, Catherine, Nasir, Shelley, their children. Everyone.

For Sarah, alone in a world of grandiosity, life is better than ever. Anything is possible. But Daniel and Genya's world is becoming increasingly difficult, a labyrinth of dead-end results accompanied by diminishing options, as time is narrowing down to a single, upcoming page on their calendar marked "Departure."

* * *

The days spent at the side of the Indian Ocean recede, and the party of three returns to Nairobi.

Sarah has convinced Daniel to take his scheduled departure and Genya to stay on; in return, she promises to accompany Genya home in another week. A deal is struck.

After her brother is well on his way back to the United States, Sarah continues her purchasing odyssey on the pretense of finishing her Christmas shopping while still in Kenya. She and Genya visit shops with African artifacts, clothing, novelties, and household goods. Gift merchandise crowds the Presidential Suite, competing with Sarah's previous acquisitions.

Toward the end of what is to be Sarah's final day before a temporary departure, hotel management abruptly informs her that she must put her belongings into storage so they will be able to rent the suite until her return. This is a maddening request Sarah has not anticipated.

Nasir and Shelley help in the packing. Whenever they must attend to their shop, they send up their general errand boy, Sammy. He works at carefully packaging the heavier items, such as the books, while Sarah buzzes around him trying to determine which president or biblical figure he was named for.

Genya is assigned the Christmas presents, wrapping them and putting them into piles Sarah has designated by name, each corresponding to someone who will realize the bounty of Kenyan crafts. Sarah has purchased a wide variety of large straw purses—the sort that had caught Julia's fancy—and each pile of goods is ultimately coaxed into these receptacles. Once they are finished, Nasir is dispatched to buy several pieces of inexpensive luggage to transport the handbags filled with gifts.

The cost of the multiple gifts, purses, luggage, and the airline's overweight penalty Sarah will incur at the airport makes the overall price of each gift outrageous in comparison to its usefulness or the extent to which it can be appreciated. The volume of these things will be added to the entirety of all the other items and issues Sarah must deal with upon her return home. The totality will be far more overwhelming than she can appreciate in her present state. The burden of distributing the gifts will be excruciating, for it will occur at the same time Sarah descends the steep slope that follows an exaggerated mood elevation. It is an altitude that, in Sarah's case, is higher than a desperately discharged rescue flare.

* * *

"I want to take you to the airport tonight."

"Brandon, I appreciate your kindness, but Nasir has already offered, and the children are looking forward to seeing Genya and me off. Besides, if Adele is getting worse, then your place should be at her side. You never know what's going to happen at this stage of her illness."

"I shall return to Adele after I have seen you off."

"Let's compromise. Why not come over now and keep me company while I finish packing? When it is time to leave, Nasir can take me."

"I can be there in twenty-five minutes."

"Who was that?" asks Genya.

"It was Brandon. He's on his way over here. I know you're dying to meet him, but do me a favor."

"What?"

"He is going through hell right now and I don't want him to feel as if he has to be a personality tonight."

"It's not a problem. I don't really want to hang around here anyway. I'm planning to go down to the lounge, order a few drinks, and smoke my brains out. I'm so nervous about flying."

"Perfect. But stay to meet him first."

"Sarah, don't be absurd. I wouldn't miss it for anything."

"Why are you giving me that look?"

"What are you talking about?" Genya asks, feigning innocence.

"There is nothing going on. Nothing. It isn't what you think. I'm not sure what it is, but I certainly know what it is not. He saved my life, though no one will ever understand that. He came out of nowhere at exactly the right time and he knew just what to say and do to keep me from entirely falling apart."

"Does he feel anything for you?"

"I think he feels I'm a kindred spirit since we've both come close to going over the edge. He's been there too. While Peter and Max were against everything about me, Brandon is able to accept me as I am."

"I understand. I don't want to ask an obvious question, but does he have money?"

"Yes and no. He makes a great deal of money, off and on. But he lives a highly visible and fairly trendy lifestyle. He's always coming and going. Then there are the galleries he owns. He's got children in private schools. It takes money to be Brandon Howard, a substantial amount of money. The answer is, I don't believe he has money for any great length of time."

"Don't you think he finds your money attractive?"

"God, no! People with real wealth, substantial assets, old money, and good genes surround him. I don't fall into any of these categories. I'm just a woman he met with a broken wing. He tried to help mend it and discovered he still enjoys the bird now that it's trying to fly again. He'll let it go at some point, I suppose."

"What about you? Are you ready to be set free?"

"No. Not so free as to never see him again. I must confess that in the relatively little time we have spent together, I have developed a serious fondness for him. When I come back, I am going to buy a home here. I want to establish a nonprofit organization. We may have some sort of working relationship, if he agrees to my proposal that he become involved as the primary speaker for my foundation."

Several strong raps on the door and Brandon's presence greets them. He envelopes Genya with his abundant personality, as if he accepts her as an extension of Sarah.

"Okay, I am going down to have a drink. Good-bye, Brandon. It was a pleasure meeting you." There is a sliver of sarcasm in her voice. "Sarah, I'll be downstairs until we're ready to leave. I'll call you when Nasir and Shelley get here. You really need to finish packing and get your bags to the lobby so we won't be rushed at the last minute. We can't miss that plane." "Right."

"Your friend is quite nice," Brandon offers genuinely.

"Please don't mind her. She's like a mother to me and very protective. I suppose it's difficult for her to assimilate everything going on. I've got to pack up the bathroom. Do you mind following me in there? You can sit on the can or something."

"I don't mind at all. Just go about your business and I'll try to stay out of your way."

"Don't stay too far out of it."

Brandon takes a seat on the marble tub platform and his eyes watch Sarah's every move. When she reaches for a large comb, she looks at it with a detached fascination. "You're a comb for someone who has hair. I don't have any hair, so I guess I won't be needing you."

Brandon laughs.

Sarah reviews a jar of Vaseline, contemplating if she should toss it in her purse to lubricate her chapped hands while on the plane.

"I've been using a lot of that lately!" Brandon sighs.

"Oh? Oh! Do you want this?"

"No, I have my own supply."

They both laugh leisurely, as if the reason he has a supply of Vaseline is not related to the fact that Adele is physically incapable of making love at this stage of her illness.

Sarah moves into the bedroom, deciding to leave whatever remains in the bathroom for the maids.

Brandon follows close behind and lies down on the bed. "My back is acting up again. I'm under too much damn pressure, and it's all in my bloody back."

"I'm pretty good at giving massages, but there's no time for that now. How about an IOU?"

"I'd like that. When shall I have it?"

"Upon my return."

"And when will that be?" There is a note of abandonment in his voice.

"As soon as I have an opportunity to wrap things up at home and to make the necessary arrangements to move here. I am not quite sure how long all that will take and what it will entail, but I hope the process won't be too lengthy."

"They say that the best way to avoid jet lag is to get back on the plane just as soon as possible and return from whence you came."

"With all the traveling you do, I expect you would know if that is true. Is it?"

"Yes. I believe it is, actually."

"I dislike jet lag intensely, so I shall return as soon as possible." Sarah begins to laugh.

"What's so funny?"

"Nothing. It's just that you said, 'They say.' Peter's mother always used that expression whenever she wanted to press a certain point. Every time she did, we would demand to know, 'Hey Mom, who's "they"?' Of course, she couldn't identify 'they,' so she would become even more dogmatic, as if the tone of her voice was somehow the answer."

Brandon studies her, trying to discover the same source of humor she has found in her recollection. Sarah, realizing this is yet another of the cultural gaps they have experienced in their limited time together, goes on. "You wouldn't understand. It's a Jewish mother-in-law thing. Oh, never mind. I don't have time to bridge our great cultural divide!"

"When you return, my dear, I am going to teach you to speak proper English. We shall understand each other so much better if you learn to speak correctly."

"Yes, what was it Winston Churchill said? Something about two great nations separated by a common language?"

The phone rings, disrupting banter that is becoming increasingly difficult for Sarah. It is Genya calling to inform her that Nasir is in front of the hotel and has just sent a bellman up for Sarah's luggage. There is a double-martini urgency in her voice.

"Well, Brandon, it's showtime. I must go now. Do you want to continue lying down for a while?"

"No. I need to get back to Adele. Come, let's go down to the lobby together. But first, I must ask you for a favor."

"Anything. What do you need?"

"I want to buy tents for a camp on some property I own in Tanzania. I shall live there part of the time in a tent while building a small home, and tourists will be able to stay in the others. I want the fees from these people to pay for the building materials I shall need. I would consider this just a loan, not a gift."

"How much do you need?"

"Forty thousand should do it."

Too confused to reason how tents could cost so much, or to question whether he is asking for the money in dollars or shillings, she begins to write the check for forty thousand dollars. Her script is unintelligible and she wonders if Brandon will be able to cash the check. But Brandon is persuasive and will find a way to have it drawn on the Barclays account she opened recently. She had created such a scene about having her money transferred from her account in the United States, she is certain they will remember her.

* * *

The lobby teems with activity despite the relatively late hour. Several groups have just arrived from the airport, ready to check in for their one-night stay before beginning their safari tomorrow. Sarah envies them their start.

Brandon leads Sarah by the arm to Nasir's car. Genya has tucked herself into the backseat. The luggage has been squeezed into the trunk. There are no excuses for lingering.

"Good-bye, again."

"Good-bye for now, you mean," Brandon corrects her, clenching her arm.

"It will be easier for me to get in the car, Brandon, if you let go of me."

"Ah yes. Yes, indeed." He leans down and whispers something in her ear, causing Sarah to smile with the serenity one enjoys when someone unexpectedly says, "I do love you, you know."

Nasir guns the accelerator and the car lurches forward, dislodging Brandon, who has been leaning on the frame of the open window. Nasir appears nervous about the possibility of Brandon's influence over Sarah. He can smell, taste, and feel this well-known man's power. Nasir is already planning how to extricate Sarah from Brandon's considerable charms. If a spell is to be cast, it is he who has won that right, through his many acts of tedious devotion. Nasir has received well over one hundred thousand dollars for his back rent and business ventures from Sarah in the final week of her stay. When she comes back, there should be more. Inshallah.

CHAPTER 31

THE DIAGNOSIS

Sarah, her chronic cough having been misdiagnosed in Nairobi, now awaits an opportunity to learn what is actually wrong with her. She is in the office of her general practitioner, a friend and confidant for many years.

"Everyone suspects I've lost my mind, considering that I've filed for divorce, taken a lease on a Beverly Hills condo, bought new furniture, and am now making plans to return to Kenya. Do you think there's something wrong with me?"

"Yes. You have mycoplasma pneumonia. It can be difficult to diagnose, which is why the doctor in Nairobi did not know what it was. Otherwise, you're fine. I think I understand what you're doing. You want to be free and be your own person. You are financially independent, so I don't think moving to Beverly Hills and buying furniture is abnormal. But for now, you must slow down and fully recover or you're going to wind up in the hospital. I want you to get this prescription filled, go home, and don't get out of bed for about twelve days. I'll see you then."

"That's it?"

"That's it for now."

* * *

"Sarah, the doctor would like you to come back into the office this afternoon. He's cleared his calendar for you. Can you be here at four?" It is the head nurse at her doctor's office. The same doctor who had told her yesterday to remain in bed for twelve days.

"What for? He told me yesterday to stay in bed. Can't he just talk to me on the phone?"

"No. He wants to see you in person. He's cancelled all his appointments after four."

"All right. I'll be there," Sarah says, desperate to know what has been determined in the last fifteen hours. Her mind runs at a frantic pace, fearing a blood test might have revealed AIDS. How could the results be back so soon? AIDS would certainly be serious enough to warrant having a sick patient get out of bed. Sarah has always known the doctor to be correct in his diagnoses. She knows he is right about the mycoplasma pneumonia. But what else has he discovered?

* * *

The doctor appears more solemn today. "Sarah, last night I took your file home and reviewed it carefully. As I thought more about what you said happened in Kenya and put it together with the notations in your folder, including your father's suicide and your own attempt, I realized that you experienced all the classic signs of manic behavior while you were there. You've always talked fast, but now your speech is so rapid, it's almost impossible to understand you. This is an indication of a manic high. After carefully considering everything, I came to the conclusion that you're bipolar; that is, you're manic depressive. Maybe I should have realized this before, but your symptoms were never as exaggerated as they are now. What I had thought of as just your particular personality, I realize now, because of your exaggerated state, is a definite disorder."

"I've never heard of anything like that. You mean when I'm depressed, I get very depressed?"

"That's just part of it. You can also have periods of extreme highs, such as you had in Kenya."

At this point, the doctor removes the pen from his shirt pocket. He begins drawing a diagram of peaks and valleys over the white paper spread out on the examining table. As he expands the illustrations of brain patterns, Sarah inches backwards, nearly falling backwards.

"It means you will have to take medication to control exaggerated mood swings. I am going to put you on lithium, which you'll take daily. We'll need to draw samples of your blood on a monthly basis because there's a narrow range of effectiveness; below the appropriate level, the dosage is worthless, but above it, it can be lethal."

Sarah is impervious to the doctor's words, considering only the limitations. "How will that work—the testing and monitoring—if I am going back to Africa?"

"You won't be able to go back. And Sarah, if you did, nothing would be the same. You experienced Africa in the particular way you did because you were in a manic state. If it hasn't started already, you'll soon go into a serious state of depression. You're going to need constant medical attention for many months."

"You don't understand. I am going back to Africa. I have to go back. I have a journal that I am going to turn into a book. I've arranged for a four-month lease on an apartment in Nairobi and I'm going to be spending time in a tent in Tanzania with the famous wildlife photographer Brandon Howard. He's buying the tents now. I'm taking a secretary with me. She's already bought two computers, printers, and all the supplies we shall need. I have made loans to be paid back and I must be there to collect the money. My personal things are still there. My friends are there. I gave my word that I'd come back, and I can't disappoint them as have so many other foreigners. My bags are already packed and I've bought the tickets and—"

"Stop, Sarah. Listen to yourself. You're almost unintelligible. You're not even going to be capable of traveling when you begin coming down from your manic high."

"How can you be so certain of your diagnosis? Why isn't there any room for doubt? Is it just that open and shut?"

"It is. Of course, you can consult any number of psychiatrists if that will help you accept what I'm telling you, but you've exhibited every symptom. When you add your father's suicide to your own attempt on your life, along with the depression I've been treating you for and the behavior you exhibited in Africa, there's just no other conclusion. This diagnosis is correct. It's textbook stuff. Pure textbook stuff."

"You don't understand. My father had good reason to kill himself. I had reasons. Let me explain."

"No, let me explain something to you. There are no good reasons for someone to try to kill themselves. The rational mind would have considered many possibilities and weighed each one. The sound mind would have evaluated alternatives. Despair would not have reached a point where the only solution considered was suicide. The normal mind would not have allowed things to get as far as they did.

"Don't misunderstand me. After you've adjusted to the lithium and weathered the depression, you can lead a perfectly normal life. But first, you must go through a very tough time, a phase of the illness that will be completely different from the high you've experienced. You won't feel the euphoria and sense of power and invulnerability that you've known recently. In fact, you'll probably be unable to do much of anything for a while. I'm going to give you a stronger antidepressant. You'll have problems sleeping, so you'll also need sleeping pills."

"How long will the depression last?" Sarah asks.

"I don't know exactly, but it will be several months. Maybe as long as a year."

Sarah is more afraid of the depression than of the label that has just been affixed to her. She tries to stretch her mind around the doctor's words, but is unable to expand it sufficiently to understand the scope of the illness. "I must talk to Peter right away. He needs to hear about this," she says, beginning to feel dread at the prospect of her illness's imminent toll.

"Despite how he has treated you all these years, Peter doesn't want to lose you and he definitely does not want a divorce. Peter has been absolutely devastated. Come here, I want to show you something." The doctor takes her outside, where he points to a brick wall parallel to his office building. "We were sitting right there, together.

He was so distraught I had to give him a prescription for Valium to calm him down."

The doctor has succeeded in getting Sarah's attention.

"I have to go to him now. Can we come in tomorrow morning so you can explain what has happened to me?"

"I can slip you in ahead of the other appointments if you can be here at eight thirty sharp."

"We'll be here."

* * *

When Sarah reaches the second-story master suite and finds Peter, she sees someone who has aged considerably in the last three months. Feeling as if she is entirely responsible for his condition, she is swamped with guilt, love, and a desperate longing for him to forgive her.

They walk towards each other, arms finding and encircling the other. They rest upon each other in exhaustion, tears mingling. Peter is the first to step back, looking at Sarah's wan face and tortured expression, her spiked hair and the makeup he has rearranged with his kiss.

"Oh God, Peter, what am I going to do? I'm sick. The doctor will explain it all to you tomorrow. You'll understand why I've acted the way I have. I must have been awful. I've spent more money than you can imagine . . . I have no idea how much, but it never stopped. I've loaned enormous amounts to people. I've gotten myself into a one-year lease on a condominium in Beverly Hills and purchased thousands of dollars' worth of furniture. I have to go back to Africa because my things are there, things I've had sent from here and things I purchased there. I've hired a secretary and bought computers so I can write a book, and . . ."

While she is flooding him with details, Sarah senses Peter's demeanor change as he steadies himself to take command of a situation that is no longer out of his control. He appears invigorated with purpose. "Sarah, slow down for Christ's sake. We'll take this one step at a time. The first step is for you to get some sleep. Tomorrow you'll go back to your condo and get as many of your things as possible and leave everything else."

"Then what?" Sarah asks, bewildered.

"Then get back here as fast as possible."

It is a perfect moment of acceptance and support. A moment that will be treasured forever. A moment, Sarah does not yet understand, that cannot last, because, being human, they will have to destroy it.

EPILOGUE

As predicted, it is not long before Sarah descends into a depression that catapults her into a personal hell of isolation. She is unable to think or talk intelligently. Her eyes cannot focus, rendering the simplest reading impossible. She can neither concentrate nor remember anything from one moment to the next. Her hands tremble constantly, making it difficult to write, hold a glass upright, or maintain a grip on utensils, thus robbing her of the small dignity of properly negotiating her way through a meal. Lithium is at work.

Days are spent almost entirely in bed, covers pulled high. In the late afternoon, she rises and sluggishly attempts to make herself presentable. When she greets Peter upon his return from golf, tennis, the racetrack, or one of his other diversions, she acts as if she has been productive during his absence. The evening lasts a torturous three or four hours, during which time all her energy is directed to behaving as if she is normal, though the glazed expression on her face belies her efforts. Then, thoroughly drained by the charade, she slips into bed and lies awake, unable to sleep, wondering if the lithium spell will ever lift.

Over the course of the first several months, Peter regularly forces Sarah to meet with their accountant to go over her credit card bills and check register in order to explain each of the expenses associated with her three-month manic high. The job proves to be a formidable undertaking, for she had spent hundreds of thousands of dollars; each attempt to recall the reason for the expenditure is forced through a prism of self-recrimination. Because her handwriting had deteriorated and was unintelligible in her check register, she never has to admit she had given Brandon forty thousand dollars. She is enormously grateful for this reprieve, for it would be outrageous, she knows, to have to clarify his need for tents in Tanzania and her need to subsidize them.

After nine months, her doctor finally agrees to put her on Depakote. The nadir of depression gradually lifts, and Sarah slowly relegates her illness to its proper place, denying it center-stage status. She reads Dr. Kate Redfield Jamison's books, *An Unquiet Mind* and *Touched By Fire*, and decides being bipolar puts her in very good company. Life assumes a dull but safe rhythm.

Her loans to Nasir are not repaid, nor could any monies be recovered, for he had woven a fabrication of corporations designed to insulate both him and his assets. She manages to reach Brandon once, and he gently informs her that the tents intended for Tanzania have not been purchased and the money is forever gone. He later writes her a loving letter in handwriting so indiscernible that Sarah diagnoses him as also being bipolar.

Relatives of many of the friends she had made write to her for sponsorship, making Sarah a magnet for some who consider her their only chance to escape poverty. George writes her asking for books to feed his voracious appetite for knowledge and Sarah happily complies. Max e-mails her that he has used the camera equipment to bribe officials in return for reinstatement of his papers and status in Kenya.

As she ascends from the bowels of depression, she discovers that Peter is once again involved in a series of relationships unrestricted by the constraints of marriage. He had seen her through her suicide attempt and the diagnosis of manic depression and it has taken its toll. He advances the idea that Sarah should simply accept his various liaisons so as not to lose her status as his wife, and although she loves him enough to seriously consider the prospect, she instinctively understands that it would be impossible to watch him walk out the door every morning and not know who he was with. After twenty years of marriage, she finally draws the line and, lacking any viable alternative, they divorce.

She spends two Thanksgivings, two Christmases, and two New Years' Eves entirely alone before she is able to consider steps to create a new life. For Sarah, this first means returning to Kenya and facing Max. It means going on a safari with him and discovering if the experience would be different now that she is well. It means learning if his behavior toward her will be more civil in Peter's absence. It means not obsessively trying to track down Nasir for money he will never repay. Most painful, it means giving up the aching compulsion to see Brandon, a man she now knows is himself a poor bird with a broken wing, whom, she allows, other women will always attempt to fix.

Life mysteriously accommodates Sarah's intentions to move forward, beginning with an invitation to a wedding of a long-time friend in Washington, DC. She decides to attend the celebration and then, the following day, to start the journey to Africa.

At the wedding, the groom introduces Sarah to another guest, a man with both feet so obviously planted solidly on the plush carpeting of the Ritz Carlton Hotel that she initially finds it foreign and disconcerting. Although it feels unusual to be in the company of one so collected, it is strangely attractive. He wears a constant smile with his dark suit, as if it is a flag he pins on each of his lapels. He is attentive but easygoing and reminds her somewhat of the "okay world" she still aspires to inhabit.

Sarah and this man e-mail each other daily while she is in Nairobi. The day she leaves the city for the safari, she rolls the dice and writes to him about being bipolar. Clicking "Send," she takes a deep breath, turns off the computer, and walks outside.

The Land Rover is already parked in front of the hotel. Max jumps out and greets her with an exonerating kiss on her cheek. "Come on, we're outta here!" He makes it sound as if there has been no time nor distance between them, as if there has never been any profound touching of each other's lives.

* * *

The ever-changing animal life is intriguing, but this time, Sarah, finding no further need for her journal, uses a camera to capture their images. Max takes every opportunity to demonstrate that he has not changed, and by the end of the safari, Sarah realizes he is simply a very competent guide with chauvinistic tendencies that have endured since her last visit.

When she returns to Nairobi, she drops her duffel bag in the hotel lobby, rushes into the business office, and turns on the computer. Here she finds a response from the new man in the "okay world." It is entitled "I'm Still Here." He believes everyone is slightly crazy to one degree or another. He does not mind the fact that she is bipolar, and he wants her to return to the United States as soon as possible.

Eleven months later, they are married.

ACKNOWLEDGMENTS

Although a few trusted friends and confidants read this book and gave me very positive feedback, a few people in particular merit special mention. Most significantly, I want to acknowledge J. A. Ted Baer, an entertainment attorney and best friend who saw the potential of *Mad Mischief* from his first read in 2010. He continued to give me confidence when my own was flagging, and he never wavered in his belief that this book was a great read. He helped me every step of the way to ensure the book's publication, a process I could not have navigated by myself.

Also deserving of my acknowledgment is my first editor, Aviva Layton. Ms. Layton went beyond her normal editing advice to urge me to pursue all avenues to achieve the book's publication. In her words, "This book deserves an audience, and I don't normally say that."

Of course, every book needs a publishing team extraordinaire, and I have had the good fortune of Mark Levine's invaluable team at Hillcrest Media who shepherded Ted and me along the way, including Athena Currier with her creative and innovative cover ideas, Ali Mcmanamon who managed the process with aplomb and was assisted diligently by the keen oversight of Emily Keenan and Aaron McMenamy, who effectively solved issues, all in synchronization with Kate Ankofski's remarkable, sensitive, razor-sharp editing of my manuscript.

Then, with the incredibly able assistance of Lindsay Jones, the COO of Hillcrest, I segued to Salem Publishing to complete the task of publishing and guiding *Mad Mischief* into the marketplace. At Salem, Chandra Thomas, their thoughtful and adept Author Services Manager, provided her expert guidance, along with the indefatigable Krystle Prashad, our Project Coordinator, and the extraordinarily talented Kimberly Ludwig, Salem's Senior Marketing Sales Strategist, both of whom gave me key insights, advice and counsel for creating my social marketing program to support the distribution of *Mad Mischief* on a plethora of platforms and media outlets. Ultimately, Taylor Reaume (Search Engine Pros in Santa Barbara) brilliantly created, energized and guided a multi-faceted, laser-pinpointed social marketing campaign with his unique insight and creativity.

Finally, I thank Samantha Bonavia for her help and creative consulting on my overall marketing, and Alicia St. John and Christian Maurer for their efforts to help me find the perfect typeface—the Hanoded Font Quid Pro Quo brilliantly created by David Kerkhoff—to give my title, *Mad Mischief*, exactly the right panache!